THE PARIS GOWN

ALSO BY CHRISTINE WELLS

THE
PARIS
GOWN

A Novel

CHRISTINE WELLS

ωm
WILLIAM MORROW
An Imprint of HarperCollinsPublishers

THE PARIS GOWN. Copyright © 2024 by Christine Wells. All rights reserved. Printed in the United States of America. No part of this book may be used or reproduced in any manner whatsoever without written permission except in the case of brief quotations embodied in critical articles and reviews. For information, address HarperCollins Publishers, 195 Broadway, New York, NY 10007.

HarperCollins books may be purchased for educational, business, or sales promotional use. For information, please email the Special Markets Department at SPsales@harpercollins.com.

FIRST EDITION

Interior text design by Diahann Sturge-Campbell

Library of Congress Cataloging-in-Publication Data

Names: Wells, Christine, author.
Title: The Paris gown : a novel / Christine Wells.
Description: First edition. | New York, NY : William Morrow, 2024.
Identifiers: LCCN 2024004866 (print) | LCCN 2024004867 (ebook) | ISBN 9780063336889 (paperback) | ISBN 9780063336902 (ebook)
Subjects: LCGFT: Novels.
Classification: LCC PR9619.4.W447 P37 2024 (print) | LCC PR9619.4.W447 (ebook) | DDC 823/.92—dc23/eng/20240209
LC record available at https://lccn.loc.gov/2024004866
LC ebook record available at https://lccn.loc.gov/2024004867

ISBN 978-0-06-333688-9

24 25 26 27 28 LBC 5 4 3 2 1

To my beloved father, Ian—lawyer, author, historian.
You have always been an inspiration to me.

THE PARIS GOWN

PROLOGUE
Claire

Paris, France 1950

Three young women stood arm in arm on the avenue Montaigne, breaths clouding together in the crisp air, shining faces lifted toward a display window at the House of Dior.

"That one!" Claire flung up her free arm as if she were on a stage, introducing the star of the show. "That is the one."

Gina, a cool, tanned blonde, lifted one eyebrow. Dark, lively Margot nodded vehemently. "Oh, yes! Most definitely. You must have this one."

Window-shopping just as the twilight hour settled like a soft veil over Paris was a habit the three friends had turned into an art. They met once a week to stroll the fashionable boulevards and feast their eyes on the sumptuous creations displayed in the atelier windows. But for Claire, visits to those other couturiers were mere flirtations; no one compared to Dior.

"Only look at the embroidery," she breathed, gazing up at this latest creation on display. "And the sequins. There must be thousands of them." The gown's train was made of cascading scalloped layers, dotted with sequins, and feathered at the edge with iridescent, pale pink paillettes designed to shiver and shimmer as one moved. The bodice was strapless and the whole effect suggested a goddess emerging naked from the sea at dawn. "How long must it take to sew a creation like that?"

"Some girls change lovers with the seasons," said Margot with a twinkle in her eye. "Claire has passionate relationships with dresses."

"At least she's monogamous," Gina pointed out.

"Mon-og . . . *comment*?" Though Parisian to the core, Claire had fallen into the habit of speaking English when she was with her friends. Claire's mother had been an Englishwoman. She had passed on her language to Claire along with her red hair and her fiery temper, but still there were some words that Claire did not understand.

"One gown at a time," explained Gina. "And one couturier. Always Dior."

Claire sighed and shook her head. "I could never afford it." How many times had she said this now?

Margot gave her hand a sympathetic squeeze. Claire, an apprentice chef from a middle-class family, was no more likely to purchase this gown than she was the many other creations they'd sighed over together on their outings during the past two years. Gina's Connecticut ancestors had sailed on the *Mayflower* and Margot's family wealth derived from the Australian wool trade. Their closets were full of couture dresses, which they insisted Claire borrow when they'd taken her out to society events with them. But she'd never had a stitch of clothing from Dior to call her own.

The three young women had met at Le Cordon Bleu cookery school, from which they had since graduated—though goodness knew how Gina and Margot had managed it. Gina didn't care about food or cooking. She'd spent each lesson lost in thought about the novel she was writing, so her soufflés fell and her sauces split.

Margot had been as mercurial in the kitchen as in everything else. Revolted by the prospect of spatchcocking a chicken or gutting a fish, she was a maestro with pastry and chocolate, and had even managed to win praise from their exacting instructor, Monsieur Guillaume.

Only Claire was serious about the culinary arts. She'd practically grown up in the family brasserie, after all. Unlike Margot and Gina, Claire had soon developed ambitions well beyond a cookery course that was expressly designed to prepare rich young ladies for marriage. After finishing the introductory course, she'd barged into the professional chefs' class and refused to take no for an answer. Eventually her persistence had been rewarded. Claire had become the lone female student amid rows of arrogant, dismissive men.

But now that their "finishing" was complete, Margot and Gina were returning home. This was the last time the three of them would gather together in front of La Maison Dior.

As she stared up at the window display, Claire bit her lip. Gina was heading back to New York, where she hoped to become a journalist while writing the great American novel on the side—not to mention avoiding the eligible bachelors her family insisted on introducing to her. Determined to find her Prince Charming back in Sydney, Margot had set her heart on marriage and children. With her warmth and charm, Margot would make the perfect society wife.

Claire did not dream of marriage. She was practical down to her bones, but she had two dreams that were highly *im*practical. One, to run a Michelin three-star restaurant in Paris one day. The other, to own a Dior evening gown.

Considering the misogyny embedded deep in the restaurant trade, the latter was the more likely to happen, even though a creation like the one Claire was sighing over must surely cost tens of thousands of francs.

"Bonsoir, mes petits lèche-vitrines!" said a voice behind them. *"Ça va?"* They turned to see Deidre Vaughn, elegant in a pale blue coat with a black velvet collar and large black buttons. Rich, stylish, and highly eccentric, Madame Vaughn balanced a slightly beaky nose with a pair of enormous blue eyes framed by thick black lashes that could not possibly be real. She had a wide, generous mouth and a strong jaw. Her chestnut hair was thick and lustrous—a testament to her hairdresser's skill. She was somewhere in the region of forty years old (or so Claire had guessed). If she had once been married, she never spoke of it to Claire, yet it had always seemed more appropriate to call her "madame" rather than "mademoiselle."

Madame Vaughn was American, but she spoke French like a born Parisienne. Ever since Claire could remember, Madame had lived alone in the apartment above Claire's family's brasserie and had become something of a benefactor to Claire over the years. She'd insisted on paying for Claire's courses at the Cordon Bleu and backed Claire's bid to become the next Escoffier when her father kicked up a fuss about her striking out on her own instead of working in the family brasserie.

"Did you just call us 'window lickers'?" demanded Margot, with dawning delight.

Madame spread her hands. "That's the literal translation. Isn't it a hoot?" Madame had a wide grin and long incisors that made her look slightly wolfish. Eyeing Claire, she jerked her head at the display window. "Your latest crush?"

"Isn't it marvelous?" breathed Claire. "This model is called 'Venus.'"

Madame Vaughn turned her head to eye the dress critically. "Hmm. Stunning, of course. But that color . . . What is it, now?" She tapped her chin and tilted her head to the side. "It's a *pale* pink, but it leans slightly more toward salmon. I'd call it 'blush.'" Her gaze traveled to Claire and back again to the display. "No. I don't think it would suit you, Claire. Pink can be stunning on a redhead, of course, but not *that* particular shade. Not for you."

Crestfallen, even though she'd never had the remotest intention of buying the gown, Claire said, "Well, it's only a silly dream, anyway." And if she *were* dreaming, she might as well change her own coloring into the bargain, mightn't she? Curly red hair, dark blue eyes, a dusting of freckles across her nose . . . She'd give anything to be an elegant blonde like Gina or dark and gamine like Margot. Or what would it be like to have Madame Vaughn's particular style of je ne sais quoi? But no. The level of sophistication Madame Vaughn possessed was unattainable, even in Claire's most fanciful daydreams.

"How lucky we ran into you," Margot said to Madame Vaughn. "This definitely calls for champagne."

"You always say that about everything," said Gina.

Margot winked. "And I'm always right, aren't I? Come on! Madame, you'll join us, won't you?"

The older woman shook her head. "I have a prior engagement,

my dears. Have fun!" Laughing, she waved off Margot's attempts to persuade her, and went on her way.

As the three friends turned toward Margot's apartment and the promised champagne, Claire took one last, lingering look at the Venus gown, with its sparkling romance and its soft allure.

One day, she said to herself. *One day*.

Chapter One

Claire

Paris, France 1956

C laire was in the brasserie kitchen, cutting a sheet of sweet pastry into perfect rounds on the marble counter's cool, floured surface, when Tante Vo-Vo slapped a bundle of letters down by her elbow with a loud *thwap*. "Mail!"

A great puff of flour swirled into the air. Claire jumped and her hand slipped, ruining her work.

That had been deliberate. Claire bit back a curse and scowled after her relative. Her aunt's real name was Véronique, but Margot had dubbed her "Vo-Vo" after some kind of Australian cookie, and the nickname had stuck. Far from remaining the sweet, funny aunt of Claire's childhood, since taking on the role of hostess at the brasserie, Vo-Vo had become grouchier by the day. All her life, she'd steadfastly refused to work at Le Chat-qui-Pêche, the family's brasserie in Saint-Germain-des-Prés. Only her fondness for her brother, Claire's papa, had made her relent. But Vo-Vo's affection had not extended to shouldering the burden with any outward appearance of good cheer. Every day, her lament was the same: she could be sunning herself on the Riviera by now, if only it weren't for *this place*.

"Well, why doesn't she go sun herself, then?" Louis, a student they employed as *plongeur* and general dogsbody, bore the brunt of Vo-Vo's temper and often muttered a rejoinder to these complaints. "She's rude to us and even ruder to the customers. Me, I'd do a better job of greeting and seating than Madame."

"Hush." If Vo-Vo were set free tomorrow, Claire doubted she'd go. And though frequently irritated and provoked by the older woman's contrariness, Claire doubted they could manage without her, particularly when Papa was at his worst.

When Maman died two years before, Papa had crumpled. Age had seemed to catch up with him overnight. He became stooped and thin, the wrinkles around his eyes more pronounced, his cheekbones more prominent now that they had less flesh to plump them out. Papa had lost his English rose, his sweetheart, the woman who had shared his bed, his work, and all of his sorrows and joys for the past twenty-seven years. Watching him force himself to work at Le Chat every day despite his grief broke Claire's heart.

The family had rallied to keep the brasserie going. Without a second thought, Claire had quit the restaurant where she'd managed to work her way up to the position of *chef de partie* and put her ambition for that coveted Michelin three-star rating on hold. The brasserie served traditional, hearty French food. It was the best of its kind, but still, haute cuisine it certainly wasn't. Claire had to work doubly hard to keep up the skills she'd developed in the years since she'd finished at the Cordon Bleu, practicing diligently after closing, or early in the mornings, always sacrificing sleep in pursuit of excellence.

Her return to Le Chat's kitchen was meant to be temporary, until Papa was back on his feet. But all of the sound and fury had left the big ox of a man when his beloved wife died. Now, two years on, Claire had begun to wonder if he'd ever regain his former ebullience. She wished she knew how to make everything better for him, but grieving, as Vo-Vo said, simply could not be hurried.

Claire swept together the wrecked pastry dough and shaped it, ready for rolling again. Papa had hit the bottle hard last night, so it looked like she would have twice the work in the kitchen today. She wanted to get a few preparations out of the way early, before the sous-chefs and the waiters came in.

Working with quick, light hands, so as not to transfer too much of her own body heat to the tender pastry, she glanced at the pile of mail Vo-Vo had so carelessly delivered.

The letter that met her eye had American stamps and was addressed in Gina's handwriting. Claire exclaimed in delight. How long had that taken to reach her? She'd almost given up waiting for a response to her previous letter, which she'd mailed almost six months ago, and wondered if, like Margot, Gina had finally ceased to think of her Parisian friend and stopped writing altogether.

Finishing off the tart cases as quickly as she could, Claire shoved them into the oven for the blind bake, rested one hip against the flour-strewn counter, and ripped open the envelope.

A stiff cream stock card accompanied the letter. She slid it out of the envelope. An invitation . . . to Gina's wedding! Well, well. A lot must have happened since her previous letter, when Gina had mentioned the young man she'd met. He worked at the State Department in Washington, and their respective fathers were business associates—two strikes against him, in Gina's eyes. She must have changed her stance dramatically since last she'd written. Gina had fallen in love.

Married. Gina had sworn she wouldn't settle down until after she'd made a name for herself as a writer, and certainly not with any of the eligible young men in her father's social set. This Harold Sanders must have something special.

Eagerly, Claire slid Gina's letter from the envelope. A small photograph fluttered out and she crouched to pick it up. Not the formal engagement picture Claire expected to see but one of the happy couple smiling and windblown aboard some kind of boat—a yacht, Claire thought—Gina's hand on the big wheel, Hal's arm slung casually around her shoulders. On the back, Gina's bold scrawl: "Gina & Hal, Summer '54." Hmm, yes. This fiancé was certainly handsome. They made a stunning pair, both blond and tanned and athletic, their faces alight with happiness and hope.

Suddenly wistful, Claire returned the photograph to the envelope with the invitation. She was thrilled to think of Gina being so happy, but for Claire, traveling to the wedding in Connecticut would be impossible. She could never afford it, and anyway, she couldn't leave Papa or Le Chat. Claire turned her gaze to the letter, scanning the initial greetings and inquiries after herself and her family.

As always, Gina wrote in English, and Claire read each sentence carefully. *We plan to have the wedding in the spring. Much as I would give for you to be my bridesmaid, dear Claire, I know you won't be able to attend. But if the mountain wouldn't . . . Guess what? We are coming to* you! *We'll honeymoon in Paris, and Hal is even talking about getting a posting there. Can you believe it?*

Claire exclaimed aloud in delight, eagerly devouring the rest of her friend's news. Gina had a punchy, entertaining style—no doubt honed as a political correspondent.

But enough about me. Tell me about you, ma chère. *I know you are busy with Le Chat, but why no mention of anyone who might have caught your eye? Can it be that there are no attractive men left in Paris? Impossible!*

Attractive men? Claire thought about her wasteland of a love life with a grimace. She didn't have time for anything but this place.

Gina told her all about the wedding plans. She was going to wear her mother's dress. She didn't care if it was old-fashioned, she'd felt close to her mother the second she'd put it on—as if Rose had enveloped her in a loving embrace. That's right, thought Claire. Gina was motherless as well. Something they now had in common.

Still nothing from Margot on my side of the Atlantic, added Gina. *What has happened to that girl? She was the busiest correspondent back in Paris.*

That was true. It was most unlike Margot simply to stop writing. And equally unlike her to turn her back on her friends. Claire hoped nothing bad had happened to her. She wished there was a way to find out, but she didn't know anyone else in Sydney, not even the address of Margot's family home.

Eagerly returning to the start of the letter in case she'd missed anything, Claire's gaze snagged on the date. Five months ago! Somehow Gina's news had been severely delayed in the post. So her friend hadn't forgotten her. In fact, Gina must be wondering by now whether Claire had stopped writing to her. Had something similar happened with Margot, perhaps? Maybe she ought to begin writing to Margot again, just in case.

With a happy sigh, Claire finished a second reading of Gina's letter and put it in her apron pocket. Then she moved swiftly to rescue her tart shells from the oven before they burned. She left them to cool, their sweet scent filling the air, while she prepared the crème pâtissière for the strawberry tarts. "Louis?" she called. "Come clean this up, please!"

Receiving no answer, Claire washed and wiped her hands and went out into the brasserie, which was empty of patrons. She loved this time of day, when she had the place mostly to herself. Gentle sunlight streamed through the art nouveau swirls in the stained-glass windows, scattering color like gemstones across the tiled marble floor. Brass gleamed; bentwood chairs and wood-paneled walls glowed with polish; banquettes covered in burgundy moleskin were clean and free of crumbs. Outside, café-style chairs all faced the street beneath the dark red awning, like a theater awaiting an audience. The round tables, marble-topped and banded with brass, were bare.

And there was Louis, loafing on the sidewalk beneath the brasserie's old-fashioned sign of a tabby cat with a fishing rod and line. He leaned on the top of his broom handle and smoked a cigarette as he chatted to another young man, a fellow student Claire vaguely recognized.

"That boy!" muttered Claire. "I don't know why we pay him good money to stand about, blaguing with his friends." Then she caught herself. She was beginning to sound like her aunt. Louis was young and cheerful and industrious most of the time.

Claire decided not to roust him, but she kept an eye out to see if he would go back to his work. Soon enough, the other young man loped off in the direction of the Métro station, and Louis resumed sweeping.

Sometimes, one's faith in people was justified. With an approving nod, Claire was about to turn away when she caught sight of the brasserie's upstairs neighbor, Madame Vaughn, who was hurrying past the brasserie with her head down. Claire couldn't have said precisely why, but she sensed that Madame was distressed. She didn't seem to notice Louis's greeting and had entered via the building's lobby door before Claire might have stepped out to call hello.

Claire thought about darting out via the side door of the brasserie into the stairwell to catch Madame there before she went upstairs to her apartment, but something about the determination in the older woman's gait and the way she hadn't so much as glanced in at Le Chat made her think better of it. Had it been Margot or Gina, she wouldn't have hesitated to barge upstairs and demand to know what was wrong, but although she'd come to know Madame quite well over the years, theirs was not that kind of friendship. As the years had gone by, Claire had revised her estimate of Madame's age downward—at a guess, she was possibly ten or fifteen years older than Claire's twenty-six—but there was still enough of a gap that Claire didn't like to overstep or presume.

A rap on the service entrance door goosed Claire out of her reverie. Her truffles! She hurried back to the kitchen, eager to catch Madame Theroux, whose specially trained pigs snuffled out these earthy, scented fungi beneath the floor of an oak forest in Sorges. Claire loved to listen to Madame speak so knowledgeably about truffles and mushrooms and other forage, which she brought, packed in their native soil, to Paris with her throughout the season.

"Coming!" Claire called, as the rapping sounded again. She opened the service door to the alleyway and stepped back with a gasp.

Gina stood in the doorway, a slim suitcase in hand.

Gina

S ur-prise . . ." The word came out deadpan rather than with the festive lilt their reunion deserved. It was patently redundant. Plainly her sudden arrival had floored her friend. If it had been summer, Claire would have caught several flies in that gaping mouth of hers by now. The alley where Gina stood was full of trash from the neighboring shops and apartments, as well as from the brasserie itself.

"But—but how?" Claire reached into the pocket of her apron and fished out a letter, which Gina recognized as one she'd sent ages back. "The wedding's not till May."

"The wedding's off." The short declaration burst from her like a firecracker but the glib story Gina had rehearsed fizzled on her tongue. She couldn't make herself explain why she had arrived in Paris months before her projected honeymoon. Not right off the bat, anyway. And she was certain that by now, her pale blond hair was falling out of its chignon, and beneath her eyes were dark thumbprints of fatigue. Before Claire could think of how to respond, she asked, "May I come in?"

"Oh! Yes. Of course," said Claire, stepping aside. "Sorry. It's just that I had no *idea* . . ." She stopped abruptly, perhaps sensing Gina's reluctance to expand on her short statement. She didn't ask why on earth Gina would wish to enter the brasserie via the alleyway, and Gina didn't enlighten her.

Gina had caught sight of the inimitable Madame Vaughn in the street, and the presence of someone connected to her own circle of acquaintance back home had made the humiliation that had simmered inside Gina for weeks now rise up again, ready to blow the top off her composure. Madame Vaughn would either congratulate or commiserate, depending on how busy the gossips had been on this side of the Atlantic, and Gina couldn't bear to receive either.

Without thinking, she'd ducked into the alley to avoid that encounter. Then she'd shrugged and picked her way along the dirty cobbles until she'd found the brasserie service entrance. She'd stepped in something noxious—yet another low in a succession of nadirs she'd suffered lately.

Nadirs. You *could* have more than one. Always precise with language, Gina had actually looked it up. Family, love life, career, finances . . . Every one of them gone down the pissoir. It had all happened so quickly—shock after shock—and yet she could scarcely remember the woman she'd been before her perfect life had come crashing down.

The sight of Claire standing there—the same warmhearted Claire she'd always known, with her wiry, active frame and her ruddy round cheeks and her mad red hair—made Gina's heart lift a little. Carefully she wiped her shoes on the doormat and took off her winter coat and hung it on the coatrack by the door. Then she stepped into the warm, comforting embrace of the brasserie kitchen, with its long, ancient farm table laden with baskets of fresh vegetables and its Carrara marble benches and gleaming copper pots and pans. She set down her suitcase—or tried to—but Claire swooped on it before it hit the floor. "Mind, there's flour everywhere! I'll put it in the office for you."

When she returned, Gina said, "Sorry to land on you like this but I couldn't wait. Don't let me interrupt your work."

"Did you only just arrive in Paris? You must be hungry," said Claire. "Let me fix you something."

"Bless you!" Gina took a seat at the end of the table. "I have to admit I'm famished." The relief of having arrived finally in Paris, of sitting with Claire again in Le Chat's cozy kitchen, was so strong, she could have cried.

Claire seemed to size her up as a couturier might size up a client before a formal fitting. Only with Claire, it was less a measuring and more an intuition, a sixth sense. She always gauged precisely what someone was hungry for. Snapping her fingers, she exclaimed, "Cassoulet!"

Gina's heart sank a little. A hearty dish, but *un petit peu compliqué* to make. Gina knew from experience that there were several steps involved in assembling the traditional casserole. Right now, she could eat the leg off a table. If she had to wait for cassoulet she might faint.

She needn't have worried, however. Claire whipped out a glazed pottery dish that had been sitting in a warm oven. She set it on the kitchen table in front of Gina, then grabbed a bottle of wine from a rack by the door and poured a generous glass.

"Oh, no! I can't. It's far too early," Gina forced herself to protest.

"Pfft," said Claire, gesturing with her free hand as she topped up the glass a little. "It will put some color in your cheeks. Go on. Drink."

The wine was a light, zingy claret that perfectly complemented the rich meal. A combination of pancetta lardons, spicy Toulouse sausage, duck, lamb, and white beans in a thick gravy that came with a topping of herbed golden-brown breadcrumbs, the cassoulet was hearty and heartening. For once Gina forgot about her waistline and ate with relish and gusto. She couldn't remember the last time she'd consumed what Claire would call a proper meal.

Her friend kept up a stream of chatter, now and then eyeing Gina with a puckered brow when she thought Gina wasn't paying attention. Yes, Gina thought wearily, she must explain about the wedding, about all of it. But she was so tired, and the wine was weaving a web of lassitude through her body, and right now she couldn't bring herself even to begin.

"Gina—" Claire broke off as her aunt erupted into the kitchen, muttering about early bird customers, and grabbing menus.

"Look who has come to visit, Tante," said Claire.

Her aunt stopped short, then her scowl turned into a beaming smile with almost comical swiftness. "Is it you, Gina? *Mon ange!* Why didn't you tell us you were coming?"

"Vo-Vo!" Gina stood and leaned over to kiss the older woman on both cheeks. Claire's tiny aunt took Gina's shoulders in a firm grip, looked her up and down, and said, "You need some meat on those bones! You're as bad as this one." A jerk of her head in Claire's direction. Then she rounded on her niece. "And don't even think of asking for the night off, *mon chou*. We're fully booked!"

As Vo-Vo stomped from the room, Gina couldn't even summon the energy to ask why she was in such a bad mood. Claire started making some kind of custard—Gina knew she really ought to remember the name of it—working as she talked.

Unable to focus on what her friend was saying, Gina went back to eating. As her stomach filled with the warm heaviness of Claire's delicious cooking, another strong wave of fatigue washed over her. Was this what it was like to be swept away by the tide, to swim against it until your arms and legs gave out? After all of that struggle, to succumb and let the undertow drag you down . . .

"Ah, Gina, *ma pauvre,* you're falling asleep sitting up!" Claire exclaimed. "Why don't you check into your hotel now, get a good night's sleep, and then we'll meet up tomorrow morning—the usual time and place. I'll get Louis to hail you a taxi."

"My hotel." Gina swallowed. "Well, you see—"

"Orders!" Vo-Vo bustled back in, ripped a page from her little notepad, and rammed it down on a spike that sat by a stack of menus on the counter. She went out again, muttering curses about customers who came demanding to be fed well before Le Chat was even open.

Under Claire's sympathetic gaze, it took every ounce of strength Gina had not to weep the whole sorry story into her wine. She made herself smile at her friend. "You're busy. I'll go." Forgoing the rest of her meal and half of the claret, Gina got slowly to her feet.

She began to clear, but Claire said, "Leave it. Louis will do that. Oh! And here he is now. *Finally*," she added, as he popped his curly head around the door and gave Gina a nod and a shy smile. "Louis, help Gina with her suitcase and find her a taxi, will you?"

Claire gave Gina another hug and whispered in her ear, "I'm so sorry, I can't stop. But we'll talk properly, yes? Come around tomorrow morning, early as you can, and we'll go somewhere we won't be interrupted."

Aware that Louis was waiting for her, Gina gave him a perfunctory smile and followed him out. "Don't worry about the taxi," she told him. "I'll walk." She deliberately left her suitcase behind.

Was it the lack of sleep, the wine, or the heavy meal? Her brain felt sluggish. All the way to Paris, her mind had raced with worry. Once there she'd had no thought beyond getting to Claire. Now even deciding which direction to take seemed beyond her. Feeling Louis's interested gaze upon her as she hesitated, Gina randomly turned left and walked purposefully away from him.

The movement of her body seemed to turn the gears of her mind. Her brain started to churn, her thoughts spinning around and around. She needed coffee. She needed to find someplace to live, a job. Most pressing of all, she needed a place to sleep that night.

She couldn't remember ever seeing a realtor in Paris, though they must surely exist, mustn't they? Or did one inquire of the concierge at each building if there were any apartments there to rent? She didn't know. She'd never had to worry about any of the practicalities of life before. For someone who'd always prided herself on wanting independence, she felt stupid and naïve, and very alone.

Once out of sight of Le Chat, Gina slowed her pace, wandering until she found a public bench by an allée where a group of old men were playing pétanque. She sat down and tried to order her thoughts. She had some money saved but she needed to be careful with it until she secured some form of employment. Journalism—freelancing—wouldn't pay immediately. Once she'd found her feet, she'd knock on some doors, but full-time employment for English-speaking journalists in Paris was scarce. She'd probably have to find something else in the meantime. She wished she hadn't been forced to leave her typewriter behind.

All right. She'd find a place to stay. Then she'd look for a job. It could be anything. She hadn't been too proud to wait tables at Le Chat when Claire was shorthanded, years ago. She knew how a restaurant was run. Maybe she could find a place that would hire her. Or she could try retail—she'd never served customers in a boutique before, but how hard could it be? Although she might need a résumé for that, and she didn't have any relevant experience. She didn't have a work visa, either. It would have to be somewhere they didn't care about visas. When she got back on her feet, she'd buy a typewriter, try to sell some articles freelance. One of the editors she knew might support her visa application. Maybe she could talk to someone at the embassy. She had a few contacts there.

But first, Gina needed somewhere to stay. She wandered the streets of Saint-Germain-des-Prés, inquiring at different pensions, but all of the more respectable places were beyond her budget. The tariffs were even higher in the hotels, and anyway, if Gina was going to make her home in Paris, what she needed was an apartment. By the time she'd worked her way to the edge of the arrondissement, she was nearing despair. Her feet ached and she felt weary down to her bones. If only she'd swallowed her pride and admitted everything to Claire.

The idea of begging for charity from her friend made her feel nauseous. Gina gritted her teeth and went on. At what seemed like the hundredth place she tried, the concierge asked about her budget.

The concierge seemed kind, but Gina had to swallow past the lump in her throat before she could bring herself to disclose how much she could afford to pay. The woman's eyebrows drew together. "Are you in some kind of trouble, mademoiselle? Pardon me for saying, but you look as if you could afford far better."

"I'm afraid I only have limited resources at the moment." She thanked the concierge and was about to leave, when the woman said, "Let me show you a room. It won't be what you're used to, but it is cheap."

They took the elevator as far up as it would go, then climbed a winding staircase to the top floor of the building. The concierge produced a bunch of keys and found the correct one. "Here."

She held open the door for Gina to come in, but Gina didn't follow her. The room was so small it would have felt crowded if the two of them had stood together inside it. There was a bed and a dry washstand and little else. Nowhere to cook or eat food, no running water. Nowhere to hang her clothes.

It was a *chambre de bonne*—a maid's room—the concierge said.

"And the bathroom?" Gina inquired.

"Public baths down the street," said the concierge. "The shared lavatory is down the hall." She nodded to a small cabinet against the wall that Gina hadn't noticed. "There's a commode, as well."

Gina had not realized people went to public bathhouses actually to bathe. If she'd thought about them at all, she'd imagined they must be much like a day spa. And the commode . . . She shuddered. She couldn't stay here long. But it was only temporary, after all. Surely she could get enough work to dig herself out of here.

In any case, she had little choice in the matter. It was the first place in a decent neighborhood that she could afford. "I'll take it," she said. She'd retrieve her suitcase from Le Chat and then tomorrow she'd try her best to find a job.

Orienting herself, Gina realized that after all of that wandering, she had ended up only a couple of blocks away from Le Chat-qui-Pêche. She checked her watch. Hmm. It was almost five o'clock. Claire would be busy preparing for the dinner rush. Maybe she could slip into the office unnoticed and retrieve her suitcase.

A light drizzle began. She put out her hand, palm up, to feel the tiny spots of rain and thought of her umbrella, which was of course packed in her suitcase. At least, she hoped it was.

As the rain intensified, she stepped under the awning of the shop next door to her apartment building for shelter. Then she realized she stood outside a bookstore. Of course! She knew this street well. She had visited this establishment countless times, because it stocked a selection of books that were in English as well as a large array of new and used ones in French. She could never decide on her *absolute* favorite bookstore in the city because each district of Paris yielded some fresh and interesting find, not to mention the fascinating and eclectic bouquinistes who peddled all kinds of literature from stalls along the quays of the Seine. But Florie's was one of the best. Gina decided to take refuge from the rain there and forget her troubles for a while.

Simply entering a bookstore never failed to make her feel better. The look and feel and smell of books—whether leather-bound and tooled with gilt or dog-eared and warped from many readings—she loved them all. But what she loved even more was what the books represented. Take one set of black marks on a bound stack of paper from the shelves, and you held an entire world in your hands. It was the only kind of magic she believed in, the ability of authors to fling her into other places, other times, other people's minds and hearts. She had always burned to weave that magic, too. A dream that would have to be put on hold while she earned a living.

As she went inside, a bell tinkled cheerily overhead and a sight greeted her that was familiar and almost as comforting as Claire's embrace. An elderly, wirehaired fox terrier lay by the feet of an even more elderly bookseller, who was cradling a steaming mug of coffee in his liver-spotted hands.

"Mademoiselle Winter!" The bookseller's face lit with a smile that was all the more charming for being unexpected. With his heavy eyebrows and downturned mouth, Monsieur Florie always appeared grumpy when his face was at rest. "It has been too long."

The warmth of his welcome was a balm to Gina's ragged soul. "Bonjour, Monsieur Florie. I trust you are well." Pricking up his ears at her voice, the fox terrier, whose name was Ricki, hauled himself to his feet and came to her. She crouched to greet him, scratching the place on his spine that he couldn't reach, which always turned him into a shaggy little puddle of bliss.

As she fussed over his dog, Monsieur told her all about his latest acquisitions, and which books might suit her taste. Gina's fatigue, coupled with the time she'd spent away, made her a little slow to catch the meaning of his rapid, guttural French, but she did her best. "You will want to see all of the new stock," he told her, rising from his chair. "Come, let me show you."

"Actually," said Gina, struck with inspiration, "I was wondering if you might have a job for me, Monsieur."

Claire

In the short lull between the lunch rush and dinner preparation, Tante Vo-Vo jerked her head at Claire. "Come sit down with us for a minute. Your papa has something he wants to say."

Surprised, Claire took off her apron, wiped her hands on it, and followed her aunt to the booth closest to the office. It was seldom that the family had the time to sit down together but whenever they did, it was always at this booth.

Papa shuffled up to them, looking sorry and sheepish, but much more alert than when she'd looked in on him that morning, still in bed after an evening of miserable drinking, tears staining his cheeks. He was a big man, and before her mother's death, he had been the epitome of the garrulous Parisian host. Now, he seemed nervous and tongue-tied. He crushed his chef's hat between his hands and twisted it.

Wary of his hesitancy, Claire glanced at Vo-Vo, whose expression seemed curiously benign. Her aunt nodded at Papa.

"Mignonne," he began, "I know now isn't a good time, but . . ." He trailed off.

"Sit down, Papa." Claire smiled up at him encouragingly and slid over so he could take a seat beside her. Perhaps if he wasn't obliged to look her in the eye he'd find it easier to come out with whatever it was he needed to say. The suspicion that he'd bought a fancy new oven they couldn't afford or forgotten to put in the produce orders crossed her mind, but neither transgression would make her aunt look so happy. Claire turned to Papa and placed a gentle hand on his arm. "What's on your mind?"

When he continued to hesitate, Vo-Vo said, "If you don't tell her, I will."

"We're leaving Paris," Papa blurted out. "Your aunt and I. We're selling Le Chat."

Chapter Two

Claire

Selling? But . . . but this place has been in the family for over sixty years!"

Papa put his big, warm hand over hers. "I'm sorry, my dear, but it's for the best."

"And it's not as if *you* want to take over," Vo-Vo put in.

Papa held up a hand. "Now, now. Let's not get into all of that. I've made my decision." He patted Claire's hand. "When you get used to the idea, you'll see it's for the best. We needed the money from the restaurant and the apartment in order to retire. Claire, the truth is that I couldn't have passed it on to you even if I'd wanted to."

"*Needed*?" Claire fixed on his choice of words—he spoke in the past tense. "You mean you've already sold the place?"

She didn't have to hear his answer to realize the truth. Knowing Papa, he had put off telling her until the very last moment. At least he'd done it before the new owner swept in and took command of her kitchen.

"But when must I leave?" Claire put her fingertips to her temples. Where would she live? More to the point, where would she work? Despite all her talk of haute cuisine and her efforts to keep up her skills, she felt blindsided by this news. Her dream of running a Michelin-starred restaurant had begun to seem far off in the distance, no less a mirage than her dream of owning a Dior gown.

"You'll be kept on here, of course," said her father. "That was a condition of my selling." He hesitated, then added hopefully, "Or you could come with us?"

She couldn't. She had so much still to learn and besides, all of her contacts in the restaurant trade were in Paris.

"Of course she doesn't want to come with us," scoffed Vo-Vo. "You can live with Cousin Juliette until you find a place of your own, Claire. She'd be only too happy to take you in."

Ugh. Cousin Juliette would expect her to cook for her enormous family. *No, thank you.*

Claire wanted to protest. Didn't she get any say in this? But she couldn't help but think of the worried creases in her father's brow, his sad eyes and the weariness behind them . . . What could she do but reassure him?

She would be fine. Better than fine. At last she would be free to pursue her dream, leave the cozy nest of the brasserie, and aim for the pinnacle of the restaurant world. Her father had given her that sudden, stomach-dropping push. Now it felt like falling, but soon enough she would gather her strength, spread her wings, and soar.

"Don't worry about me, Papa," she said, turning in her seat to hug him. His arms closed around her and he squeezed her tightly. She felt him tremble a little as he let her go with a gasp that sounded very like a sob. He wouldn't like her to see him in tears, so she turned to her aunt.

"Where will you live?" As if she needed to ask.

"As soon as you're settled, your papa and I will go down to Nice," Vo-Vo replied. "I have my eye on a nice little villa overlooking the sea."

Papa added, "We will take care of each other." He paused. "I do hope, my dear, that one day you will achieve your dreams. In the meantime, there are worse things than working at the best brasserie in Paris, you know."

Claire tried to smile but she couldn't quite manage it. That Le Chat-qui-Pêche was the best in Paris had always been her father's grandiose claim to patrons; over the years it had become his and Claire's little joke. And of course he was right about there being worse things. The war and its privations lived on in Claire's memory, even though she'd been young and shielded from the worst by her doting parents. And it was true. Le Chat *was* easily among the best of its kind. It was just that ever since she'd discovered that cooking could be elevated to the level of art, Claire's dream had been to pursue a career in haute cuisine.

Papa eyed her warily. "You know, I would have been happy to have stayed on and put you in charge if I'd thought—"

"Don't worry, Papa." She cut him off, leaning over to kiss his cheek. "You did the right thing by selling. I'll be fine." It occurred to her that he had made a huge sacrifice. The brasserie had been in the family for generations. If Papa had come to her first with the proposition of selling, she would have felt honor bound to offer to take over the brasserie herself. But he'd given her no choice in the matter, and thereby relieved her of guilt. It was only the suddenness of it that left her feeling as if she had a rock in the pit of her stomach.

The apartment was another thing. When would she have to move? As soon as possible, by the sound of it.

Gina

Gina arrived back at the brasserie exhausted but mildly trium-phant. In one afternoon, she had secured for herself a job and an apartment. Not a very nice apartment and not a very well-paying job, but if she worked hard to bash out some feature articles in her spare time, she might just make ends meet. Maybe even get ahead. As a privileged young woman who had never been obliged to give a second thought to the sordid question of money, she might be for-given for feeling a smidge proud.

The brasserie was packed with patrons and full of noise and color, the glow of candles and leadlight shades lending warmth and intimacy to the scene. Gina stopped short outside. She must look a complete mess right now. It was getting dark, and who knew what she might step in this time, so instead of using the alley again, she headed into the lobby of the building.

After she'd paid Madame Pipi to use the restroom, tidied her hair, and reapplied her lipstick and powder, she felt slightly more like herself, though still grubby from travel and weary down to the marrow of her bones. She would be glad to get to bed that evening, even if it was in that cupboard of a maid's room.

As she left the restroom, a loud *bang* coming from above made her look up.

Bang . . . bang . . . then a crack of splintering wood. It sounded like it came from Madame Vaughn's apartment upstairs.

Forgetting her earlier reluctance to encounter her fellow Amer-ican, Gina climbed the stairs two at a time. On the second-floor landing, she saw the door to Madame's apartment leaning drunkenly off one hinge, and the backs of a couple of men in suits as they filed inside.

The click of her heels on the tiles must have alerted one of them. He turned and frowned at her, saying in French, "Go away, mademoiselle. This is a private matter."

She'd been undecided whether to butt in, but the arrogance of his command made her stand her ground. "Madame Vaughn is my friend. I demand to know what you mean by breaking into her apartment." She raised her voice and craned her neck to see past him, adding in English, "Madame Vaughn? Are you there? Is everything okay?"

"You're American," said the man with something of a sneer.

"Yes," said Gina. "How do you know Madame?"

"That's none of your concern." His jaw tightened. "Mademoiselle, you must leave."

Gina's journalistic instincts rose like the hackles of a cat, but her foremost concern was for Claire's neighbor. She wouldn't leave this spot. Not without a reasonable explanation.

Gina had doorstepped lots of people and talked her way into many homes in the course of her short career in journalism. However, the man who blocked the narrow vestibule to the apartment seemed immovable in every sense of the word. He was built like an American footballer, padding and all.

She narrowed her eyes. "How do I know you're telling the truth? You could be anyone." When he simply folded his arms in answer in the manner of a bouncer at a nightclub, she added, "If you don't tell me exactly what's going on, I'll call the flics."

She ought to have run off and called the police straightaway. If these men were up to no good, it was probably stupid to tip them off as to her intentions. The man swore under his breath. "That would be a big mistake, Mademoiselle . . . ?"

Before Gina could answer, she heard another voice, quiet and precise. "If you please to step aside, Monsieur Limeaux."

The big man stepped out of the way and a small older gentleman shuffled out of the apartment, a slim black attaché case in hand. He looked pale and the waxed ends of his moustache seemed to droop dispiritedly, but he had such an air of gentle dignity that it required only the lightest touch on the elbow and an inclination of his neatly barbered head before Gina found herself back on the landing outside the apartment again.

"What is it?" she whispered. "What's happened to Madame Vaughn?"

"Nothing terrible, I assure you," came the calm reply. "I was concerned for Madame Vaughn when I hadn't heard from her for some days, but it seems I was, er, overreacting." A glance at the splintered doorframe and a self-deprecating moue made light of the situation. "I will have this repaired immediately."

As Gina hesitated, he added, "Please, Mademoiselle . . . ?"

"Winter," she supplied.

He nodded. "Mademoiselle Winter. A call to the gendarmes would only result in the kind of fuss Madame Vaughn would abhor."

If he was a con man, he was a highly accomplished one. Mollified by his air of respectability, Gina asked, "Perhaps you have a card?"

He handed her a business card and it all looked legitimate—the neat, bold engraving of his name, vocation, and address seemed to tally with his fine grey suit and the understanding in his dark eyes. The man's name was Maître Bosshard and he was a lawyer. At least, that was what his card said. He certainly seemed respectable, despite having broken into an apartment.

The lawyer deflected further questioning by holding up one hand. "If you will excuse me, I must find a locksmith before he closes for the day." He retreated back into the apartment and pulled the door shut behind him, effectively ending the conversation.

Lost in speculation, Gina slowly descended the marble staircase and let herself into the brasserie's office by the side door that gave onto the foyer of the apartment building.

She peeked into the kitchen, which was buzzing with noise and movement. Chefs barked orders from their various stations, waiters loaded their arms with dishes and whizzed past. And there was Claire at the center of it all, fully in command, conducting her staff's movements like a maestro. Catching sight of Gina, who was standing by the door, Claire acknowledged her friend's raised eyebrow and jerk of a chin with a nod and a shooing gesture that said, *I'll be with you when I can.* The next moment, Claire was leaping over to the stove to pour brandy into a fry pan and tilt it to the heat. Flames whooshed upward, then slowly died. Gina retreated to the office to wait.

Now that she'd recovered from the effects of Maître Bosshard's reassuring calm, doubts began to surface in Gina's mind. Had she been a fool to trust him? He could be a confidence trickster or a thief. Or even if he was genuine, perhaps he had broken in precisely because something awful had befallen Madame. Was she lying up there in her apartment, lifeless, right now? Gina shivered, biting her thumb and thinking hard. She shouldn't jump to conclusions, but how could she fail to fear the worst when the two men had forced their way in like that? What had made them do it? Madame had been out and about only that morning. It wasn't as if she'd been missing for days. A frisson of dread ran down Gina's spine.

Impatient to speak with Claire, she paced the small office. At least Claire might know if this Maître Bosshard was legitimate or not.

A knock fell on the door that led from the office to the apartment building lobby. Gina wasn't sure if she should answer, but it might be important. She wrenched it open. Maître Bosshard was standing there, without his sidekick this time. "Oh!"

He seemed equally surprised to see Gina. "I realize it's a busy time, but might I speak with Mademoiselle Bedeau? It is very important."

Just then, Claire bustled in, carrying a plate of steak frites. "Gina, you *must* eat! . . ." She faltered and stopped short as she noticed Gina's companion. "Maître Bosshard! What are you doing here?"

Then he had been telling the truth about his identity, Gina thought with relief.

"I realize now is not a good time, but . . ." the lawyer began, then hesitated. "I thought it best to give you this tonight." He handed Claire an envelope. "From Madame Vaughn. She left it for you."

"I don't understand," said Claire. Taking the letter, she put Gina's dinner plate down on the desk, then ripped the envelope open and fished out a brass key. "What is this? I only saw Madame this morning. She could have . . ." But her words trailed off as she scanned the letter.

Maître Bosshard waited. "Anything . . . anything I should know?"

None of her business, of course, but Gina was desperate to hear details, too. Why would Madame take off like this, and leave Claire her key?

Claire reread the message, thrust it into her apron pocket, then held up the key. "She wants me to look after her apartment. Says she won't be back again for some time—maybe a year—and would I please stay there until she returns. She says not to worry about her, that she's fine, but something came up suddenly and she needed to leave Paris straightaway."

"She didn't tell you what the emergency was?" demanded Gina.

"You know how she is," said Claire with a shrug, her eyes shifting to the side. "She said she simply had to see Africa before she died. I believe she's on her way to a safari in Kenya as we speak."

"Africa." The lawyer nodded. "Yes, that's it." He inclined his head at Claire. "Madame left me similar instructions. To clear out her belongings for you to move in, and to pay any utilities while she's gone. Only, she forgot to leave her key under the mat as she'd promised." He made an apologetic gesture toward Gina. "My associate and I were obliged to break in."

Claire's eyes were great, wide pools of blue, and her usually ruddy cheeks were pale. Was it the prospect of caring for Madame's extravagant apartment upstairs that she found so daunting? Or had there been something else in the letter that had shocked her?

The lawyer smiled reassuringly at Claire. "If there's anything else you need, please call." Maître Bosshard handed Claire his card and left.

Gina watched her friend stare down at the lawyer's card for some time before putting it in her pocket with Madame Vaughn's letter and key.

"I hope it's nothing serious?" Gina ended the statement on a note of inquiry that bordered on interrogation. She couldn't help it; she was incurably curious. It was what made her such a tenacious journalist.

Before she could reply, Vo-Vo stuck her head into the office. "Claire!" she barked. "What are you doing back here?"

Claire started and put her hand to her chest. Then she drew a long breath. "Coming." She made a face and squeezed Gina's hand. "Let's talk tomorrow, yes? And make sure you eat your dinner!"

"JUST LIKE OLD times," Gina murmured the next morning as they stood looking up at the new Dior window display.

Finally she would have Claire's full attention. Or at least the part of it that wasn't contemplating the fashions. The window contained a tableau of store mannequins in day suits. The creations were black, elegant, and completely beyond Gina's budget. She'd never truly understood Claire's yearning for couture until now, when it had been whisked so far out of her reach.

"Not quite like old times," answered Claire. "I miss Margot."

"Me, too," said Gina. "She made everything more fun, didn't she?" She sighed. "And boy, could I use some cheering up right now."

"Maybe she'll come back for a vacation sometime," said Claire. "I suppose you sent her an invitation to the wedding?"

Gina nodded, frowning. "Though heaven knows if she got it or if she'll ignore that like every other letter I've sent. Have you heard from her?"

"No." Claire's mouth twisted. "Not for years. But wouldn't she at least respond if it was about your wedding? That's important. I still can't believe she stopped writing."

Gina didn't immediately reply. Margot's silence had hurt her as much as it had hurt Claire. She'd hoped very hard that a wedding invitation might prompt Margot to get in touch. "Well, just in case, I need to get word to her that the whole deal's off. What if she tries to surprise me and I'm not even in the country?"

"Margot would write," said Claire. "She'd send an acceptance. She might be flighty, but she always had good manners."

"There isn't anywhere to send an acceptance anymore," said Gina, sighing. However, she had set up mail redirection before she'd left home, so hopefully any correspondence from Margot would still reach her via the local post office in Saint-Germain-des-Prés—if belatedly. "I'd better send her a telegram," she said. "'Wedding's off.

Meet me in Paris.'" The telegram would be expensive but she couldn't let Margot set off for the States on a fool's errand.

"What happened with you and Hal?" asked Claire.

But it wasn't something Gina wished to talk about openly in the middle of the street. She linked arms with Claire and said, "Come on. Let's find somewhere we can talk."

As they turned to go, one of the mannequins, a slight figure dressed all in black, seemed to animate inside the Dior window, then disappear. Gina frowned, about to remark on it to Claire. Then she shrugged. Her eyes were playing tricks on her. Either that or one of the Dior employees had been making some adjustment to the window display. She'd had a fleeting sense of the familiar—in fact, for a wild moment, she'd thought she'd glimpsed Margot—but it was gone.

The two friends strolled for some time, and Claire told Gina about the brasserie and Papa Bedeau's decision to sell.

"That's so sad!" said Gina. "Won't it be awful to see Le Chat under new management?"

"It is sad," Claire agreed. "I wish my brother was interested in taking it on but he has a family of his own now, and a business to run. Still, I can't help feeling a little relieved. I can finally get my career back on track."

They chose a small café and ordered. As they discussed Claire's plans and Gina told Claire about the job she'd landed at the book-shop and the apartment she'd found, Gina drank black coffee and nibbled on a corner of Claire's croissant. For Claire, it was a hot chocolate sort of day, with lashings of whipped cream on top.

"But enough about all of that," said Claire. "What happened to you, Gina?"

Gina pressed her fingertip into the croissant crumbs on the table. Claire's large eyes were fixed on her with expectation and sympathy. But now that it came down to it, Gina found that she couldn't go into all of the heartbreak. Humiliation seemed to rise up through her chest and close a hand around her throat like a vise.

"Tell me," said Claire, "what did Hal do?" When Gina didn't immediately answer, she asked, "Did he break off the engagement?"

"No, I did." In her mind's eye, Gina saw the scene once more. A private dining room at the club, all dark wood paneling and gleaming silver. Joe, Hal's father, treating Gina to lunch, before telling her over cigars and brandy that she must now break off her engagement with his son. Her father had lost all of his money, and was in bad odor with his investors, including Joe himself. Such a fall from grace could not help but taint his daughter. Hal was being groomed for politics—to enter the White House one day had always been his dream. But to achieve the heights of power, he needed the right woman by his side. And Gina must see that she was no longer that woman. Well, Gina had seen it. And she had done what she'd needed to do.

"So do we hate him, this Hal?" said Claire. She always liked things spelled out in black-and-white.

"Not at all," said Gina. She still loved him, and that was why it hurt so much. Hal had fought hard to keep her. In the end, she'd only escaped him by leaving the country. "It just wasn't meant to be."

Claire reached for Gina's hand and gave it a squeeze. "Maybe it's for the best, *hein*? You never truly wanted to be married, did you, Gina? You always dreamed of independence."

Gina agreed, though her bruised heart robbed her words of conviction. When, exactly, had she lost sight of her dreams? Sometime after meeting Hal. He'd been so persistent, so perceptive and genuine. Despite her reluctance to marry someone from her parents' world, Hal had gotten under her skin. By the end of it, she'd done the thing she'd vowed never to do. Allowed her love for a man to temper her ambition. Let herself lean on him. But then, she reminded herself, even as a single woman she'd never been independent in any meaningful way. She'd always had family money to cushion her fall.

"I didn't know what I was talking about back then," she said at last. "True independence means earning a living. Writing novels doesn't pay the bills—at least, not immediately. Right now I simply can't afford to have dreams."

"Nonsense!" said Claire. "You can do anything you put your mind to."

Gina blinked at her friend's certainty. Dryly she replied, "Thank you for the vote of confidence, but it's not that simple."

"It is exactly that simple," said Claire. "Do you think I let being trapped at Le Chat stop me pursuing my dream? Every spare moment I have, I am practicing my skills, perfecting recipes. If I can do that *and* run a brasserie, then you can write a few pages of your novel every day."

How to explain that the emotional upheaval of the past few months had left Gina drained and desperately uninspired? She needed to survive before she needed to be a novelist.

"We'll do it together," said Claire. "You move in with me to Madame's apartment. I'll cook. You write."

Gina stared at her. "But wouldn't Madame mind?"

"Of course she wouldn't!" said Claire. "And if it makes you feel any better, I shall ask permission of Maître Bosshard. And I won't tell him what a slattern you are."

"Slattern?" Gina retorted, indignant. "Where did you pick up a word like that?"

Claire grinned. "I know it because my mother used to call me one."

Gina laughed. "That all sounds marvelous but I really don't have time to work on a novel. I need to establish myself here as a free-lancer on top of working at the bookstore."

"Then break up the day," said Claire. "Come to the brasserie for your dinner, go upstairs and work on your articles at night, then write your novel first thing in the morning before you go to work. I'll check on you every day, make sure you stick to the plan. And you can do the same for me."

The instinct to argue against what Claire was saying was so strong, Gina was surprised at herself. Why was she fighting it? Did she want to write a novel or not? Gina stared at her friend. "Why are you so good to me? I must seem like a walking disaster, and a sad, moping sack of potatoes into the bargain."

Claire laughed. "Sack of potatoes? You?" She shook her head. "You've had a terrible knock but you're a strong, clever woman, Gina. You'll get back on your feet. I'll help however I can, cheer you on, nag you—even if it makes you hate me."

Gina stared in wonder at her friend. The experience of someone showing her possibilities instead of throwing obstacles in her path was so novel, it took her breath away. More energized than she'd been for months, she laughed and looked at her watch. "I guess if I'm going to write some pages of that novel before work, I'd better make a start." There had been an idea brewing in her mind for some time . . . A book about a young American woman in Paris.

"There! You see?" said Claire with a radiant smile as they left the café. She turned and gave Gina a hearty hug, rocking her back and forth a little in her excitement. "I'm so glad you're back, *mon amie*. We'll make everything work, you and I. We'll achieve our dreams, no matter how long it takes or how hard it gets. Just you wait and see."

Margot

Margot MacFarlane had been at work early, swapping out the accessories on the store mannequins in the Dior display window, when who should stroll along, then stop to stand peering up at her, but Claire and Gina.

She was hovering behind a display mannequin that was slightly taller than she was and trying to fix a tricky catch on a necklace when she heard their voices, muffled a little by the glass—Claire's heavily accented English and Gina's louder, faintly raspy tones. Startled, she'd peeked around and caught sight of her friends. What was Gina doing in Paris?

Instinct made Margot duck back behind the mannequin and hold herself frozen in place. Her face wasn't visible to Claire and Gina because they'd halted squarely in front of the window. If they were to walk on and stare back in at an angle, they would spot her, but for the moment, she was safe. She merely had to stand very still with her arms in the air for as long as it took for them to move away.

From past experience, that could take a while. In front of this display window was where the three friends had always exchanged good news, the highlights of their day, and everything that was right with the world. Right, because Margot had made a rule that nothing negative must ever pass their lips in front of Dior. The atelier was like a shrine at which the only acceptable offering was happiness.

Oh, dear! Margot heard Madame Renou, her supervisor, call her name, and squeezed her eyes shut. She couldn't move in case Gina or Claire spotted her, but if she didn't come on the double when called, she'd receive the sharp edge of Madame Renou's tongue.

"Where *is* that girl?" she heard Madame say to one of the others. "I told her to switch out the hat display half an hour ago."

"Maybe she has gone to use the convenience," volunteered Delphine, a sweet young assistant who always tried to defend Margot.

"Well, go fetch her back," said Madame. "She has a way with the hats."

Margot was glad to hear the compliment, though Madame would not have said it to her face. Monsieur Dior himself had praised Margot's sense of style. She had a knack for making unusual pairings work, of avoiding the obvious, the cliché.

Changing the hat display in the boutique had been only one item of a long list Madame had given her that morning, a list that Margot had been working through efficiently and diligently. She disliked the way Madame always tried to make out that she was scatterbrained and feckless. Perhaps she had acted like that once upon a time, largely to amuse her friends. But that was back in the days when she could afford to be taken for a delicious featherhead. She had shed that version of herself long ago. Or rather, had it stripped from her, piece by piece, like the bark from a tree.

Margot ventured a quick peek at Gina and Claire over the mannequin's shoulder. Both women had grown thinner, she thought.

Both looked far more serious than they ought, particularly while on pilgrimage to Dior.

How she had missed them and wondered about them, and dreamed of what their lives must be—almost as if by willing them both to enjoy a happy and fulfilled existence, she might somehow borrow a little of that happiness for herself.

Was Claire a chef in a great Parisian restaurant these days? Granted, it was too early in her career for Michelin stars, but Margot had no doubt that with Claire's talent and diligence, she would be well on her way up the culinary ladder by now.

And what about Gina? Margot would have heard if Gina had achieved her dream and published the great American novel. A compulsive reader with wide-ranging tastes, even in the hardest of times, Margot had managed to buy, beg, or borrow most of the books she'd wanted to read. On her weekly visits to the bouquinistes, she had always searched for a cover with Gina's name on it but never heard of one coming out. Maybe Gina had stuck with journalism, after all, or maybe she was still waiting for her big break as a novelist.

Seeing her best friends in the world together like that, without her, hurt with an exquisite, pleasure-laced pain. Margot had spent years believing they had forgotten all about her, that to the other two young women, their time together in Paris had been a pleasant interlude, nothing more. Doggedly, she had gone on writing to them long after their letters had ceased to arrive. Reminding herself again and again that she must have been mistaken about what their time in Paris had meant did not seem to lessen the sadness and feeling of betrayal. Now, here the two of them were together. Maybe it was only Margot they hadn't valued as much as she had valued them.

Regardless of the past, she couldn't let her friends see her now. She couldn't rush out the door of the atelier and yell, "Surprise!" and assault her dearest friends with hugs and kisses. She couldn't link arms with them and stand out there in front of the display window as the three of them had done so many times in the past, discussing the world and all of the good things in it.

Longings crowded her mind—a thousand "if only"s that all focused on one dagger-sharp regret. If only she'd never met *him,* everything would be different.

Stop it, Margot! But before she could catch the runaway train of her thoughts, his voice echoed through her mind. The trembling started, the pounding of her heart.

She'd tried so hard never to think about it, to block all of it from her memory. She couldn't let that helpless, hopeless feeling take over. If she did, she simply would not be able to function.

Her arms, held up for so long, began to tremble. She needed Claire and Gina to go. *Why didn't they leave, for goodness' sake?* Clenching her hands into fists, she squeezed her eyes shut and deliberately slowed her breathing. Her arms ached but she dared not move or even rest them against the mannequin that hid her from view, in case she knocked it over.

Think good thoughts, she told herself. Margot's rule had been to talk only about delightful things at Dior. Champagne and beauty and dreams and lovely young men. No, not men. She shuddered. Never again.

Deep breaths, her father would have said. With a supreme effort, she focused on the jacket on the model in front of her, on the weft and warp of the superfine wool, the precise line of the shoulder seam. When she'd managed to calm herself enough, she ventured another look over the mannequin's shoulder at Claire and Gina. "Finally!" she whispered. The two of them were moving off.

Carefully, Margot turned, shuffled along to the side, and pushed open the concealed door that led to the fashion house. Without a backward glance, she slipped through it, her heart beating hard.

Next time she had to dress the window, she'd make a more careful reconnaissance. But the knowledge, always held but now concrete, that Gina and Claire still existed in the world without her—and worse, that they were now together, here in Paris, while she couldn't go to them—made her terribly, sickeningly sad.

Chapter Three

Claire

Two weeks passed before Claire and Gina moved into the apartment above the brasserie. Maître Bosshard had requested Madame Vaughn's former housemaid to remove all of the personal belongings Madame hadn't taken with her and spring-clean the apartment until it was ready for new occupants.

Claire took one horrified look at the shoebox of a room where Gina had been living for the past two weeks and wished she'd insisted on having her stay with her family until Madame Vaughn's apartment was free.

"Are you *sure* Madame won't mind?" Gina asked for the twentieth time. "I wouldn't want to impose."

"Maître Bosshard has granted his approval," said Claire. "And Madame did say I was to treat the apartment as my own."

Gina sighed. "Thank goodness for that. It has been pretty bad, I admit. And I just heard from my father. He's in Paris at the moment on business, so it would be nice if he didn't see his little princess living in squalor."

As they approached the door to the apartment, Claire felt in her coat pocket for the key, and thought once more about the secret

Madame had entrusted to her in that letter. Did Maître Bosshard know the reason Madame had left Paris? The fact that he'd been worried enough to break into the apartment might suggest that he did. It would be easier if Claire could tell Gina the truth, but she couldn't break a confidence.

The brass key had a satisfying weight to it, with curlicues on the bow and a patina that suggested it might be as old as the building itself. Claire unlocked the door and she and Gina moved in single file through the narrow vestibule.

"Wow." They emerged into a light-filled space—one could only describe it as a drawing room. Gina turned around in a circle. "It's like a penthouse." She headed deeper into the apartment. "Two large bedrooms. Bathroom. Galley kitchen—not that I'll be using *that* . . . And a great view, too!"

Gina pushed open the French doors that gave onto a small balcony, where window boxes would spill crimson geraniums throughout the summer and fall, and a small circular table with two wrought iron chairs awaited. Claire joined her friend outside. They weren't high enough to see above the rooftops but she enjoyed feeling part of the bustle and color below. The plane trees lining the street were bare now, but soon they'd be covered in pale green leaves. Looking down, she saw the top of Le Chat's dark red awning and the traffic passing by, the patrons coming in and out of the Tabac across the street.

It was the edge of winter, and a chill wind blew, so they retreated inside and went out to the landing to bring in their luggage. Gina had just one suitcase. Claire had taken a couple of days to sort through her belongings and brought with her only what she needed, plus a few keepsakes. At the end of that exercise, she'd realized with some satisfaction that she had never been much of a pack rat. Her life was in the kitchen. She didn't spend money on frivolous things.

"I knew Madame had style, but this apartment is something else," said Gina.

Madame's panache was everywhere—in the bold pieces of art she had chosen with obvious care, abstracts mixed with Renaissance nudes and striking modern sculptures, in the eclectic yet harmonious mix of modern furnishings and antiques. The handsome fireplace, the high ceilings, the gorgeous, floaty pale green silk drapes.

"Beautiful," agreed Claire, though privately she thought with trepidation of all the dusting she'd have to do.

"And will you look at that?" Gina crossed the room with her long, decisive stride. "A desk *and* a typewriter! Oh, and it's a beauty, too." She looked up. "Do you think she'd mind if I used it?"

"Of course not," said Claire. "You know how generous she is."

Gina kissed her fingers to their absent benefactor. "Bless you, Madame Vaughn. I'll buy a new ribbon and paper first thing tomorrow."

Claire's focus shifted to the correspondence that lay propped against a small bronze art deco dancer.

Gina stopped talking and followed her gaze. "Ought we to open them? Did she say anything about paying bills and so forth?"

"All mail should have been redirected to Maître Bosshard," said Claire. "I'll see that he gets this one."

"What *did* she say in her letter to you?" asked Gina. "Did she give any explanation at all about why she left so suddenly?" This wasn't the first time she'd asked the question.

"No," said Claire a trifle wearily. "But it sounds as if she might be away for close to a year."

Madame had written a long letter, but other than one solitary sentence, it had all been instructions about taking care of the apartment and its contents. And about a certain couture gown . . .

No. Claire was not going to think about the gown. It was too much all at once, on top of this fabulous apartment. She simply couldn't.

Gina's unpacking took all of ten minutes. She emerged from her designated bedroom dressed in a brunch coat, clutching a towel and her toiletries bag. "If you don't mind, I'm off to have a luxurious, long soak," she said gleefully, and sped to the bathroom.

Claire chuckled. Public bathing was not something to which Gina had grown accustomed while living in her tiny maid's chamber. No doubt Claire wouldn't see her friend again for some time.

It didn't take Claire long to unpack her personal belongings, but cooking implements were another matter.

The galley kitchen was small, and by the looks of it, Madame had rarely used it for more than boiling a kettle. However, it had a decent amount of storage space, so Claire decided to unpack the essentials. She was just sorting her saucepans and hanging them up on the pot rack when the telephone rang.

"I'll get it!" Gina called. She must be out of the bath.

Claire didn't hear more than a murmur. After a short conversation, Gina popped her head into the kitchen. She had a strange expression on her face. "It's for you, Claire. She says she's from La Maison Dior."

"What?" Claire hit her head on an open cupboard door and yelped. Rubbing the spot that smarted, she added, "For me?" This was too quick. She still hadn't decided how to refuse Madame Vaughn's parting gift.

"Well?" said Gina, her voice laced with excitement. "Aren't you going to come to the phone?"

"Oh!" Claire felt heat rush to her face. "Yes. I suppose I'd better."

Claire crossed the drawing room to the telephone table and lifted the heavy receiver. The instrument was ivory and gold, and even had a matching gold dialer. Claire picked up the dialer and tapped it on the message pad. Tentatively, she said, *"Allô?"*

"Is this Mademoiselle Bedeau?" said a husky female voice on the other end.

"Yes, this is she."

"Ah, thank goodness! I have been trying to reach you for the past few days. Mademoiselle Bedeau, Monsieur Dior is ready for your fitting. May I arrange a suitable time for you to come in?"

"Oh!" said Claire. "Oh, I . . . er, that is to say, I don't think I can . . ."

Before she could finish, Gina snatched the receiver from her, continuing the conversation without missing a beat.

When she hung up, she turned to Claire, beaming. "You have an appointment for three o'clock on Tuesday the twelfth. That's in two weeks so you have plenty of notice to ask for time off. And I'm coming with you to make sure you go through with it. What on earth, Claire? This must be Madame Vaughn's doing, mustn't it?"

Like an automaton, Claire nodded. "She wants *me* to have this gown. A Dior gown!"

"You mean you knew about it already?" Gina put her hands on her hips. "Why didn't you tell me?"

Claire sighed. "Madame was having a gown made at Dior but she won't be here in Paris for the final fittings and where she's going . . . safari in Africa, you know . . . Well, she won't have occasion to wear it. You know how she likes to have only the latest fashions, so if she doesn't wear it this season, she never will. So . . . she wanted me to have it." Claire wished she could share Gina's excitement. "The gown is all paid for. I just need to go to the fittings and . . . and that's all. But I don't have anywhere to wear a gown like that. And it's a bit much, don't you think? I mean, minding the apartment is one thing. But accepting a couture gown . . ."

Gina tilted her head, considering this. "It certainly is true that Madame Vaughn would never wear last season's couture. I don't see what's wrong with not wanting the gown to go to waste. Still, it makes me even more curious about what came up that made her take off like that."

Claire rolled her eyes. "This again!"

"I know, I know. It's just so strange, don't you think? Running off to Africa without a word to anyone. And about the gown—don't be silly, of course you must accept it! I will come with you to the fitting and live vicariously through you and fantasize about all the beautiful dresses that might have been." She laughed. "Just think, Claire! Your dream is finally coming true."

"Yes. Yes, I suppose it is." Inwardly Claire balked. How could she accept such a generous gift, even if it might never be used otherwise? Imagine only wearing a dress that expensive for a single season!

No. She couldn't do it. Gina might think it silly to refuse, but something about it didn't seem right to Claire.

She glanced at the telephone. She ought to call back and cancel the appointment, tell Dior to keep the gown until Madame Vaughn's return. But not in front of Gina. She didn't want to have to argue about it anymore. Someone who was accustomed to wealth would never understand how staggering it was to be presented with such an astonishingly expensive gift. Even if Claire longed to accept, she simply couldn't. She'd find a quiet moment when Gina wasn't around to telephone Dior. Then she'd cancel the appointment.

Gina

Gina Winter, you are not going to be a pushover this time. She'd run away to Paris to escape temptation. Now Jay was dangling it before her eyes once more. "Father, I can't."

J. Wadsworth Winter wasn't used to hearing the word "no"—especially not from the women in his life. Despite his recent troubles, he looked as rakishly handsome as ever, with his pencil moustache and brushed-back hair and his immaculate grey suit with one perfect pink rosebud in the buttonhole. It took all of Gina's strength to harden her heart against him.

Hurt surprise shone in his vivid green gaze. "But, Gigi, you *have* to. Everything depends on it. Don't you see?" Jay put his hands on her shoulders, then cupped her face in his big palms. "Do me this one favor and everything we lost can be ours again."

Not everything. Not the most important thing. Her mother would never smile her enchanting, dreamy smile, never pen another word of verse, never lay her gentle hand on Gina's forehead. Rose Winter had died when Gina was ten—of heartbreak over Jay's many affairs, everyone had said. No one knew that beneath that gentle exterior beat the strong, whole heart of a lioness. Cancer had ravaged Rose's body, but her mind had been keen until the last. She had pressed a small book of poetry into Gina's hands and told her to leave home as soon as she could. *"Live,"* she said. "Go to Paris and live." Her wasted hand made a gesture around at their magnificent apartment, with its lofty view of Central Park. "You don't need all this."

At the time, they had divided their year between a sprawling mansion in Connecticut and an apartment in Manhattan; the luxury that surrounded her was normal for Gina and she hadn't understood. It was only after they lost it all that she heard the plea beneath those words: *Live the life I should have had.*

Even when her father had lost all of their money and more on a risky business deal, she hadn't obeyed her mother's urging. Gina had left Washington, where she'd been working as a correspondent, and come home to be with her father, only to find that she had no home left. Jay had moved into the Manhattan apartment he'd bought for Marly Madison, his current mistress. The apartment was in Marly's name, so it had escaped the creditors. There was no room in that apartment for Gina.

That had severed the last, frayed thread that had tethered her to America. Finally Gina obeyed her mother. She sold everything she owned that was of value, bought a ticket to Paris, and left.

The only item of real value she'd managed to keep was Rose Winter's gold fountain pen. She wrote with it every day, and the memory of her mother lent her strength.

Working what amounted to three jobs now, Gina was tired—more tired than she'd ever been—but she felt something she hadn't even experienced when she'd received her first paycheck from her first job at a magazine. She was making her own way, her own money, relying solely on herself. Free accommodation at Madame Vaughn's apartment was a huge help, that was for sure, but she planned to save a nice cushion so that when she and Claire eventually had to leave the apartment, they could afford to move somewhere decent.

Now her father promised restitution. A rise from the ashes. But it all depended on Hal. "I can't go to the embassy ball, Father," said Gina. "Please don't make me see him."

Hal was in Paris. Did he even know she was here? Contradictory emotions battled inside her. She hated that, along with the horror and fear of meeting him again under such humiliating circumstances, she still held a shameful hope—that he had, indeed, come to persuade her to marry him after all, that their reunion would be like a scene from a movie, that he'd call her a little fool and sweep her into his arms . . . She made a face. She was a fool, indeed, to believe that love could conquer all. If only there was a switch she could flick to turn off the love she still felt for him.

The worst part? Hal hadn't done anything wrong. It was his tough-as-nails father, Joe, who had pointed out to her—quite rightly—that Jay's predicament had made Gina an unsuitable wife for a young man with political ambitions. Until Jay's fall from grace, Gina had possessed the connections and the finances to support Hal's rise to the very top. Now, however, she had neither.

Had it been Joe alone who had wanted the White House for his son, she might have refused to give in. But Hal was talented and driven, and passionate about eradicating the many injustices that prevailed in America right now. He could achieve great things—as long as he didn't have Gina holding him back.

Perversely Gina resented Hal all the more for his naivety in refusing to give her up, for making it so very hard for her to do what was best for him and break off their engagement.

Now Hal was in Paris and Jay expected her to attend a ball where everyone would know her history. On top of that, she was supposed to cultivate Hal, to persuade him to invest his money with the man who had lost Hal's father a fortune. With a handsome inheritance from his maternal grandfather, Hal was a wealthy man in his own right.

"Please, Gigi." Desperation lurked behind Jay's hundred-watt smile. "Do it for me." When she continued to hesitate, he added, "Just get Hal to agree to meet with me. I'll do the rest."

Gina couldn't imagine anything worse. A ball at the United States Embassy, where everyone would know and gossip about her family's fall from grace. Of course they all thought Hal had jilted her, which made things a hundred times worse. And to meet him there again, in front of them all . . .

Gina squeezed her eyes shut, her entire body clenching with humiliation. She hadn't bought a new dress for months, and nothing she'd brought to Paris was suitable for such a glittering occasion. Such a contrast to the previous visit to the fashion capital of the world, when she'd purchased gowns and jewels without a second thought. The jewels were long gone, the gowns snatched out of her closet by the burly men who had come to collect on her father's debts.

And yet, if only Jay *could* reclaim his position in the world, if he could make this new business venture a success, then perhaps Gina could be with Hal after all. She shouldn't allow herself to hope, but didn't love make fools of everybody?

"I don't have anything to wear," she said at last. Her resistance was crumbling, and they both knew it.

Jay, who cared more about appearances than her mother ever had, nodded slowly. "You'll need couture to make the right impression. Can't you borrow something from that friend of yours? What's her name . . ." He frowned in an effort of remembering and Gina tried not to roll her eyes. He'd met Margot many times, but he never remembered a woman's name unless he wanted to romance her.

"Margot went back to Australia years ago." She wished Margot were here now. Not for the dresses, but she could use her friend's unique blend of tact and ruthless determination to extricate her from this excruciating conversation.

"Well, isn't there anyone else?" said Jay. "You used to have a lot of friends in Paris."

"No." She couldn't bring herself to renew her acquaintance with her friends from before. Claire was the only one she wanted to see.

She blinked. There it was. The solution to her dilemma was obvious, wasn't it? The Dior gown . . . But how could Gina wear it before Claire had the chance to do so?

Jay's defeated expression, when she knew for a fact that he bought couture for his current girlfriend, stung. But unlike Marly Madison, Gina did not want Jay to go deeper into debt on her behalf.

Still . . . was she relieved or disappointed when he didn't make the offer?

She shrugged. "I guess I'll work it out somehow."

"So you'll go?" Her father's face lit up, like a small boy's at Christmas.

"Yes. I'll go." If there was any chance she could help her father get back on his feet, she would have to try. And she couldn't deny it. She longed to see Hal again, despite knowing the encounter would be painful.

Jay pulled her into a mighty bear hug that reminded her of happier days, when money worries happened to other people. He drew back, his brow furrowed. "You'll need an escort, of course."

Gina's heart sank at the reminder. She'd intended to avoid her fellow Americans altogether while in Paris. Now she'd have to beg someone to go with her to the ball.

Casually her father added, "Why not ask Hal?"

Jay's tactless suggestion made her want to scream. If this was all a ploy to bring her and Hal back together, she'd never forgive him. Biting back the scathing response that leaped to her tongue, she said, "I'll find someone." Then, because he seemed to brighten, she added, "Don't get your hopes up, Father. I don't think this will work."

But Jay was having none of her pessimism. "Of course it will. The boy wanted to marry you. He would have, too, if the old man hadn't nixed it. He'll be putty in your hands."

There was no sense arguing, and Jay had already moved on. "What was the other thing I meant to ask you?" Jay clicked his fingers. "That's right. Did you see the new Mellifleur anthology is out? Do you have a copy in that bookstore of yours, by any chance?"

She did indeed. In fact she'd just bought it—a little gift to reward herself for sticking to her daily writing schedule. One of his saving graces, and what had attracted Rose to him in the first place, was Jay's love of literature.

"I'll get it for you."

After finding him the poetry collection he wanted in the book-case in her bedroom, Gina brought it back into the drawing room, to see her father standing over her desk.

"Oh, don't!" She hated people reading anything she wrote before it was finished. It felt like a violation that he would casually glance through her work, as if he had the right. As if it wasn't the most important thing in the world to her, and intensely private until it was done.

He turned, his cheeks flushed. "Sorry, Gigi. I couldn't resist." His eyes grew moist, and her heart melted once more. "There's so much of your mother in you."

He drew a large cream stock card from an inner pocket of his coat. "Here's the embassy invitation. The ball is six weeks away.

I trust that's sufficient time to . . ." He trailed off. "Look, I know things are tight now. Maybe I can—"

"It's fine." Gina stared down at the card. It had her name on it. That meant her father had already solicited the invitation without asking her first. The elegantly engraved script blurred. Her hands grew clammy at the thought of facing them all. Not just Hal, but the society gossips as well. Carefully she propped the card on the mantelpiece. "I'll work something out."

Satisfied, her father left. She stood by the window to watch him go. The brasserie awning briefly hid him from view but then she caught sight of him continuing up the street, the slim volume of poetry she had given him in hand, a jaunty quality to his walk. She might have been mistaken, but she thought she heard the faint whistle of his favorite tune.

Gina turned away, feeling the weight that had seemingly lifted from Jay's shoulders settle onto hers.

If only Margot were here in Paris. Then at least the problem of the gown would be solved.

Still, casually sharing clothes was one thing; admitting to Margot that her family was too broke to buy her a couture gown for the embassy ball would be something else.

What was Margot doing now? Living the life of a social butterfly back in Sydney, no doubt. Gina smiled a little, picturing her as she continued to flit about the place, doing not much of anything except bringing sparkle and fun to every occasion. Gina had always wondered if that kind of life could be truly fulfilling for someone like Margot. There was a sharp mind behind all of that froth and bubble. Still, convention was a difficult thing to kick against. Even Gina, who had begun with high ambitions, had gladly agreed to marriage once she'd found love with Hal.

Now she thought about the Dior gown Claire was about to receive from Madame Vaughn . . . No. It just wasn't right. Gina shouldn't even raise the issue because she knew Claire's generous heart would prompt her to lend the gown to Gina at once. Only how could she go to the embassy ball if she had nothing to wear?

Chapter Four

Claire

The brasserie was quiet that morning, so while she waited for the last trays of croissants to puff up and turn golden in the oven, the whorls of their laminated layers as intricate as fingerprints, Claire jotted down all of her contacts in the restaurant world. Most of these were fellow classmates from the Cordon Bleu or chefs she'd worked with at different restaurants, but one name stood out—Monsieur Thibault. He had opened two restaurants now, and each of them had been awarded the coveted three-star rating in the Michelin Guide. Unfortunately she'd been fired from Monsieur Thibault's kitchen at the Meurice for insubordination, so he would be unlikely to hire her again.

Reluctantly she crossed him off her list and then arranged the names in order of preference. Claire didn't get a day off until the following week, but she'd begin working through her list, trying to schedule interviews for that day.

With a jolt, she remembered she still hadn't canceled the appointment at Dior.

After the morning's baking was done, Claire slipped up to the apartment. She'd telephone La Maison Dior and tell them she wasn't coming, ask them to put the gown away for when Madame returned.

Upstairs, she found Gina pacing, her arms crossed and her fingertips digging into the flesh of her upper arms. Gina's blue eyes seethed with emotion, but the rest of her face remained expressionless. She had always carried herself like a dancer, her posture almost too correct. That hadn't changed, but her body seemed more rigid than usual.

"What is it?" asked Claire. "What's wrong?"

Gina blew out a breath. "My father came to see me this morning."

"I'm sorry to have missed him." Claire had met Jay Winter a few times. She knew the type: charming but with an underlying ruthlessness she wasn't sure Gina had ever fully recognized. "Did he come to take you back home?"

Gina shook her head. "No. No, he didn't try to do that, at least."

"Then what?" asked Claire gently.

"Oh, it's nothing, really." Gina drew a deep breath and seemed to gain control over her emotions. With folded arms, she faced Claire. "It's Hal. My father wants me to cultivate him. He needs Hal to invest in his business."

Claire gaped at her. How could Jay ask something like that? She didn't yet know the details, but she could tell the end of their engagement had hit Gina hard. "Must you be involved? Why doesn't your father ask him directly? Surely—" Claire broke off at the look on her friend's face, which had shuttered once more. It seemed terribly selfish and insensitive of Jay to expect this of his daughter, but perhaps there was some deeper reason for his involving her. One that Claire didn't know about. Maybe he hoped to bring the two of them back together?

Gina gave a quick shake of her head, as if to dismiss Claire's unspoken objections. "I need to be prepared when I see him. I need to be armored with perfect makeup and fabulous hair and a glorious gown." Her determined smile went awry. "I sound pathetic, don't I?"

Claire searched her friend's face. An angry and disappointed admirer had once likened Gina to a marble statue, her heart as hard and unresponsive as her perfectly carved features. Gina was the strongest woman Claire had ever known. Now, she sensed the vulnerability beneath Gina's flawless exterior. She wished she could say something to make it all better, but she couldn't.

She ventured on the obvious solution. "Maybe you should just tell your father no."

Gina seemed to freeze. Then she said, "I can't. I know that I should, and I know he is taking advantage of me, but I just can't, Claire." She swallowed. "And I hate to admit it, but . . ." She drew a deep breath. "I want to see him again."

The pain and hope in Gina's eyes caught at Claire's heartstrings.

Gina gave a wry smile. "The only catch is, I don't have a stitch to wear." Claire's face must have registered shock, because Gina spread her hands. "We're broke, you see. The creditors took everything we owned that was worth a dime."

Claire knew Gina was short of money, but she'd assumed that was because she'd left New York without her family's blessing. She hadn't explained that part. "*Mon Dieu!* But why didn't you tell me?"

So Gina related the whole story—her father losing all the family money, Hal's father giving her an ultimatum. The excruciating task of breaking Hal's heart.

Claire had never been able to comprehend the extent of Gina's family wealth. It was impossible to imagine a debt so great that it would swallow up every house, automobile, and boat, every stick of furniture they owned.

What must it have been like to go from luxury to penury in an instant? The debt collectors had even taken the most valuable of Gina's clothes.

Inspiration struck. "But of course! The Dior gown! You should have said something. Why didn't you?"

Gina's shoulders slumped. "I couldn't ask that of you. I'd feel like a complete heel."

"But no! Why should you?" demanded Claire. "I was about to telephone Dior to say I didn't want the gown. But for you, dear Gina, I will be pleased to accept. And *you* can go to the fitting, all right? And I will come with you."

Gina started to argue, but Claire held up her hand. "*Chut!* I don't want to hear it. How many times did I borrow your frocks, back then?" Those frivolous days filled with parties and fun seemed like a long-lost dream, but she would never have enjoyed such a life without Margot and Gina towing her along and foisting their clothes upon her so she didn't feel out of place.

"Oh, I'm so happy to do this!" she said gleefully. Accepting Madame Vaughn's generosity for herself had seemed too . . . Well, it just wasn't right. But for Gina, she most certainly could.

Gina eyed her in wonder. "You were really going to turn down a Dior gown? After all those years of yearning?"

Claire shrugged. "Where would I wear it, anyway? In the kitchen at Le Chat?"

It was true that Claire never went anywhere fun these days. Gina would have to see what she might do to change that. Slowly she shook her head. "I will never cease to wonder at your generosity and goodness, my dear." She gripped Claire's hands tightly in hers. "Thank you, my dearest friend. I will try my very best to repay you."

"No thanks necessary. I shall love seeing you in all your finery." Claire smiled, but suddenly she felt as if sobs burned in her throat. She couldn't for the life of her work out why.

Gina

On the morning after Jay's visit, Gina rose early. The bookstore didn't open for another two hours. A perfect amount of time to spend writing. Hopefully working on her manuscript would take her mind off her father's upsetting visit.

Spurred on less by Claire's nagging than by Claire's example—sometimes Claire would get up before dawn to practice her skills in the brasserie kitchen below—Gina had not missed a day of writing since her second morning in Paris.

Madame Vaughn's desk was so elegant, it was a pleasure to use. Her typewriter was top-of-the-range, too, as one might have expected—very different from Gina's battered old Corona. At first, Gina had only used the typewriter for her freelance articles, but later she'd taken to correcting the handwritten pages of her novel and then typing up the corrected version. The view from the window facing her might have proven distracting to another writer. But whenever Gina worked, she was so focused, she could be anywhere. Her surroundings didn't matter at all.

She picked up the pages she'd written the day before and immediately saw a word she wanted to change. Eyes still on the page, she groped for her pen, but the cool, sleek gold casing did not meet her questing fingers. Impatiently she looked around the desk. Her mother's pen wasn't there.

Anxiety clutching her chest, she checked under papers, shaking them a little in case the pen had been caught among them. The desk drawers yielded no result. Gina got down on her hands and knees to search the floor surrounding the desk. Nothing. Could it be somewhere else? But she hadn't worked anywhere in the apartment other than at the desk.

She made the search anyway, but after she'd looked under the sofa and coffee table and behind the curtains on either side of the desk, she'd exhausted the likely places. Nonetheless she went through the entire apartment, dumping out the contents of her purse and sifting through them, peering under each of the twin beds in her room, rummaging through her dresser drawers. She even glanced in at Claire's room in case she'd borrowed the pen without telling her—unlikely, but by now, Gina was desperate.

Trying to stay calm, she put her hands on her hips, thinking back, retracing her movements. "I had it yesterday." She'd left it on the desk next to her manuscript pages after her morning's writing session. She was sure of it. She only ever used that pen for writing novels—a vow she'd made to honor her mother's memory.

The image of her father reading her work popped up in her mind's eye. Maybe Jay had jotted something down with her pen and absently put it in his pocket. Yes, something like that must have happened. She prayed that it had. She could not bear to lose her one tangible reminder of Rose.

Would Jay have arrived back at his hotel yet? Gina telephoned the Meurice and asked to leave a message for her father. He called back almost immediately.

"You haven't reconsidered about the ball, have you, darling?" Jay's voice was strained.

"No, nothing like that," said Gina. "It's just that I've lost my gold pen. You didn't happen to see it when you were here, did you?"

"No, I can't say that I did," said Jay. "Where did you have it last?"

"I thought I'd left it on the desk in the apartment," said Gina, frowning in an effort to remember exactly the last time she'd put it down. "I'm *sure* I . . ." She trailed off.

"Well, I do hope you find it, darling," said Jay. "Sorry. I have to go. Was that all?"

"Yes," said Gina, staring at the desk. "That's all."

Claire

Claire had tried every contact she knew in Paris, but few were hiring at the moment. Throughout all of those early mornings and late nights working on her skills, she had never once considered that upon being set free from the brasserie, she would find it difficult to get a job.

"You are being too picky," said Vo-Vo when she heard about Claire's struggles. "You've been out of the game for two years. Did you think they'd let you simply pick up again where you left off?"

"You mean I'll have to start over?" Claire was horrified at the thought.

Vo-Vo shrugged. "Just get a foot in the door. You'll prove yourself soon enough."

But Claire had her pride to consider. She couldn't possibly accept a position that was too many steps lower on the ladder than her peers'. If certain people ever found out she'd been forced to go back to being an apprentice, for pity's sake, she'd never live it down.

But when she attended the first round of interviews she'd organized, she discovered that Vo-Vo was right.

Her first port of call was the Auberge du Vert-Galant on the Île de la Cité. She'd managed to beg and plead with a *demi-chef* she'd worked under at Le Meurice to get her an interview.

When Claire arrived at the Auberge, with its wide terrace and its view of the Palais de Justice, her heart was pounding so hard, she thought she might faint. It was one thing to hold in her heart an ambition to be one of the best chefs in Paris; it was quite another to actually present herself for inspection at one of the city's premier restaurants, having not worked in the kitchen of a great chef de cuisine for more than two years.

You can do this, she told herself sternly. Don't be one of those people who are forever talking about what they *might* have done, their lives full of "if only." Don't leave yourself with regrets.

Claire was thoroughly prepared. She'd worked harder than ever, practicing her sauté skills, perfecting her stocks and sauces. She knew she would not be appointed saucier straightaway at a place like the Auberge, but she hoped very much to be made a *demi-chef,* in charge of one of the smaller stations of the kitchen brigade. She knew that she was likely to meet with arrogance over her interlude at Le Chat. She held ready several arguments against such prejudice. If she had to compromise, she wouldn't even mind if they took her on as a lowly *commise*. She'd show them what she could do soon enough and be promoted, just as Vo-Vo had said.

What she did not expect was to be rejected out of hand. From the beginning, she got off on the wrong foot. Her interviewer, pristine in chef's whites with a red kerchief tied at his throat, was the sous-chef, and not the man she'd expected to see.

"But where is Monsieur Bos?" she asked, naming the chef de cuisine.

"Do you think Chef has the time or inclination to trouble himself with someone of your experience?" demanded her interviewer, outraged.

A bad sign that Chef had not bothered to meet her. Worse that she'd managed to offend this man into the bargain. "Mademoiselle Bedeau," said the sous-chef with a haughty sniff, "it is clear to me that you do not have the requisite commitment to *la cuisine* for the Auberge. You have not worked at a decent restaurant in years."

"Well, you see, family circumstances led me to—"

"I'm sorry," the sous-chef interrupted with an arrogant wave of his hand. "There is no place for you here."

And so it went, at interview after interview. Her brasserie experience counted heavily against her—far more heavily than she had guessed. It was so unreasonable! It wasn't as if she was seeking some exalted position. Or were they just making excuses not to hire her? Many kitchens simply didn't hire women, it was true.

Would it have been better to have left the brasserie off her résumé entirely? But then she'd have to explain the gap in her work history, and it would mean telling lies. That wasn't the way she wanted to begin with a new employer.

In desperation, Claire begged to be given a trial period. She offered to work as an apprentice, but even that position was denied her. "Your skills are clearly more suited to a family brasserie," said the final chef who interviewed her. "Go back to Le Chat, mademoiselle. This is not the place for you."

Gina

On the morning of their proposed visit to Dior, Gina dressed carefully and applied her makeup with a well-practiced hand. She was competent enough at dolling herself up, but she wished Margot had been there to do the honors. Margot was a genius with makeup and hair.

In Paris, Gina missed Margot more than ever. Everywhere she went, she was reminded of all the good times they'd spent together, of Margot's funny sayings and irreverent quips. She missed their shared love of literature, too. Claire wasn't much of a reader, mainly because training to be a chef had never left her much leisure time, but Gina and Margot could talk about their latest literary discoveries for hours. No one else had ever filled that gap.

With grim determination, Gina returned to the matter at hand: the vexed question of what one ought to wear to a fitting at a fashion house. She ended the agony of decision by putting on her best sapphire blue suit and hat, but she couldn't help making a face at herself in the mirror. It was a Schiaparelli, and the attendants at Dior would see at a glance that it was from two seasons ago, but why let that bother her? This happened to be her favorite outfit, one she'd purchased with her own money, what was more.

Gina slipped down to the brasserie a little before the appointed time and caught the *plongeur* sweeping the sidewalk, a hand-rolled cigarette stuck to his lower lip. "*Bonjour,* Louis!" she called.

He returned the greeting and went on with his work. Gina cleared her throat. "Uh, Louis? May I ask you something?"

He grabbed his cap and pulled it from his head, then dashed his hand through his hair a couple of times. He was a handsome lad but very shy. Gina smiled kindly at him but found it impossible to continue.

A kernel of suspicion had grown into a dreadful likelihood. Having searched everywhere, even on the brasserie floor, Gina had not been able to find her gold pen. Then she realized that not only was she missing the pen but also its tooled leather case, which she always kept in the desk drawer in the apartment. That told her she hadn't simply lost the keepsake somewhere. It had been taken. The word "stolen" was too harsh to contemplate.

Only two people besides Gina had been in that drawing room, and she'd already asked Claire. In any case, Claire was above suspicion. Sadly, if past experience was anything to judge by, Jay Winter was not.

The image of her father bending over her manuscript pages kept coming back to her. Had he been reading her work that morning, as he'd claimed? Ever since their last telephone conversation, he'd proven elusive. She had called and left messages, and even visited his hotel to try to see him, but he was never in. Only once had he returned her call—and that conversation had been so hurried and short that Gina had failed to work up the courage to ask again about her pen.

Sometimes, she convinced herself that she was a traitor even to consider that her father might have taken such a precious keepsake to pawn or sell. Maybe someone had come into the apartment when Gina and Claire weren't there. Maybe someone else had a key.

At Gina's hesitation, Louis raised his eyebrows and nodded encouragingly, waiting for her to continue.

"It's nothing," Gina said with a quick, pained smile. "Never mind."

She'd been about to ask Louis if he knew of any pawnbrokers nearby. But she was a horrible, disloyal daughter even to think of such a thing. Jay would never do something like that. Not to her. He'd never sell the one thing she had left of her mother. She'd have to accept the loss.

"Ready?" Interrupting her brooding, Claire strode up and linked her arm in Gina's. Laughing, Claire lifted her shoulders in excitement. "I can't wait to see what Monsieur Dior has in store for us, can you? *On y va!*"

Claire

Claire and Gina took a taxi to Dior. Gina insisted on paying for it, and Claire, seeing that she needed to do this out of pride, simply thanked her.

The familiar stone edifice with its black railings and revolving door, and its pearl grey awning with "Christian Dior" lettered in white, made Claire's heart rush up to her throat. Excitement and nervousness warred inside her, even though she wasn't the one to be fitted today.

Hardly noticing the window displays this time, Claire followed Gina inside. They were met by an elegant woman, dressed in black, who greeted Gina by name.

While the other women exchanged pleasantries, Claire stared about her. She'd seen photographs of Dior parades in magazines, of course, but she'd never been inside the fashion house before. An air of hushed elegance pervaded; the walls, painted a dove grey with white detail, seemed the epitome of sophistication, a plain but subtly stylish backdrop to the wonderful gowns the house had to offer. A small boutique full of hats and gloves and other exquisite accessories caught her interest; maybe they'd visit after the fitting. She didn't want to miss a single thing.

"And this is my friend Claire, who made the appointment for me today," Gina said. Hearing her name, Claire wrenched her attention from their surroundings, smiled, and greeted Madame Vincent.

Madame was most probably baffled by the way Le Patron's work of art was being passed around like a parcel at a children's party, but she did not show it by a flicker of an eyelid. She conducted them upstairs, to a spacious room with one mirrored wall, a collection of clothes racks, and various accoutrements ranged along shelves: shoes, hats, and scarves. There was a screen in the corner and a round dais next to it. This must be where the magic would begin.

Madame indicated a pair of pale grey medallion-backed chairs and invited them to be seated. "I'll arrange for your gown to be brought in."

With rising anticipation, Claire turned to Gina. "I can't wait to see it! I wonder what Madame chose?"

"Remember the Venus?" said Gina. "Maybe it's something along those lines."

"Oh, that would be magnificent." Claire made a face. "I'm glad you're to wear it, in that case. I would feel . . . Oh, I don't know . . . Unworthy of such a gown."

"But that's ridiculous!" said Gina. "You are worthy of the very best—"

She broke off as Monsieur Dior himself entered the room. He was smiling and dapper and gave a softly spoken introduction to the creation they were about to see. "I do not usually like to do things this way, you understand," he said with only a gentle note of complaint. "But Madame Vaughn was most insistent."

"Ah!" said Monsieur Dior. "Here we are."

At last, in came the gown, carried with care by a gloved assistant. Both Gina and Claire stood up as it entered, as one rises for a bride to walk down the aisle.

And this was a gown worthy of respect. It was a magnolia dream of silk organza, opening over a satin skirt embroidered with gold thread, mother-of-pearl, beads, and sequins, with a flourish of chiffon at the shoulder. Even Claire, so often awkward and gangling in dresses, would be sure to feel like a fairy queen in this gown.

"It's even better than I'd hoped." Gina was aglow. She turned to Claire. "Isn't it stunning?" In a lower tone, she added, "How can you bear to let me be the first to wear it?"

"But of course I can," said Claire when she found her voice. She smiled as brightly as she could, to show she meant it. "Go. Try it on."

Madame Vincent explained that the gown came as a separate bodice and skirt. "If Mademoiselle permits, I will help you to put it on."

When Gina emerged from behind the screen and stepped up onto the dais, it was only the hem that needed letting down and the bust letting out the teeniest bit.

"Oh, you look ravishing!" said Claire. "Like Queen Mab or Empress Joséphine."

Gina turned to Monsieur Dior. "*Absolument parfait,* monsieur! This gown is a tour de force!"

But the couturier himself only acknowledged her gushing with a shy, almost embarrassed smile. With his slightly beaky nose, he looked like a large bird of some sort as he tilted his head this way and that to scrutinize the fit of the gown. Using a long white stick, Dior pointed here and there, murmuring instructions to the seamstress, who was pinning the material in the places he indicated. He checked that the skirt fell properly, that the bodice and its fastenings were perfect.

"Bon!" he said. "Mademoiselle is truly ravishing in that gown." He observed Gina, and she noticed he was holding a sprig of lily of the valley, twisting it this way and that as he pondered. "If I might suggest, long white gloves, a delicate diamond necklace with this gown. Perhaps earrings. Nothing more. And also . . ." He clicked his fingers. "Madame Vincent, send down to the boutique, will you please? I want the embroidered stole. Marie will know the one."

Gina waited, turning this way and that, admiring herself in the full-length mirror at the end of the room. Claire said, "It is even better than I'd dreamed. How can that be?"

Impulsively, Gina turned to the couturier. "Monsieur, would you allow my friend to try—" But as the door to the fitting room opened once more, she broke off, her eyes widening and her lips parting in surprise.

Claire turned to see that it wasn't Madame Vincent who had entered with the required stole draped carefully between her outstretched hands.

She was thinner and her hair was different—blond—what on earth had she done to her beautiful dark hair? But there was no mistaking the identity of this sales assistant.

It was Margot.

Chapter Five

Claire

"Ah, Marie!" said Monsieur Dior. "Thank you, *ma petite*. Bring it here."

Claire's mouth fell open. She looked to the doorway beyond Margot but there was no one else the couturier could have been addressing as Marie.

Maybe this gaunt, blond version of Margot wasn't their friend at all, but a doppelgänger. Stranger things had happened, surely. But from the sales assistant's aghast expression, and the tremor in the hands that held out the stole, Claire knew she wasn't mistaken.

When the shock wore off, Claire was still frozen in place. She couldn't decide whether she was more furious or delighted. She wanted to shake Margot until her teeth rattled and hug her very tightly at the same time.

Most of all, she wanted to ask why.

Why had Margot apparently been in Paris long enough to obtain a job at La Maison Dior and not come to see Claire? Why had she dyed her hair blond, of all things? Or was that a wig? Claire couldn't tell. And why was Monsieur Dior calling her Marie?

Claire sent a wild, questioning look to Gina, but Gina was clearly as stunned as she was, although the subtle hardening of her features told Claire she felt no ambivalence about Margot's sudden appearance in their midst.

The stole glistened with beading and gold thread. As their friend arranged the garment around Gina's shoulders, Claire couldn't help but notice that Margot's shoulder blades were pronounced beneath the severe black dress she wore and that about her mouth and eyes there were signs of habitual strain.

Gina watched her in the mirror with queenly disdain. "Thank you . . . *Marie,* is it?" That devastating eyebrow was raised.

"Oui, mademoiselle." The answer came out softly and there was a pause, a moment of communion between the two women.

Suddenly Gina's face transformed, softening, and her hands stretched toward the other young woman, but with the slightest shake of her head, Margot stepped down from the dais. As Margot turned to leave, Claire received her second shock of the morning.

Margot didn't look flustered or ashamed or even mischievous, as if this was all a joke she'd gleefully planned to play on them.

She looked terrified.

While Monsieur Dior discussed shoes with a distracted Gina, Claire slipped away and followed Margot. She saw her descending the elegant staircase and hurried down after her. "Margot, wait!"

Her friend stopped, then slowly turned around. With a resigned sigh, she replied, "Hello, Claire."

"But what are you doing here?" Claire demanded.

Margot gave a faint smile at that. "I work here. Isn't it obvious?"

"Since when? I—I don't understand—"

"Mademoiselle Foulon, you are needed in the boutique." Madame Vincent was coming up the stairs toward them. Clearly she was addressing Margot, and Margot's eyes closed for a moment, as if to acknowledge that she'd been thoroughly exposed.

Claire stared at her friend. Was she working here under a false name? Why on earth would she do that?

"I have to go," said Margot, turning away.

Claire grabbed her elbow. "Come to Le Chat tonight, when you get off work," she begged. "Margot, *please* . . . We need to talk."

Margot hesitated but seemed to sense that Claire wouldn't let go until she agreed. "All right. All *right*." Pulling herself free, she hurried off downstairs.

In a daze, Claire returned to the fitting room to find that Gina was behind the screen once more, getting changed. Monsieur Dior took his leave and Madame Vincent whisked the creation away for the final alterations. Gina's earlier suggestion that Claire try on the gown seemed to have been forgotten, and Claire could only be grateful. She was too upset to enjoy the experience at that moment. She was too worried about Margot.

Why had she come to Paris without telling Claire? And why was she working at Dior? The shock, hurt, and anger Claire had felt upon first catching sight of Margot had now turned to worry. What on earth had put that look of fear on Margot's face?

The second they set foot outside Dior, Gina exclaimed, "Did you *see* the way she looked at us? She genuinely did not want to run into us, did she?"

"Do you think that's what it was?" asked Claire. "I don't understand."

Gina drew her gloves from her purse and put them on, frowning. "I don't know. I mean, at first I thought she was just embarrassed at being caught working. I thought, maybe she's in dire straits financially and didn't want us to find out." She made a wry face. "Something we have in common, if only she knew. But no . . . There was more to it than that, wasn't there?"

"I think so, too," said Claire. "She looked scared to death."

"Well, now we know why she didn't write. Who knows how long she's been here in Paris, right under your nose."

"There's something else," Claire said. "She's using a false name."

"You mean Monsieur Dior calling her Marie?" Gina shrugged. "I wouldn't set any store by that. I understand he often gives people pet names."

"But it's her *nom de famille* that's changed, too," said Claire. "I heard Madame Vincent call her Mademoiselle Foulon."

"That *is* strange. Although maybe it's because 'MacFarlane' is too hard to say?" Gina glanced up at the store window into which they had gazed so many times in the past. "You know, I thought I was imagining things when I thought I saw her the other day in the window. I guess I really did."

"Come on," said Claire. "I've asked her to visit us at Le Chat tonight. Let's plan our strategy. I think she needs our help. But first we need to get her to tell us what's wrong."

"*If* she shows," said Gina.

"At least we know where to find her if she doesn't," said Claire. "I'm not giving up, even if I have to drag her out of La Maison Dior kicking and screaming."

Gina jutted out her chin. "I'm so mad at her, I could spit. She owes us an explanation, and I'm going to get it."

Claire wondered who would come out the victor in this encounter. Gina, with her habit of drilling down to the crux of the matter, or Margot, who danced lightly around the truth and could be as elusive as French perfume when it suited her. Claire, ever the peacemaker between them, expected to have her work cut out for her tonight.

Margot

Margot couldn't stop trembling. Sheer delight at seeing her friends again had quickly switched to anguish. She would have to go to Le Chat tonight as Claire had demanded, but she needed to slip in unnoticed. And she needed to make it clear to Gina and Claire that she couldn't resume their friendship, no matter how much she wished she might.

The sight of Gina standing there resplendent in a Dior gown evoked so many wonderful memories of their time together in Paris, back when Margot had been clean and whole and the world was her oyster. If only she'd stayed. If only she'd chosen independence, like Gina and Claire.

She never should have come back to Paris—it was a fairly obvious bolt-hole to those who knew her history. But in London, she hadn't felt quite safe. Paris, at least, was unfamiliar to the man who was looking for her, the language a barrier for him but not for her. And even if she couldn't go back to her old friends and her old haunts, at least Paris felt like her second home.

Of course she had expected to run into acquaintances at Dior, but she'd managed to dodge anyone she knew well so far. She tried to stay in the background, replenishing stock, arranging displays, serving customers in the boutique only when she couldn't avoid it. Wearing a blond wig helped somewhat. And the fact that wealthy clients rarely took a second look at the help. Add to that a new name—Marie Foulon—and an address where no one asked questions and no one would think to look, and she felt safe. Or as safe as could be expected when one resided in the Pigalle, the famous red-light district of Paris.

"Mademoiselle, a word?" Madame Vincent crooked a finger. "Follow me."

Up in the fitting room, a gentleman turned as they approached. He was, she judged, in his late twenties, early thirties, perhaps. He was tall and strikingly handsome, as pale and patrician as a vampire. Dark eyes glittered beneath the black fringe waving over his brow and his cheekbones were prominent in his lean face. She might be imagining it but she thought his mouth held a hint of cruelty. Only a pair of broad shoulders seemed at odds with the aristocratic visage. He seemed to size her up, as if he were a self-appointed judge of the physical attributes of every young woman he came across.

Margot bristled. This fellow had "lady-killer" written all over him, and her natural inclination was to take him down a peg, as the Australians would say. However, she prided herself on being professional, so she wouldn't utter any of the rudely deflating things that came to mind.

The gentleman didn't seem to be accompanied by a lady. Was he looking for one of Le Patron's silk ties, perhaps? Then why had Madame brought him up here?

"Mr. Mountbatten, this is Marie. She will assist you," said Madame in English, gesturing to the rack of sample garments that stood beside the dressing screen.

Margot eyed the row of five women's suits, then returned her gaze to their male guest. In French, she said, "But I don't think any of these will fit Monsieur."

Madame Vincent looked aghast, but their client laughed, and his dark eyes crinkled attractively at the corners. Oh, drat, Margot thought. When he laughed, he became another person entirely. A person she could like.

So Mountbatten understood French, did he? Then she would continue to speak it. He was British. Of course he was, with that name. Like any other girl in Australia, ever since Margot could remember, she'd followed avidly everything the British princesses, Elizabeth and Margaret, did. Queen Elizabeth had married Prince Philip, whose adopted surname was Mountbatten. Was this man a relation? She thought he might be.

He tilted his head, as if regarding her with new interest. "The clothes are not for me, you understand," he answered her in excellent, if formal, French. "Forgive me. I must seem rude, but I saw you in the boutique downstairs and you reminded me of someone. I took the liberty of asking Madame if you might model a selection of these garments for me. It's a gift," he explained, perhaps seeing that she was still puzzled. "For my sister," he added, as if he felt the need to explain himself to her.

She wasn't sure she believed that last part. Instinct urged her to get away from him, to tell him firmly that Dior had house models to show clothes, that it was not appropriate for her to do the honors. But she was certain Madame had already made similar representations to him and he looked like a man who habitually got what he wanted. It wasn't Margot's place to object.

Then, too, trying on beautiful clothes, even if she could never afford such luxury again herself, would be a pleasure. The admiration in the gentleman's gaze, though . . . She didn't want it. Contrary to appearances, he seemed charming and perfectly respectful, but somehow, he made her feel anxious rather than flattered. A sorry end for a girl who once had been the most accomplished flirt in Paris.

Madame hovered, for which Margot was grateful. It made her feel safe. She hadn't willingly been alone with a man in months, except for Monsieur Dior when they read their horoscope together.

"Which suit would you like me to try on first?" she asked, trying to sound businesslike. She chose a suit at random. "This?"

Mountbatten surveyed the garment she held up with a slight frown between his flyaway brows. "Is this the one *you* like best?"

She hesitated. Her mind had been awash with worry about Gina and Claire, and now she must cope with the unsettling undercurrent from this rather disturbingly charismatic individual before her. She hadn't truly looked at the garments until now. "Uh, well . . ." Ordinarily when a customer asked her this question, she preferred whatever was most expensive. But something about this man made her answer honestly. "This is my favorite."

The suit was one of the A-line dress and jacket combinations that Monsieur Dior had designed for the spring–summer season. The black dress was short-sleeved and gently skimmed the body, culminating in a calf-length skirt that had a satisfying swing to it. The jacket was double-breasted with shiny black buttons.

Madame Vincent's brow puckered, and she was about to speak when Madame Bricard called her away. With an apology to Mountbatten and a promise to return, Madame left them alone.

Suddenly the air felt thin. As unobtrusively as she could, Margot took several deep breaths to steady herself. It helped. A little.

"Why don't you try that one on for me and I'll be able to judge better," Mountbatten suggested, indicating the suit she'd recommended.

She went behind the screen to change. As she undressed, she tried to force her mind to be practical, but it felt oddly intimate and frightening that there was only a screen between this disturbing man and her unclad body. Of course, she wore underwear and her slip covered everything, but still . . . The circumstances evoked the intimacy of marriage, or more likely, an illicit liaison. Her hands shook so much, she had trouble doing up the buttons on the jacket.

A cold inner voice cut through her agitation. *He's not interested in you. He's buying this for his sister or his mistress or his wife—and it's absolutely no business of yours who it's for, anyway. Just smile and pose and walk to and fro and sell this outfit so you don't have to try on anymore. You are nothing to him. He'll forget you the second he leaves.*

You're not Somebody anymore. You never were.

Stop it! The longer Margot had been away from home, the better she'd become at noticing that the voice in her head that criticized and undermined her confidence at every turn was *his* voice and not her own. If only she could banish it, once and for all.

Still, she was not going to flirt with Mountbatten or allow him to see how he affected her. She'd had quite enough of men for the foreseeable future. Anyway, it was never wise to encourage a client to become too familiar.

Lifting her chin, Margot arranged her features in a remote expression and stepped out from behind the screen. Taking care not to meet Mountbatten's gaze, she walked forward and executed an elegant twirl, just as she'd seen mannequins like Anna and Yvette do. Then she unbuttoned the coat, her trembling fingers making the process take a little longer than strictly necessary, shrugged it from her shoulders, and let it fall to the floor. She walked another couple of steps forward, turned, and put her hands on her hips.

Silence. It stretched for so long that in spite of herself, her gaze went in search of the man sitting in the chair watching her.

A jolt went through her the second their eyes met. She felt herself flush.

"Tell me," he said. "Do you like yourself in this costume?"

Do you like yourself? What a question to ask her. *No,* she wanted to answer. *I have not liked myself for a very long time.* Undoubtedly it was his slightly imperfect French that made it sound more personal than the question needed to be.

"I—it is not up to me," she said.

"Still, you have an opinion," he insisted. "Let's hear it. Or perhaps you'd prefer to try on the others before you decide."

"No! I mean, I . . . I love this one, monsieur. It is by no means the grandest of the selection, but it is so modern and chic. The fabric is exquisite and I feel . . . very feminine in it, but also powerful, somehow."

"Powerful?" He leaned forward. "How?"

"It's the skirt, you know, and the lightness and lack of constriction about the waist. It has this movement when I walk that makes me feel . . . spirited and free." If only she could feel like that always, but even the magic of Dior couldn't lift the lead weight from her heart.

He was watching her intently. Had she said too much? She probably had. Why could she never seem to remember that people did not appreciate it when the old Margot peeked through the cracks in the shopgirl façade?

She tilted her head. "Does Monsieur wish me to try on something else?"

He took a moment to answer. Then he let out a breath. "No need. I'll take this one."

Jubilant and relieved, Margot did not entirely forget her sales technique. "Oh, and I must not forget the hat!" She went to the shelf where she had set out the accessories she had chosen for each ensemble. Taking a wickedly sharp hatpin and a smart white pillbox hat with black trim, she looked in the mirror and pinned it on. "A pearl choker, like this . . ." She clasped the faux pearls around her throat. "White gloves." She put on the pair of short white gauntlet gloves with the slightest flare to them that she'd chosen to finish the outfit and turned back to show the completed look.

Staring beyond him at her reflection in the mirror that spanned the opposite wall, Margot almost felt like her old self, and she nearly smiled in delighted recognition. But it was a fleeting sensation. She returned her attention to Mountbatten. *No.* She would not think of him by name. She would think of him only as "the client," nothing more.

She turned around again, feeling even more self-conscious, and a little clumsy, as if her feet had decided to rebel against the messages from her brain. She cleared her throat but her voice came out in a husky murmur. "Do you think you've seen enough, monsieur?"

She hadn't meant it to sound suggestive, but her words hung on the air like a sultry perfume. Heat flooded her cheeks. She hoped her flush wasn't apparent to him.

But either he didn't catch the double entendre or was too gentlemanly to give any sign that he had. "Yes, thank you," he answered. "I'll take it. And the rest of the ensemble as well."

Grateful to have the matter settled with such expediency, Margot went back behind the screen, making herself move with slow, deliberate steps instead of fleeing, as she dearly wished to do. Hurriedly, she changed and hung up the suit, which was a model that had been worn in a recent show and not for sale.

When she emerged, she saw that Madame still had not returned. The client was standing, waiting for her. "Mademoiselle will need to make an appointment for a fitting," said Margot.

"Of course," said the client, and she made herself ignore the glitter of anticipation in his eyes. "She was supposed to accompany me today but something came up. Shall I make the next appointment with you, or . . . ?"

"Please. If you will accompany me to her office, Madame Vincent will accommodate you."

Margot led him to Madame Vincent's office. As she turned to leave, he said, "Thank you, Mademoiselle . . . ?"

"Foulon," she supplied. Somehow her mouth had trouble forming the false surname. She had never liked lying but she rarely felt this guilty about it.

The client tilted his head as if considering whether it suited her. "Foulon," he repeated, and the way he said it made her wonder, Was he committing it to memory? Did he mean to ask for her next time? It was clear that he intended to accompany his sister for her fitting.

If the woman really is his sister. How many brothers bought couture for their sisters, after all? Though usually it was older, married men who claimed kinship with women who were, in fact, their mistresses. And in that case, usually they called the young women their nieces.

"I shall look forward to seeing you next time," he said, putting on his hat, tipping the brim, and giving her a smile that would have melted the polar ice caps.

There won't be a next time, said a voice in her head. *I'll make sure of that.*

When closing time came finally and Margot had replenished stock, dusted the vitrines and display cases, and generally restored order in the boutique, she retrieved her hat and coat and purse and set off for Le Chat.

What a day! Not only had she been caught out hiding from her two dearest friends but she'd met easily the most handsome man she'd ever seen in her life—and the most unsettling one. She must not let herself be swayed, however, or dwell on his dark attractions. Men like Mountbatten never meant anything by it when they toyed with shopgirls like her. Monsieur Dior protected his *"petites filles"* from the more predatory of the men who tended to try their luck, but it was very French to flirt, and even the older sales assistants indulged in sophisticated banter with male clients when required. They all knew, however, that it was usually the woman who was blamed for going beyond flirtation. If a sales assistant got herself a reputation for stealing the husbands and lovers of Dior clients, she was likely to be dismissed.

Regardless, Margot wasn't interested in Mr. Mountbatten. She'd sworn off men forever.

The defiance in that thought gave her some pep in her step, as Gina might have said. But the ache in her heart returned as she thought of Gina and Claire and the fun they used to have. She'd never found another friendship like it—not that she'd been granted the opportunity. Once upon a time she'd thought she made friends easily but experience had shown her that the only true friends she possessed were the ones she must not see.

How to explain it to them without explaining it at all? No matter how close the three of them had been once, Margot was a different person now. She couldn't bear for Gina and Claire to know the truth of what she had become. She was only going to Le Chat for two reasons: One, because if she didn't, she knew those two would be back at Dior the very next morning, demanding to know why. The second reason . . . She had to beg them both to stop seeking her out, to pretend they'd never seen her at all.

Trying to avoid focusing on the forthcoming confrontation, Margot made herself live in each moment, observe acutely the beauty

of Paris that surrounded her. It was a trick her father had taught
her once, a way of letting worries fall away by living in the present.
Worry was all about the future, after all. The practice had saved
her sanity time and again. In fact, she wasn't completely certain
she *was* sane, but at least she was strong enough to carry on with
life, such as it was, and to keep her wilder, more self-destructive
thoughts contained.

In this moment, what do you see? she imagined her father saying
to her, his voice deep and comforting.

*In this moment, I see a street vendor packing up his wagon, a small
boy selling* Le Monde *newspapers, belting out the headlines, a calico
cat slinking behind a dustbin.*

What do you hear?

*I hear the clock tower somewhere nearby chiming the hour. I hear
the coo of pigeons, the honk of a car horn, and the rev of an engine.*

What do you feel?

*I feel the soft texture of my kid leather gloves, the humidity inside
them from my nervous perspiration. I taste the wind off the Seine on
my tongue.*

Or was that the sour tang of fear?

Banishing the stray thought, on she went, across the Alexandre
III bridge, over to the Left Bank, past Les Invalides and the As-
semblée Nationale. By this time, she was regretting having decided
to walk in favor of the Métro, but doggedly, she went on, until she
came to the familiar streets of Saint-Germain-des-Prés.

Darkness had fallen, and Paris had lit up, sprung to life, but by
the time she reached Le Chat, Margot was weary. As the noise and
movement and the aromas from the brasserie reached her, she felt
almost faint with hunger, but then nervous tension gripped her

vitals and she knew she couldn't eat a bite. Not even of Claire's delicious cooking.

Avoiding the main door of the restaurant in case she saw someone she knew, Margot entered the lobby of the building. She was about to make her way to the restaurant's side entrance when a voice said, "Margot?"

Gina was coming down the stairs, presumably from the apartment above. Madame Vaughn's apartment—at least, it had been Madame's years ago.

Margot swallowed. No turning back now. "I—can we please go to the office?" She felt a fool for asking. "I don't want anyone to know I'm here."

Gina gave her a strange look, then shrugged. "We were going to bring you upstairs anyway."

Margot glanced up. "Oh, but . . . I don't want to see Madame Vaughn."

Gina regarded her for a long, sober moment. Then she said, "You won't. Follow me."

As often as she'd visited Le Chat in years gone by, Margot had never been to Madame's apartment before. She liked Deidre Vaughn but she hadn't known her as well as Claire and Gina had.

"Madame's gone away for a while," Gina explained, as they crossed the landing. "Claire and I are taking care of her apartment."

That was excellent news. Margot counted on Gina and Claire to keep her secret but she wasn't so sure about letting anyone else into the circle of trust.

"You're living here?" Margot exclaimed when she'd followed Gina inside. "It's a palace!"

"We like it," said Gina with a slight smile.

It certainly was a palace compared with the cramped room Margot had found in a boardinghouse in the seedy part of town. The advantages of living there were that the landlady had not cared to ask Margot for identification of any kind, it was cheap, and the residents kept themselves to themselves.

Claire emerged from what appeared to be a small kitchen, untying her apron. Her apple cheeks were flushed and rosy, which made her eyes a brilliant blue. She reminded Margot of a Pre-Raphaelite painting. All she needed was to let that glorious red hair come tumbling down.

"Come here and let me hug you," said Claire, opening her arms wide.

The relief of such a warm welcome after years of estrangement made Margot throw herself into Claire's embrace. For good measure, she reached out an arm and hooked a reluctant Gina into the hug as well. Gina hadn't warmed to her yet, she could tell, but Margot would simply make her, that was all. Claire's greeting had given her just enough confidence to try to talk Gina around. Then maybe they'd remember her fondly instead of resenting her when she was gone.

"How I've missed you both!" Her voice cracked in the middle of the sentence. If she could have let herself, she would have shed a few tears then. But these days a few tears were enough to start a tidal wave.

"You're just in time for cocktails," said Gina, slipping free and crossing to a stylish chrome drinks cart. She picked up the cocktail shaker and looked back at Margot, quirking an eyebrow. "The usual?"

"Please." She'd almost forgotten what her usual had been back in those heady days in Paris.

Claire brought out a tray of canapés—tiny, perfect vols-au-vent, little pastry cups with a creamy filling redolent of mushroom and truffle, and prunes with a bacon and thyme stuffing. Not that Margot could eat a bite of anything. Her stomach kept tying itself into knots.

When Gina had distributed the drinks, she sat down on a couch, kicked off her shoes, and, knees together, tucked her legs sideways beneath her. She looked like a movie star or a mannequin at a fashion shoot, effortlessly glamorous.

Claire plumped down beside Margot. "Now. Tell us everything. How do you come to be in Paris and why didn't you tell us you were here?"

Margot took a deep sip of her drink and nearly choked. Gina had made it a double. Ah, that's right. Margot had never actually enjoyed martinis but she'd thought them the height of sophistication, so that's what she'd always ordered, back when she first hit Paris. Funny how things like that didn't matter anymore.

Nervously Margot tried to smile. "I know. I owe you an apology. I—I had good reasons not to see you. Please believe me, it wasn't at all what I wanted. It's just . . ." And suddenly she couldn't tell them the elaborate lies she'd concocted. They were too dear to her and this time with them was too precious. So she made herself smile brightly and hoped she could be convincing. "Things have been so busy ever since I arrived." The excuse sounded feeble, even to her own ears.

"But how long have you been here in Paris?" demanded Gina. "And why are you using a false name?"

Margot stirred her drink with the toothpick-spiked olive. "So many questions!" she said with a little laugh. "You certainly found your calling as a journalist. You are still a journalist, aren't you, Gina?"

If she just spent the evening with them, asked them not to tell anyone where she was or what she was calling herself these days, she would leave it there. They might think her a snob or a false friend, or whatever. She couldn't help that. She simply couldn't go into it. If there was one thing she loathed, it was people feeling sorry for her.

"Yes, I am a journalist," answered Gina. "Which is why I can tell when someone's deflecting attention and *not* answering my question."

"Gina, stop." Claire's voice was quiet but commanding and Gina subsided, glowering. Claire turned to Margot and slipped her hand into hers. "Are you in some sort of trouble, Margot? You can tell us anything. You know that, don't you?" Claire's genuine compassion tugged at Margot's resolve.

"Do you mind awfully if we don't talk about it?" Margot said with a quick smile. "I don't want to spoil the evening."

Claire stared into her eyes, as if to divine whether that was truly what Margot wanted. Disappointment clouding her face, she answered, "Of course. If that's what you'd prefer."

Gina said, "No, Claire. I think we are owed an explanation." She fixed her gaze on Margot. "You didn't write us for ages and ignored our letters. We started to think something terrible had happened to you. We were worried and hurt, Margot. And now we find you in Paris, working at Dior, of all places! Why can't you at least tell us the reason?"

"Hush, Gina!" Claire squeezed Margot's hand. "Can't you see it's upsetting her? She doesn't want to talk about it right now. Leave her be."

So they *had* written, thought Margot. She knew it! And clearly her letters hadn't reached them. She shook her head. "No. Really, it's all right, Claire. I understand. I've been a bad friend and you are confused and angry." She tried to smile. "Please believe that it was unavoidable, and that I'll explain it. I just . . . can't right now."

The *brring* of a timer from the kitchen made Claire jump up. "Dinner in ten minutes. I'll leave you two to talk. Be nice!" she admonished Gina, who made a scoffing sound and sipped at her drink.

"So . . . What brings you to Paris, Gina?" asked Margot.

"Oh, so now I'm supposed to tell you everything," Gina replied. "Well, if you must know, I'm here because my family lost all our money and I broke off my engagement. I came to Paris for a fresh start. Been here nearly a month now."

The hard way Gina spoke was one Margot recognized. She knew when Gina's attitude masked deep pain. In the past, Gina had spoken of her mother's death in exactly that tone. Still, Margot also knew it was Gina's way of saying *I have it this bad, how could you have it worse?* Well, that was a matter of opinion, of course, and Margot wasn't interested in competing. "I'm sorry to hear that," she said. "But you're a smart, independent woman with an established career. You'll be back on your feet in no time." She hesitated. "Are you still writing that novel?"

"You mean the one from back then? Goodness, no. That was trash," Gina said. "But I'm sending out freelance articles and getting some bites. And I'm working on a new book. This one is set here in Paris."

Knowing that Claire was bustling to and from the kitchen but would reject any offer of help, Margot asked Gina all about the novel. She watched with pride and envy as her friend lit up the way she always did when she spoke about her work.

What would it be like to have such a fierce passion? True, at Dior, Margot felt privileged even to exist among the most exquisite couture in the world, and there was satisfaction in putting together the perfect ensemble, but she'd lost her passion for just about anything long ago. She'd always loved reading, but it was a form of comfort and escape—an obsession more than a passion. The youngest of her siblings by many years, growing up in a house full of eccentric adults who forgot about her for long stretches of time, Margot had always found solace in reading. And books had saved her when things were at their bleakest later on.

"Tell me," Gina said, changing the subject. "What's it like to work for Christian Dior?"

"He is a dear man," said Margot, relieved to be talking about neutral topics. "Exacting and a perfectionist but so very kind to us all." Then she glowered. "It's the dragons who work under him you have to watch out for. My boss . . ." She shuddered. "I try very hard never to get on her bad side."

Claire called to them from the dining table. *"À table, s'il vous plait!"*

Usually they spoke English when the three of them were alone together because Claire had insisted she needed the practice, but Gina and Margot had made a rule that at dinner, they always spoke in French.

"If only I'd brought champagne," murmured Margot. If only she could afford it! "Oh, this looks absolutely divine, Claire! Thank you a thousand times."

Claire beamed at her and Gina like a mother whose children have all come home for the holidays. "Bon appétit!"

Claire

They managed to stick to uncontroversial topics over dinner but Claire watched Margot carefully the entire time. She hadn't liked Margot's pallor when she'd arrived at the apartment, nor the haunted look in her eyes. And her gorgeous, glossy black hair . . . Why on earth had she dyed it blond and styled it so plainly? Or was it a wig? If it was, it was certainly a good one.

Then Margot chortled and slapped the table at one of Gina's quips and for a few moments, she was their dear friend of old, sparkling and free, her cheeks flushed from the wine. But Claire was still worried about her. Despite her praise of Claire's cooking, Margot had eaten little. Gina had been refilling Margot's glass often, perhaps with a stratagem in mind. Like most Australians Claire had come across, Margot had always possessed a hard head for liquor, but she'd become quite tipsy by the end of the meal.

Gina cleared the dishes after dinner, saying, "Now I must love you and leave you, dear ones. I have an article to finish before I go to bed tonight." She winked. "Our Claire has me on a strict schedule."

Margot sent her a darkling glance. "You're just avoiding the washing up. Besides, how can you write after all that wine?"

"I'm a journalist," said Gina. "I write best when I'm drunk." She made a face. "The hangover in the morning, however . . ."

But as Claire watched Gina's retreating back, she knew Gina wasn't intoxicated, and she wasn't leaving the two of them alone because she didn't want to do the washing up. Gina had taken the wrong approach with Margot and she knew it. She was allowing Claire some time with her to try a different tack.

"My word," murmured Margot as she took in the disaster zone that was the small galley kitchen. Claire stared around her guiltily. If she had one failing as a cook it was that she was very messy. In the brasserie there was always someone else to clean up after her.

"Come on. Hand me the gloves," said Margot with a reckless air. "I'll be *plongeur*."

They scraped off all of the plates and set some of the pots and pans to soak in hot water.

The galley kitchen was quite cramped with the two of them in it but they managed. Margot washed while Claire dried and put away. As they worked, Margot said, "I'm so sorry about your mum, Claire. It must have been hard to come back to work at Le Chat with her gone."

"Yes." Claire changed dish towels as hers had become too wet to continue. "I suppose it was. But keeping busy helped, I think. And I had to be strong for Papa. It got me through." She sighed. "Now Papa is retiring and moving to the Riviera with Vo-Vo."

Margo smiled. "Dear Vo-Vo. And your papa—he is such a lovely man. I'm sorry I won't be able to—" Margot broke off. Then she gave a small shake of the head, as if to rid herself of emotion. "I expect this is a weight off your shoulders, in a way. Will you go back to Le Meurice?"

So Margot remembered. It had been a long time since Claire was an apprentice at one of the city's finest hotels. She wouldn't tell Margot she'd been fired from that job.

"No, my skills have advanced since those days, but they will still see me as an apprentice if I go back there," said Claire. "Best go somewhere new, I think."

Margot looked sideways at her as she scrubbed a saucepan. "You don't sound too keen about it."

"'Keen'?" Claire tilted her head.

"Happy. Excited. Enthusiastic," explained Margot.

"Ah. Well, a lot has happened lately," said Claire, though it sounded like a lame excuse even to her own ears. "Le Chat is busier than ever." And why was she the one on the defensive when her intention had been to weasel Margot's secrets out of her? This wasn't going the way she'd planned.

"Hmm," said Margot. She rinsed the clean saucepan of suds and put it in the drying rack. "Now tell me what you're afraid of."

"Listen," said Claire, putting her hands on her hips. "If we're talking of fear, why didn't you come to see me the second you set foot in Paris?"

"Now *you* are trying to deflect attention from the issue," said Margot. "But I'll let it pass for now." The very fact she could get that sentence out meant that she'd sobered up since dinner. Or that she had only been acting tipsy. "Please don't be hurt about my not coming to see you. I—I didn't get any letters from either of you for so long, I thought you'd forgotten about me. I didn't know if I'd be welcome."

"*Forgotten* about you?" Incredulous, Claire stared at her. "But we both wrote and wrote. It was you who stopped writing."

Margot's attention seemed absorbed in her work. "That's not true," she said quietly. "I never stopped writing even after your letters didn't come."

"But why, then . . . ?" Claire couldn't understand it.

A long pause. "Never mind why," said Margot. "Just . . . please believe me." She looked up. "I was always your friend and always will be. Even if I can't see you as often as I would like."

"What's that supposed to mean?" asked Claire. She took a pot from Margot and set it down on the counter, then gripped Margot's shoulders and turned her so that she could stare her dead in the eye. "Are you in some kind of trouble, *mon amie*?"

Those big brown eyes stared into Claire's, and that haunted look was back in them again. Margot exhaled a long breath. "Someone, maybe more than one person, is looking for me. When they come to Paris—if they come to Paris—one of the first places they will look for me is at Le Chat." She blew out a long breath. "I can't be here. I can't be around the two of you. It's the reason I changed my name, Claire. I don't want them to find me."

"But—but why? What happened to you?" It sounded like the trouble Margot was in was far more serious than she'd thought. "Did you—" She put her hand to her mouth. "Have you committed a crime? Is that it?"

With a broken laugh, Margot said, "No, no! Why would you think that?" Then she sobered. "Don't ask me any more about it. Just accept that I can't come back here again. And please don't ever tell anyone you saw me, or where I am, or that I am in Paris at all."

"Of course," said Claire. "If that's what you want. And I'll make Gina promise, too. But, Margot, one thing I can't agree to, and that's not seeing you. Maybe we don't meet here, if you think that's best, but we must be allowed to meet. I can't let you go through whatever this is on your own."

Margot's lips pressed together and her eyes filled with tears. She wrapped Claire in a tight, hard hug, wet rubber-gloved hands and all. "Thank you, my dear, dearest friend. I'm so very lucky to have you. I shouldn't accept, but yes, I will, because I've missed you both so terribly!"

Claire made her write down her address and the telephone number of the boardinghouse where she was staying. Claire stared at the address. A place like that would make Gina's maid's room seem like a suite at the Ritz. "But, Margot, the Pigalle! This is one of the worst parts of Paris. You can't live there."

"Well, I don't spend a lot of time at home," Margot said. "And I lived right on the edge of Kings Cross in Sydney, you know. I'm used to that kind of place."

Claire knew all about Doc MacFarlane's eccentricities, that the surgery at their family home had seen a colorful procession of people, from the cream of society to nightclub entertainers to king-pins of organized crime. She also knew that the physician had kept a loaded pistol in the drawer of his desk.

"No," Claire said. "I utterly forbid you to stay there."

Margot gave a startled laugh. "*Forbid* it? You've always been so bossy, Claire."

"I am when I know what's good for people." Claire folded her arms. "If you don't move in with us tomorrow, I'm going to tell the people at Dior you're using a false name."

Margot gasped. "You wouldn't! I'd be out of a job."

"I'll find you another." Claire smiled grimly. "We could use another *plongeur* at Le Chat."

"But I can't live here, Claire," said Margot, her voice rising. "I just told you I can't be anywhere they might find me."

Claire threw out a hand. "That place you're in now, you're more likely to be found knifed in an alley or robbed of all your possessions. We can keep your presence here secret, don't worry. You don't ever have to come into Le Chat. There's a separate entrance. You can come and go that way."

She could tell Margot was wavering, but then she set her jaw. "I—I can't. You don't know how much I'd love to, really love to live here with you both. I simply can't."

"We'll see about that," said Claire.

Eyes flashing with anger, Margot cried, "For goodness' sake, Claire. Will you jolly well let me be?" She took a deep breath and squared her shoulders, as if trying to get her emotions under control. In a more moderate tone, she added, "Now. I have to get back. Thank you for a lovely dinner."

As she left the kitchen, Gina emerged from her room. "I see that went well," she remarked as Margot snatched up her hat, coat, and purse.

"Goodbye, Gina." Margot crossed to Gina and gave her a quick hug. "I'm sorry."

A hug to Claire, then she left the apartment.

"We can't let her go like that, can we?" said Gina. "What happened?"

Claire relayed the conversation she'd just had with Margot in the kitchen. "She's adamant she won't live here with us," she said finally. "But I'm not giving up."

"I'm going to do some digging," said Gina. "We need to find out exactly what Margot's hiding from us and why."

Chapter Six

Gina

Gina woke early the next morning with something of a hangover. She hadn't realized she'd drunk quite so much the evening before.

Force of habit carried her through washing, dressing, and putting on her makeup. She'd taken to finding a quiet, sunny spot in Le Chat with a cup of coffee and a freshly baked roll and writing for a couple of hours before leaving for the bookstore, which opened at ten. The routine seemed to be working, and not even a hangover would prevent her from following it today.

She entered Le Chat quietly, set down her things in a pool of sunlight-tinted amber by a stained-glass window, and went to get coffee.

Usually Claire respected her need for absolute quiet on these early mornings and went about her own work without more than a nod and a smile in Gina's direction. This morning, Claire was practically bouncing off the walls.

"She simply must move in with us," she said, before even bidding Gina a *bonjour*. She was pacing with a copper whisk in hand, a great dollop of whipped cream crowning the implement. Waving the whisk, Claire added, "I mean, the Pigalle! What on earth could she be thinking?" Gina dodged a fleck of whipped cream that flew in her direction, then stepped forward to remove the whisk from Claire's grasp as if she were a police officer disarming a gangster.

"She will move in with us, don't you worry," said Gina, setting the whisk back in the copper bowl. "If she needs to keep her presence here a secret, we can do that."

Claire frowned. "I can't stop worrying about her. I lay awake all night."

Gina hadn't gone that far, and she was almost as mad at Margot as she was concerned. Gina had always believed that God helped those who helped themselves. She was impatient with any kind of martyrdom, and it seemed to her that Margot was determined to struggle rather than to accept her friends' assistance. However, she kept telling herself to reserve judgment until she knew the full story. And it hadn't been so very long since Gina had been in a somewhat similar position.

"She'll come around," she said, chiefly to soothe Claire. "We'll make her. In the meantime, I'm going to get to the bottom of what happened to Margot back in Australia." Gingerly she picked up the coffee press that, thanks to Claire, sat waiting for her, and poured herself a cup.

"How are you going to do that?" asked Claire.

"I'm a journalist, remember? It's my job to find things out." Gina tapped the side of her nose, then snatched a croissant from the tray that had just left the oven, but quickly dropped it on the counter as it was piping hot. She blew on her singed fingertips, then used a napkin to handle and plate the croissant. "Now if you'll excuse me, I have pages to write."

Despite her outward insouciance, worry and speculation about

Margot threatened to derail Gina's writing session. However, years of training herself to write at any time, in any place, and under any constraints, be they emotional or physical, allowed her to dismiss from her mind everything but the book she was working on. For the next hour or so, she slipped away to that other world in the depths of her mind, watched what happened there, and took note.

When she slid back to the present and became aware of the bustle starting up around her, it was time to leave for work.

The day passed pleasantly at the bookstore. Gina had set herself the task of taking inventory of the extensive English-language section, so that kept her busy when there were no customers to serve. She thought of her promise to Claire—to find out what had happened to Margot. It was still early enough to visit the Bibliothèque Nationale.

She loved this building, and stood for several moments marveling at its glorious oval reading room, with its glass roof and beautiful mosaics and its four stories of galleried bookshelves framed by tall Ionic columns. Anywhere there were books, Gina knew she would be at home, and among like-minded people. A friendly assistant directed her to the room she was looking for, and she began working her way through back issues of the *Sydney Morning Herald* on a microfiche machine.

If she confined herself to the years the friends had been apart, it would be like searching for a needle in a haystack, but Gina knew within a month or two where to look. Sometime between the date of Margot's final letters to her and Claire and the next date Gina judged she ought to have written back to them. Something had happened during that time. Gina had her suspicions about what. If she was right, she'd find what she was looking for tonight.

After skimming through several weeks of Sydney social pages and announcements, there it was, in black-and-white: a beautiful, if grainy, photograph of Margot and a handsome man quite a few years older than she was, if Gina were any judge. Had Margot mentioned getting serious about someone? Surely Gina would have remembered if she had. There were always multiple beaux to escort her to parties, but never anyone special, as far as Gina could make out from Margot's letters. This courtship must have been a whirlwind affair. Was that why Gina and Claire hadn't been invited to the wedding ceremony?

Gina studied the photograph closely. Margot looked enchanting. Her dark hair was piled up and encircled by a delicate tiara with a filmy white veil suspended from it. Holding a sheaf of white lilies, she stared up at her new husband with a kind of rapt admiration. He was gazing directly at the camera, a faint smile lighting his eyes. He reminded her a little of Senator Jack Kennedy, whom she'd interviewed once when she worked in D.C.

Triumph at the discovery was swiftly replaced by a churning sensation in Gina's stomach. Married. Margot had been married for three whole years. But now she was in Paris, alone, using a different name from her husband's, and she wore no wedding ring.

Had she divorced her husband and been too ashamed to admit it to her friends? Or had she simply run away?

The latter seemed more likely. Margot had claimed someone was looking for her. Someone she was so desperate to hide from that she hadn't even paid a visit to Claire as soon as she hit Paris.

Gina stared at the groom in the wedding photograph and tried to fathom what kind of man he might be. A playboy? Possibly. Definitely a charmer, popular with women. But then, all men tended to look sophisticated in morning suits, didn't they? One thing was clear to her: Margot had loved this man when she married him. There was no faking that adoring expression. What he felt about Margot, on the other hand . . . He wasn't looking at her in this particular photograph but there was a smile in his eyes. Was that significant?

Glancing at the clock, Gina realized she'd better get home before Claire sent out a search party. She copied down the details of the marriage announcement and took the Métro back to Saint-Germain-des-Prés. Emerging from the subway station, she walked slowly toward Le Chat.

What had happened to Margot in that marriage? Had her husband beaten her? Gina was experienced enough to know that this happened, even in the most unlikely and affluent of couples. It was a somewhat obvious conclusion, a good reason for Margot to run away to Paris, perhaps even to change her name. But what about her family? Margot's people were wealthy and liberal-minded and cared little about what people thought, if Margot's anecdotes were anything to go by. Wouldn't they have protected her if she'd suffered that kind of cruelty?

Well, maybe not. It never ceased to amaze Gina what hypocrites some people could be. The compulsion for a woman to stand by a husband no matter what he put her through was enshrined in the law as much as it was reinforced by society at large. Maybe Margot hadn't found a safe harbor at her childhood home.

One thing was for sure—Gina had been too hard on Margot last night, too unforgiving. It was a terrible trait, one she'd thought she'd overcome when she'd fallen in love with Hal. But there she went again, judging those closest to her and finding them wanting.

She needed to see Margot and try to persuade her to let her friends help. She didn't need to face whatever it was alone.

Margot

Days after her visit to Claire's—or rather, Madame Vaughn's—apartment, Margot had not regained her equilibrium. However, there was a new influx of stock that needed to be inventoried and new displays to execute for the Dior boutique, and many errands to run that necessitated traipsing up and down the many flights of stairs between the boutique and the ateliers several floors above.

For the past week, stomach flu had cut a large swath through the staff, and their collective absence had increased Margot's workload. She could only be thankful, both for her own good health, and for the way the added busyness filled her days. It kept her mind off other things.

The service door buzzed and Margot, stripping off the cotton gloves she used when handling Monsieur Dior's creations, hurried to answer it. A bouquet of flowers bigger than the deliveryman's head, complete with its own vase, was thrust into her arms. Before she could ask for the recipient's name, the deliveryman had gone.

Margot shut the door with her hip and carried the flower arrangement to the counter where another of her duties was to wrap parcels for delivery.

How lovely! At this time of year, flowers were terrifically expensive. Who were they for? Probably one of the mannequins who had featured in Dior's last show, or maybe for Monsieur Dior from a grateful client. The heady scent almost made her dizzy as she searched for a card. She found a little envelope nestled in the arrangement and plucked it free.

It was addressed to her.

Dropping the envelope without reading the card, Margot backed away, her hand to her mouth. Then she realized. Pink peonies. Her favorite flower. Or it had been once.

"Watch out!"

She turned to see that Madame Vincent had come up behind her. She'd stepped on Madame's toe.

Babbling apologies, her heart beating wildly, Margot's instinct was to flee. But Madame said sharply, "One moment. Who are these for?"

Before Margot could answer, Madame Vincent had stooped to pick up the card Margot dropped.

Oh, no! If only she'd shoved it in her pocket instead! Squeezing her eyes shut, Margot waited for the anvil to drop on her head.

"For *you,* Mademoiselle Foulon?" Madame sounded incredulous and affronted. She riffled inside the small envelope. "From Monsieur Mountbatten!"

It took several seconds before that sank in. *Mountbatten* had sent her the flowers! Relief flooded her entire body. She felt limp with it, and made the mistake of laughing out loud. At the expression on Madame's face, she quickly sobered. "Sorry, Madame. I swear, I did nothing to encourage him. I—next time you see him, will you please explain to Monsieur that it's not appropriate?" Surely Madame would oblige her in this. Monsieur Dior frowned upon any relationships beyond light flirtation between clients and staff.

"Actually, he will be here very soon," said Madame, checking her watch. "His sister is coming for her fitting at two. You can explain it to him yourself."

"Oh! But you must understand . . . I can't see him," said Margot. "It would be too awkward."

"Well, I don't know who else will look after his sister," said Madame. "I have to leave for London in fifteen minutes. This trip couldn't have come at a worse time."

Tempted though she was to fake a stomachache and pretend that she, too, had succumbed to the virus that was going around, Margot knew such behavior was unlikely to earn her a reprieve. "Madame, it is uncomfortable for me to attend to Monsieur Mountbatten." She gestured to the flowers.

"I hardly think he'll cross the line. Particularly not with his sister there," said Madame. "And anyway, there is no one else."

"But, Madame—"

"I don't have time for your nonsense, child," said Madame. "Do as you're told!"

Margot frowned as Madame hurried away. It wasn't right for Mountbatten to use his status as a client to pursue her, knowing that to keep her job she must keep him happy. In her experience, such men were too arrogant to understand that their attentions might be unwelcome.

If she were completely honest, part of her did welcome his interest. The foolish part of her. The part that, despite everything, still had not learned its lesson.

With Madame gone, Margot went to the desk in her small office and checked the appointment book. Monsieur Dior was away at his Riviera house, dreaming up new designs. With Madame gone, Margot would have to oversee this fitting, but one of the tailors would be there with her to make the necessary adjustments. At least, she hoped so.

Margot returned to the boutique and restored order there following the exodus of a gaggle of young ladies who had come in to try on hats. Leaving Delphine in charge, she climbed to the top of the *maison,* where usually she found a hive of activity.

Today, only a few workers remained, one of whom was her friend Béatrice. The tailor was pinning a suit skirt made of toile on a mannequin and standing back now and then to view it from different angles. All of Le Patron's designs were made up in this inexpensive fabric first so as to judge how the garment fell, what details might be added or removed, and how the construction of the garment might best be achieved. Sometimes at this stage, Monsieur Dior would scrap a design entirely from the collection when the reality did not match up to the fantasy he had created with his sketches.

"Thank goodness you haven't gone down with flu," said Margot, clutching her friend's hands. "Will you do the two o'clock fitting for me? Pretty please?"

Béatrice chuckled, showing dimples. "But of course. I hear the English aristo has a crush on you, *ma petite.*"

Margot felt heat rise to her cheeks at this unexpected teasing. "Who told you that?" Even with a skeleton staff today, it seemed news of Mountbatten's floral tribute had spread up and down La Maison Dior.

Béatrice tapped the side of her nose. "I have my sources. And now I get the opportunity to see your admirer's beaux yeux up close. How could I miss it? See you at two."

Beaux yeux. Margot sighed a little, wistful for the days when a pair of beautiful eyes would set her own heart aflutter. And it was true that Mountbatten's were particularly fine—the color of maple syrup with the kind of thick, dark lashes that many women might envy. But it wasn't the color or shape—it was the understanding in those eyes that hit her hardest. She had the strangest feeling that he saw through all of her pretense, even though he couldn't possibly guess at the truth of her recent history. He unsettled her and she didn't like that sensation at all. Well, she would make it clear to him she wasn't interested. A gentleman would give up and move on.

At ten minutes to two, Margot was ready and braced for combat.

Miss Mountbatten was as elegant as Margot had expected, but she had a twinkle in her eye that drew Margot to her immediately. She was younger and fairer than her brother, and although she lacked his charisma, the resemblance in facial structure was strong. "I'm here for my fitting!" she announced merrily in poorly accented French as soon as she walked in the door.

"Good day, mademoiselle," said Margot, also in French. "My name is Marie Foulon and I will be assisting you this afternoon."

"I can't wait. A Dior suit!" The young woman grabbed Margot by the elbow as if they were friends off to do some shopping together. "Isn't my brother too, too marvelous for words?"

When Margot didn't answer for a moment, a little taken aback by this ebullience, Miss Mountbatten tilted her head toward the staircase. "Shall we?"

"But what about Monsieur? I thought he was . . . ?" Margot trailed off, flustered.

The other girl laughed. "Oh, I told him not to bother coming along. Men are no fun to have around when one is buying dresses, dear as they might be."

Margot tried to mask her emotions, but she was caught off guard. She'd done her best to fortify herself against the man's visit and now it seemed there had been no need. She ought to be relieved.

As they moved to the staircase, Miss Mountbatten darted a mischievous sidelong glance at Margot. "Disappointed? My brother is *very* handsome, isn't he?"

"Would you prefer to speak in English, mademoiselle?" Margot asked, switching languages and hoping to avoid answering the question.

"Oh, yes, please. And I wish you would call me Charlie—short for Charlotte, you know. I hate standing on ceremony. I'll call you Marie, if I may." Without waiting for an answer, she added, "You're Australian, aren't you? I can tell by the accent, though yours isn't very strong. How splendid." Though what was particularly splendid about it, Margot had no idea.

Margot laughed. "In my experience, the British are more likely to view my compatriots as uncouth colonials."

Another sidelong glance. "Now I think I understand what my brother meant."

Surprised, Margot nearly missed her footing on the stairs. Had Mountbatten mentioned her to his sister? Unable to think of anything to say in response, she pushed open the door to the fitting room, where Béatrice was waiting with her tape measure.

"Here we are," Margot said. "We will make the suit to measure, of course, but this model will give you an idea."

"Oh! I love it. It is utterly perfect." She turned to Margot. "Andrew said you chose it. Thank you! Goodness knows what I would have ended up with if he'd been responsible. It's a birthday gift, you know. I'm turning twenty soon. Well, in a few months, actually, but my brother's leaving for Bermuda shortly, so he wanted to do this before he goes."

All of this gushing was making Margot uncomfortable. What on earth had Mountbatten said about Margot to his sister for her to react like this? Surely his family would disapprove of his interest in a mere shopgirl, even if she did work at Dior? True, Le Patron tended to hire society ladies in the knowledge that they would attract the right clientele to his boutique, but the Mountbattens were related to royalty. Trying not to appear as flustered as she felt, Margot gestured toward the changing screen. "If you would like to try on the suit? Béatrice will measure you first."

Béatrice had been agog, watching their exchange as if it were a gripping tennis match, but she understood virtually no English, so hopefully she wouldn't get the gist. However, when Charlotte retreated behind the screen, Béatrice widened her eyes and raised her eyebrows, as if she'd at least understood the tenor of it—that the client was being unusually familiar with a member of staff.

After Charlotte's measurements had been taken, she changed into the suit—the same model that Margot had shown to Andrew Mountbatten.

When Charlotte stepped out from behind the screen, Margot couldn't help a pleased exclamation. "You look utterly divine."

Turning this way and that so that the A-line skirt swished and swung, Charlotte chuckled. "I do, don't I? Simply smashing!"

Having admired herself some more in the full-length mirror and tried on the hat and gloves Margot recommended to go with the suit, Charlotte slipped back behind the screen to change. When she emerged, and Béatrice had left with the dress and jacket, Margot said, "If you wish to take the hat and gloves, shall I order them for you, mademoiselle?"

"Yes, please. Oh, but I do wish you'd call me Charlie because I want us to be friends."

Friends? Margot stared at her in surprise.

Her expression must have betrayed her because the other young woman's smile faltered. "Don't you want to? I was hoping— I don't know an awful lot of people in Paris. Well, I do," she corrected herself. "But I don't count most of them as friends. Not *real* friends, anyway." She pursed her lips and flared her eyes. "I know!

I'm having a small dinner party next week and I'd love you to come."

This was so strange, Margot decided to be blunt. "It's not that I don't want to, mademoiselle. It's just that I'm so . . ." What was the word? "Flabbergasted"? "Dismayed"? "So flattered. And you are very, very kind, but I'm afraid it's not appropriate."

"What nonsense!" said Charlotte. "Oh, I suppose you are thinking we're stuffy because of the family but Andrew and I don't care a fig about that." Some of her brightness faded a little. She gripped her hands together and tilted her head, as if trying to decide how to phrase a difficult statement. "I suppose it does seem incredibly odd and forward of me to ask you to be friends, and I can't explain it now, but . . . Will you think about it? I love my brother dearly, and I know he would be so pleased if you'd say yes."

Without waiting for an answer, she took out a pencil and scribbled the details of the dinner down on a visiting card. Then she hesitated. "I didn't ask if you intend to bring an escort. You aren't attached, are you?"

Without answering that question, Margot glanced at the card. "I'm afraid I can't join you on Friday evening. I have a prior engagement."

"Oh?" Charlotte tilted her head as if debating whether to challenge this fairly transparent untruth. Then she nodded. "Another time, then. I won't forget, mind!"

Charlotte left Margot with much food for thought. If she were honest, she had been disappointed Andrew Mountbatten hadn't attended his sister's fitting at Dior. But the knowledge that he'd told his sister—what? Something about his encounter with Margot?—unsettled her. She couldn't go to any dinner party at the Mountbattens'. What if she ran into someone she knew?

Besides, she couldn't befriend Charlotte while lying to her about who she was. And she certainly couldn't do anything to encourage Charlotte's brother.

Years ago, Margot would have accepted the Mountbattens' friendship without a second thought. She'd always loathed the very idea of social hierarchy. Be they prince or pauper, they were all just people, weren't they? She took everyone as she found them, but with her money and connections she'd rarely been on the receiving end of snobbery. It had been humbling to accept that, now, things were different. At Dior she was obliged to swallow some of the stinging retorts that rose to her tongue in response to clients' rudeness, not to mention Madame Renou's barbs, for the sake of keeping her job.

She managed to compartmentalize, to separate the servile Marie from the real Margot lurking inside, treating her job as an actress might treat a theater role to be performed in a long-running season. And now, here came Andrew and Charlotte Mountbatten to upset that careful balance.

No. She couldn't risk it. She couldn't let this house of cards she'd so gingerly constructed come tumbling down around her for the sake of a new friendship and a disturbing pair of beaux yeux.

Chapter Seven

Claire

"I'm offering you two whole weeks' vacation, Claire. Why won't you take them?" The furrows in Papa's forehead deepened. He was shifting from foot to foot, a clear sign he was keeping something from her. "You need a break." His expression turned hopeful. "Or maybe you could use the time to look for a new position at one of your fancy restaurants?"

"Are you trying to get me out of the way for some reason?" Claire narrowed her eyes. Her father's startled reaction showed she'd hit a chord. "You are, aren't you? Come, Papa. What is it? Don't you think I can be civilized toward the new owner? Do you think I'll make trouble for him?"

Papa opened his mouth, shut it again, and shook his head, looking helpless. Surely she wasn't so formidable that he was scared to tell her something important? What could be as earth-shattering as the news that he was selling the brasserie out from under her?

No. Not selling it out from under her. He was setting her free. Why couldn't she remember that?

If Vo-Vo were here, she'd tell Claire the truth straight out, but she'd left for Nice to close on the purchase of her new villa. In fact, the thought of heading down to Nice for some warmth and sun once her father and aunt were settled was very appealing. But Claire couldn't go now. She wanted to ensure the handover to the new owner went smoothly. Not only that, she wanted to make sure the new owner didn't intend to sweep away all the hard work her family had put into Le Chat over the past six decades.

It didn't seem as if her father would ever get to the point, so Claire said to him, "Come, Papa. This dough won't knead itself." She'd been using the lull before the evening rush to make a batch of dinner rolls now that the dough had had time to prove.

She dumped the risen bread dough out on the counter in front of her father. Patently grateful for the change of subject, he washed, dried, and floured his hands, then set to with a will.

Side by side, they worked together in companionable silence, kneading and shaping rolls. Her father's hands were still big and strong beneath the dusting of flour. When the rolls were shaped and ready for the oven, Papa slid in the trays, and with that final action, a wave of sadness came over Claire. Their time working together like this would soon be over for good.

Claire had joined in with the staff who had begun prepping for dinner, when her father said, "Claire, I need to talk to you."

She paused in the act of showing an apprentice the correct way to julienne carrots. "Yes?"

"I don't quite know how to say this." Papa hesitated. "It's about the new owner."

"Why?" asked Claire, her brow furrowing as she continued to chop the carrots into perfect, slim straws. "What's wrong?"

"Claire, will you put down the knife, please?"

The faint note of panic in his voice made her stop work and carefully place the knife on the counter. "Papa?" She was filled with foreboding. Come to think of it, wasn't it odd that they had never mentioned the new owner's name to her? "Tell me."

"He's someone you know," said Papa, licking his lips.

"Really?" Claire did not like the sound of this. Difficult though it was to give up the brasserie to a stranger, wouldn't it be worse if she had to watch an acquaintance, or even perhaps a rival, take over the place?

"He offered us a generous price, and he agreed to keep you on here for as long as you wanted," said Papa. He spread his hands pleadingly. "Give him a chance, Claire."

"*Who is it, Papa?* Tell me!"

Suddenly the flurry of activity in the kitchen halted. Apprentices and chefs put down their implements and stared past her at the doorway.

Claire turned to see what they were looking at. Her jaw dropped open. She couldn't seem to draw in any air.

A large form hulked in the doorway, almost filling it. His shaggy hair untamed, his five-o'clock shadow standing out starkly against his lantern jaw, he clearly hadn't cared about the impression he made on the staff. Or maybe he knew his unkempt appearance made him more intimidating.

Hervé Gabin. The bane of her existence.

His eyes were a startling, clear blue, and heavily lashed, the one refined thing in that mountain range of a face, with its beaky nose and prominent cheekbones and its strong jaw roughened by stubble. He stood easily six-foot-two and had to stoop over the stove in most kitchens, but he never tried to hide his height elsewhere.

Claire froze, remaining silent as her father introduced Hervé around. He was giving her time to absorb this ridiculous, heinous news.

She had worked as an apprentice under Hervé at the Meurice—the best and worst time of her life. That man hadn't let a day go by without finding fault with her. Time after time, she'd nearly given up because of him. And now he was going to be her boss in her own family's restaurant? It was too much.

The chefs were all bowing and scraping to the new owner in a way they had never done to her. Hervé gestured for them all to go back to work. Finally he glanced at Claire, gave a self-deprecating shrug.

Papa turned to her. "And here is my daughter, Claire, whom you know already. Claire, a bottle of our best wine, I think, and three glasses, to celebrate. Shall we go into the office?" He gestured in that direction.

Claire gaped at her father. After turning her world upside down, he expected her to bring them wine? Claire ripped off her apron, scrunched it, and threw it in the corner. She stormed out the service door into the alley. She needed to walk and fume and be alone for a while with her raging thoughts.

To be fair, Papa didn't know the truth: that she had harbored a secret admiration for Hervé for all of the years she'd been his apprentice. Her crush had been a natural combination of hero-worship of Hervé's advanced skills in the kitchen and the sight of his well-muscled forearms as he'd worked the grill station. She hadn't actually minded how tough he'd been with her. He was no more exacting than most chefs, after all. It was the fact that he'd never once thought of her as a woman that had grated on her. Everyone else had noticed her crush, however, and when the other apprentices had teased her about it, she'd realized that Hervé must have known about it, too, and that had been mortifying.

She'd reacted by behaving in such an obnoxious and insubordinate manner to Hervé that even the sous-chef had noticed, and fired her.

"Face it," Claire told herself. "You can't blame someone for not liking you back." But did she really have to put up with him running her family's brasserie?

And what had happened to Hervé's grand ambitions? Why would he settle for owning a brasserie rather than becoming chef de cuisine at a first-class restaurant?

Now that this thought had occurred to her, curiosity burned even more brightly than her anger. After a few more strides, she turned around and headed back to Le Chat. It had been childish to flounce out of there, particularly when she knew how hard all of this was for Papa. Surely she'd grown out of such schoolgirl tendencies long ago. And besides, she had no time for romance if she wanted to get to the top, so Hervé had done her a favor all those years ago.

She'd just have to find a new job sooner than she'd planned, that was all. There was no way she was going to work for Hervé again.

When she arrived back at the kitchen, she found things humming along without her, so she squared her shoulders and lifted her chin and marched straight to the office, where her father and Hervé were enjoying a glass of wine together.

"Am I interrupting?" She was pleased to find that her voice sounded calm.

"Ah, my dear," said Papa. "Come, join us." He poured her a liberal glass of wine and brought it to her. "Take a seat."

The two men occupied the only chairs in the room. She could take the sofa, but it was low to the ground and set against a wall, a little apart from the desk. Sitting there, she would feel at a disadvantage.

Instead, she perched on the edge of her father's desk, the way she used to do when she was a child. Only now, she felt Hervé's gaze graze the line of her legs as she crossed them before he transferred his attention to the dark dregs of his glass. She was wearing a comfortable pair of cigarette pants, so there wasn't a lot to see, but somehow she felt a little better that she'd caught him looking.

Papa leaned forward to refill Hervé's glass. The wine was excellent and should have been decanted and left to breathe but her father had never been a patient man. It was an aged burgundy as smooth as velvet, but heavy. One sip and it went straight to Claire's head, reminding her that she hadn't eaten all day.

Claire set her glass down on the desk and eyed the bottle, which was more than half empty already, and hoped Papa would not overdo it and grow maudlin. "So has the sale gone through, then?" she asked Hervé. "You are the new owner of Le Chat?"

"Some final details to clear up, but yes," said Hervé. "I start next week." He hesitated. "Your father tells me you're taking some leave."

"Did he?" Her anger might be in abeyance but with the wine, a certain recklessness was taking over. "He was mistaken. My vacation is not due until the spring."

She would take leave when she wanted to, not to make it easier for this man to usurp her authority and bulldoze his own changes through. "I suppose you'd prefer it if I were out of the way," she added with the suspicion of a sneer.

He shrugged. "If you're determined to make things harder for yourself, who am I to stop you?"

Claire glanced at her father, who ordinarily might have intervened to make peace between them, but Papa wasn't listening. Somehow he had refilled his glass without her noticing and now a brooding look fell like a pall over his face.

She slid off the desk and jerked her head at Hervé. "Can I speak with you alone?"

She'd only wanted to keep Hervé from seeing her father at his most vulnerable. Once they emerged from the office, she wasn't sure what to say or do. Hervé was so large, and . . . and *unwieldy,* she thought resentfully.

"Do you want me to show you the ropes?" she asked after a long, uncomfortable pause, which was all the more awkward for her because he seemed completely at ease. That was something she remembered about him. He was comfortable with silence.

He shrugged. "Not much to it, is there? I'll figure it out."

"You need to watch Basil," she warned in an undertone. "He makes trouble if you don't keep an eye on him. Skimming from the supplies, taking bribes from tradesmen. I have nearly fired him countless times, but . . ."

"He has a light hand with pastry, and his mille-feuille is like an angel's wing," said Hervé, nodding, a gleam in his eyes that was almost a smile. "Your papa told me."

She hated the idea that Papa had been meeting with Hervé behind her back. Anger flared again. "Why did you do it?" she blurted out. The question had been playing on her mind. "Why this brasserie? Why Le Chat?"

His eyes did that not-quite-smiling thing again. He rubbed his shadowed jaw. "Someone told me it was the best brasserie in Paris."

She rolled her eyes at the well-worn joke. "But you were going to be the next Escoffier," she said. "Why settle for this place?"

"I don't know," said Hervé with a short grunt that might have been a laugh. "I've been asking myself that question every single day."

FAR FROM ACCEPTING her father's offer of vacation time, Claire worked harder than ever during the transition in ownership from Papa and Vo-Vo to Hervé. The long hours helped to plug up the moments where her guilt and regret seeped through.

It was the end of an era. Somehow she'd thought her papa would go on forever, that she could leave Le Chat safe in the knowledge that it would continue without her. Grandpère was in his eighties before he relinquished his grip on the place. She'd expected Papa to be the same. He probably would have carried on happily, had Maman not died. And had it not been for Vo-Vo's constant grumbling.

Well, Vo-Vo had finally got her way and Claire had to hope, for their sake, that it was all for the best.

Uncharacteristically Hervé insisted on throwing the pair a private farewell dinner, to which all of the staff were invited. Gina came as well, and murmured to Claire, "I can't help but feel someone is missing."

Margot. She had always been a favorite with Claire's family—with Vo-Vo in particular. It was such a shame not to have her there.

Yes, they needed to do something about Margot. Busy as she'd been with the brasserie, Claire hadn't given up hope of persuading Margot to come and live with them at Madame Vaughn's.

Vo-Vo, who had dyed her hair pale pink once more, made Claire promise to visit them on the Riviera soon. "You'll be working your fingers to the bone for some demanding prima donna of a chef soon enough. Take a vacation, refresh yourself, before you begin. Bring Gina, too."

Claire looked around at the waitstaff and the handful of regulars, some of whom had been eating at Le Chat for longer than she'd been alive. "Where has Papa got to?"

She found him in the kitchen, an apron around his waist, hopping from stove to oven and back again with all of his old vigor. Hervé was busy flambéing steaks as if he were just the grill chef. She smiled and refrained from scolding. Then she grabbed her apron from its hook and stepped in to help. It was the final time they would work together and she intended to make the most of it.

As the meals sailed out to the tables in the hands of the waiters, all of the chefs and apprentices put down their tools and followed. Claire dragged her father out and they went together, arms about each other's waist. On the threshold of the dining room, they paused. Everyone was seated, chattering and passing bread and pouring wine, their faces lit by candles and the mysterious, shifting, colored lights from the stained-glass windows.

"Fifty years," said her father, shaking his head and smiling, his eyes shining with unshed tears. "This place has been my whole life."

The noisy, vibrant restaurant radiated the joy of celebration and frivolity, but as the staff and patrons caught sight of Papa, the room fell silent.

Claire hugged him and reached up to kiss his cheek. "Come, Papa," she said. "They're waiting for you."

As she watched him take his place at the table and raise a glass for a toast, Claire's eyes misted over. It was the end of a long family tradition. What would become of Le Chat under Hervé? How on earth could she bear to leave the brasserie in his hands?

Chapter Eight

Gina

Gina went alone to her second fitting at Dior because Claire couldn't—or wouldn't—take time off from the brasserie. In Claire's present state, it seemed useless to remind her that she was free now to find work elsewhere, to pursue her own ambition. There was a definite frisson between her and this new owner, Hervé. Gina saw through Claire's protests, but for once, she held her peace. She only hoped Claire wouldn't sacrifice her own ambition in some misguided attempt to save the brasserie from whatever havoc Hervé might wreak upon its traditions.

"Persuade Margot to come to us," said Claire, as Gina left the brasserie. "I've tried time and again, but she won't listen to me. It might carry more weight coming from you."

Gina made a wry face. "I hardly think so, but I'll try."

The date of the embassy ball was fast approaching. Gina had kept herself busy, using her freelance work to keep her mind off the upcoming event. She wanted to pitch a feature about the "lost years" in Paris, about the Fitzgeralds and Hemingway and Gertrude Stein, and the preliminary research was consuming a lot of her time.

Her novel was not moving forward as smoothly as she wanted, and she was starting to suspect she'd have to scrap everything and begin again. But sometimes, if she walked away from the book and thought about something else for a while, suddenly inspiration would strike.

The second Dior fitting turned out to be an inconvenience, requiring her to cross town on her day off when she should be working on her next piece. She was hoping to get this one published in the *Paris Review*.

If she had the opportunity to speak with Margot, well and good. If she didn't, she'd go to a nearby café and write for a while, then lie in wait for her friend to leave work for the day and catch her as she came out.

When Claire had told her about Margot's new address in the Pigalle, the red-light district of Paris, Gina couldn't help experiencing a sympathetic shudder. At least her maid's room had been clean and situated in a safe neighborhood. Margot must be broke and friendless to live in that part of town.

But the Margot she had known had never been friendless in Paris—she'd always been at the center of the social whirl. Now she was living under an assumed name in a seedy part of the city and shunning her dearest friends. What had happened to her? Was she hiding from her husband?

Stepping into the exquisite hush of La Maison Dior lifted Gina's mood, almost in spite of herself. Now that she was here, she might as well dismiss everything from her mind except her enjoyment of the experience.

A sense of luxury pervaded the air and seeped into her bones as she climbed the marble staircase to the fitting room. The gown was brought and an assistant helped her into it, but she did not catch sight of Margot.

The boned, silk-lined bodice of the gown felt perfectly comfortable and cool against her bare skin. The layered skirts were a regal weight on her hips, made heavy by the lavish beading. As the seamstress fussed about her, smoothing and tweaking the fabric so that it draped the right way, she had a childish urge to twirl and let her voluminous skirts flare around her.

"One or two more adjustments and it will be *parfait*," said the seamstress, sticking in one final pin.

Gina changed back into her own clothes and went downstairs. As she moved into the foyer, she said to Madame Vincent, "Before I go, I'll just stop in at the boutique and take a look around." With a nod and a smile she extricated herself from Madame.

She walked into the boutique and found herself in a wonderland of accessories. So many beautiful things, all in one little jewel case of a showroom covered in toile de jouy. But today, Gina's focus was Margot. She'd caught a glimpse of her friend before she'd scurried into a back room to hide.

Undeterred, Gina asked of the young assistant, "Might I see ..." She caught herself about to give Margot's real name. "Marie, I think her name was? She assisted me last time and I need to ask her a question."

"I'll just fetch her for you," said the assistant. With a smile, she hurried away.

Margot emerged from the back room, her carriage stiff. *"Oui, mademoiselle?"* Her tone was exquisitely polite, but her dark eyes glared. "How may I assist?"

Gina cleared her throat, somehow nervous. But what did she have to be nervous about? "Good day, Mademoiselle . . ." Gina stopped. What was the surname Margot went by here? She couldn't remember. "May I see the stole you brought to my fitting the other day?"

Margot regarded Gina stonily, clearly resenting being ordered about by her old friend like this. "It's just an excuse to talk," Gina hissed, with an eye out for the other assistant, who had left the boutique and disappeared into the back room, but who might return at any moment. "I couldn't care less about the stupid stole."

Margot thawed a little, but she said, "Of course, mademoiselle. I'll fetch it for you." She brought the stole and unwrapped it from its tissue paper. Under her breath, Margot said, "Not here."

Gina scowled at her. As if she didn't know that. "What time do you finish?"

"Six, but—"

"No 'but's," whispered Gina. "We're going to sort this out, once and for all."

"Well . . ." Margot looked up, the old spark lighting her eyes. "If you're buying, I'll come."

Gina pursed her lips. "I'm buying, but I warn you, I'm broke, so there won't be champagne of any description."

"Well, I don't actually like martinis," Margot said. "Just so you know."

Gina snorted and was about to make a rude retort when the other assistant returned with her arms full of hatboxes.

Loudly, Gina said, "This is not quite what I had in mind, lovely as it is." She had no idea of the garment's price but she probably couldn't even afford to buy a ribbon from the Dior boutique, much less an exquisite wrap like this. Not after purchasing shoes and a clutch bag to go with the gown.

She left the atelier and took herself off to write in a café nearby until six.

When at last Margot came out of the atelier, wrapped in a sable coat that clearly belonged to a different lifetime, Gina had formulated a plan. She would not nag or interrogate. She'd tell Margot her own story in the hope that she'd reciprocate.

So often in the past few months, Gina had longed to pour out her troubles to Margot, who was familiar with the kind of rarefied society to which Gina's family had belonged. She would understand how Gina felt to have that world turn its back on her.

As they lingered over cheap glasses of wine at a sidewalk café near Dior, Gina told her all of it, about her father, about Hal, everything. Margot listened with a sympathetic ear, but she didn't share anything of herself. She said, "My father is a wise man. You know what he always told me? That everything always turns out the way it's meant to be." She touched the rim of her glass, traced it in a circle as she stared into the light red wine.

"I don't believe that." Gina frowned. "And what good does it do to think that way, anyway? If you believe everything is fated, planned out in advance, why would you ever strive to do anything?"

"I don't think he meant it like that," said Margot. "I think he was talking about acceptance. Life teaches us lessons. Harsh ones, sometimes. And sometimes the situations are of our making, sometimes they aren't. But wherever we end up, that's not a mistake. That's where we are supposed to be, and we can either use the opportunity to adapt and grow, or we can stay stuck in regret and blame and self-recrimination."

"Are you trying to tell me losing all of our money and my broken engagement was a *good* thing?" Gina demanded.

Margot shrugged. "Adversity makes one a bit of a philosopher, I find. Maybe it's too soon for you to see the bright side."

"What happened to you, Margot?" said Gina quietly. "Why won't you come back and stay with me and Claire?"

Margot gazed far off into the distance. "No," she said. "I can't, Gina. Thank you for your concern, but the answer is still no."

Something Gina had learned about Margot was that she was very decisive. Once she'd made up her mind about something, it was difficult to shift her. If it weren't for that gown . . . Gina straightened as inspiration struck. "Will you at least help me get ready for the embassy ball? I can't afford a hairdresser and no one does makeup like you."

Margot eyed her for a moment. "I know what you're doing."

Gina gripped her hand. "Magoo, I really need your help."

The old nickname made Margot's lips tilt up in a reluctant smile. "All right, then. Just this once, mind." She sighed. "Oh, but Gina! In that gown, you'll be the belle of the ball. I hope you're ready for Hal to fall for you all over again."

Gina tried to smile at Margot's words but she couldn't take any pleasure in anticipating Hal's admiration. She'd need all of her strength to resist giving in to the feelings he still stirred up inside her. If he tried to persuade her to come back to him, she knew her heart would shatter all over again.

Thank goodness Margot and Claire would be there to pick up the pieces when she came home.

Margot

You want *me* to take charge of an entire department at the Grande Boutique?" Margot couldn't quite believe what she was hearing. Trade at Dior's Grande Boutique had been booming ever since it opened its doors the previous June. While an artist in every sense of the word, Christian Dior was also an astute business-man and he had seen very quickly the advantages of producing a ready-to-wear line of clothing that was affordable for teenagers and young women.

Perfumes, accessories, homewares, and even men's accessories and gifts were available for purchase at the new boutique.

Excitement and apprehension went to war inside her at the idea of running a department there. "But surely someone with more experience—"

"No, no," said Le Patron. "Of course it must be you, *ma petite*. The Grande Boutique is where young ladies come to purchase ready-to-wear fashions and accessories and perfume. I must have chic young ladies like you to assist them and show them how to wear my creations." Monsieur Dior's eyes twinkled. "Birds of a feather flock together—do you see? And you are an excellent sales-woman, according to Madame Renou. You will do well."

Monsieur Dior's offer was tempting. Margot did have a head for figures and she'd learned much from Madame Renou while she'd worked in the boutique downstairs. She *knew* she was capable. But that old voice inside her whispered, *Of course you couldn't take on an important role like that. Who do you think you are?*

Monsieur Dior regarded her for some time before he said, "I want you to go to see Madame Delahaye for a reading. Perhaps she can provide reassurance." He felt inside his coat and took out a card. "Madame is greatly in demand, but as a favor to me, she will make you an appointment. The address is on this card."

Margot stared at the card he handed to her. Madame Delahaye was Monsieur Dior's trusted clairvoyant, who had guided the couturier's decisions throughout his career. Most significant, she had correctly predicted the safe return of Monsieur Dior's sister Catherine from the German concentration camps, a foretelling that had given him immense comfort and hope throughout the tense months of Catherine's detainment by the Nazis during the war.

"That is kind. Thank you, monsieur." Margot only half believed in astrology. She was the daughter of a man of science, after all. But she couldn't deny she'd be fascinated to meet the legendary Madame Delahaye.

"Now." Monsieur Dior smiled at her and took up his newspaper. "Shall we see what our horoscope says today?"

"Ooh, yes, please," said Margot, skirting the desk to look over Monsieur Dior's shoulder. They were both Capricorns, which Monsieur had been pleased to discover when Margot had expressed an interest in the couturier's mystical side.

"'You will enter a new situation,'" he read out. "'Do not be timid but be bold in every undertaking to achieve your true purpose.'" He smiled. "There you are."

Bold? It was the opposite of how Margot felt. But she was determined to rise to the challenge Monsieur Dior had set her. For him, she would be the best saleswoman the House of Dior ever had. "If you really think I could do it, monsieur, then I accept."

"Excellent!" said the couturier, setting the newspaper aside. His desk was covered in sketches for the autumn/winter season. It was to feature two lines, as always: the A-line, and a contrasting Y shape—broad, accentuated shoulders, a tiny waist, the slightest flare at the hips, and a narrow pencil skirt.

"Do you see anything that catches your eye?" he asked, as he saw Margot perusing the sketches.

"Oh, everything," she said frankly. "These are all superb, monsieur."

"But no, you must not flatter me," insisted Le Patron. "Which is your favorite?"

It wasn't flattery; there was not a single design she would not kill to own herself. But she knew he wanted her to choose, so she said, "For me? This one, I think."

It was an exquisite sleeveless black dress, the neck a deep V, the skirt tight and tapered. It was probably the most unobtrusive of the garments whose sketches lay scattered over the baize leather desktop, the only one she could envision herself wearing in her present circumstances.

"*Vraiment?*" He stared up at Margot, then his eyes narrowed. "*Ma petite,* you are far too young and beautiful to hide your light like this."

She stared at the couturier. What did he see that no one else could?

"I know women—oh, but very well, you see," said Monsieur Dior, as if in answer to her unspoken question. "And I see you sparkle in the company of other jeunes filles, yet you shrink in the company of men. You are comfortable in the black clothing of the assistant, and in this you hide away, but you were born for more than that, my dear Margot." He pointed at her. "You know it, too."

She gasped. He'd used her real name. "You *know* me?" She thought she'd fooled everyone. It didn't occur to her to deny it, to keep up the pretense. She'd always hated and despised herself for lying, to Monsieur Dior most of all.

But if he'd known all along, wasn't he angry with her? Why, he'd even given her a promotion!

Dior smiled. "But of course. Me, I remember every woman I design for. Besides, it would take more than a change of hair color for anyone to forget Margot MacFarlane."

Suddenly she was aghast. "Then Madame Renou and the others . . . ?"

"Madame Renou will keep your secret," said Dior. "The others do not know, but that is because so many of them are new since you used to come here." He smiled. "Think on what I've said to you, my dear. You only get one chance at this life, remember. It cannot all be at an end when you are still in your twenties."

Shocked and upset at this sudden revelation, Margot hurried from the room, clutching the clairvoyant's card so tightly, it crumpled. She thought of her horoscope. *Be bold in every undertaking to achieve your true purpose.*

But Margot wasn't in the least ready to throw off the fragile protection of her new identity. Not when she still looked over her shoulder everywhere she went. And how could she shine her light, as Monsieur Dior expressed it? She couldn't revert to the person she'd been before. Not while *his* voice was still the voice in her head.

Claire

I guess I'll have to lower my sights, that's all," said Claire glumly that evening to Gina. They were huddling under a blanket with hot cocoa warming their hands while Claire told Gina about the rejections she'd received from the best chefs in Paris. "I can't believe none of them even wanted me as a *commise.*"

"They've got rocks in their heads, that's all," said Gina. "They'll be sorry one day."

"Yes," said Claire, raising her mug to Gina in a toast. She sighed. "But until that day arrives, I guess I'll have to stay at Le Chat. With *him.*"

Gina tilted her head. "Would that be so bad? I mean, I know you want to be the best, but it seems like a very hard life, being a chef de cuisine. And working your way up to that point seems even harder."

"Yes, but it's what I want," Claire insisted. "No, not want. It's what I *need*. It's . . . oh, it's like asking you if you want to write stories for your county newspaper instead of for the *New York Times*."

Gina smiled a little. "When you put it like that . . ."

Claire gesticulated wildly, nearly making her half-full cocoa spill. "I want to hone my talent to the sharpest point. I want to astonish and delight my patrons with edible fantasies, invent new dishes, write recipe books. I want my name to be synonymous with haute cuisine, like Carême or Escoffier, or . . ." She blew out a breath. "I've lost too much time. I'll never get there at this rate. I need more practice." She jumped up, flinging off the blanket, and making Gina protest. "What am I sitting around here for, feeling sorry for myself, when there is work to be done?"

"It's past midnight," said Gina. "Can't you cool your jets until the morning, at least?"

She frowned at Gina. "Cool my jets? What does that mean? No! I cannot wait till morning. There is no time to lose." She rummaged around inside the blanket for the shawl she'd discarded but couldn't find it, so she ran into her room to get her coat.

Gina laughed and shook her head, holding up her hands in surrender. "All right, all right. But can you keep it down? I have to be up early in the morning to work on *my* particular obsession."

Claire found her slippers and shoved her feet into them. "Don't worry, I'm going downstairs. I'll be sure not to disturb you when I return."

"But, Claire, do you think you ought to? The brasserie is Hervé's now."

Claire wasn't listening. She was going to work on her sauces tonight. And a good sauce was made with an excellent stock. Fortunately, she had some that she had rendered from beef bones already. To make a truly excellent beef stock, one needed the bones of a mature beast, but these were impossible to come by because the animals were butchered when young enough for their meat to be tender. The answer was to strain the first rendering and then simmer it down to reduce the stock to an intense flavor. Then you were ready to use it in a sauce. She had made a great quantity of stock, intending to practice all of the sauces she knew, and the pot still sat on the stove in the galley kitchen.

Claire grabbed the keys to the brasserie and shoved them in the pocket of her coat, then retrieved the stockpot, throwing a dishcloth over the top so as to prevent spills.

"Let me get the door for you," said Gina. "Watch yourself down the stairs."

"*Oui, Maman*," said Claire with a happy grin. "*Merci, Maman.* Don't wait up!"

She heard the apartment door close behind her as she made her way downstairs to the brasserie, careful not to spill any of the precious stock. The place was dark. It was a rainy, cold night, belying the signs of spring that had arrived throughout the city. It looked like Hervé had closed and sent everyone home. Claire set the stockpot on the floor and tried the door handle. Locked. Good. That meant she'd have the place to herself.

She let herself in and went straight to the kitchen, turning on the lights as she went. With the illumination of the immaculately clean bench tops and gleaming copper pots and pans, a sense of rightness and anticipation flooded her. She never felt so at home anywhere as in a kitchen, but at the same time, there was no more exciting place on earth.

She set to with a will and lost herself in the fierce concentration her work deserved.

She made demi-glace and Bordelaise. She made mushroom sauce and red wine sauce. She even made a sauce that was her own invention, a variation of sauce espagnole, which she flavored with her own combination of aromatic herbs, adding finely chopped bacon to the mirepoix—a delicious combination of diced carrots, celery, and onions, which she sautéed to tenderness before adding the stock and other ingredients. Later, she would strain out the mirepoix, leaving behind the intense, savory sweetness of their essence.

The sauces were in small white jugs, all standing in a row, and she was sitting on the counter, eating the delicious bacon mixture that she'd strained from the final sauce, when she heard a noise—the scrape of a key in the lock of the service door.

Caught red-handed, as Margot would say.

There was no time to conceal either herself or her creations. Hervé's massive presence filled the doorway to the alley. He was dripping all over the floor.

The oddest feeling of tenderness washed over her. "Oh, just look at you!" She slid from the counter and went in search of towels. "Don't you own an umbrella?"

He wrestled himself out of his coat and hung it up, then shook water from his shaggy hair. He was like an overgrown dog, she thought, but she couldn't help but be aware that her pulse had kicked up when he'd come in, and it wasn't because she was afraid of what he might say about her blatant misuse of what was now his kitchen. She had the strangest impulse to take care of him, which was foolish and unnecessary. He was the most self-sufficient, self-contained man she knew.

Ignoring the towel she offered, he wiped his shoes on the large mat and advanced into the kitchen. "What's all this?" Then before she could answer, he took spoons from the cutlery drawer and began to taste each sauce.

"Hey!" But she could hardly object, could she, after using his kitchen to make everything? And secretly she burned to know what he thought. Hervé had an excellent palate. She ought to know. He'd been intensely critical of her when she'd worked for him at the Meurice.

He made no comment—which for him, was high praise—until he got to the sauce she'd invented herself. It didn't stray too far from the classic, but just far enough that he would be sure to notice.

"This is good," he said. "I want to put this on the menu, serve it with the roast beef." His eyebrow quirked up. "Can you bear to have your creation appear on such a lowly menu?"

"Well . . ." Claire pretended to consider. She would die rather than show it, but Hervé's praise had sent tingles all the way down to her toes. She knew her sauce was good, but to hear him say it! And why was she still looking to him for approval after he'd sold out like this? She scowled. "It's not a lowly menu. You've got me all wrong on that. And yes, you can use the sauce, but you have to call it . . ." She mused for an instant. "Sauce Claire."

"Not Sauce Bedeau?"

"No. They will think it's my father," she said. "This one is mine."

"All right, then," said Hervé. "Done. Teach Jacques how to make it, as well."

Since Jacques was the *saucier* at Le Chat, this ought to be a given, and yet it troubled Claire. She'd made no secret of the fact she wanted to leave the brasserie as soon as she could, but did Hervé have to act as if it was a foregone conclusion that she wouldn't be around to make the sauce herself?

"You can't wait until I'm gone, can you?" she said. The words came out in a hard tone because she was trying not to sound hurt.

He stared at her. "I thought *you* were the one on edge here. I'm surprised you haven't left already."

She flushed. "Turns out it's not that simple." Her shoulders slumped and she heaved a great sigh. She might as well admit it. "No one wants to hire me. No one worth working for, anyway."

If he took that as a subtle insult, he didn't show it. He tilted his head, considering her. "You know who owes me a favor?"

She shook her head.

"Thibault."

It took several seconds for his meaning to sink in. "So . . ." Her eyes widened. "You would do that? For me?"

He grunted. "Why not? If it gets you out from under my feet."

"I would still be living upstairs." She didn't know why she said it. To goad him?

The corners of his eyes crinkled while the rest of his face remained immobile. It was a peculiar trait he had, this warming of the eyes that you might miss if you weren't paying attention. But Claire caught it. She knew. And her heart gave one strong beat before resuming its usual rhythm.

"You'd better go up and change before the others arrive," he said, and for the first time, she remembered she'd shed her coat at some stage and now stood before him in her nightdress, an apron tied hastily around her waist.

Flushing, she grabbed her coat and was about to flee when he said, "I'll see what I can do about Thibault."

Cheeks flaming, she called, "Thank you!" over her shoulder as she sped out the door.

Chapter Nine

Gina

The following evening, when Gina arrived home from working late at the bookstore, she found Margot already in the apartment, waiting for her.

Margot looked up from Hemingway's *For Whom the Bell Tolls*. "Claire let me in."

A flock of butterflies set up a ruckus in Gina's stomach. She'd been doing her best to avoid thinking about the ball but finally, the evening had come. She was going to see Hal. Worse, she'd have to try to persuade him to meet with her father. How had she been weak enough to agree to that? Why could she conduct hard-hitting interviews with politicians and doorstep con artists but she couldn't stand up to her own father?

Still, she was glad to see Margot. She hadn't been sure her friend would come. "Thanks. I owe you one."

She wasn't looking forward to taking a great big bite of humble pie in front of Hal with a large contingent of their acquaintance in Paris watching her smile and grovel. Well, call her vain and frivolous, but it was a comfort knowing she'd look absolutely stunning while she did it.

"I've been looking through magazines," said Margot. "And I came up with this for your hairstyle." She showed Gina a picture of Grace Kelly in a scene that Gina recognized from *To Catch a Thief*.

"Oh, yes. I like that." The cares of the day began to fall away. How could she fail to get excited about primping for a ball after all this time spent in worry and struggle?

In Gina's experience, her slightly-longer-than-chin-length blond hair did not lend itself to much variety in styles, but Margot achieved a sleek, sophisticated look that emphasized Gina's cheekbones and gave her a modern edge. She nodded with approval. "You are a genius. I don't know how you do it."

"Didn't I tell you? I used to be friends with a hairdresser at Kings Cross in Sydney. She styled all the famous drag queens, though of course they all wore wigs. Such a hoot. She taught me everything I know."

The makeup went on next, a lightly applied base of Max Factor pancake foundation, a hint of powder, a touch of rouge, misty-grey eyeshadow, and black mascara that Gina saw at once brought out the green grey of her eyes. A careful slick of coral lipstick and Margot was done.

"I don't know." Gina tilted her head. She had always been partial to a red lip.

"Trust me." Margot stood back, surveying her work. "When you put on the gown, you'll see."

Margot went to the drawing room and brought back a slim, square case. "This is not ideal," she said, "but since you don't have any real jewels to speak of and neither do I, let's use costume jewelry. On loan from Monsieur Dior." She pulled out a necklace made of clear rhinestones, slender and elegant. "They complement the beading on the gown."

The problem of her lack of jewelry had been needling at Gina on and off for weeks. "Margot, you are a wonder. They're perfect."

While Gina doubted any woman in her family had ever eschewed real gems for fake, it had become the fashion to wear costume jewelry, even with evening wear, so she wouldn't look out of place. As Margot put the necklace around her throat and worked on the clasp, Gina couldn't help but think, wistfully, of the diamonds she'd inherited from her mother. Gone now, of course, to pay her father's debts.

"I still feel guilty," she said. "Wearing the gown before Madame Vaughn or even Claire got the chance."

"Well, don't." The clasp clicked into place and Margot squeezed Gina's shoulders lightly. "Claire would have refused it altogether if it weren't for you. After you've worn it, we can get it altered to fit Claire. I have a friend at Dior who will do it for us cheaply, as long as we don't tell anyone."

"Truly? How marvelous," said Gina, brightening. "That makes me feel better about the whole thing. Still," she mused, "I wonder why Madame Vaughn took off in such a hurry. Do you believe this story about her going to Africa?"

Margot shrugged. "Why not? It sounds like exactly the sort of thing she would do. Gosh," she added, checking her watch. "Look at the time!" Margot closed the jewel case and placed it on the vanity table. "You need to get dressed."

"Oh! So I do." Gina inhaled a long breath, then exhaled. She set her shoulders back. "Right. Squire, bring me my armor!"

"Let's put your shoes on first," said Margot. "I'll do it. You don't want to ruin your nails."

She kneeled on the floor and helped Gina into her shoes, fastening the straps for her. The shoes and clutch purse were the only items Gina had permitted herself to purchase for the evening, because she'd brought nothing suitable with her to Paris, and a pretty penny they'd cost her.

"Take off your robe and I'll get the gown." Margot plucked a pair of cotton gloves from her pocket and hurried away to Claire's room, where the closet was tall enough to accommodate Dior's creation.

Gina shed her outer layer and instantly felt the goose bumps rise on her flesh. She couldn't afford to buy the stole Monsieur Dior had recommended, which might have given her some warmth. She'd have to wear her plain winter coat and take it off as soon as she arrived.

Returning first with the bodice, Margot settled it against Gina's torso, then fastened it at the back. Because the corset foundation had been made especially for Gina, it was far more comfortable than an ordinary brassiere. It almost felt like she was wearing nothing at all.

"Now the skirts. Gosh, they're heavy," panted Margot, holding out the voluminous garment for Gina to step into it.

Once the skirt was secured, Margot gave Gina's hair a quick tidy and checked her makeup. "Come into Claire's room. There's a full-length mirror there. You can admire yourself while I call down to the brasserie and bring her up."

Gina did as she was told, and couldn't help a gasp of wonder when she saw herself properly. Somehow the fittings hadn't prepared her for the sight of this queenly figure in full makeup and with her hair so much more elegantly styled than usual.

Gina stared into the mirror until Claire's voice came from the doorway. "Oh, Gina! It's magnificent. Truly."

Gina turned to face her. There were tears in Claire's eyes, but they seemed to be happy ones. Awkwardly, Gina said, "I'm glad you . . . I mean, I'm glad it's all right."

"Of course it is. Have a *wonderful* time," said Claire. She started forward as if to embrace Gina, but stopped, laughing. "I shouldn't mess up your makeup." She blew a kiss instead. "You will be the most beautiful woman there by far."

It was typical of Claire's generous heart that she would not let anything overshadow Gina's night. No reference to the fact that the gown had been meant for Claire, not Gina, crossed her lips. Claire had always been the sort of person who wanted more for her friends and family than she ever sought for herself. Sometimes that level of selflessness troubled Gina, but tonight she could only be grateful. Only now that she was ready did she begin to feel nervous about what lay ahead.

Chin up, Winter, she told herself. "I'll just get my coat."

"Wait!" Margot put out her hands. "I have something for you."

She went out, then returned with her own sable coat. Carefully, she settled the soft fur over Gina's shoulders. "There! Now you won't freeze to death."

"I feel like a proud *maman,* sending my daughter off to her first party," said Claire, pretending to wipe away a tear.

"Knock him dead, kid," said Margot in a very bad American accent.

Gina raised one eyebrow. "Don't you mean 'knock *them* dead'?"

Margot smiled. "I know what I meant."

Margot

I'll wait up for you to come home and help you out of the gown, all right?" Margot said to Gina as she left the apartment for the ball. Not to mention that she had to return the costume jewelry to Dior, and she'd need her coat back, as well. The sable was the only winter coat she owned. Though they were halfway through March already, the night air still held a chill.

Gina and Claire had insisted that Margot stay the night, and Margot had given in.

"Thank you, my dear, darling Margot!" said Gina. "I couldn't have done it without you."

In a rare show of affection, Gina bent to kiss her, but Margot ducked away and waved her off. "Don't you dare mess up that lipstick! Have a *wonderful* time."

As Margot watched Gina sweep out of the apartment behind Claire, who had to return to the brasserie, a wave of sadness hit her. She closed the door and pressed her forehead against it. What was this emotion? Surely she wasn't jealous!

No, not jealous, precisely. She had never been fond of formal affairs like the embassy ball, where there was a set program and everyone was dull and behaved with the utmost decorum. Her kind of party had always been a little wilder than that.

But it wasn't the parties she longed for so much. That gown, with its Cinderella enchantment, reminded her painfully of the young woman she had once been, a girl who had always secretly believed her prince would come. Her mother had raised her to be a society wife, like herself. It had never occurred to Margot to pursue higher education, though she'd always read widely. She'd never considered pursuing a career, either, even though her two best friends had set highly ambitious examples she might well have followed.

No. Margot MacFarlane was always destined for marriage. She was going to be a society hostess, throw the most marvelous parties in the world, use her talent for making fast friends out of strangers, for connecting people and making them laugh.

She'd pictured herself becoming an asset to her husband, helping him make business contacts and being the person to whom he'd confide all of his hopes and fears. She would listen and dispense sage advice, and he would respect her opinions. She would be the woman behind the man and content to be there. That was how it had worked in her family, and that was how she had expected her life to be.

But life had taught her a brutal lesson. Despite being surrounded by their beauty on a daily basis, she, Margot, would never wear a Dior gown again.

That bleak reflection sent her into a frenzy of tidying up. Gina was as messy in the rest of the apartment as Claire was in the kitchen. What a pair they were! Margot collected brassieres and knickers and stockings from the floor and tossed them into the laundry hamper.

How she longed to take up Claire's offer to move in. They would have such fun together here, even if Margot did have to do most of the housework.

But she couldn't risk it. She'd told him all about the brasserie and he had a mind that retained details like that. If she lived above Le Chat-qui-Pêche, there was the chance that he'd come there to inquire about her, and then the game would be up.

If she moved in with Claire and Gina, the constant state of vigilance and fear that had only just begun to lessen after six months in Paris would return. Irrationally, Margot still felt as if she were being watched, and a constant voice inside her head criticized everything she did and thought. But at least she could soldier on and fight each battle as it came, doggedly correcting the criticisms with her logical mind each time they arose. Somehow, she managed to keep going, almost sure that he would not find her.

She knew she needed to gather the courage to step out of hiding eventually. The new position in the Dior boutique that Le Patron had offered her would expose her to a greater risk of discovery. But she couldn't refuse it. The salary would be higher, her role more diverse and challenging, with greater responsibility than before. And she couldn't let Monsieur Dior down.

Margot retrieved a hanger from the closet and picked up Gina's heavy winter coat, which she'd slung over the chair at her vanity. On top of the vanity was a small selection of cosmetics but also a stack of typed pages, with the title printed in bold capitals. "LIBERTY." Gina's new manuscript.

To dust the vanity, Margot would have to clear off the surface. She hesitated, but only for a moment. She couldn't help herself. As she picked up the typed pages, her gaze swept over the first one. A bookworm from her earliest years, Margot was a speedy reader. In the time it took to move the manuscript from the vanity to the top of the chesterfield, she had skimmed the opening paragraphs of Gina's book.

"That's my girl," Margot murmured to herself. Gina's prose was punchy and simple, but full of color and bold turns of phrase. Already drawn in, Margot was sorely tempted to stop what she was doing and sit down to read. But Gina would kill her, and Margot hated to leave a task unfinished, so she resumed dusting, her mind ticking over with what she'd just read.

Humming to herself, she removed everything from the vanity and dusted the mirrorlike surface. She replaced lipsticks and nail varnishes, powder and face creams in an orderly fashion. She rummaged in the dining room bureau and found a pretty little Limoges dish to hold odds and ends like hairpins and a pair of earrings Gina habitually wore. She set it on the vanity as well, filling it with small treasures.

Pleased with her work, Margot tidied the books on Gina's night-stand, resolutely ignoring the pull of those typed manuscript pages that seemed to shine like a beacon from Gina's vanity. Among Gina's books was *Lord of the Flies*. Margot picked it up and read the jacket. She hadn't been in the mood to read a book like that when it was published to such acclaim but maybe now . . . She'd borrow it, give it a try. Then she caught herself. She kept falling into the habit of believing the three women's friendship would continue on the same footing as when they were in their early twenties. After to-night, she couldn't let herself visit here again.

The thought drove her to the laundry basket she'd seen in the living room, where a mound of freshly washed and dried clothes waited to be ironed. After hunting through the apartment, she found an iron and a small board and set to with a will.

Unlike other domestic chores, Margot found tidying and iron-ing relaxing, an almost meditative practice. But as she worked, her mind kept straying to Gina's manuscript. She used to read pages for Gina all the time in the old days. Knowing her friend as she did, she was well aware that Gina hated people reading her work before she was ready to show them. It would be a violation of her privacy for Margot to do so now.

Then again, Margot had made up her mind to break contact with Gina and Claire after tonight. If she didn't read now, she never would—not until the book was published, anyhow. And Gina didn't ever need to know . . .

"I'll just finish the ironing," she said into the quiet of the apartment. If her conscience hadn't won the fight by then, she'd read it. Gina would have wanted to show the manuscript to her anyway, when she was ready. The only trouble was that Margot would no longer be around when that time came.

Right. She returned to Gina's room with a cup of tea and grabbed the manuscript. From the fact that one of the twin beds was perfectly made, Margot deduced it wasn't the one Gina slept in, so she set her cup down on the bedside table, propped up a couple of pillows at the headboard, and settled down to read.

The first two chapters were close to perfection and Margot wanted to rush over to the embassy to tell her friend immediately how much she loved them. Gina had clearly worked hard on every last word.

The next pages were rougher and bristled with corrections. As Margot read, her fingers itched for a pencil, to add comments of her own. She rubbed her chin. Would Gina hit the ceiling if she found that Margot had marked up these pages? Well, what was the worst she could do?

Margot refreshed her tea and found a pencil by the message pad on the fancy telephone table in the drawing room, then she went back to the bed and Gina's story.

It was an allegory of sorts—following the Statue of Liberty from France to the United States of America, with a parallel narrative of a young American woman who seeks to escape the stifling mores of modern American society by running away to bohemian Paris.

The story was so engrossing that when Claire stuck her head around the door and called a cheery *"Bonsoir!"* Margot half levitated off the bed in fright.

Her heart pounding hard, she said, "Oh! Don't *do* that! You scared me out of my wits."

"Sorry," said Claire. Then she caught sight of the bundle of pages Margot had clutched to her chest and her eyes widened. "That's not Gina's book, is it?"

"Yes," said Margot with determined unconcern. "I'm editing it for her."

Claire's mouth dropped open. "Won't she be mad? Gina hates it when—"

"I know, I know." Margot shrugged. "She'll be mad at first, but then she'll thank me. You'll see."

Claire looked unconvinced. "Better you than me." Then her brow puckered. "Have you eaten? Would you like me to fix you something?"

At the mention of food, Margot's stomach gave an audible rumble. She chuckled and rubbed her bleary eyes. "What time is it?"

"Past midnight."

"So the brasserie is closed and everyone has gone home?"

Claire nodded, then she eyed Margot warily. "Why do you ask?"

Margot sent her a mischievous grin. "Do you still have a key?"

Laughing, Claire put up her hands, palms out, and waved her off. "Ah, *non, non, non.*"

"*Mais oui, oui, oui!*" said Margot, her eyes dancing. "Give me five minutes to finish this and then we'll go down."

Chapter Ten

Gina

"Hello, Frank." Gina smiled at Frank Fielding, a handsome if stolid young man she'd met while she was a reporter in D.C. and Frank was working for the State Department. "Thank you for escorting me tonight."

She'd chosen him because he seemed safe and because he didn't belong to their social circle. Hal was immensely popular with Gina's friends, both male and female, and he seemed to have kept every single one of them after their breakup. Thank goodness for Claire and Margot, who were hers alone.

Frank stepped back, surprised, as Gina came down the stairs to greet him. "I would have come up to knock on your door like a gentleman. There was no need to meet me in the lobby." He smiled indulgently, as if he were many years her senior and not her contemporary. "But I suppose it's not every day a girl gets to attend a ball at the United States Embassy."

Gina stopped herself from rolling her eyes. She hadn't forestalled him due to eagerness, but rather because Margot didn't want anyone else to know she was in the apartment. Margot was as jumpy as a cat on a hot tin roof, so Gina had decided to save her friend the anxiety, no matter how misplaced it seemed.

She forced a smile. "Shall we?"

A car with diplomatic plates and a driver awaited them in the street outside. So Frank must rank quite highly now. Amazing how quickly mediocre men rose to the top at the State Department these days, she mused. But she should stop criticizing. He was doing her a favor. If it weren't for Frank, she might have had to go to the ball alone.

He helped her into the car and she did her best to arrange her skirts so they wouldn't get crushed. Luckily there was plenty of room on the wide back seat for both her gown and her escort, who slid into the other side.

"You look beautiful tonight, Gina," said Frank.

"Thank you."

He seemed to want to say more, then to think better of it. She was glad. Her nerves were stretched so tightly, she felt nauseated. Making small talk was the last thing she wanted to do.

They cruised through the streets of Paris, crossed the river, and headed toward the Place de la Concorde. The Chancery was a large stone edifice on the northwest corner of the square. It had been built in the 1930s to the Americans' requirements, but its façade held a grandeur and elegance that harmonized with the neighboring Hôtel Crillon, which had been built for Louis XV centuries before.

As their driver waited in the queue of automobiles to pull up outside the embassy, Gina pinched the inside of her wrist in an effort to focus on something other than her fears, but her gloves dulled the effect. Her stomach churned. The image of Hal rose before her, his face ravaged with pain, his hand gripping her wrist. The dreadful sensation of wrenching free. The stomach-dropping feeling of step-ping off a cliff, being swallowed by the darkness that was her future without him.

"Gina?" Frank was waiting to help her out of the car. It felt wrong to take his hand and step onto the red carpet. Frank placed a hand on the small of her back, as if she needed his help to get to the front entrance.

"Mind the gown, Frank," she said, eluding his touch and whisk-ing her skirts to the side.

"Oops. Sorry about that."

"Perhaps if you weren't so close," she said, as he attempted once more to shepherd her up the steps.

"Sorry." Letting his hand drop, he shuffled a little to the side. They joined the queue of guests that was inching toward the recep-tion rooms.

Frank's ineptitude somehow made everything worse. She just needed to get through the next couple of hours. Once she'd spoken with Hal and arranged a date for him and her father to meet, once she'd made it through the formal dinner, she could plead a head-ache and go home.

As they entered the embassy, Gina took in the opulence of the new building, with its parquetry floors and molded ceilings, its gilding and Louis XV furniture. She'd been brought up to disdain replicas, but she couldn't deny that despite being newly built, the embassy might have graced the Place de la Concorde since before the revolution.

"Miss Winter." Gina turned to find Tommy Ledbetter at her el-bow. A contemporary of Hal's but not a friend, he was employed by Hal's father, Joe, as some kind of general factotum. "Fancy meeting you here."

Frank took her coat with an air of one laying claim over private property and passed it to a waiting attendant. Gina made the introductions.

"Well, well." Stepping back, Tommy looked her over from head to toe with an insolence that made her wish she had a drink to throw in his face. "You certainly pulled out all the stops tonight." He quirked an eyebrow. "Dressed for revenge?"

Gina pressed her lips together. "I don't know what you mean."

Had she overdone it in an effort not to appear pathetic? Looking around, she saw that the other women present were dressed as extravagantly as she was. Balmain vied with Balenciaga, Schiaparelli, and Givenchy. She recognized other models from Dior's Automne/Hiver collection. Gina was not at all out of place in this company.

Frank cleared his throat, holding out his arm to her. To Tommy, she said, "Excuse me," and placed her hand on Frank's arm, preparing to enter the ball and work their way down the receiving line. Tommy didn't take the hint, but instead took possession of her other arm and linked it with his. Her skin crawled but she didn't want a scene. She just wanted this over with as quickly as possible.

"Standing guard?" she murmured, for his ears alone. "You needn't bother."

"On the contrary," said Tommy. "I'm here to help you."

Shocked, Gina covered her reaction with difficulty. "Why would you do that?"

"The king is dead. Or very nearly," Tommy replied. "Long live the king. And our soon-to-be new monarch insists on having his queen." At her scoffing reaction, Tommy added, "Why do you think he's in Paris? It's not for the escargots."

So Hal had followed her. Had he somehow orchestrated her presence at the ball tonight? Surely that had been Jay alone.

As she glided over the red carpet into the reception room between two handsome young men, Gina should have felt like a million dollars. If the admiring glances cast in her direction were any indication, she looked like a million dollars, too.

She ought to feel satisfied, exhilarated, even. Yet for perhaps a full minute, everything inside her froze: her bones, her blood, her brain.

What on earth had she been thinking, agreeing to come here tonight?

Finally Gina admitted it to herself. She was terrified. She was so afraid of meeting Hal here tonight that if she weren't rooted to the spot, she would turn on her heel and flee. How could her father put her through this? Or had her hard-as-nails act fooled him, as it did most everyone else?

Neither gentleman seemed to notice her reluctance and swept her along between them. With the greatest exercise of will she had ever accomplished, she forced herself to hold her head up and look around her, a slight challenge in her gaze. No escape now.

They ran the gauntlet of the receiving line, which was made up of dignitaries and officials. Gina didn't pay much attention to any of them. Every sense was on the alert for Hal.

While Frank was busy greeting some acquaintance or other, Tommy seized the opportunity to steal her away. "I want you to meet some people."

She wanted to protest. Tommy was a snake, and he clearly had some plan in mind that involved using her. However, she'd lost sight of Frank in the crowd and did not want to be left alone in a sea of strangers.

Despite the fuss over her gown, Gina had forgotten what elaborate affairs embassy parties could be. Before the dancing, there would be a formal dinner with many toasts, and before that, a cocktail reception. She accepted white wine from a proffered tray, feeling the need of liquid courage. "A Californian chardonnay, mademoiselle," said the waiter.

"Bold choice," Gina said to Tommy. "Serving American wine to the French." She sipped and the chardonnay was buttery smooth. She eyed her glass. "It's very good."

"Not that you'd catch any Frenchman admitting as much," said Tommy.

He introduced her to many of the guests, always circulating, always amusing and saying exactly the right thing. He'd make an excellent campaign manager when Hal ran for office. Although her senses were on high alert for him, she still hadn't set eyes on Hal.

Tommy introduced her to an American businessman and his wife, expatriates who had lived in Paris since the end of the war. "Came here for a vacation and never left," said the man, chuckling.

"We simply fell in love with the place," his wife gushed.

"Paris will do that," said Tommy. He glanced at Gina. "Miss Winter certainly couldn't stay away. Isn't that right, Gina?"

She gave a start. "Yes. Oh, yes. It is the most marvelous city in the world. Have you become true Parisians, then, and secretly despise the tourists?"

The couple laughed. "Only when the tourists behave badly." Mrs. LeBlanc had a pleasant southern drawl. "I am positively *mortified* on occasion, let me tell you. Why, only the other day . . ."

Gina did her best to listen as the lady recounted an example of her compatriots' egregious behavior. She didn't succeed. She caught sight of a tall, blond man who might have been Hal. A surge of anxiety flooded her chest, only to recede again when it turned out that it wasn't him, after all. She felt unsettled, jittery, ready to turn and bolt from the room.

For pity's sake, get a grip, she chided herself. She had a purpose in coming here tonight and she refused to be diverted from it. Hadn't she always prided herself on possessing nerves of steel? She'd interviewed movie stars and senators, doorstepped fraudsters and white-collar criminals, but now her stomach felt fluttery and her lungs were tight. She was acutely aware of the silk lining of her gown, which lay cool against her skin. Despite the heat of the room, goose bumps broke out on her shoulders and arms.

". . . and then he said, 'But ours is bigger!'" Mrs. LeBlanc finished her story on a triumphant note, and her audience burst into laughter.

Gina joined in, though she had no idea what she was laughing about. She scanned the crowd once more. She needed to get this over with. She needed to find Hal and talk to him without his minder present.

Still smiling, Gina said to the group, "Will you excuse me?" In an aside to Tommy, she explained, "Powder room," because it appeared he intended to stick to her like gum on a shoe. She headed in the direction of the ladies' retiring room, but moved slowly, scanning the crowd for Hal.

"Gina Winter, as I live and breathe!"

She knew that voice. The remark was so loud, Gina couldn't pretend not to hear. Bracing herself, she turned to see Laurel Chapman, a woman she'd known all her life. But Gina's gaze rested on Laurel only briefly. Her attention was immediately captured by Hal, who stood beside her.

It wasn't that Gina had forgotten how handsome he was, but she was startled by him, nonetheless. He had a kind of star power that more properly belonged to Hollywood heartthrobs than to politicians, and even though she'd attempted to prepare herself for this encounter, she might as well have spent her time buffing her nails. It was impossible to remain unaffected by him—at least, it was for Gina. No matter how much she might shore up her defenses in his absence, when he appeared before her, larger than life like this, her heart began hammering in her chest.

Hal's blond, tanned perfection, the whiteness of his teeth, were a startling contrast to the black dinner suit he wore. He patronized a London tailor and she could tell at a glance that his dinner suit was of the finest quality. She preferred him in an old fisherman's sweater and faded shorts.

On that thought, the memories flooded back, so exquisitely painful that she could scarcely catch her breath.

"Hello, Gina," said Hal, and there was a warmth in his tone that made her insides twist. Their eyes locked for a moment, before his smile went awry and he cut his gaze away. "Drink?" He signaled a waiter and without asking her preference, took a glass of chardonnay and handed it to her.

"Champagne for me," said Laurel. Lips compressed, Hal procured a flute of sparkling wine for her.

Murmuring her thanks, Gina sipped the wine, unable to meet his eyes.

This was excruciating. Laurel jumped into the awkward silence, relating a long story about her and Hal's running into each other in Paris. Clearly the object of the tale was to drop all kinds of hints about the nature and closeness of their relationship. Staking her claim, was she? As if such posturing was necessary. Gina's so-called friends had informed her months ago that Laurel made a play for Hal the second that Gina was out of the picture.

Gina remained silent, allowing Laurel to rattle on with some anecdote that was clever and amusing, no doubt. All the while, Laurel's attention darted between Gina and her former fiancé but Hal's gaze never wavered from Gina.

Perhaps sensing that she was only betraying insecurity by remaining by his side when he clearly didn't want her there, Laurel said, "But you two must have a lot to catch up on. Excuse me."

Hal didn't answer her. Gina wished with all of her heart that she could walk away, too, but she needed to fulfill her promise to her father. She tried to gain the upper hand with her emotions. "It's been a while," she managed. "How are you?"

"Gina, we need to talk," said Hal in a low voice. "But not here." He sipped his drink, watching her over the rim of his glass. "May I see you tomorrow?"

Before she could answer, Tommy appeared at Hal's elbow. "There you are! I've been looking for you all over."

Hal didn't take his eyes from Gina's face. "Go away, Tommy."

There was a note of steel in his tone. Tommy backed off, palms turned outward. "Fine, fine. I'll leave you two lovebirds to catch up."

Gina tried to keep her expression neutral, aware that many eyes were upon them. For a second, she wished they could have met in a less public setting, but immediately thought better of it. Being alone with him would be dangerous.

"How long are you here?"

"A couple of weeks." He gave a grim smile. "I'm expected back home to run things at the company. My father is . . . he's dying, Gina. The doctors have given him six months. A year at the outside."

"*Oh.* Oh, no." So that's what Tommy had meant with his talk of kings. The need to hold Hal was so strong, she had to clench her hand into a fist to fight it. "I'm sorry." And she was sorry, even if the curmudgeonly old coot had destroyed her happiness.

"Thanks." His mouth formed a brief grimace, as if he was suppressing strong emotion. In spite of herself, Gina felt her insides soften. She was so mad and hurt but none of it was his fault. Then he added, "I know you haven't always seen eye to eye."

That was an understatement. Did he know what his father had said to her? No. Of course not. Joe would have wanted to remain the benevolent patriarch in his son's eyes. He wouldn't have told Hal about that time he'd invited Gina to his country club and laid down the law. To be fair, it hadn't been Joe's fault she'd broken it off. True, he had warned her off, but in the end, she'd made up her own mind about that.

She stared at the deep golden color of her wine, half wishing she'd allowed Tommy to rescue her from this difficult conversation, half wanting to hold on to this moment in spite of all the reasons she shouldn't.

"You're looking . . ." Hal tilted his head as if to take all of her in. "That dress, Gina. It sure is a knockout." He didn't sound too thrilled about it.

"I'll be sure to tell Monsieur Dior you said so." Then, regretting her dry response, she added, "How do you like Paris, Hal? Is it all that you thought it would be?"

His blue eyes burned into hers, then he lowered his gaze to his drink. "I guess you know the answer to that."

She had told him often of her magical interlude in Paris in her late teens and early twenties, and how she longed to share the delights of the city with him. They were supposed to have explored Paris together on their honeymoon, married at last and free to enjoy each other in every way. Was he doing all of that with Laurel now? The idea hurt so much, Gina thought for one searing moment that she might never feel whole again.

But no one died of a broken heart, or of humiliation, she'd discovered. Life went on, and the brokenhearted either wallowed and declined or picked herself up and got on with her life.

Finally he said, "You were always a straight talker, but you were never cruel, Gina." His jaw set hard—more Marlon Brando than Troy Donahue now. "Money isn't everything, you know. I hope you won't let what happened to your father sour your outlook on life. You're worth a hell of a lot more than that."

She was so flabbergasted, she could only stare at him in utter shock, but he was already walking away.

She wanted to stomp after him and sock him in the jaw. *She* was the one who cared too much about money? How dare he, of all people, lecture her about that? The sheer audacity of it took her breath away. Why was he acting like the injured party in all this? When she'd done something utterly selfless for the first time in her life?

But wasn't that Hal all over? The golden boy, still believing he could have it all.

Suddenly she remembered her original purpose in attending the ball. She was supposed to ask Hal to consider investing in her father's new venture, arrange a meeting between them. If she'd ever been going to do so, she couldn't possibly broach the subject now. Not after what Hal had just said.

She shouldn't stare after him like a lovelorn fool, but she couldn't help following his retreat as he weaved through the crowd to rejoin Laurel. With a supreme effort, Gina wrenched her gaze away, again conscious of the other guests' attention. Gossip would be rife tomorrow, no doubt.

It had been cruel to send her here, just as she'd been finding her feet again in Paris after the rug had been pulled out from under her. Then she thought about Joe and his illness. Had her father known Hal was taking over? Was that why he'd grabbed the opportunity to secure Hal's help? Her stomach turned at the thought.

"You two sure can put on a show." As if he'd witnessed the scene and come to her rescue, Tommy took her empty glass and nodded to a passing waiter. "More wine?"

"Thank you. Or no. Maybe something stronger."

"Hold that thought." When he returned with a glass of cognac, she accepted with thanks. "Why are you doing this? Being so good to me?"

He cocked his head. "Can't you guess?" He gestured toward where Hal stood, unsmiling, in a group of laughing young people. "He means to have you, come hell or high water. And Hal always gets what he wants."

Her heart was breaking all over again. The cognac went down painfully past the lump in her throat. Hoarsely, she said, "Well, he won't. Not this time."

"You know, you're really something," said Tommy. "If I hadn't just seen the two of you together, looking like you'd rip each other's clothes off the second you were alone, I'd believe you. But there's something you need to remember about Hal Sanders. He might come across as an Ivy League poster boy, but there's more of old Joe in him than you'd think."

She stared at him. Was Tommy trying to explain Hal to her? A man she knew inside and out? "I'll keep that in mind," was all she said.

Gina became aware that the guests were moving through to the dining room, and quickly drank the rest of her brandy.

"Where's your escort?" said Tommy, taking her glass from her.

"Over there. Studying the seating chart."

She turned to go, but Tommy said suddenly, "The two of you can still work it out. Let me help."

There was only one way she would agree to marry Hal, and that was if her father won his way back to affluence and into the good graces of his peers. That wouldn't happen if she couldn't even work up the courage to ask Hal to meet with him. Without answering, she left Tommy to find Frank.

Dinner seemed interminable, with speech after dreary speech, but the evening picked up again when the dancing commenced.

The ambassador had called in a favor and brought in the great Duke Ellington and his band to entertain them, and soon Gina's foot was tapping. She couldn't resist Frank's invitation to take the floor. Ellington kept the party in full swing, and Gina waltzed and rumba'ed and fox-trotted with so many different partners, she couldn't remember them all.

Gina had just sat down and kicked off her shoes under cover of her gown to release her aching toes from their merciless pinch, when someone touched her shoulder.

"Mademoiselle, may I have this dance?"

That voice. She felt it like a kiss on her bare nape, sending shivers down her spine. Turning her head, she looked up at Hal and instantly regretted it. When he smiled at her like that . . . She couldn't be this close to him and not burn to throw herself into his arms.

She wanted to get up and walk away, but barefoot as she was, she couldn't immediately escape. She felt around with her right foot and wedged her toes into her shoe. Wrong one. She slid it off and put her left foot into it, felt the sting where her heel had rubbed raw. Then she felt about with her right foot again, but the right shoe continued to elude her.

"Come, Gina. Please. Dance with me." Hal held out his hand to her as if in command, but his expression was entreating. The anger she'd seen there earlier seemed to have melted away. He'd had a shade more to drink than was wise, she realized. She hoped he wouldn't make a scene.

"No, Hal. I'm not going to dance with you."

"Then can we just talk? May I?" Without waiting for an answer, he pulled out the empty chair next to hers and sat down.

A little breathless, she replied, "All right." Wasn't this what she'd come to the ball for in the first place?

With one fingertip, he traced the silvery pattern on the damask tablecloth. "How's the novel coming along?"

She was surprised he asked. "For once, it's going quite well, thank you."

"Good, good. What's it about?" he asked, then gave a wry smile and held up his hand. "I know, I know. You refuse to talk about it until it's finished. I always loved your writing. I miss talking about books with you. I just . . ."

This was excruciating. If Jay had wanted to torture her, he couldn't have devised a better method. "My father wants to meet with you," she blurted out. "On business." There. That ought to kill the mood. She'd do her best to persuade Hal to meet Jay. Then she could get out of here and never set eyes on Hal Sanders again.

She'd expected reluctance, but Hal didn't skip a beat. "Sure. Is Jay in Paris, too?"

She nodded. "At the Hotel Meurice."

"Then I'll give him a call."

Gina hesitated. It might be disloyal of her, but she didn't place any confidence in Jay's new scheme. The way her father made money involved complex financial arrangements, and it all seemed like smoke and mirrors to her. "Don't let him talk you into anything just because . . . you know."

"I won't." Hal might appear easygoing but Tommy was right. He'd learned business from his father, and he was no pushover. He added, "I think everyone deserves a second chance. If it wasn't for . . ." He ran a hand through his hair and narrowed his eyes as if at a painful memory. "Well, I should have got in touch with your father sooner." He drew a deep breath and took her hand in his. "I've missed you, Gigi. I've missed you so much. Won't you please come and dance with me?"

Didn't he *know*? Couldn't he tell how much she ached to walk into the warmth of his arms, feel his strength surrounding her, experience the certainty and security she'd felt whenever she was with him? But that wistful longing only made it more imperative to refuse.

"Bad idea." Gently she drew her hand away. All the while, she'd been searching beneath her skirts for her right shoe, but in vain. She wanted desperately to get up and leave if he wouldn't go away, but she couldn't. Not missing one shoe like some pathetic, modern-day Cinderella.

She felt around the carpet in a wider arc, accidentally kicking her shoe beyond the shelter of her skirts. It landed between Hal's feet.

Surprised, he looked down. With a grin, he bent to pick it up.

He ought to have had the decency to discreetly shove it back under all those layers of silk and tulle, or at the very least, hold it out like a prince in a fairy tale so she could slip it on.

Instead, he held on to the shoe as if taking it prisoner, blue eyes alight.

Tightly, she said, "Don't be an ass, Hal. Give me the shoe."

"Not unless you promise me a dance."

"Ugh! You are such a little boy sometimes." She made a grab for the shoe but he whisked it out of her reach. "Just give me the—"

"Everything okay here?"

Gina looked up to see Laurel Chapman. Her lips were smiling but her eyes were firing bullets.

Hal's gaze was fixed on Gina, and he took a beat before he turned his head to acknowledge Laurel's presence. "Everything's fine," he said. "I'm holding Gina's shoe hostage, that's all. She's refusing to dance with me."

"That's not very gentlemanly of you, Hal. You ought to be more generous. Or do I mean *charitable*?" With a drag on her cigarette and a pitying smile, Laurel sauntered away.

Furious at the implication dripping like poisoned honey from those words, Gina reached out and snatched her shoe from Hal's grip. "Leave me alone, will you?"

Without bothering to be subtle about it, she stuck her shoe back onto her foot, got up, and stalked away to find Frank and ask if he was ready to escort her home. She had never been so glad to leave a party in her life.

Hal wouldn't be in Paris too much longer, she consoled herself. She only needed to get through a couple of weeks and then he'd be gone. Out of her life forever.

Chapter Eleven

Margot

Nostalgia hit Margot hard as she entered the brasserie kitchen for the first time in years. In the old days, after a night on the town, the three friends would plunder the larder with gleeful abandon, but in the knowledge that Papa Bedeau would have stern words to say to them the next day.

Now that Hervé owned Le Chat, raiding the provisions felt more transgressive. But if Claire's complaints about the new chef held any merit, he deserved to have his feathers ruffled a bit.

"There shouldn't be so much surplus food here," said Claire, frowning. She stood inside the enormous storeroom, surveying various covered meats and cheeses and a large gateau with only a quarter missing. The gateau, at least, would keep. "We always pack up the leftovers and take them to the nuns to feed the poor."

"Ought we to do that now?" said Margot. "It's late, but I'm game if you are."

Claire shook her head. "No, it will have to wait until tomorrow." She frowned. "I hope this isn't a sign of things to come."

She continued to take inventory, and Margot heaved a sigh. "I don't feel so much like gorging on leftovers now. Let's just have some bread and cheese and wine, and we'll pay for it, too. I don't want you to get into trouble for pilfering."

But Claire was still rummaging around in the larder and not paying attention, so Margot busied herself cutting a generous portion of cheese from a massive wheel of Brie, then hacked into a block of Gruyère. She added muscatels and some preserved figs dripping with vanilla-scented syrup and grabbed the rest of the water crackers Claire had made that day. Those would taste like cardboard by tomorrow, anyway.

All of it looked rather delicious, arranged artfully on a small platter, and she was pleased with herself. "Wine?" she asked Claire. "You'd better take care of that. I know almost nothing about wine, yet instinctively, I always choose the most expensive bottle." She shrugged. "It's a gift."

"Hmm?" Claire's unseeing gaze shifted to Margot. "Sorry, what did you say?"

"What's up with you, Claire?" said Margot. "Brooding about Hervé?"

Claire flushed. "Of course not. Only I didn't think he'd overturn *all* of our practices the minute he got here."

Margot caught the waver in her voice. Then the truth dawned. Softly, Margot said, "It was your mother, wasn't it? She made sure the leftovers reached the people who needed them." Claire didn't often speak of Madame Bedeau, but she must miss the big-hearted firebrand of a woman who had run Le Chat with such warmth and charm.

Claire nodded, but she gave a small shake of the shoulders as if to throw off a weight. "I'll get the wine."

They were sitting down at the big kitchen table when a key scraped the lock and the door to the apartment building creaked open. Margot jumped, her entire body racing with fear. Claire put a hand on her arm. "It's all right. That's probably Gina. I'll go look."

When she returned, Gina was with her, Dior gown and all, wrapped in Margot's fur coat. Her expression was difficult to decipher, but it certainly wasn't a happy one.

"You look like you could use a drink," Margot said, grabbing another glass and pouring her one.

"Could I ever," said Gina. She sat down and accepted her glass, then raised it. "Cheers, girls. And no, I don't want to talk about it."

Claire regarded her for a moment as if undecided whether to accept this statement. Then she said, "All right. But *ma chérie* . . ." She turned to Margot and her expression held deep concern. "I'm sorry, but I must say it. I cannot bear to watch you jump at every shadow without knowing why. It kills me to see you like this. Won't you please tell us who or what you're hiding from?"

Claire's question caught Margot off guard. Her pulse, which had just begun to slow after discovering Gina to be the intruder, kicked up again. How did she explain it so they'd understand? Did she even want to make the attempt?

Margot took a long sip of wine, hoping that familiar soft, slow feeling of alcohol-induced calm would steal over her. But she couldn't be calm about this. She wanted to tell them. She'd intended to do so before she left, if only to make their parting more final. If Claire and Gina understood her reasons for remaining apart, surely they would be less likely to insist on including her in their lives.

But where to begin? As she tried to frame the words, a sick, frantic feeling made her blood fizz and race. She couldn't seem to open her mouth. She'd only ever told one person—her mother—and while loving and ultimately supportive, her mother had clearly thought her fears the product of neurosis.

"I know you got married," said Gina with more gentleness than she usually showed. "I found the notice in the Sydney paper."

A jolt of surprise made Margot stare at her friend. Her mouth twisted. Trust Gina to ferret out the truth. The marriage notice. Margot squeezed her eyes shut. Her wedding day. The best and worst day of her life.

"You looked so happy in that photograph," Gina said softly. "What went wrong?"

Margot swallowed. "Well, I *was* happy. Deliriously happy, in fact." She tried to smile but she couldn't. "'Delirious' is a good word for it, actually. I—I don't think I was quite in my right mind." She tried to calm herself, to take a deep breath. What had her father always told her about breathing? But her voice trembled and the words came out all in a rush. "I always thought I was such a good judge of character. It was one of the things I really prided myself on, you know? But he . . . He was not a good man, even if everyone around him thought he was a god."

"Did he hit you?" Claire's eyes filled with sympathetic tears.

Margot shook her head. "I used to think that in some ways, it would have been easier if he had. It was never clear-cut like that. But it was . . . hell, all the same."

How to explain it? The way he had treated her like a queen when they'd first met, not just showering her with gifts, which wasn't a new experience for her, but showering her with attention, with deep understanding, which had been far more seductive. Men so rarely *listened*. He'd told her his darkest secrets, his greatest fears, and she'd reciprocated—of course she had. She'd never met a man so open and honest. Even now, he was the only one in the world who truly understood her. It was the very thing that made him so dangerous.

Later—too late—she'd discovered that on his side, it was all lies. Sometimes she'd allude to a deeply emotional confidence he'd made, and he would look at her strangely, as if he had no idea what she was talking about. He'd been playacting, coaxing her to reveal herself, only to use her fears against her.

He hadn't even waited for the honeymoon before it began.

At first, it was small things. A little joke in his wedding speech that at last Margot was completely in his power, which later did not feel like such a joke. Criticizing the way she walked—she'd looked so dear and precious, coming down the aisle with her funny little duck walk, hadn't she? That comment, though couched in such affection, had taken the shine off the entire day. Her friends assured her she walked perfectly normally, but she couldn't shake the worry that they were just being nice. After that, she couldn't take a single step without feeling self-conscious. His voice in her head: *Toe to heel, not heel to toe, my dear.*

Then she began to find that unless she expressed herself with the succinct precision required of his medical students at the hospital, he pretended not to understand what she meant. He would question her as if employing the Socratic method until finally, he comprehended, or alternatively shook his head in frustration and gave up the attempt. By then, all of the color and sparkle had leached out of what had been, she'd thought, a very amusing story. Why was he the only one who couldn't seem to follow what she said? She began to edit every sentence before it came out of her mouth. Sometimes, Margot caught herself silently rehearsing what she wanted to tell him beforehand. And it was exhausting, truly, to live like that, but it never occurred to her to rebel. He was so clever, and she needed him to respect her intelligence, too. But somewhere along the way, it simply became easier not to talk much at all. Before her marriage, Margot had delighted in her reputation as a raconteur, but her funny anecdotes went untold in that house.

Sometimes, absorbed in a fairly mundane task like cataloging his extensive record collection, he would ignore her all day, or for several days, even when she tried to speak with him about something important. Later he would tell her how much he loved her, that she was the only woman for him, and bring her bunches of her favorite pink peonies, or some gift that was so specific and thoughtful and tailored exactly to her taste that she remembered how well he knew her. It would seem as though he truly loved her, that his occasional lapses and small cruelties were merely the product of his highly stressful profession as a pediatric surgeon.

But more seductive than the compliments and the gifts was the sudden, razor-sharp focus on her and her alone. She would feel loved and wanted, drenched in happiness, until inevitably— with unpredictable timing—the coldness set in again, making her frantically search her memory for something she must have done wrong. Sometimes he seemed to go out of his way to disrupt her plans or behaved with a complete lack of consideration, woke her in the middle of the night to ask her something that easily could have waited until morning. If she complained about it, he did it more often. She learned not to object at all.

When Margot tried to put into words the way things had changed between them, her mother would say, "He's a busy man, darling. You have to be accommodating. And you can be such a flighty thing at times." Her elder sister, whose husband had run into money troubles, sourly told her to count her blessings.

Looking around at her friends, she started to notice that the wealthier a husband was, the more his wife was obliged (or willing) to put up with. Had she become one of those wives? Surely she had more pizzazz than that. It was what he'd loved about her, he'd said, the way she challenged him. Only they didn't seem to have those kinds of conversations anymore.

By nine months into their marriage, Margot was terribly confused, but she hardly knew what she was confused about. Only after she'd left, when she thought hard about how it had all unfolded, did she see the pattern emerge. At first, he encouraged her to be extravagant. His money was hers, after all. He only required her to keep every receipt and explain to him what each purchase was and where it had come from and why she needed it. He never told her she couldn't. He wasn't at all mean. Somewhere along the line, however, he explained to her his philosophy about money and the unimportance of material things, and that he wanted to build their wealth so that he could retire early and spend more time with her. Ergo, her spending money equated with not wishing to spend time with him. Secretly she *didn't* want to spend time with him anymore, but guilt made her all the more determined to prove otherwise.

Without being explicitly told to do so, she found herself scrimping on the household expenses and proudly presenting to him her latest savings. She stopped buying new dresses—he never liked the new ones anyway, and who else did she have to impress? He preferred her to be natural—she was so beautiful, after all—and he mocked her gently for her vanity whenever she primped in front of a mirror, stared at her blankly if she asked him how she looked.

So she stopped going to the beauty parlor as often, and opted for plainer styles, with a view to sinking into the background instead of becoming the life of the party as she had once always been. He didn't seem to like extroverted women, and visibly winced whenever Margot's more ebullient friends opened their mouths to speak. They irritated him so much that Margot began to see them only on her own, and then, slowly, not at all. The ones he did like seemed to turn against Margot, ever so slightly. She'd realize it was happening again when they began to parrot his criticisms of her, like ventriloquist dummies with his hand up their skirts.

Yet if anyone dared to criticize him or his treatment of her, she bristled and cut the acquaintance. She was too deluded, or perhaps too proud, to admit they were right. One day, Margot looked around her and realized she had no friends of her own. As a couple, they only ever saw the people who were acceptable to him.

So she wrote to Claire and Gina every week, clung to their friendship like a lifeline, even though their letters had stopped coming after she wrote of her marriage. His courtship of her had been a whirlwind, lasting less than a month. Although she'd begged him to wait until Gina and perhaps even Claire could fly out to join them for the wedding, he had refused, saying he couldn't wait another minute more than necessary to have her to himself. Maybe Claire and Gina had been offended not to have been invited to the wedding? Or maybe they hadn't taken note of her new address? He had arranged for all Margot's mail to be redirected from Margot's little apartment, in any case.

Then her husband bought a small farm in the highlands only a couple of hours' drive from Sydney. It was idyllic, a perfect weekend retreat, with log fires and exquisite gardens and views forever. Somewhere she could read a dozen novels and go for long walks in solitude and bring up their children. She wanted children, didn't she? Of course she did. She was aching for someone to love. Her failure to conceive had been a source of tension between them for some time.

Margot's acquaintances oohed and ahhed over the highlands property and told her she was lucky. But when he suggested that they move to the farm permanently, she clung to one last vestige of self-preservation. She refused to go.

It was the first time she'd openly defied him, and though afraid, she'd been unprepared for his reaction. Before, he had undermined her confidence subtly, chipping away at its foundations. This time, he demolished her character, her family, her friends. From the vitriol that spewed from his lips, finally she understood what a well of hatred he harbored for her—for all women, in fact. He was a completely different man from the one she had adored, calling her names she had only heard from the dockworkers who visited her father's surgery in Kings Cross.

Painfully she was forced to accept it: She'd loved a mirage. That man did not exist, and never had. For the first time, she saw him clearly. Now that she had, she couldn't bear to live with him anymore.

Always attuned to her moods, he seemed to sense he'd gone too far. For the first time ever, he apologized. She was too frightened not to pretend to be swayed by the assault of his charm, but the entire time he was attempting to beguile her back into submission, the poisonous words he'd uttered to her wound themselves into her brain and writhed there like a parasite. Even now, half a world away and six months down the track, something would remind her and she would hear that venomous speech again, as clearly as if he were in the room with her. The lovemaking that followed his apology had felt like a rape.

She couldn't remember much about the weeks that followed. She had trouble with her memory these days—whole tracts of time had been lost to fear and constant vigilance. The slam of a door, the jingle of keys—that meant he was home. Like a starter's gun, those sounds would set her heart racing.

Seeming to forget she had ever refused to move to the country, he put their house in Sydney on the market and told her to oversee the packing. Suddenly the fog that had invaded her brain lifted. At the thought of being cut off from the city she loved, from her family, alone with him, she panicked. She was drowning, and she knew that if she did not act to save herself, if she didn't leave, her very self would be obliterated.

So she waited until he left for the hospital. He had a full patient list that day. It was a sweltering November morning but she put on her fur coat and packed as much as she could carry without alerting the staff, who she was convinced watched her on his behalf. She had no money of her own—he made sure of that—so she sold her jewelry to pay for a ticket to Paris. Thank goodness, she'd renewed her passport.

She'd been of two minds about whether to tell her mother, but she couldn't leave without a word and have her worry herself sick. "You can't tell anyone I've gone out of the country. Not even Father," she said to her mother before she left. "Promise me you won't. Not under any circumstances."

Her mother didn't understand any of it, but she seemed to sense Margot's urgency and fear, so she promised and pressed into Margot's hands what money she had put by. "Oh, darling! I hope you know what you're doing. It's a big step, running away like this. How will you live?"

"I have friends in Paris. They'll help me," Margot lied. She had no intention of seeking out Claire, in case he found her through her friend. She had no idea how she would function without a husband to support her—he had undermined her self-confidence in every possible way—but if she thought too much about that, she'd never leave. But she'd done it. She'd gotten away. And she'd come to Paris, managed to wrangle herself a job at Dior.

"And the rest, you know," she finished finally, her voice hoarse from all of that talking.

THERE WAS SILENCE in the brasserie kitchen. Suddenly Margot couldn't bear to hear Gina and Claire's reaction. If *they* dismissed her pain, there was nowhere left to turn.

She took a deep breath and rose to her feet. "So you understand," she said, staring at her hands, "why I can't live here with you. Why I have to stay in hiding. He knows I'm in Paris. I told him all about you and Le Chat and the wonderful times we had here. If he comes after me, it's the first place he'll try." She had deliberately not looked at either friend while she told them. It was Gina's opinion she feared the most. Surely she would despise the cowardly way Margot had accepted such awful treatment.

There was a long pause. Then, "Oh, honey," Gina said. With a scrape of her chair, she launched herself at Margot and wrapped her arms around her tightly, all expensive scent and soft fur. Claire joined in, wiry and strong, and they stayed like that until Margot managed to whisper, "I never got your letters. I realized what happened as soon as you told me you never received mine. He must have taken them before they got to me and intercepted the ones I sent to you. I was so stupid! I used to leave them for the house-keeper to mail, but she always did his bidding."

"You were *not* stupid," said Claire. "You are one of the cleverest people I know. And when someone tells you they love you and marries you, how could you possibly suspect they would do such horrid things? It's like something out of a movie."

"He sounds like a master manipulator," Gina agreed. She stepped back and put her hands on her hips, her face the picture of an avenging goddess. "I hope he *does* come looking for you. I'd like to give him a piece of my mind."

"*I'd* gut him where he stands," said Claire with relish. "And you know I have excellent skills with knives."

Margot gave a broken laugh and wiped the tears from her cheeks with the back of her hand. "It's so hard to explain what it's like. It all happens so gradually, and before you know it, you're trapped." In a small, strained voice, she added, "Even my father . . ."

That had been the hardest of all to take. Her husband had established such a rapport with her father that he could do no wrong in Doc MacFarlane's eyes. A generous donation to each of the welfare organizations her father championed in Kings Cross, and he'd cemented himself in the Doc's good books. Margot was too proud to complain to her father of the treatment she'd received from him, having encouraged and delighted in their close relationship. To turn around and debunk the myth she'd built would have made her look unstable at best, and at worst, a malicious liar. She'd left Australia without even bidding her beloved father goodbye.

"He isolated you from everyone who cared about you," said Claire. "He wanted to make you alone and afraid. I'm *sure* your papa would have been on your side."

"That's just it," said Margot huskily. "Every month, I've telephoned home to let Mother know I was safe. Last time I spoke with her, she admitted she'd finally told Father where I was. I begged him not to pass it on to my husband, but he . . . He said it was his duty. He said it was my husband's right to know. So you see why I've been so jumpy. I keep expecting him at any moment."

"Well, I'm glad you told us," Claire said, at last. "But it makes it all the more imperative that you come live with us, right this minute. We'll stand by you, no matter what."

"Of course we will," said Gina. "We can keep a secret. Besides, he might have decided not to come after you. A man like that . . . Wouldn't he be too proud?"

"Yes!" said Claire. "And even if he does find you, what can he do? He can't drag you all the way back to Australia."

"Not in this day and age," Gina agreed. She tapped her chin. "Let's look into the legalities. Maybe Maître Bosshard can help you with a divorce. Then you can make a plan and set your mind at rest—on that front, at least."

Margot gripped a hand of each of her friends. "Thank you!" She couldn't quite explain how deep her fear of her husband was, nor that Gina's practical solution, while well-meant and eminently logical, did not reassure her. It wasn't over her body but over her mind that he held such power. Somehow—she didn't know how—he would get into her head and persuade her or subtly coerce her to return to Sydney with him. And then she would be lost.

Claire squeezed her hand. "The way I see it, if you keep living in hiding, then he's won, hasn't he? And I do *not* want him to win."

"No matter what, you can't stay in the Pigalle," said Gina. "I won't allow it. And you know," she added, "the more I think of it, the more I doubt he'll follow you to Paris. He's probably preying on some other poor victim by now."

That idea made Margot see a glimmer of hope for the first time. If he had found someone else, he wouldn't come looking for her. Of *course* he would have found someone else! Why hadn't she thought of that before?

"We'll help you move tomorrow," said Claire.

"But you have to work," Margot objected.

"Don't you worry about that," said Claire a trifle grimly. "I'm taking some time off from the brasserie."

Margot looked from one friend to the other. They were striking down all of her fears. And although she knew those fears would rise up again, like the undead in a horror movie, it was such a relief to let her friends make the decision for her, to borrow some of their courage. She was so very tired of struggling alone.

Suddenly seized with her old brand of recklessness, Margot drained her glass and held it out for more. "To us! The best friends in all the world!" she cried, holding up her glass in a toast.

"To us!" chorused Claire and Gina. They clinked glasses, then fell to planning Margot's move.

Chapter Twelve

Claire

Hervé greeted the news that Claire needed the day off without apparent chagrin, or even much interest. He was in the office, writing up the new menu. As she approached his desk, she tried her best to read *la carte* upside down—she'd definitely need to critique it thoroughly once it was finalized—but his handwriting was atrocious.

"Don't bother," Hervé said without looking up. "You will know what's on the menu when everyone else does."

"You aren't even going to ask for my opinion?" Claire would have reached over the desk and snatched the menu from him, only she probably couldn't read his writing when it was the right way up.

His eyebrows lifted and his intense blue eyes met hers. "I'm sorry—aren't you leaving Le Chat as soon as you can find a position somewhere else? How's that going, by the way? Have you called Thibault yet?"

She avoided his eye. True to his word, Hervé had given her Thibault's number and told her to call. She hadn't quite worked up the courage to do it.

Throwing down his pencil, Hervé relaxed back in his chair and put his hands behind his head. She couldn't help but be aware of the strength in his bare forearms, with his sleeves rolled up to the elbow like that, nor the bulge of the biceps that strained against the fabric of his pale blue shirt. He wasn't wearing the traditional chef's whites—never had, even when he'd worked at the Meurice.

Claire shrugged, dragging her gaze away from his physique. "I bet you can't wait to have me gone."

"When did I say that?" He frowned. "You're in a mood today. What's up?"

So he'd noticed. Well, good. "I came in last night and found the larder overflowing with leftovers." The words shot out of her mouth like bullets.

He tilted his head. "Huh. I thought someone had been in the kitchen after lockup." He quirked an eyebrow.

She flushed. *She* was not the one in the wrong. "You did say I could let myself in to practice my skills."

"I did, didn't I?" The look in his eye told her he knew she hadn't been practicing last night. "So. Leftovers."

"We *always* take them to the nuns at St. Catherine's," said Claire. "Change the menu all you like, but I can't believe you would change that." She gave him a scornful look. "Soon you'll be calling the place Hervé's and turning it into some fancy showpiece. Drive all our regulars away."

Hervé rubbed a hand over his face and sighed. "I told your papa it was a bad idea to keep you on here."

Claire threw up her hands. "Oh, here we go! I knew it would only be a matter of time." She smacked her palm on the desk and leaned in. "You need me, Hervé. You've only ever worked for other chefs. What do you know about running your own restaurant?"

"I know enough. And what I don't know, I'll learn my own way, in my own time." He picked up his pencil. "Now if you'll excuse me, I have a menu to plan."

"And my day off?" asked Claire. *Just see how you do without me,* she thought. "Make it a week."

"Take a month. What do I care?" He crossed something out on the menu and scribbled something down.

Furious, she stormed out of the office and headed straight to the kitchen, where the chefs were busy with the morning preparation. "Louis!"

The *plongeur* was doing the washing up. At her sharp command, he dropped a plate with a clatter. Muttering something under his breath, he scooped up the plate and turned his head. *"Oui, mademoiselle?"* When had he stopped calling her Chef?

"Last night's leftovers," she began. "I—"

Louis's shoulders slumped. "Not you, too! I've already been yelled at for that."

She moved closer. "What? By whom?"

He threw up a hand, and a spray of water arced in the air, narrowly missing her head. "By Chef, of course. He left me to close up last night but I had to go straightaway. My girlfriend was waiting for me, and it was late, so . . . I forgot to take the surplus food to the nuns. I'm sorry, okay?" He seemed to pluck up some courage and stuck out his chin. "But . . . but you're not the boss here anymore, so . . ." He trailed off, faltering beneath her frown.

She jabbed a finger at him. "I'm still the boss of *you,* Louis. And don't you forget it."

Claire turned away before he could see her cringe at the thought of all she'd said to Hervé. Ugh! Even worse than butting heads with the brasserie's new owner was the realization that she'd wrongly accused him about the leftovers. It made her want to shrivel where she stood. She'd have to apologize.

With dragging feet, she went back to the office and looked in, but Hervé wasn't there. The menu he'd been working on sat on his desk.

Claire glanced around. No sign of him. Truly she would have to be a saint to miss this opportunity.

She went to the desk and picked up the pages he'd written, with much crossing out.

"Aren't you supposed to be taking the day off?"

She jumped. Hervé leaned over and snatched the menu from her, then slapped it face down on the desk.

"I couldn't read your writing, anyway," said Claire. Although she'd deciphered several of the dishes, and one in particular—the sauce she'd developed. He'd included it in the description of the roast beef as "Sauce Claire" just as she'd insisted, and circled her name three times. It was a strange and giddy feeling to have a sauce named after her. Even though she'd demanded it, she hadn't really expected him to comply.

Her face was hot. She put the back of her hand to it, and hoped he hadn't noticed. And then she realized a reddish tinge burned along his high cheekbones, disappearing into his stubble.

"I came to apologize," she said quickly. "Louis explained about the food surplus." How much easier was it to say she was sorry than to dwell on the cause of their mutual embarrassment?

He grunted. "Fine. Maybe next time you'll give me the benefit of the doubt."

Claire's gaze went to the menu. Maybe she would.

Gina

Gina woke late the next day with a headache and a vague sense of foreboding. She sat up and drove her fingers through her hair, then grimaced. After whatever magical potion Margot had put through it to create those sleek blond waves last night, today Gina's hair needed a wash.

Margot. Her story had made a few lost millions seem like a blip on the radar. Margot was scarred from that marriage in ways that weren't visible. Thank goodness she'd agreed to come live with them above the brasserie. She needed to stop hiding herself away.

They were moving Margot out of her Pigalle boardinghouse today. She'd better get up and find a cure for her hangover before they left without her.

The bed next to Gina's was neatly made. It was Saturday, yet Margot never seemed to deviate from her morning routine, no matter what went on the night before. That hadn't changed, at least.

Something else hadn't changed. The way Hal had looked at Gina last night. The way he'd made her feel. A weaker woman would have danced the night away in his arms and to hell with the consequences. She ought to feel glad she'd resisted him. Because the fact remained: She was not the right wife for him. He needed a girl who had the money and connections to help his political career. She was no longer that girl.

Gina stretched, felt pain grip her brain at the movement, and was tempted to lie down and close her eyes again. Sleep would stave off the pain, both in her head and in her heart. She didn't want to think about Hal.

But she'd never been one to run from the truth no matter how ugly it might be. And besides, she'd promised to help Margot move. Gina swung her legs over the side of the bed and cautiously stood up. She hadn't drunk that much at the ball. It had been the shared bottles of red in the brasserie kitchen that had done it.

She rummaged in the drawer of her vanity and found a medicinal powder she always took on mornings like this. As she straightened, she saw the typed pages of her manuscript and her gaze snagged on a penciled annotation. "Perfect!" had been written above the opening paragraph. Gina's eyes narrowed. She knew that neat, bold cursive.

Snatching up the manuscript, she turned page after page. Deeper into the story, Margot's commentary riddled the text. In the margins, "Awkward phrasing" and "Why??" and "Oh, I like her!"

"Margot!" Gina yelled. Head pounding now, she pulled on a robe, grabbed the manuscript, and stormed out of the bedroom.

She found her friend in the kitchen, slicing *pain de mie.* The air was redolent of cooking. Several rashers of bacon sizzled in a large fry pan.

"Morning," said Margot, smiling. She reached for the coffeepot. "Want some?" Her gaze flicked to Gina's manuscript and back to her face, her expression turning wary.

"What I *want* is for you to tell me what the heck you mean by reading my pages!"

"Oh, that." Margot swiveled back to the pan to turn the sizzling bacon rashers, one by one. She reached for an egg, cracked it in. "I couldn't resist." She blew out a breath. "Well, if you must know, I was bored waiting for you to come home from the ball and the manuscript was just sitting there, so . . ." She shrugged. "Don't be cross, darling. You know I'm the best editor you've ever had."

"But I wasn't ready to show anyone yet. I don't—"

"It's the finest work you've ever done," said Margot simply.

Gina stared at her, all the wind taken out of her sails. Damn the woman. How could Gina stay mad when Margot said something like that? She swallowed. "You really think so? I mean, I can never judge a book when I'm in the middle of it."

"I know so. And I never say what I don't mean. Not about books."

Disarmed, Gina turned away, groping for the water jug and a glass. She poured herself some, tipping the headache powder in and stirring it with her finger. She chugged down the concoction.

"By the way," Margot said, plucking two slices out of the toaster, "your father called."

Gina grimaced as the bitter dregs of the headache powder caught on her tongue. "Thanks, I'll call him later." Her father would want to know whether last night's mission had been a success. He'd find out soon enough when he received Hal's call.

"Now come and eat," said Margot. "Claire left for the brasserie so I thought I'd do the honors." Onto a plate, she placed a piece of toast, then doled out crispy rashers of bacon, glistening with fat. She slid a spatula under a fried egg and then shimmied it carefully onto the toast. "Don't look so worried! I'm good at a fry-up."

Gina's stomach churned, but the scent of bacon was so enticing that she began to feel ravenous at the same time. "I don't know whether to bless you or curse you," she said.

They took their plates onto the terrace. The weather was still chilly of a morning but the day was clear and bright. Too bright. "Ugh," said Gina. "I need sunglasses."

They both bundled up warmly and put on sunglasses. Gina sat down and watched the street below for a few moments. Le Chat was already busy with weekend patrons enjoying the pleasant weather.

She couldn't see beneath the awning of Le Chat but she could hear the chink of cutlery on plate, the buzz of conversation. Farther up the street, a group of boys were rolling a large hoop along the sidewalk, calling good-natured taunts to each other.

Margot returned from the kitchen, holding up two glasses filled with thick red liquid spiked with bright green celery sticks. "Virgin Bloody Marys," she said. "Best thing for a hangover." She set them on the table and sat down.

Cautiously Gina sipped. To her surprise, Margot was right. The savory tang of the tomato juice concoction with its hint of heat and spice settled her unruly stomach somewhat. She stirred the drink with her celery stick.

Margot took up her knife and fork. "Do you feel like talking about what happened at the ball last night?"

Gina's throat tightened. "There isn't much to tell. I saw Hal. It was excruciating. He agreed to meet with my father. That's about it."

"You're not going to see him again?" Margot's attention was on her plate and her tone was casual—as if she could fool Gina.

"Not if I can help it." Gina paused. She needed to change the subject, so she heaved a sigh. "All right. Out with it."

Margot's head snapped up, her eyes wide. She swallowed. "Out with what?"

"The manuscript," said Gina. "You've told me the good. Now give me the rest." Margot would have criticisms. She always did, but it was hard to resent her for it; she invariably knew how to make a story ten times better. And anyway, arguing with her would take Gina's mind off Hal.

"Okay, I will." Margot put down her knife and fork. "The opening is strong, and I expect that's because you've worked on it the most. But later on, I need . . . more. More emotion. More description."

Margot gestured around her and flung a hand toward the street. "I want to *feel* like I'm in Paris. But I know you always layer the detail in later, so I'm not too worried about that." She frowned. "It's the friend. Marcie. She's too passive."

Gina felt herself prickling up like a porcupine, the way she always did when her work was criticized. She made herself take a pause to think about Marcie. "But she's there to provide a foil for Laura." Laura was the central character of the novel.

"I know that, but she feels two-dimensional to me," Margot argued. She sipped her own Bloody Mary. "And if she's such a milquetoast, why on earth is a firecracker like Laura friends with her?"

Gina had to accept the sense of this.

"What if . . ." Margot began, and with that, they were away, brainstorming, arguing, and laughing together, just like they used to do all those years ago. And the more they discussed the characters of Gina's book as if they were real people—friends to gossip and wonder about—the more vivid and real they became.

It was precious, so precious, this thing she and Margot had together. Precious and rare. No one had ever cared as much about Gina's writing as Margot. Hal had been supportive and a good listener, but he was more of a sounding board than an active participant. Besides, her fiction had taken a back seat since she'd returned to America and become a journalist. Margot might not have gone to university, but she had read extensively and she was analytical about her reading. Not only could she tell Gina what she did and didn't like about a book, she could tell her why. She could even make suggestions about how to fix it, some of which Gina took and most of which helped her to come up with her own solutions.

Despite herself, Gina began to feel confident. Not only would she finish this novel, this time, she would send it out to publishers and see what happened. She'd only tried to get a novel published once before, and the many rejections she'd received had so disheartened her, she'd decided to focus on journalism for a while. Confident to the point of brashness in other areas of her life, when it came to her fiction, she was as tender and vulnerable as a newborn.

When she'd finished her breakfast, Gina reached across the table to grip Margot's hand. "I'm so glad you're here."

Margot smiled but her eyes glistened with tears as she returned Gina's grip. "Me, too."

Claire

Right," said Claire, her hands on her hips as they stood outside the run-down boardinghouse where Margot had been staying. "That's all done. I gave the key back to that horrible landlady and you are now officially moved out!"

Margot hadn't bought much furniture since her arrival in Paris—an armchair for reading, a cheerful rug, and a faux Tiffany lamp. Louis had driven off with Margot's scant possessions in the brasserie van. Now the three women had the evening to themselves.

"Golly, look at the time." Gina was checking her watch. "I didn't realize it was so late. Is there somewhere good to eat around here? I'm starving."

"Let's celebrate," said Margot. There was a reckless air about her, as if, having agreed to move into Madame Vaughn's apartment, she had thrown away the last vestiges of caution. In for a penny, in for a pound.

They dined at the Petit Moulin Rouge, and lingered over their wine. There was so much to catch up on, and now that Margot had finally confided in them about her marriage, she had much to tell of her adventures back in Sydney before she got married.

"I suppose we ought to go home," said Claire, checking her watch. She had to be up early in the morning if she wanted to stick to her self-imposed cooking regime.

"Oh, come on!" said Margot. "It's my last night in the Pigalle and I want to go out with a bang. *I* know! I'll take you to my favorite club." Her eyes sparkled with that naughty mischief Claire had come to know and half love, half dread in the past. Now she was glad to see animation replace the fear in those lovely eyes.

"I thought you were lying low," said Gina. "How is it that you're still going to nightclubs?"

But Margot gave her a mysterious, sidelong glance and tapped the side of her nose.

A short walk took them deeper into the seedy streets of the nightclub district. They came to a building that looked half derelict, with its windows boarded shut.

With an exchange of dismayed looks, Claire and Gina followed Margot down a stone staircase to basement level, where the squeak and rustle of rats could be heard.

"Yikes," said Gina as they picked their way along the alley. "Do you think it's safe? This place looks likely to fall down with us in it."

"Hardly," said Margot. "It survived the war. It's not likely to collapse now."

Claire thought this showed a blithe lack of understanding for the principles of engineering and construction but she didn't want to rain on Margot's parade, so she swallowed her protest.

They reached an iron door that looked so impenetrable, it should have led to a bank vault. Margot pressed the worn buzzer on the wall beside it. A small panel in the door at eye level slid open. Margot mumbled what Claire assumed must be a password, and the door swung open.

Admitted to a dimly lit, smoke-filled club, they were greeted by the wail of a jazz trumpet. Claire stared about her, wide-eyed, at the gathered crowd. Some were gyrating to the music. Some were seated at tables, apparently engaged in intense conversation.

"I've never seen so much black outside of a funeral," said Claire.

"Beatniks," said Gina. She raised an eyebrow at Margot. "I didn't know this was your scene."

"Why not?" Margot shrugged. "The wine is cheap and the conversation can be interesting. And nobody cares who I am or where I come from in this place."

"Why do you need a password to get in, though?" asked Claire. But she was to be left to find that out for herself. Gina smirked and Margot said, "Come on!" She turned to lead them to the bar.

They ordered drinks. Gina and Claire sipped cautiously while Margot downed hers in one long swallow and ordered more. Someone shouted, "Marie!" and suddenly they were surrounded by several of Margot's acquaintances, drawing them deeper into the club. The supper tables were bare and scarred, and the only available chairs were milk crates and rickety stools, but Claire found she didn't mind at all.

They talked and laughed and danced and the hours passed by like minutes. Claire enjoyed a fascinating conversation with one gentleman who turned up on the small stage half an hour later dressed in a blond wig and black sequined gown with a split to mid thigh, giving a marvelous impression of Marlene Dietrich.

Claire glanced at Margot to see her friend grinning at her. "Isn't she brilliant?" Her eyes were heavy-lidded and Claire guessed she'd had one too many glasses of bordeaux.

But when the song ended and the applause died, Margot stood up. "And on that note, it is time for us to leave."

Forgetting she'd wanted to be up early to work on her skills the next day, Claire objected. "But we're having such fun!"

"My dear, one should always, always, *always* leave a party when one is most enjoying it." Margot flung out a hand. "Let us unto the starry night be borne!"

Dryly, Gina said, "Looks like we'll have to carry this one out of here."

Between them, Claire and Gina helped Margot upstairs and out into the street. After walking some distance, they managed to hail a taxi.

"But my place is that way!" protested Margot, lurching away from them.

"You're not going to your place tonight, remember?" said Claire, pulling her back. "You're coming home with us."

Claire chuckled to herself as she shut the taxi door on Margot and went around to slide in the other side. All three of them under one roof. She loved the idea. Despite Margot's troubles and the need for secrecy, they were going to have a lot of fun. And hopefully, in time, Margot would relax her vigilance and allow herself to return to normal life.

Smiling, Claire glanced over at Margot, who had closed her eyes and seemed to have fallen asleep.

When they arrived back at Le Chat, the restaurant lay in darkness, a nearby streetlamp throwing a gentle glow onto the sign of the cat and the fishing line.

"I'm all right. I'm all right." Her hands in the air, palms outward, Margot refused help to alight from the taxi, but as Claire turned to the apartment building, still laughing and feeling for her key, Margot let out a hoarse scream.

A man had stepped out from the shadow of the doorway. "Sorry." Pulling his hat brim lower over his eyes, he brushed past Claire, and sauntered up the street.

"It's all right, Margot." Claire put her arm around her friend and rubbed her shoulder. "He wasn't here for you."

Gina was staring after the stranger as he vanished into the darkness. "Then what was he doing here?"

Shrugging, Claire unlocked the door and they headed upstairs.

By the time they reached the apartment, Margot had calmed down and seemed to have sobered up a little as well. "I overreacted," she said. "Still jumpy, I guess."

"I don't blame you," said Claire. "He gave me quite a fright." But, she wondered, as Margot shuffled off to the bedroom she shared with Gina, what would it take before Margot felt safe?

"We need to help her get this divorce," said Gina quietly, as if she'd read her mind.

Claire nodded. "I'll call Maître Bosshard in the morning."

As she turned to go, Gina said, "Claire? Did you hear what that man said when he pushed past us just now?"

Looking back, she answered, "Yes. He said . . ." Claire's gaze met Gina's. "He said, 'Sorry.' He said it in English."

"English, but with an American accent," added Gina. "There aren't any other Americans in the building, are there?"

"He could have been visiting," suggested Claire. She frowned. But had the man actually come out of the apartment building? Or had he been skulking in the doorway for some reason? If he'd been coming out, wouldn't he have held the door open for Claire and her friends?

Gina's face was stony. Claire asked, "What are you thinking?"

Gina shook her head and wriggled her shoulders a little as if shaking off a disturbing thought. "Nothing. I'm sure it's nothing. Good night."

Chapter Thirteen

Margot

.

"S uperstition," Margot's father, who was a physician and a scientist, had always said, "is born of ignorance."

But her father had not been brought up among a phalanx of crazy great-aunts, the way Margot had, and in a house that was part museum, part mausoleum into the bargain. They'd all lived together on the cusp of the most colorful, sinful part of Sydney, Kings Cross. Margot had seen and heard things for which there was no apparent, logical explanation. She was willing to believe in . . . something beyond the physical realm.

When she heard of Christian Dior's strong metaphysical leanings, Margot was intrigued. She was agnostic when it came to the spiritual, but willing to be convinced, and always curious to learn more.

Monsieur Dior went to a clairvoyant who, it was whispered, had predicted correctly that his sister Catherine, a heroine of the Resistance, would return alive from her ordeal in the German concentration camps. It had been an unlikely eventuality, although her father would have said any charlatan would guess they had a 50 percent chance of being right, and probably would not have wished to foretell the opposite in case such an eminent client withdrew his custom.

Be that as it may, when Monsieur Dior told her he'd arranged for her to visit Madame Delahaye, Margot had jumped at the chance. She was about to leave Dior for her appointment when she nearly collided with Charlotte Mountbatten in the foyer.

"Oh, it's you!" Charlie gripped Margot's shoulders and leaned in to kiss her cheeks in the French way. "I've just had my final fitting. Where are you off to?"

There was something so disarming about Charlie's friendliness, that despite her wish to keep her distance from the Mountbattens, Margot found herself explaining her mission.

"Oh, that sounds like fun. Can I come?" Without waiting for an answer, Charlie linked arms with Margot. *"En avant!"*

Margot laughed and found herself accepting Charlie's company. "Don't you have a lunch date?" Young women like Charlie always had a full social calendar.

"I have now. With you and Madame Delahaye," Charlie responded. "Come on!"

Madame's lair was in the fashionable 16th arrondissement. "Madame is doing well for herself, I see," Charlie observed with a waggle of her eyebrows. "Bilking the innocent public of their hard-earned centimes."

"If you're a skeptic, you'd best stay out of the consultation," said Margot. "You'll ruin the . . ." She waved a hand. "I don't know what it's called. The vibrations? Something like that."

Charlie eyed her quizzically. "D'you mean you believe in that tommyrot? You are a funny one, aren't you, Marie? I never would have guessed."

"Let's say I am open to possibility," said Margot. Desperate, more like.

"Well, all right. I will stay outside if you'd prefer," said Charlie. "I'd probably start giggling in the middle of things and end up getting cursed or something."

They climbed the winding staircase to the fortune teller's apartment. A housekeeper admitted them and they were asked to wait in an anteroom.

Charlie cast a glance about her. "I have to say, I'm disappointed. I expected something more exotic."

"Me, too," whispered Margot. The fortune tellers she'd come across before had festooned their dens in gaudy, floating materials and cluttered the space with symbols of the occult. This apartment was decorated tastefully in muted, neutral tones. She couldn't decide if the ambience made Madame seem more or less legitimate.

After a short wait, Margot was conducted inside.

"Good luck!" Charlie called after her, crossing her fingers and nodding encouragingly.

The room where Madame's reading took place was no more remarkable than the rest of her apartment. Margot recognized the influence of Dior's taste and noted several decorative items that had come from his Grande Boutique.

Madame herself was a commanding presence, with eyes that were at first dark and penetrating, then seemed to release their grip. "Come, my dear. Sit down," she said, gesturing to the seat opposite her. The table between them was covered with a cloth of rich crimson velvet, the only touch of color in the buff-toned room.

"I am grateful to you for agreeing to see me, Madame," said Margot.

The older woman waved away her thanks. "Monsieur Dior would not rest until you came," she said. "He's highly sensitive, you know, and attuned to the mystical. He believes you are some sort of a lucky charm." She spread the cards out before her. "Your situation troubles him."

Margot had wondered why Monsieur Dior would go to such lengths on her behalf, even paying Madame Delahaye for the reading. Now she understood. Maybe he wanted Madame Delahaye to tell him whether he was right to give Margot a promotion.

She held herself at the ready to choose three cards, the way she'd been asked to do back in Sydney. But the clairvoyant did not invite her to do so. Instead, she stared deep into Margot's eyes, and drew a series of cards without looking, put them face down on the table, and swept the remainder of the fanned cards up and set the deck aside.

There were ten cards in total, five set out like a Maltese cross with a sixth placed diagonally over the middle card of the cross. Then to Madame's right, another four cards were placed in a vertical line beside the cross.

Margot waited, holding her breath, while Madame Delahaye turned each card over. Her hands fluttered over the tarot and she mumbled to herself, "King of Cups. But then there's the Devil, right there . . ."

Suddenly Margot wondered if this had been a very bad idea. If the clairvoyant concluded that her future did not turn out well, did she want to know? Was her future set in stone or might she take action and change it?

She made the supreme effort to remain quiet while all of this cogitating went on. At last, the clairvoyant sat back, as if exhausted by the reading she'd just done. *"Bien,"* she said. "You may go."

Margot stared. "That's it?"

Madame said, "The reading was for Monsieur Dior, not for you, my dear. But I shall tell you this: You are not meant to stay at the House of Dior. Your destiny is closer than you think."

Margot came away from the reading confused and worried. Would Monsieur Dior fire her on Madame's say-so? That would be a disaster. She wished she'd never agreed to come.

"I'm famished!" Charlotte announced when Margot rejoined her. She checked her watch. "Let's go to a little place I know. It's not far. My treat."

"Why not?" Margot shrugged, happy to go along with Charlotte. "I don't have to be back at Dior this afternoon." A meal in Charlotte's company might take her mind off the fact that she was likely to be unemployed soon. She sent a dark look up at the clairvoyant's window as they left the apartment building.

"You seem put out," said Charlie. "Didn't the reading go very well?"

"The reading wasn't actually for me, as it turned out," said Margot. "It was for Monsieur Dior."

"Bit strange, isn't it?" said Charlie. "Well, don't worry. It's all a load of rot, anyway."

"Perhaps, but it happens to be rot Monsieur Dior believes implicitly," said Margot. "I might be out of a job tomorrow." Maybe Hervé would employ her in the brasserie. She made quite a decent *plongeur,* if she did say so herself.

"Well, lunch will cheer you up," said Charlie. "I know a place with the best bouillabaisse in town." She hailed a taxi and directed the driver to a quiet, unassuming restaurant near Dior. It was more intimate than Le Chat, with low ceilings and small, cozy booths. The air was redolent of garlic and fine cheeses, with a faint hint of truffle. Margot's stomach growled. She'd skipped breakfast that morning, as usual.

Charlie was craning her neck to scan the crowd. "Ah!" She grabbed Margot's wrist. "There is my brother. Come on."

"What?" Margot planted her feet, resisting the pull of Charlie's hand. She'd assumed the restaurant had been a random choice on Charlie's part, not an appointed rendezvous with Mr. Mountbatten. "Goodness, is that the time? I really ought to head back."

"You just said Monsieur Dior gave you the afternoon off," Charlie pointed out with a grin. "Don't be a cowardy custard, Marie. Come on. He's seen us now." She waved enthusiastically at Andrew Mountbatten, who was sitting in one of the booths, a newspaper and an empty coffee cup before him, as if he'd been waiting for some time. At the sight of them, he smiled and rose to his feet.

Charlie started forward, then looked back at Margot. "Come *on*," she repeated. "He won't bite."

Margot followed Charlie to the booth. She ought to be annoyed with the other girl but she couldn't help the small flutter of gladness that she felt at seeing Mountbatten again. And what harm could a lunch in this out-of-the-way place do, after all?

"Look who I have here, Andy!" said Charlotte.

"*Bonjour, monsieur,*" said Margot with a smile. She continued in English. "I hope I am not imposing."

"On the contrary," he replied. "I cannot tell you how delighted I am to see you, Mademoiselle Foulon." The warmth in his gaze made her believe him to be sincere. "We missed you at dinner the other evening. I do hope next time you'll accept."

Charlotte put out her hand and gripped Margot's wrist. "Yes! Do come. You absolutely must. We'll set another date before we leave today." She picked up the carte du jour and perused it intently.

"I don't know why you bother to look at the menu," remarked her brother. "You always order the same thing." In an aside to Margot, he added, "Watercress salad. And then she makes me order the bouillabaisse and eats half of mine."

"How else am I to keep my figure?" Charlotte grinned back at him. "Stolen calories don't count." She turned to Margot. "You must try some, too. Even the broth is divine."

"Oh!" Margot laughed, inwardly balking at the idea of sharing a bowl with Andrew Mountbatten. "The poor man will have none for himself."

"I wouldn't mind," he said mildly.

"I know!" said Margot. "Let's order several dishes and share them among the three of us."

"Share?" said Charlotte.

"Yes, the way they do in some other cultures." The closest Margot had come to these other cultures was eating out in Chinatown back home, but she'd always loved the variety and informality of the way the meals were served there. As a child, she'd been fascinated by the massive lazy Susans, revolving round platforms on top of each table that one could spin to bring dishes closer. "I'll do the ordering, shall I?" Margot perused the menu, then rattled off the orders to the waiter, along with instructions to bring extra utensils and plates.

The waiter looked down his nose at her and said coldly, "Mademoiselle, this is not how we do things in France."

Margot replied, "Yes, but today, it is the way *we* do things in France." She smiled winningly up at him. "Won't you please let us have our little bit of fun?"

Thawing a little, the waiter bowed and said he would see what he could do.

When he had left, Margot sat back, satisfied. Then she noticed that brother and sister were regarding her with curiosity and surprise. Oh, dear. Somehow the old Margot had taken over, the one who always made a party out of the simplest gatherings and a picnic out of the most formal ones.

Always have to make yourself the center of attention, don't you? Again, that voice in her head, reminding her that she wasn't the one footing the bill for this meal, that she hardly knew the Mountbattens, that she was only a shopgirl from Dior. Margot felt the heat rise to her cheeks. "Oh, gosh, I'm so sorry! I've overstepped. I shouldn't—"

"If we are staring, it's because we are in awe," said Andrew Mountbatten, his dark eyes alight with amusement and, perhaps, she thought, with admiration?

"Yes, that was masterly!" Charlotte picked up the wine list and held it out to her. "Now do it with the wine."

"Not such a good idea to mix and match those." Andrew intercepted the printed card. "If I may?"

"Please," said Margot, only slightly reassured by their acceptance of her boldness.

He decided on a light pinot noir, which would best complement the variety of dishes she'd ordered. "Unless you prefer white?" he asked Margot.

"Not at all."

"Don't I get a say?" Charlotte put in.

Her brother glanced at her sidelong. "Your taste in wine is about as good as your taste in men."

"Oh, that's a bit harsh, isn't it?" said Margot.

"No, no. He's right, drat him," said Charlotte with a sigh.

"The latest was a poet," Andrew informed Margot. "And it's all my fault, apparently. He's one of mine."

"What do you mean, one of yours?"

"Oh, I'm an editor," said Andrew. "At least, I'm on sabbatical at the moment, but I work at Viking in New York."

"Oh, blast," muttered Margot. Could this man be any more perfect? Not only was he warm and amusing and kind to his sister, but he loved books, too?

"Sorry, I didn't quite catch . . ." The poor man seemed mystified, as if he'd heard what she said, but couldn't understand it.

Margot hurriedly covered her slip. "I meant about Charlotte and the poet. In my experience, poets can be extremely tiresome. They tend to forget everyone else for days at a time."

"Yes, but you see, he thought I was his muse," said Charlotte mournfully. "It was utterly exhausting. I wish he *would* forget me, quite honestly." She sighed. "Anyway, Andy warned him off, didn't you, big brother?"

He shrugged. "I merely told him I couldn't act as his publisher while he was with my sister. It's a conflict of interest, you see. The lover and the artist went to war inside him for all of five minutes, I'd say. But the artist won, so that's that."

Their savory courses arrived all at once, as Margot had instructed, and they had terrific fun, picking and choosing and passing plates.

Margot questioned Andrew so closely about publishing that he asked, "Why? Do you have an interest in that world?"

"I love books, you see." Margot dabbed at her lips with a serviette. "And I have a friend, Gina Winter, who is writing a novel. No . . ." She held up a hand as Andrew went to speak. "I do *not* expect you to publish it or even to read it. I would never impose like that. But I think this book is going to be terrifically good—I mean, it's really got something special—and I happen to have excellent taste. So I was wondering how I might help her to get it published."

"Really?" Mountbatten leaned forward, as if intrigued. "Perhaps I can help point you in the right direction." They embarked on a thorough discussion of the publishing industry and its foibles. Margot was so absorbed and fascinated, she forgot about the time, until Charlie dabbed at her lips with a napkin and said, "Well, I must be going. I have an appointment." She waved an encouraging hand at them and gave Margot a knowing smile. "But you two carry on."

Reluctantly, Margot decided it would be dangerous to remain alone in Mountbatten's company. The gleam of appreciation in his eyes when he looked at her, his dry wit and self-deprecation, his keen observations about books and their authors . . . She was beguiled by him; she had to admit it, if only to herself. All the more reason to keep her distance. She stood to accompany Charlie. "Thank you for lunch, and for telling me all about publishing. I'll pass it along to Gina."

"Publishing houses aside," said Mountbatten, rising as she did, "your friend's best bet would be to interest a literary agent." He thrust a hand into his pocket and said with studied nonchalance, "Listen, I'm having a gathering of sorts next week. Authors, editors, agents who are all here for the Festival du Livre. You and Miss Winter would be most welcome to join us."

In the interests of self-preservation, she should have declined. She couldn't afford to fall for anyone right now. She couldn't trust herself to choose wisely. But she wanted this opportunity almost as much for herself as for Gina. She needed to find a publisher for this book. "Thank you," she heard herself say. "We'd love to come."

But when she broached the subject with Gina upon her arrival home, her friend was far from appreciative.

"The book's not done yet."

"You'd only be meeting people, not handing them your manuscript," argued Margot. "According to Andrew Mountbatten, writing a good book is only half the battle."

"Yes, I do know how it works in the publishing industry, thank you very much."

"I think you're wrong to say no to Mountbatten's invitation, Gina," Margot insisted. "It's a great opportunity for you. Andrew said you need a literary agent, that these people work for you to sell your book on commission."

"I know what a literary agent is," said Gina. "I've been rejected by enough of them."

"Well, that's their bad taste and nuts to them because I *loved* your pages. And if I loved them, so will tons of other readers." Margot tapped the side of her nose. "You know I can pick a winner from the outside. Mark my words, Gina. Your book is going to be a big hit. We just need the right person to represent you."

"What we *need* is for the book to be finished," said Gina. "And I'm a little preoccupied with other things right now."

"Well, that's not going to cut the mustard, my dear," said Margot. "If you want to be a published author, you need to do whatever it takes to get those words on the page."

The plain truth of that statement made Gina even madder. Margot could see by the way her nostrils flared and her eyes flashed with annoyance.

"So you're going to this soiree, then, whatever I say?" Gina demanded.

"Yes," said Margot. There was nothing to stop her talking to everyone in general terms about Gina, even if her book wasn't ready yet. "I certainly am."

Only later, once the excitement of the day had worn off, did Margot realize what she'd done. She'd agreed to attend a cocktail party full of all kinds of people with Andrew Mountbatten, a man who didn't even know her real name. What if an acquaintance spotted her and spilled her secret? Could she bear seeing the look on Andrew's face when he found out the truth? What if this one evening brought her all of the trouble she'd been trying so hard to avoid? What if her husband finally found her?

Margot drew in a deep breath and let it out again. Let him find me, she thought. I refuse to live in fear anymore.

Claire

A week was too long for Claire to stay out of the brasserie kitchen. Of course it didn't help that she lived upstairs.

"Again?" Early one morning, Hervé eyed her as they both set to work. He wiped down the marble-topped bench, floured the cool, clean surface, and began the bread-making with which he always started the day.

As Claire was assembling ingredients to make her strawberry tart shells, the door to the alley opened and one of the waitresses came in. Mélanie was a pretty young woman, dressed that morning in black cigarette pants and a tight black sweater and sporting a swinging high ponytail. She called a greeting as she hung up her coat, then poured herself coffee. Claire noticed Hervé's gaze follow the waitress as she took her cup out to a sidewalk table to enjoy her morning cigarette before starting her shift.

Though accustomed to thinking herself plain or even freakish because she had inherited her mother's red hair and fair skin, Claire had never begrudged other women their beauty. But just some-times, when she saw a man like Hervé give a woman like Mélanie an appreciative look, she did wish that she might command similar admiration.

"Did you get in touch with Thibault yet?" asked Hervé, bring-ing her back to earth. "He's been expecting your call." His strong hands worked quickly, shaping, kneading, in a well-practiced rhythm, his muscles flexing as he drove the heel of his hand into the soft dough.

Without meeting his eyes, Claire said, "I wanted to make sure my consommé was perfect first. You know what a stickler he is." A lame excuse. "And you know better than anyone that I was fired from his kitchen, so I don't hold out too much hope."

"Your consommé is not the problem," said Hervé. "And if Thibault held your previous misdemeanors against you, he wouldn't have agreed to meet."

Claire felt a peculiar warmth seep into her chest at his words. "I suppose you're right, but—"

"Don't wait too long." Hervé covered the bread dough and set it aside to prove. "He's about to announce the new restaurant. You know what it's like. As soon as they hear the news, everyone will be begging to work there."

Claire quirked an eyebrow. "Can't wait to be rid of me, hmm?" As soon as she said it, she knew she sounded ungracious. Hervé was putting his own reputation on the line by recommending her. No one else had wanted to hire her, and Thibault was one of the best. She was unlikely to have another opportunity like this, so what was stopping her? Fear that all of those other chefs were right. She'd been out of the game for too long. She wasn't good enough.

Claire touched his arm. "Sorry. I really am grateful. I won't let you down. It's just that right now, I feel . . ." "Terrified" was the word.

"Don't tell me I'm going to have to fire you," Hervé growled.

Laughing for what seemed like the first time in weeks, Claire put up her hands in surrender. "All right, all right. I'll call him tomorrow. Happy?"

He grunted and turned away. "Ecstatic. Now get back to work on those tarts, will you? We're running behind today."

She did as she was told, kneading the pastry dough a little before rolling it out to a uniform thickness. They continued in silence for some time before she said, "What made you decide to buy Le Chat? I thought you aspired to be the next Escoffier."

"Me?" Hervé began slicing onions so quickly, you could hardly see his hands move. "I'd never thought of owning a restaurant like this until I heard it was for sale." He cleaned off the board with his knife, sweeping the diced onion into a bowl, then got to work on a bunch of carrots. Ordinarily this was the job of apprentices, but Hervé seemed to like to have a hand in everything, once in a while. She liked that about him. He had never thought himself too good for any kind of kitchen work.

"So what made you decide to buy it?"

He shrugged. "I'd just come in to some money from my grandfather. It seemed like fate."

As she turned that over in her mind, she sensed him watching her. "You believe in fate?" she asked.

He cut his gaze away. "I guess we'll see if I was right." After a few moments, he added, "At first, I admit I came here expecting to change everything. But you know how I trained under the great Mère Brazier?"

"Really? I *didn't* know that." Brazier was the first chef to be awarded six Michelin stars—three at each of her two restaurants. A legend in the industry. Hervé had never mentioned he'd begun his apprenticeship with her.

"La Mère taught me that simple meals made with the finest produce are best." He reached for another onion. "Besides, Le Chat has a dedicated clientele and I don't want to mess with that."

"But?" Claire sensed he was trying to decide how to say the next part.

He blew out a breath. "It might take me some years but I want to make Le Chat so profitable that I can open another place. A small, exclusive restaurant that serves only the finest cuisine."

She stared at him. "But that is what I've always wanted, too. Only I need a lot more experience first."

"Not so much more," he pointed out. "You already know all about the business side. And you've organized this kitchen as well as any hotel restaurant, taught your chefs superior skills. You already invent your own dishes. A couple more years working with the best, and you will be ready. And then," he added matter-of-factly, "I will steal you from wherever you are, and you will come and work with me."

She nearly dropped the tray of tart shells she was holding. "You have all of this thought out?"

He spread his hands. "I'd ask you to stay, but I don't think it's what's best for you. You need to prove to yourself you can cut it out there before you settle for something else."

Slowly, she said, "I don't think I'd see it as settling." Somehow she couldn't look at him. She felt as flushed and giddy as if he'd just proposed marriage. It was all so confusing. She'd thought she was over her feelings for Hervé . . . But she shouldn't get ahead of herself. His interest in her was purely professional, just as it always had been.

"Why don't you finish up here and give Thibault a call?" Hervé said. "You know you're only putting it off because you're scared."

That fired her up. "I am not scared!"

"Oh, yeah?" He laughed. "Prove it."

"All right," said Claire, ripping off her apron and throwing it at him. "I will."

Snatching the apron from the air, he gave her a wolfish grin. With the knife in his other hand, and with that shaggy hair and stubbled jaw, he reminded her of a pirate. A very annoying one.

"Bonne chance, ma chère."

"Oh, go jump in the lake!" Claire muttered in English.

As she stomped upstairs to find the card Hervé had given her with Thibault's details, she realized what he'd done, and got mad at him all over again. How easily she'd fallen for his goading! She huffed out a sigh. Only an idiot refuses to do what they should do just because an extremely provoking person has told them to do it.

Her annoyance receded, but anxiety about what she was going to do took its place. Her shoulders tense and her throat tight and dry, she had to force herself to cross to the ivory-and-gold telephone and dial Thibault's number.

Maybe he wouldn't be at the restaurant. Most chefs at the top of their profession did not have to arrive early to prep the kitchen the way their underlings did.

"Allô?" a female voice answered.

She had to clear her throat before she could get the words out. "May I speak with Monsieur Thibault, please? It's Claire Bedeau calling. Hervé Gabin recommended me."

This time, she was not fobbed off on the sous-chef. Monsieur Thibault himself came on the line.

"Ah, yes. Hervé's protégée," said the chef de cuisine. Either he didn't remember her being fired from his kitchen all those years ago or he was too polite to mention it. "I'd like to visit this brasserie of his I hear so much about. Why don't I make a reservation and we can discuss?"

Chapter Fourteen

Gina

Gina was still stewing over Margot's stubborn refusal to leave her to work on her novel in peace when she joined her father for cocktails that evening at Chez Julien.

As soon as she set eyes on Jay, all thought of her book and Margot fled. She'd asked for this meeting so that she could have a difficult conversation with her father. Had he insisted on such a public venue to discourage her from speaking her mind?

Well, it wouldn't. He was so hard to pin down these days, she couldn't let the opportunity pass by.

The restaurant's terrace, bordered by plane trees, with the gothic bulk of Notre Dame looming above, seemed a tranquil oasis, set back from the busy street.

"Darling." Jay stood to kiss Gina's cheek. He smelled pleasantly of lemon verbena, a scent that shot her straight back to her childhood. He drew back, eyes crinkling as he beamed at her. "You are looking beautiful today."

Jay looked as dapper as ever, his moustache trimmed, hair perfectly styled, his jaw as closely shaven as if he'd just stepped out of the barbershop.

When they were seated and he'd ordered them each a dry martini, Jay said, "I can't wait to tell you all about this new venture, Gigi. All it took was for Hal to make a few calls and I've been busier than ever. I'm flying home to New York on Monday."

"Monday?" repeated Gina, startled. "But I've hardly seen you."

"Never mind. I know you're busy," said Jay, as if she had been the one to duck his calls, rather than the other way around. Knowing her father, she'd have to get to the point straightaway or risk his leaving Paris without her ever broaching the subject of Rose's pen.

Maybe he hadn't taken it, she thought, as the waiter arrived with their drinks. Or maybe he'd taken it by mistake. But she knew that couldn't be right. Otherwise, the case would still be in her desk drawer where she always kept it.

As soon as the waiter left, she plunged in. "Father? I wanted to ask you . . ." She hesitated. She ought to have rehearsed how she'd phrase this. "My gold pen went missing a while back. You know, the one Mother gave me?"

His eyes went wide. "Your *mother*?" he repeated, as if it was the first time he'd heard of it. "Rose gave you that pen?"

How could he have forgotten that? It was her most treasured possession. Gina's heart started to beat fast. She began to tremble and her voice came out shakily. "Did you happen to see it when you came to the apartment?"

There was a long silence. Jay seemed to be staring into the past, and his eyes filled with tears. A lone, sweet birdcall sounded far above.

"Daddy?" Her voice sounded small and she hated it, but she couldn't control her emotions this time. She hoped she wouldn't burst into tears surrounded by all of these people. "Did you take my pen?"

His voice was husky with emotion. "Oh, honey. I'm so, so sorry."

It was as if an ice pick had pierced her chest so cleanly, she felt the cold of it before she felt the pain. She tried to steady her voice. "Where is it now?"

He buried his face in his hands. Then he dragged them down his cheeks and answered her. "I took it to a pawnbroker to sell." His tears were spilling over now. He'd never been one to hide his emotions. Whipping the spotted handkerchief from his breast pocket, he dabbed at his eyes and gave a sniff.

Gina was stunned into silence. Even though she'd suspected that her father had pawned the pen as he had done with so many other valuables before the bailiffs had come, hearing him admit it made her reel. "Which pawnbroker did you visit?" she demanded when she could speak again. "Please, Father. Give me the address."

"Why, I don't exactly recall," her father said, still dabbing at the corners of his eyes. "It was a couple of streets away from your apartment. Next door to a Tabac. Let me think . . ."

He couldn't remember the name or precise location of the place he'd sold her most prized possession, though he did recall that the Tabac next door had carried his favorite brand of cigarette. He trailed off, perhaps realizing how that sounded to Gina.

The silence stretched, and Gina couldn't dredge up an adequate response. She couldn't put what she was feeling into words.

"Gigi?" His lips trembled beneath his dapper moustache. "Gina, my dear, are you okay?"

But Gina didn't answer him. It was too late to visit any pawnbrokers, but she couldn't stay here another minute. Gina snatched up her purse and muttered, "I have to go." Ignoring his protests, she headed for the restaurant's entrance, charging past the other diners, nearly colliding with an affronted waiter. On the street outside, as she turned toward the nearest Métro station, she came face-to-face with Hal.

"What a delightful—" Hal broke off, the smile dying from his eyes. "Gina, what's wrong?"

It couldn't be a coincidence. "Did my father ask you to come here?" she demanded.

"Why, yes, but I didn't know you'd be here, too, I swear."

Gina wanted to wring her father's neck. She was so confused and hurt and the idea that he'd used their one time together before he left Paris to further his own agenda made her furious. "He's trying to get us back together," she said. "Don't fall for it."

"But I want us to get back together," Hal said, his eyes searching her face. "I thought you knew that."

She couldn't look at him. He had always been a man who knew what he wanted. He'd come to Paris to make sure he got it. But this time, he was in for a disappointment. She couldn't trust Jay to make things right again. She'd thought she could. She'd begun to hope he'd come through for her, that she could marry Hal with her head held high.

"Anyway," Hal was saying, "that's not what has you all upset. Did your father say something to distress you? I know he can be a little . . . single-minded."

That was putting it politely. A wave of shame washed through her. How could she admit to Hal what her father had done? After all that had led to her breaking their engagement, how could she make herself look even more pitiful?

"It's nothing," she said, turning away. "Please leave me alone."

He caught her arm in a hold that was gentle but firm and pulled her back to face him, his blue eyes blazing. "Gina, I'm not the enemy here. And I'd appreciate it if you'd stop treating me like one."

Tears sprang to her eyes, and she saw his face soften. "Oh, honey," he said, and his voice was a caress. "What's wrong?"

If only she didn't feel like this. If only she could hate him, or be indifferent. But he cared about her, and the look in his eyes made her long to tell him everything, to solve this problem together, as they always had in the past. Why did he have to come to Paris and test her like this?

"I can't!" She yanked her arm free and took off, running. She heard him call after her, but she didn't stop. When finally she slowed her pace and threw a glance behind her, she realized that he'd let her go.

Margot

Margot couldn't stop smiling. She was in her element among the elegant surroundings of Dior's Grande Boutique. While retaining the hushed, exclusive atmosphere of the atelier, the emporium was not a little jewel box of a shop tucked in beneath the stairs in the foyer of the Maison Dior, but a large and expansive set of departments housed in a seven-story building full of exclusive ateliers.

At Monsieur Dior's urging, she had left her blond wig at home and fixed her dark hair in a less severe, more becoming style. It felt like a huge step to come out of hiding like this, but Claire and Gina were right. She couldn't hide away forever, jumping at every shadow. A new look and a new position would be a start.

She would miss working with Delphine and Béatrice and even the difficult Madame Renou at Maison Dior, but as head of the department of young saleswomen selling the most beautiful and exclusive accessories in the world, Margot felt a new sense of purpose, and she was determined to make Monsieur Dior proud.

She wondered what exactly Madame Delahaye had said about Margot's future to make him so easily award her this position of responsibility, but Le Patron didn't explain and she didn't dare ask. He did, however, say to her, "You must come to me of a morning, *ma petite,* same as always, and we will read our horoscope together."

In spite of herself, his singling her out in such a fashion made Margot feel special and fortunate. She knew she was the envy of some of the other, more experienced girls, but she shrugged off a momentary twinge of guilt. Life simply wasn't fair. She'd discovered that soon enough. You were forced to take a bad hand when it was dealt; if a good hand came along once in a while, what a sad sack you would be to refuse it.

Charlie Mountbatten soon ferreted out the news of Margot's change in role and brought along a group of young friends, who fell upon the offerings in the accessories section like hungry wolves upon hapless prey.

"I love what you've done with your hair!" she exclaimed. "I hardly recognized you with it like that."

Margot smiled and wished she could be honest about everything with Charlie. She liked her very much. As for Charlie's brother . . .

"Aren't these sweet?" Charlie indicated the purses that had just come in for spring. They were made of wicker and shaped like different breeds of dog. "This one looks just like my Woodruff," said Charlie, picking up a pointy-eared canine with a long, boxy snout. "Oh, and look! This is like a West Highland terrier. I'll take that one, as well, for Gan-Gan."

While her friends swarmed like locusts through the rest of the store, Charlie drew Margot aside. "You will help me plan my birthday party, won't you? It simply must be spectacular."

"*Me*?" She knew Charlie tended to be impetuous but this request seemed like a shot out of the blue. Margot was already regretting agreeing to attend Andrew Mountbatten's literary soiree.

"Yes! You made lunch the other day such fun. Imagine what you might do with a party. And besides," Charlie added blithely, "if I have you to back me up, Andrew will say yes and amen even to the most outrageous request."

Margot pursed her lips. "I hardly think my opinion would carry weight."

Charlie stared into her eyes. "You really don't see it, do you? Andrew is absolutely smitten with you, but it's as if you have blinkers on when it comes to him." She gripped Margot's wrist. "You will at least come, won't you? Promise me you will."

The event was to be a Venetian ball. They would all be masked, so what was stopping her? And really, hadn't she taken the risk and decided not to hide anymore when she'd accepted this role at the Grande Boutique? She might not wish to encourage Andrew Mountbatten—she was still a married woman, after all—but couldn't she simply go to a wonderful, magical party with a friend and enjoy herself for once?

Then she realized. She had absolutely nothing to wear.

"I'll think about it," she promised.

"You will?" Charlie beamed at her. "Oh, that would be utterly brilliant. I'll send a car for you and everything. And clear your diary for this weekend. We have an event to plan!"

Before Margot could protest that she hadn't actually said yes, either to attending the ball or to planning it, Charlie had turned away to examine the vitrines full of costume jewelry, exclaiming over the stunning parure of aurora borealis rhinestones that Swarovski had made in collaboration with Christian Dior and supplied to him exclusively. The shifting pinks, golds, turquoise blues, and violets of the specially treated rhinestones were magical and the clientele were wild for them.

"Can I try the necklace on?" she asked Margot.

"Of course," Margot replied. "But the stones change color depending on what you're wearing, so to get the best effect, you really need to wear them with an evening gown. Why don't I find something suitable for you?"

Charlie ended by purchasing not only the aurora borealis necklace, bracelet, and earrings, but a sweet, ready-to-wear cocktail dress in turquoise that matched her eyes and set off the jewelry to perfection. A pair of Roger Vivier heels in toile de jouy and a bright pink evening clutch completed the look.

When Charlie's friends saw her preening in front of the mirror, they wanted to have Margot put together complete ensembles for each of them. Margot was run off her feet and blessed Charlie three times over for allowing her to hit her first week's sales target in a single afternoon.

Buoyed by this success, Margot's confidence spilled over. She would go to the masquerade, by hook or by crook. But working at Dior, she felt rather like the Ancient Mariner in that poem: "Water, water, everywhere, and not a drop to drink." What could she find to wear?

The obvious solution to her problem had not escaped her, but it would be indecent even to ask Claire if she might borrow The Gown. She'd have to think of another way.

Chapter Fifteen

Claire

Five years?" Margot jumped to her feet and started to pace the plush Persian carpet of the lawyer's office. "I have to be separated for *five years* to get a divorce?" She'd expected it to be difficult, but this?

The rest of them sat at one end of a mahogany board table with Maître Bosshard at its head. The lawyer spread his hands in apology. "I'm not qualified to advise you in the New South Wales jurisdiction, you understand, but I am told that's the case." He sighed. "Unless you can prove habitual drunkenness, adultery, cruelty—"

Claire jumped in. "But he *was* cruel to her. Margot just told you that."

The lawyer shook his head sadly. "I'm afraid we have no proof. And even if we did . . . Sadly, the behavior you describe is not enough. Not nearly enough for a divorce."

"You mean he would have to have beaten her," Gina said. "Then, what about adultery? Couldn't we pay a private detective to follow him, catch him in the act? I mean, surely by now . . ." Claire sent her a warning look and Gina closed her mouth.

"But I don't have any money," said Margot, her lips pressed together. She was fighting not to cry and Claire's heart ached for her. She wished more than anything she could do something to help but the law was against them.

"What if *you* were the one to get caught?" suggested Gina.

"W-what?" Margot looked mystified, then horrified. "You mean have someone take pictures of *me* in bed with some man? Are you out of your mind?"

"Gina, you're not helping," said Claire.

"Sorry." Gina sat back in her chair. "I just hate that Margot's being held hostage like this." She swiveled to see Margot properly as Margot continued to pace. "Will you stand still a minute? Could you contact your husband through Maître Bosshard and see if he'd be willing to come to a resolution? You might find he wants to move on, too. You know, in America, couples will agree on a scenario where the husband hires a woman for the night and gets the pictures taken, and it's all fixed, no fuss."

"He'd never agree to that," said Margot. "And besides, proving it would mean going to court, wouldn't it, and facing him? I can't. Really, I can't." Margot crossed her arms and lifted her shoulders a little, as if the thought chilled her.

After a few moments of silence, she blew out a long breath. "I suppose I'll just have to wait the five years."

They thanked Maître Bosshard for his help and rose to leave.

He had stood also but before Claire could go, he said, "Mademoiselle Bedeau? A word?"

It was clear he wanted to speak with her alone. With curious glances at Claire, the others filed out. Claire sat down again.

The lawyer began to clean his spectacles with a white handkerchief. "I understand from Madame Vaughn that you are aware of the reason she left Paris."

Warily Claire answered, "She told me in her letter. Yes."

Maître Bosshard smiled and hooked his spectacles over his ears, then pocketed his handkerchief. "Madame wanted me to let you know that she is well. She found an excellent spa in Switzerland where she expects to stay until the baby is born." He hesitated. "As you know, Madame is unmarried and it does not appear that this is likely to change. Initially she was planning to put the child up for adoption, but she has since changed her mind. That being the case, Madame intends to return home to New York with the child and pretend that she has adopted him. Or her, as the case may be."

Claire was overjoyed to hear this. "Don't worry. I won't betray her secret."

"I'm sure her secret is safe," said the lawyer, smiling. "Which brings me to the reason I wished to speak with you." He steepled his hands together. "Madame wishes me to assure you that you may remain in the apartment for as long as you like. She will honor her original promise of nine months, rent-free. Then if you want to stay after that, she will charge a reasonable rent, outgoings and so forth, which we will talk about closer to the time. Does that sound acceptable?"

"That is too generous of her," said Claire, relieved that she and her friends could stay. "May I write to thank her?"

"Address all correspondence to me and I'll make sure she gets it." The lawyer stood as Claire did. "Take care, mademoiselle. I am sorry I did not have better news for your friend."

Gina

Much as she was itching to get started on the search for her gold pen, after the early meeting with Maître Bosshard, Gina had to go to work. Fortunately the bookstore was quiet that day, so with Monsieur Florie's permission, she took the afternoon off to hunt for the pawnbroker that had bought her gold pen from Jay.

Upon inquiry, Louis had known of a pawnbroker next to a Tabac only a couple of streets away, so she followed his directions and found it without too much trouble.

The shop looked like a respectable-enough establishment if one disregarded the fact that the large picture windows were fortified by wrought iron grilles. Gina pushed open the door and in the broken afternoon sunlight that streamed through the barred front window, dust motes whirled around her. The place smelled musty and damp, as if someone had died and left the place closed up and neglected for months.

"This establishment could use a good airing," she told the flashy, middle-aged individual behind the counter. He wore a sharkskin suit and loud necktie, perhaps to distract from his pugilist's face and balding head, across which he had combed several strands of hair. His hands sported several gold signet rings and an expensive watch. Had he gleefully put on each piece the second the door closed behind the poor individual who had sold it to him? Had the gold been warm still from the customer's body?

"What can I do for you, mademoiselle?" With a hacking cough, the pawnbroker felt about in his pockets, then produced a cigarette case and lighter.

Gina decided not to explain her quest. "Do you have any gold pens for sale?" On a cursory glance through his display cases she couldn't see any pens at all.

"No, mademoiselle." Puffing belches of smoke into the fusty air, he added, "Gold watches, plenty. Rings, necklaces, bracelets. We have one gold cigarette case—*very* nice, that one. Tie pins, cuff links . . . No pens."

"Would you remember if one had come in and since been sold?" Most likely she was already too late.

The man rubbed the side of his nose. "A gold pen, I'd remember. But we have several other kinds if that's what you're looking for. Steel, silver-plated . . ." He reached beneath the counter and pulled out a wooden tray, plonked it on top. "There's sure to be something you like."

A cursory glance told her that Rose's pen was not there. "Thank you, no." Ignoring his attempts to persuade her, she left the shop.

Gina sighed. *Of course it couldn't have been that easy, could it?* She tried two other pawnbrokers in the vicinity with no luck.

Had the man in the sharkskin suit lied to her? Or had Jay been mistaken about which pawnbroker he'd visited?

She returned to the first one she'd tried. This time, it was not the man in the sharkskin suit who served her, but a woman in a stained mackintosh and a shapeless knitted cap, like the French revolutionaries had worn. Maybe this woman would remember the pen. Perhaps a female might be more sympathetic to Gina's situation and try harder to recall than her colleague had.

The woman's smile was more of a grimace, glinting with gold fillings. Her shrewd eyes examined Gina from head to toe while Gina explained the story behind the pen. "So you see, the pen was brought here by mistake," she concluded, unable to bring herself to say it had been stolen by her own father. "If you sold it, perhaps you might tell me to whom?"

The woman behind the counter tugged at her woolly hair and her eyes held an anticipatory gleam. Gina knew that look. She'd bribed enough people in her time as a journalist.

Loath as she was to part with her hard-earned money for what might turn out to be a trick, she drew a small wad of francs out of her pocketbook. Offering them, she said, "I'd be grateful for any information."

The money disappeared into the woman's pocket. She smacked her lips and jerked her head back, as if the cash had jogged her memory. "There *was* a gold pen, yes, yes. But I sold it last week, mademoiselle."

Another offer of cash only elicited a shrug. "It was a man, that's all I know. Not a regular. We don't take details of our customers, my duck. We just take the money."

Nothing Gina could say or offer had the power to extract any further information, and she was forced to conclude that the woman truly didn't know any more.

That was it. Her mother's pen was gone forever. She would never get it back. Gina managed to hold herself together until she made it out of the pawnbroker's shop. Striding away, she dashed her hand across her eyes as great, wrenching sobs tore at her throat.

Margot

As she walked the short distance to the club where Andrew Mountbatten was holding his literary soiree, Margot was so sick with nerves, she was tempted to turn around and run home. That awful voice in her head had nearly stopped her going altogether, and Claire had spent more than an hour convincing her to leave the apartment. Apprehensive as Margot was, she knew she needed to do this. Not just for Gina, but to take one small step toward overcoming her fears for good.

She wore a cocktail dress she'd saved up for months to buy—a simple black tulip dress with spaghetti straps. Around her throat gleamed her grandmother's pearls, the only jewelry she couldn't bear to sell. Her hair was piled high, with one silky tendril on either side of her face spiraling free.

As the evening deepened, the streets of Saint-Germain-des-Prés came alive with light and music spilling out of the cafés and bistros. Once she'd felt an integral part of this vibrant, joyous nightlife, so blithe and carefree, swept up in the giddy period where the main object of Parisian youth was to forget the deprivations and humiliations of the war.

It was the first time she'd been to any kind of party since she'd arrived back in Paris. The only reason she'd let herself agree to come was to try to make contacts in the publishing industry. She'd told herself she was doing it for Gina, but that wasn't the whole truth.

A strong breeze flirted with her coiffure but that was securely pinned in place and in no danger of tumbling free. She felt more vulnerable without her blond wig, however. Maybe it had been a mistake to banish it to a hatbox in the closet.

Would Mountbatten admire her as a brunette? She shouldn't concern herself with what he thought, but she couldn't help it. He'd made it clear he found her attractive as a blonde.

She couldn't deny she was drawn to him. His dark good looks had struck her as rakish when he'd watched her play the mannequin at Dior—the wicked tilt to his eyebrows, the glint in his dark eyes, the slightly cruel slash of his mouth. But sometime during that lunch with Charlotte, he'd shown a warmer, more relaxed side. If she were honest, this made him even more compelling, and more dangerous to her peace of mind.

She couldn't trust her feelings anymore—she had to remember that. Not after falling for a man who had nearly destroyed her.

She entered the club and handed her things to the coat-check girl. The hard thump of her heart echoed the beat of the music as she searched the club for Andrew Mountbatten's urbane figure. She couldn't let herself feel like this. She needed to pull back hard on the reins of her emotions. *You are married,* she told herself sternly. *You cannot be the judge of who is good for you right now.* But it didn't make a bit of difference to the way she felt.

The crowd was dotted with people whose faces she recognized from book jackets. One could make quite a game of naming them, she thought. Andrew must be a big wheel in the publishing industry to have attracted all of these people to his party.

"Marie?" A touch on her shoulder. "Hello, there."

She gave a start and turned around, kicking herself for momentarily forgetting her alias.

Andrew Mountbatten looked even better in a dinner suit than in pinstripes. His smile lit his eyes and made him seem younger. "I like what you've done with your hair," he said softly. Seemingly without thinking, he reached out and drew one sleek tendril through his fingertips, then released it. "I almost didn't recognize you."

Her pulse kicked up at the intimacy of the gesture, but somehow she couldn't bring herself to protest. Breathlessly, she said, "I thought it was time for a change."

"Thank you for coming tonight," said Mountbatten. "I'd quite given you up."

"Oh, no! If I say I'll be somewhere, I always go." *I just needed Claire and a crowbar to get me out of the apartment,* she thought. Determinedly tamping down the fluttering sensation in her chest, she added, "Will you call me Margot, please?" When he hesitated, she rushed to explain. "I know it might seem odd, but that's what my parents call me, and I prefer it."

"Very well. Margot it is. But only if you'll call me Andrew." He jerked his head. "Come and meet some people. I know several authors you'll particularly like."

In the most natural way possible, he took her hand and tucked it in his crooked arm. The fine wool of his jacket brushed her bare shoulder, sending shivers down her spine.

Fighting the effect he was having on her was almost a full-time occupation, but Margot couldn't help but be impressed by the authors who clamored for his attention. They tended to be dismissive of Margot at first, but she soon took care of that. As she and Andrew moved on from one group, which she had entertained with the story of her father accidentally shooting his own knee with the firearm he kept in the desk drawer in his office, Mountbatten said, "I think you might have found your calling. They were hanging on your every word."

"I do have an endless store of amusing anecdotes," she agreed. "It comes from living with a bunch of eccentrics on the fringe of the most sinful part of Sydney."

As he'd promised, Andrew introduced Margot to several fiction editors from across the Atlantic. She did her best to charm them, and to glean from them what kinds of books they published and what they were looking for currently.

"I notice you don't publish many books by female writers," she said, eyebrows arched at Mr. Evans, the editor from a small but venerated literary press. "Why is that?"

Evans puffed on his cigar. "I publish important literature, my dear. Most women don't have anything important to say."

Margot felt her hackles rise. "So you mean books about war and man's struggle against man, and man's struggle against nature, and so on."

"Well, er, yes."

"But women make up more than fifty percent of the population, Mr. Evans, don't they? And I believe they tend to read more books than men."

"Well . . . er, yes."

"And so wouldn't it follow, Mr. Evans, that if you published important books by women about women, you would also increase your sales?"

"She's got you there," said Mountbatten, sipping his drink.

"Faulty reasoning," said Evans, gesturing at her with his cigar. "After all, men won't read about women. But women will read about men."

Margot opened her eyes wide. "But isn't Agatha Christie the most widely read author in the world?"

"Well, but that's not literature."

Margot shrugged. "Still, it shows that men *will* read books by women. Doesn't it, Mr. Evans? It's all in the marketing, I would have thought. *I* think if you promoted a woman's book as important literature, men would most certainly read it."

Mr. Evans, running out of puff and clearly defeated, excused himself from the conversation.

Eyes sparkling with triumph, Margot turned to Mountbatten. "I cannot bear such stupid prejudice. And from someone who has every claim to intelligence!"

"You make an excellent point, though," said Andrew. He quirked an eyebrow. "Have you never thought of writing a book yourself?"

"Me? No!" Margot shook her head. "I don't have the patience and I hate being squirreled away on my own for long periods. But I do have an eye for a hit. I just knew Arnold Mathieson's *Lightning Glass* was going to be a hugely successful book well before the rest of the world caught on."

"Oh?" Andrew Mountbatten shifted position and regarded her seriously, as if he cared about her opinion. "What made you think that?"

"It dealt with one of the basic human struggles," said Margot. "And it gave us a fresh perspective on grief. Add to that an ending that was both surprising and inevitable . . ." She noticed that his eyes were brimming with laughter. "What's so funny?"

"No, don't stop! I'm impressed. With passion like that, Mathieson should hire you to be his agent."

She laughed. "Maybe he should." She tilted her head. "I know a literary agent sells a book to a publisher, but is that it?" It sounded like her idea of a dream job, but there must be a catch.

"Well, the agent gets to know all the editors, wines and dines them and learns their tastes, what they're looking for . . . Basically what you've been doing this evening on your friend's behalf. Then, when a publisher offers a deal, the agent advises the author whether to accept. There might be more than one publisher involved, and there will sometimes be an auction, which follows certain conventions and rules, depending on what kind of auction it will be. An agent needs to understand publishing contracts and how to negotiate a favorable deal."

"So basically, it's a bit like when a realtor negotiates the sale of a house?"

"*Just* like that," said Mountbatten. "Only there is a very select pool of buyers to whom you can pitch. And you have to remember that it's an ongoing relationship. Not only will that particular author continue to work with the editor who acquired their novel, but you will want to sell other books to that editor again and again. So you can strike a hard bargain, but it has to be a fair one, or it might jeopardize the relationship."

"I see." She hadn't been so excited by anything in a long time. "I'd like to know more. Maybe another time, we could . . . ?"

Mountbatten smiled. "Of course. But tonight you should make sure you meet everyone you can, while they're all here, in one place. And if you're truly interested in entering the publishing business, make sure you collect their cards as well."

The very next person to whom Andrew introduced her was an editor at a large publishing house in New York. "Seth Richards, meet Margot Foulon," he said. "She's a literary agent."

Margot's eyes widened, but she could see that Andrew was enjoying himself, so she decided to play along.

"Oh?" The editor's eyes roamed her figure, as if her literary discernment might possibly be located in her cleavage. "Which authors do you represent?"

"She's building her list," Andrew smoothly replied.

"Give me your card and I'll be in touch next time I'm in New York," added Margot.

"You're British, though?" said Richards, handing her his card.

"I'm . . . a citizen of the world," said Margot, tongue firmly in cheek. "In fact, I have just signed a brilliant author who hails from Connecticut. She's working on the great American novel right now. I can give you a sneak peek if you like."

The editor's gaze flickered to Andrew and back again to Margot. "Why haven't you already snapped this book up, Mountbatten?"

"Miss Foulon isn't officially going out with it until the fall," said Andrew. "But when *Liberty* comes on the market, you can bet I'll be knocking at her door."

"Interesting title," said Richards.

"It's an even better book," said Margot. "Poignant, tough, insightful—it's everything you want in a novel. Hits that perfect note between literary and commercial."

When the editor left, Margot raised her eyebrows at Andrew. "That was bold. How did you know I'd play along?"

He grinned. "I'm a good judge of character. Besides, you must have wanted to help your friend quite desperately to come along to this party. Because for some reason," he said, his dark eyes capturing hers, "you don't trust yourself with me."

Heat rushed to Margot's face. She hoped she wasn't blushing. "W-well, I . . ." Good gracious, she never stammered, or found herself at a loss for words, either.

Mountbatten held up a hand. "No, that was gauche of me. You don't have to answer. But I hope you know that happy as I am to talk about the publishing industry, my interest in you is strictly personal."

Her mind might be in disarray, but there was a solid, clear reason she could not allow this man any closer. She was still a married woman. She'd lied to him. Andrew Mountbatten wouldn't want her if he knew the truth.

With a great effort, Margot hardened her heart and changed the subject. "How long will you be in Paris, Mr. Mountbatten? Charlie mentioned you were leaving for Bermuda soon."

"Ah." He took out a cigarette case. "Now, I thought we'd agreed to use first names."

She merely blinked and widened her eyes, waiting for him to answer her question. She was deflecting, trying to blame him for the distance she intended to put between them, but he surprised her by shaking his head and laughing ruefully. "You know, I've been looking forward to my sabbatical for some time, and my trip to Bermuda was supposed to round it off with an appropriately hedonistic luxury. But all of a sudden, I feel as if I don't want to go."

It took her a moment to remember to breathe. "Look, Mr. Mountbatten—"

"Andrew. Please."

Margot huffed out an exasperated breath. "Andrew. Let me be frank."

"No, no. Don't do that." He was watching someone over her head. "Here comes Charlie's poet. We need to move on."

His hand at the small of her back, sweeping her clear before the poet could buttonhole him, sent shivers up her spine. He was dangerous, this man. She needed to be careful or she'd end up falling for him completely.

"I have to go," she told him firmly, stepping away and turning to face him. "Thank you for tonight. It's been marvelous, truly."

"Shall I get someone to call you a cab?" asked Andrew.

"No, I'll walk," said Margot. "It's not far."

"Then I'll walk you home," said Andrew, drawing closer when she would have moved away.

It was late and despite her misgivings, she had to admit an escort would be welcome. "Won't you be missed?"

"I doubt it," said Mountbatten with a cursory glance around at the noisy crowd. "Anyway, you said it's not far."

They emerged to find a cool, crisp night, freshened by recent rain. The wind picked up and Margot shivered.

"Wait." Taking off his jacket, Mountbatten settled it around her shoulders.

She nearly melted on the spot. The silk lining felt warm from his body. Its collar smelled subtly of shaving soap, a scent she liked better than expensive cologne.

"There." Briefly, his hot breath tickled her ear.

"Thank you," she said in a strangled voice. They walked on in a silence so crackling with tension that she nearly jumped out of her skin when a cyclist shot out of a side street in front of them as she was about to cross. Andrew grabbed her arm and yanked her back to the curb.

"Thanks," she said breathlessly, her hand to her chest. "Gosh, that gave me a fright."

"Idiot," said Andrew, glaring after the cyclist. "Are you all right?"

"I'm fine." She hitched the jacket more securely over her shoulders. "Thanks to you."

Finally they came to Le Chat. The lights were still on in the brasserie but Louis was stacking chairs on top of tables when she and Andrew reached the door to the apartment building. She turned to him. "Thank you again for a wonderful evening."

"Margot..." He trailed off. For a moment, he simply stared down at her, as the silence between them grew taut with anticipation.

"Yes? What are—" she began to ask, but he bent and swiftly kissed her cheek, and then her mouth, cutting off her question.

His warmth and the insistent, skillful pressure of his lips made her senses swoon. It seemed like a lifetime since she'd felt like this, completely swept away. She responded, winding her hands around his neck, dimly aware that his jacket had fallen from her shoulders but not caring one bit.

All too soon, he drew back. His expression thoughtful, he traced one warm fingertip along the cooling skin of her clavicle.

She let out a ragged breath, unable to speak.

"Good night, Margot." His eyes gleamed devilishly in the half-light. "See you at the ball." Without waiting for an answer, he picked up his jacket from the ground, slung it over his shoulder, and sauntered away.

Gina

You did *what*?" Gina had been putting a new ribbon into the typewriter but she whirled around in her chair and stared at Margot. She'd been writing furiously, trying her hardest to avoid stewing about her father and her lost pen. It had worked, to some extent. She was close to the end of her book, the momentum of the story carrying her through.

"Watch those fingers on the upholstery." Margot had been dusting the mantelpiece as she told her about her adventures with Andrew Mountbatten's literary set. "You've got ink all over them."

Gina glowered down at her smudged fingertips. "I ought to wrap these around your neck," she growled. "What did you say to those editors?"

Margot shrugged. She went to the desk and started laying out business cards like a hand of trumps.

Commissioning editors, publishers, vice presidents, of Knopf, Scribner, Viking, Random House, Farrar, Straus & Young. The list went on.

"I didn't say much—just enough to whet their appetites. That I had an author who was going to be the next Patricia Highsmith. And I collected all their business cards, and—"

"Wait a minute. *You* have an author? What does that mean?" Gina's mouth dropped open. "You don't mean you pretended to be my literary agent!"

"Of course I did, silly. And they are all waiting on tenterhooks for my call."

"But the book isn't finished yet!" Gina spluttered.

"Well, then, you'd better get cracking, hadn't you?" Margot replied sweetly. On that note, she picked up her feather duster, waved it at Gina like a fairy wand, and disappeared into their shared bedroom.

Gina sat down hard on the nearest chair and was about to put her head in her hands when she remembered her ink-stained fingers.

She went to the bathroom and scrubbed at her hands with soap and a nail brush, rubbing them almost raw in the vain effort to remove the shadows of black ink that seemed to have seeped into her skin.

She had to leave for work in an hour and she'd wanted to get some writing done before she left. Now Margot had totally derailed her thought process. She couldn't possibly write when she was so mad.

Margot was so impetuous and bold—and true, it was good to have the old Margot back—but why did she have to embroil Gina in her crazy schemes? And now, instead of writing this book at her own pace, she felt pressured to finish.

A bolt of excitement shot through her in spite of her exaspera-tion. What if Margot's machinations led somewhere?

No. Gina had been disappointed by rejection too many times in the past. It wasn't that simple.

The old fears that had halted her progress for several years rose up again. As a journalist, she'd developed a thick skin, but that didn't always translate to her fiction, which felt more personal and important. She needed to conquer her fears or she'd never finish this book.

Determination surged through her. She could do this. Margot believed in her. It was about time she believed in herself.

Due to Margot's meddling, she needed to double down on her writing schedule. She'd work all night if she had to. She'd get this book done and dusted in record time. And then they would see whether Margot could deliver on her promises.

Shaking her head, Gina gave a rueful grin. How was it that no matter what liberties Margot took or how outrageous her schemes, Gina could never stay mad at her? More often than not, she fell in with Margot's plans like a good soldier. Probably it was naïve to put her book in the hands of a rank amateur, but somehow Margot's enthusiasm and verve were impossible to resist.

So Gina dried her hands and sat down at the typewriter and forced herself to focus on the page in front of her. Word by word was how this book would get done.

Chapter Sixteen

Claire

"Everything has to be perfect!" Claire had not felt so nervous nor so utterly alive in years. She was to cook for one of the best chefs in Paris—which of course meant he was one of the best chefs in the world—and she needed to create the most magnificent dinner she'd ever cooked in her life if she was going to have a chance of impressing him.

Unusually for him, Hervé was being helpful. "Here." He thrust under her nose a bloody cut of beef that had veins of fat webbing through it in a patina that to a chef was more perfect and beautiful than the finest Carrara marble. "What do you think of this?"

She had already been to the butcher's and chosen what she'd thought to be the best cut, but the eye fillet Hervé proffered was clearly superior. She looked up at him, grateful for more than the beef. "Thank you."

Mélanie giggled. "You look like he just handed you a bouquet of roses, not a slab of meat." The waitress had been spending more and more time in the kitchen lately, and Claire could only conclude she was doing it to catch Hervé's eye.

Claire flushed. Annoying as she was, Mélanie was right. Why couldn't Claire swing her ponytail and bat her eyelashes like other women? Why did she have to wax rhapsodic over meat?

Hervé regarded the waitress impassively. "It takes another chef to understand."

Claire blinked. If she didn't know better, she would have thought he'd meant that as a snub. However, it hadn't escaped Claire that most of the time, Hervé didn't seem to mind having the pretty young waitress around.

"Perhaps you can teach me what's so good about it, then?" Mélanie responded pertly.

Rolling her eyes, Claire left them to it and went back to work, sorting through the cornucopia of fresh spring vegetables she intended to serve Thibault with the filet mignon that evening— asparagus, baby carrots, new potatoes, snap peas.

She'd decided on a classic main course but to add her own twists to the other dishes. For the starter, a salmon mousseline with lobster and scallops. The dessert was her own invention, an apricot Vacherin—layers of meringue with finely chopped hazelnuts through them, and a sweet puree of apricots poached in sugar syrup, swirling through a filling of whipped cream that was lightly scented with apricot brandy. There would be several amuse-bouches and palate cleansers along the way, plus a cheese platter at the end of the meal. Monsieur Thibault tended to eat sparingly but he would try at least a bite of each dish.

Laughter from the station where Hervé was chatting with Mélanie while the rest of the staff ducked and weaved about them made Claire forget what she was about to do. She looked at her hands, one of which held an egg, the other, a pastry brush, and she had to think for a moment before she remembered why. Scowling, she quickly made an egg wash and brushed it over a tray of vol-au-vent cases and slid them in one of the ovens.

"Will you help me choose the wine, Hervé?" Claire called, but he didn't hear her. He was busy instructing Mélanie about different cuts of beef.

She wiped her hands on her apron and went over to tap him on the shoulder. "Wine?" The word came out more tersely than she'd intended.

"Ah. Yes." Hervé prided himself on his palate, as her papa had before him. It was one area in which Claire wished she was better versed, but in the restaurants at which she aspired to work, there were always sommeliers, so she hadn't ever concentrated on that aspect of service.

She'd already discussed with Hervé the menu she intended to serve that evening and told him the kinds of wines she thought she wanted, but she'd left the details to him.

To his credit, Hervé had neither approved the menu (which she might have taken as patronizing) nor critiqued it (which would have made her both rebellious and anxious at the same time). He had given her some inside information on the kinds of flavors and dishes that the master chef most favored and then held his peace.

Now, he said, "Over here." Lying in a small wine rack at the edge of the workspace were the bottles he'd chosen. "The champagne is on ice," he said when she'd inspected the other wines. She followed him to the cool room and he held out the light sparkling wine he'd chosen to begin.

As they stepped outside again, she asked, "You don't think chardonnay or a white bordeaux would be better to start, and just continue with that for the mousseline?" She was conscious of the cost of this evening. She suspected Hervé would refuse to accept any payment, as he had all of the times she'd tried to contribute toward the cost of her early morning experiments in his kitchen, and she didn't want him to be too greatly out of pocket. That particular champagne appeared to be a vintage and probably carried a heavy price tag.

"You said you'd leave the wine to me," said Hervé. "Don't forget, this is my brasserie now, and I want to impress Thibault as much as you do."

"Well . . . Thank you," said Claire, feeling awkward. When he would have turned away to go back to the kitchen, she added, "I . . . I don't think I've said this before, but I'm grateful for all you've done for me."

When he'd talked about stealing her back from Thibault, she'd begun to suspect he had done more for her than she'd ever dreamed. Wary of overstepping, however, she'd kept the notion to herself.

He frowned as if he didn't understand what she meant. Claire flung out a hand. "Letting me stay on at the brasserie, letting me practice in your kitchen, putting in a good word with Thibault . . . I do appreciate it, even if it seems like I don't."

He folded his arms and leaned against the wall. "I know you do. What brought this on?" With a look of comprehension, he glanced back toward the kitchen, then grinned.

"What?" Claire stared hard at him, daring him to say it. She was *not* jealous of Mélanie.

"You're blushing," commented Hervé.

"The heat of the kitchen always makes me flushed," she snapped back.

"But we were just in the cold room," Hervé pointed out.

"I don't have time for this." Claire pushed past him and stomped back to the kitchen, where she worked faster and with more focus than she had all afternoon.

CLAIRE'S DINNER WAS a triumph by any standards. By Thibault's it was *très bon,* which was high praise, indeed. "The mousseline was a success," said the chef de cuisine. "The Vacherin shows style. But the filet mignon was the star."

Claire waited eagerly for more. A simple "you're hired" would have been sufficient, but the chef de cuisine fell into deep conversation with Hervé about where he had sourced the beef, and the subject wasn't raised again. Somehow it felt too gauche to ask.

Thibault proposed to linger over cognac with Hervé, but rather than dismissing Claire, as would have been more customary—after all, she was in no way the head chef's equal—Hervé insisted she remain with them at the table.

Happy enough merely to have been asked, Claire tactfully declined and left them to it. She was too excited to retire tamely upstairs, however, and remained in the kitchen long after the ovens were turned off and Louis had mopped up and gone to deliver the leftovers for the nuns.

Claire stood leaning one hip against the kitchen counter, a forgotten glass of cognac in her hand. She relived every moment of the night, every word of praise Thibault had spoken. While the meal she served had been a success, she still didn't know whether Thibault would offer her a job. Surely he would? But what if he hadn't mentioned the matter because, despite his compliments, the answer was no?

When Hervé came in, carrying empty glasses and a bottle that only had a slick of cognac left inside it, Claire took them from him and set them on the counter. "Well?" she demanded.

He rubbed a hand over his stubbled chin. His eyes seemed sunken in shadows. He'd been working doubly hard to make up for her absence from the regular staff while she concentrated on Thibault's meal. "Well, what?"

She punched him on the arm. "Is he going to hire me?"

Hervé looked surprised. "Didn't he tell you himself?" He rolled his eyes. "Typical."

"Argh! Just tell me, will you?" Attacked by doubt, Claire faltered. "You mean he left you to break the bad news? He doesn't want me?"

Hervé plucked the dish towel out of his waistband and threw it on the counter. "Of course he wants you. He's making you *entre-métier*." His eyes crinkled at the corners. "Congratulations, Claire. You did it!"

Claire shrieked with delight and jumped up and down. She was going to work for the great Thibault! Not only that, but she would also be in charge of preparing all dishes involving vegetables and eggs. She couldn't believe it. Far from going back to apprentice status, she had effectively skipped a step in the hierarchy of the kitchen brigade.

"Thank you!" she said to Hervé. "Oh, thank you a thousand times!" Overcome with gratitude and joy, she flew to him, took his face between her hands, and gave him a smacking kiss on the cheek. Or that was what she'd planned to do, but somehow, he turned his head a bit and she mashed her lips against his mouth instead.

Suddenly—she wasn't quite sure how—they were kissing in earnest, open-mouthed and hungry, their breaths laced with cognac. He was backing her against the counter, picking her up as if she weighed no more than a sack of flour, depositing her on the countertop so that her face was level with his.

Her hair was falling out of its ponytail and Hervé's hands were on the buttons of her shirt. If anyone saw them . . . "Wait!" Claire put her hands on his chest. Despite the strong and fiery need that coursed through her body, she felt obliged to point something out. "We still work together. I have to serve out my notice."

"Then you're fired," growled Hervé, diving for her mouth again, ripping her shirt when the buttons became too much of a bother for his usually dexterous fingers.

Claire laughed, shocked and delighted at his urgency, but also aware that he was going too fast. But then he pressed his lips to her throat, as if he wanted to feel the laughter there, and she nearly surrendered and let him do his worst.

"Wait," she whispered. Then she spoke more firmly. *"Wait."*

He stepped back, breathing hard, his gaze, bright and fierce, fixed on her mouth. "Don't tell me you don't want this."

"I . . . Yes, I do." But the words came out with less certainty than she'd felt mere seconds before. "But we need to slow down."

He ran a hand through his hair in frustration. "I've waited long enough, Claire."

She was confused. "But I . . . But you've only been here a couple of months."

He scowled, picking up the dishcloth he'd thrown down earlier. "You know it's been longer than that." He tossed the towel in the laundry basket. When he turned back, his face was stripped of its usual hardness. He looked off-balance, vulnerable, and her heart melted.

She slipped off the countertop and stepped toward him, trying not to smile. "Really?"

"Really." He put his arms around her waist and kissed her again.

"But when will we ever see each other?" Claire asked with a sigh. "You'll be working long hours here. I'll be working long hours there." She needed to throw everything behind her career now that she'd been given this golden opportunity.

"It won't be forever," said Hervé. "I'm going to steal you back, remember? In the meantime, we'll work it out."

Chapter Seventeen

Margot

Margot was attacking her housework with vigor and trying not to think about Andrew Mountbatten. Without his intoxicating presence deranging her mental faculties, she ought to be able to figure out a way to make it clear she thought of him as a friend and potential colleague, but her thoughts kept straying to that kiss.

If only she could throw caution to the wind and give in to that delicious, heady feeling. But what she wanted and what was good for her when it came to men were clearly two different things.

Her own lack of stability had been highlighted when Claire had come in late the night before, half delirious with happiness and exhaustion, telling them all about her triumph with Thibault and Hervé's declaration of love. Thrusting aside her own worries, Margot had jumped up and down and laughed and cried along with Claire, demanding to know the entire history of her romance with Hervé. She was genuinely happy for her friend, but she'd lain awake that night, sick with longing for a time when she might again feel that kind of unalloyed joy and security in a loving relationship. She'd come to doubt she ever would.

Gina had been upset about something for days now, but whenever Margot inquired, she forced a smile and said it was nothing. Gina had thrown herself into her work with almost frenzied gusto, which was good for the book, no doubt. But was it good for Gina? From experience, Margot knew that all she could do was to wait for her friend to be ready to talk. It couldn't be easy for her, what with Hal still in Paris and her father's demands.

As Margot vacuumed the drawing room, Gina was sitting at her desk, making corrections to her manuscript. Without looking up from the page, she lifted her feet so Margot could vacuum under the desk, then set them on the floor again and kept working.

At first the other two women had felt guilty about Margot's shouldering the housework alone at the apartment and tried to persuade Margot to share her duties, but she'd refused. Claire cooked and Gina cleaned and washed up after her—no small task. Margot did the tidying, dusting, vacuuming, mopping, and ironing. She liked housework, she was much better at it than the other two, and her allotted tasks were only necessary once a week, which suited her just fine.

Today was Saturday, overcast and dull, threatening rain. She would whip through her chores this morning and spend the afternoon reading as her reward.

Margot switched off the vacuum. The ensuing silence was palpable. She unplugged the appliance and hauled it into Claire's room. "Dust first," she said to herself, fetching the fancy feather duster from where she'd left it in the drawing room.

As she came back into the bedroom, the dark clouds parted, and sunshine burst through the windows, flooding the room with light.

Claire's closet door hung open—that girl was as messy as Gina!—and the glint of beading caught Margot's eye.

Leaving the feather duster on the vanity, she went over to the closet and pushed aside Claire's other dresses. The hangers screeched a little in protest. Then she took out the gown and hung it on the tall stand Madame Vaughn had kept for this purpose.

Ah, Dior. Each time she looked at this creation, it seemed more beautiful than before. In the sunshine, each individual crystal and sequin threw off a tiny rainbow. The creamy skirts gleamed as if a goddess had spun silk from champagne pearls and woven them with threads of moonlight.

A longing Margot had ruthlessly suppressed unfurled its petals and blossomed inside her. What with Gina already wearing the Dior gown before Claire had the opportunity, somehow Margot hadn't felt right asking Claire if she could borrow it.

Maybe it wouldn't suit her anyway. Maybe it wouldn't fit. *You could ask Béatrice to alter it for you,* argued a treacherous voice in her head. *Suit you? Of course it will. How could anyone not look ravishing in such an ensemble?*

As if in answer to her question, the sunshine beaming through the window intensified and the gown seemed to glow with promise, as if it were a treasure in a movie. It beckoned her to throw off the mask she'd been hiding behind for months—no, years—now, to return to her old self, the self she had been proud to be.

Spellbound, Margot started to undress.

"What are you doing?"

With a gasp, Margot spun around, her arms covering her chest. She was down to her bra and knickers and it wasn't anything Claire hadn't seen a million times, but she felt exposed.

Her heart thumping in her chest, Margot said, "I'm sorry." She snatched up her dress and pulled it over her head, wishing she hadn't given in to temptation like that.

Feeling like a child caught in wrongdoing, almost nauseous with guilt and shame, Margot would have rushed from the room, but Claire put a hand out to stop her. "Wait."

Margo halted, staring down at her feet.

Claire was laughing. "Margot! There's no need to be sorry." She nodded her encouragement. "Try it on. Come on. I'll help you."

She should have known. Claire's heart was so big, so generous, she would not even comprehend why Margot had been reluctant to ask her this favor.

"The gown is to be worn," said Claire, "not preserved like a . . . What's the word? Something in the Louvre, for example."

"Artifact?"

"*Oui, c'est ça.* 'Artifact.'" She gestured toward the gown. "Please. Let me see how it looks."

But Margot shook her head. "No, I really shouldn't. Not hot and bothered from cleaning, anyway. But I did want to ask you . . ." She bit her lip. If she asked and Claire said yes, there was no going back. She would be committed to attending Charlotte's masquerade.

"She wants to wear it to the Mountbattens' Venetian ball." Gina's drawl came from the doorway. "I *told* her you wouldn't mind."

"You're going?" Claire's delight was genuine. She pulled Margot into a tight, strong hug. "Oh, *ma chérie,* I am so pleased for you! Yes, yes, you must wear the gown. I can't believe you were finding it hard to ask. What's mine is yours, always. You know that."

"And we might not have your expertise with hair and makeup and such, but we will both be here to make sure you are the most beautiful woman at the ball." Gina's mouth quirked up. "Shouldn't be too hard, considering what we have to work with."

Margot looked from one of them to the other. Everything was falling into place as if fate were lending a guiding hand. Madame Delahaye had told her that her destiny was not at Dior. That might have been the kind of generic advice she gave to everyone—Doc MacFarlane would have argued this to be the case—but half of destiny was seizing opportunity, making the most of one's luck. That was something Margot knew how to do.

She made a sound between a gasp and a laugh. "I'm scared." Not to a living soul would she have admitted such a thing before. But these two women would never use her weakness against her. Their friendship, so easy and fun in the early years of their acquaintance, had deepened and matured with time, strengthened by the hardships each of them had faced.

Gina said, "I know it's a big step, attending Charlotte's ball. But even if it doesn't work out with Andrew, you will have the satisfaction of knowing you overcame your fear of going back to your old life, being seen by your socialite friends. You've punished yourself enough, staying hidden all this time. After the masquerade, you can start to truly live again."

Claire's arm was still around Margot. She squeezed her shoulder. "Gina's right. And who knows? You might just have the night of your life."

That felt like too much to hope for. But one thing was certain: she'd regret not taking the leap. And most wonderful of all? She knew without a doubt that her best friends would be there to catch her should she fall.

Gina

When Gina answered the telephone at ten o'clock that evening, she expected it to be Jay calling to try to make amends before he left Paris.

"Gina, hi." The voice was Hal's. "Listen, can we meet?"

"Now?" She was about to turn in for the night but she wasn't going to admit that to him. She was on the verge of finishing her book and she'd been rising earlier and earlier to get more pages done, to keep the momentum going. That meant going to bed earlier, too. Otherwise, she'd be following Monsieur Florie's example and snoozing during her lunch break at the bookstore each day.

"It's important or I wouldn't ask." Hal hesitated.

"Is it about my father?" She didn't want it to be about Jay.

"Look, I'll tell you when I get there. The brasserie, okay?"

"I guess."

"I'll be there in fifteen," said Hal.

She hung up and hurried to the bedroom, where Margot was sitting up in bed, reading more of Gina's manuscript and making notes in the margins. Margot lowered the pages. "Who was that?"

"Hal," said Gina. She was scrabbling around on the floor. "Have you seen my cashmere sweater? The cream one?"

"It was neatly folded in your drawer last time I checked," said Margot.

"Well, how am I supposed to find it there?" quipped Gina, opening the drawer and pulling it out.

Climbing out of bed, Margot found a pair of camel-colored trousers in their shared closet and threw them over a chair. "Wear these. And this scarf." She snatched a small square of patterned silk from the floor where Gina had just flung it while searching for her sweater and handed it to her.

Gina knew better than to argue with Margot over fashion. By the time they were done, Gina looked casual but chic, as if she wasn't really trying too hard—exactly the impression she wanted to give Hal.

When she'd dressed and patted on some makeup and Margot had fixed her hair, Gina looked at the clock. More than fifteen minutes had passed since she'd spoken with Hal. "I'd better go."

Down at the brasserie, she found her former fiancé sitting at a table on the sidewalk, two glasses of red wine in front of him. It was a little too chilly to sit outside but perhaps he'd chosen that spot so they could be alone. Gina took a seat to his three o'clock, but the table was so small and his legs were so long, her knees brushed his when she sat down.

Before she could say anything, he reached inside his jacket and brought out a tooled leather case, then laid it on the table.

"My pen!" She grabbed the case and opened it. The gleam of gold, the loving inscription, met her eye. "You found it! How did you . . ."

She trailed off, understanding what had happened. On the evening she'd run into Hal outside Chez Julien, he'd gone to Jay and made him explain why Gina was so upset. Then he'd gone to the pawnbroker himself and somehow managed to get the pen back for her.

"I'm sorry for calling so late," he said. "I thought you'd want it back as soon as possible." He toyed with his wineglass. "The broker had already sold it, so I had to go and, uh, persuade the man who'd bought it to give it back."

"Oh, thank you, *thank* you!" She couldn't believe it. Tears were pouring down her cheeks. Tears of relief and joy. She had this vital piece of her mother back. She'd treasure it even more now.

Hal caught her gaze and held it, his expression solemn. "I'd do anything for you, Gina. You know that."

She knew it was true and she couldn't help herself. A little awkwardly, since they were both seated, Gina threw her arms around Hal and hugged him. "You don't know how much this means to me. I'll pay you back. I—"

Her words were cut off by his kiss. The second their lips touched, she knew she was a goner. Her whole body was set alight. They'd always had this natural rhythm and fit, and they kissed greedily but with no awkwardness or hesitation at all, as if they'd never been apart. It was bliss to feel him, his solid chest against hers, his thick ash blond hair between her fingers as she plunged them through, drawing him closer.

After some time, Hal drew back and looked deep into her eyes. "Please, Gina. Please say you'll marry me. I can't live without you. I've tried." His voice broke. "I'll do anything. Please."

Guilt flickered at the desperation in his voice. She'd hurt him terribly, even if she'd meant it for his own good. How stupid would she be to pass up a man like this? "But your political career—"

"Don't you see?" Tenderly he tucked a strand of hair behind her ear. "None of that means anything without you."

He meant it. She knew that. And maybe she ought to trust that he was right, that everything would work out, if only they could be together.

"All right," she whispered, throwing away every caution and objection she'd ever thought of. "I will marry you, Hal Sanders."

Claire

On her final day off before her work at Thibault's new restaurant began, Claire slept in. She opened her eyes to bright sunshine peeping through the cracks in her curtains and kissing her cheeks. Smiling, she stretched, luxuriating in the crisp linen sheets and heavenly soft pillows, and the acres of space on Madame's four-poster bed.

What was Madame Vaughn doing now in that spa town in Switzerland? Claire had written to her, telling her how grateful she was to be living with her two best friends in Madame's beautiful apartment, assuring her they were taking excellent care of the place.

Now she had more news to share. When she thought back over the evening of Thibault's dinner, she could hardly believe all of her dreams had come true at once. And there was still so much she wanted to do. Now she would achieve all of it with Hervé by her side. She had her friends, her career was back on track, and she had a man who would support her every step of the way. What more could anyone want? She would go to Mass today for the first time in weeks and offer up thanks to God.

There was a faint scratching at her door. "Come in!" she called, knowing it would be Margot seeing if she was awake, impatient to start the day.

But it was Gina who opened the door. Over her shoulder, she called to Margot, "She's awake! Come on." Grinning widely, Gina took a running jump and landed on the bed next to Claire. "Scoot over." Obediently Claire wriggled sideways to allow Gina some space.

Margot came in, wiping her hands on an apron and shaking her head. "Gina's been like a child on Christmas morning, waiting for you to wake up."

Gina flung out an arm and beckoned to Margot. "Come here. I have something to tell you both."

Claire watched as Margot untied her apron, folded it, and put it on a chair, then boosted herself up to sit at the foot of the bed. "What is it? You are positively giddy today."

Gina's eyes gleamed. "Hal and I are back together."

"*What?*" Claire cried, hugging her. "Oh, Gina, that's wonderful!"

"How did it happen?" said Margot. "Does that mean your father is back on his feet now?"

"Well, he's getting there, apparently," said Gina. "But it's not that. I just realized all of that baloney about reputation and being the perfect political wife doesn't matter anymore. Hal cares about me more than anything else. I guess I thought I knew what was best for him but he showed me that wasn't the case." Gina beamed. "He said he's been miserable without me."

Margot laughed. "And that makes you happy?"

"I know. I'm awful." Gina sighed. "But he made me realize last night that he needs me as much as I need him. I never truly understood that before."

She told them about her mother's gold pen and about how Hal had got it back for her. "I know the fallout from my father's business failure won't magically disappear. But Hal has told his father, his campaign manager, everyone, that if he can't have me, he won't run for office at all. So they've agreed they'll make it work."

"That is a man who knows how to get what he wants," said Claire.

"But, Gina, is it what *you* want?" Margot looked troubled.

Gina's eyebrows drew together. "Of course it is, silly!"

Margot seemed unconvinced, but before she could open her mouth to argue, Claire jumped up and clapped her hands together. "I know! Let's celebrate!" She grabbed Margot's hand and dragged her into the kitchen, telling her to open a bottle of champagne while Claire whipped up some special scrambled eggs with shavings of precious black truffle.

Later, Margot insisted on washing the dishes instead of Gina so that Gina could get ready for a drive in the countryside with Hal. When the two of them were alone in the kitchen, Claire said, "What's wrong, Margot?"

"I'm happy for her. I am." Margot frowned down at the sink filled with sudsy water.

"But?" Claire prompted.

"Hal always gets what he wants," said Margot. "But what about Gina's career?"

"What do you mean?" asked Claire. "She'll still be able to write."

"Will she?" Margot regarded her gravely. "Not every man is like Hervé, Claire."

"Yes, but this is Gina we're talking about. She has a pretty strong will of her own. And you heard it yourself. Hal adores her. He'd do anything for her."

"He will now," said Margot. "But what about when things get hard?"

Privately Claire thought Margot's view of Gina's relationship was heavily colored by her own horrible marriage. She wasn't going to say it, though. "Try to be happy for her, Margot. At the end of the day, it's Gina's decision to make."

Margot looked unconvinced, but she said, "Of course I'm happy for her. He loves her and she loves him." Slowly, she added, "Only sometimes I think love means different things to men than it does to women. At least, it does to men like Hal."

Chapter Eighteen

Claire

Had it only been a few days ago that Claire had thought her life was perfect? She'd forgotten quite how relentless and exacting Thibault could be. As *entremetier,* she was in charge of a crucial link in the chain of production, and she was determined not to let him down.

Claire had taken longer than she'd expected to get into the swing of things in a new kitchen. She had to learn Thibault's system, focus on one section of the kitchen alone, and remember that her place was not to be the boss anymore or to argue when she didn't agree with something the sous-chef told her to do.

"Again." Thibault's calm order to her to make a complicated sauce again from scratch rang in her ears until she started hearing it in her sleep.

Determined to prove herself to him, Claire practiced every morning before working a long and exhausting shift at the restaurant. By Saturday evening, she was so tired, she fell asleep on the Métro on the way home and nearly missed her stop.

It was late, past the brasserie's closing time, and a fine drizzle made her glad of her raincoat. She would have let herself in to the apartment building and dashed upstairs to shed her wet things, but she noticed the office light in Le Chat was still burning.

"Mademoiselle! Thank goodness you're here!" Louis must have been lying in wait because he stuck his head out of the front door and flagged Claire down.

"Is something wrong, Louis?" Claire followed him inside, hanging her raincoat on the stand at the front of the brasserie.

"It's Chef. He's hurt." Louis threw the words behind him as he led the way.

"What?" With a surge of fear, Claire followed, her heart pounding.

"I told you not to tell her." Hervé spoke around teeth that were clenched on the end of a bandage. He'd been tying it himself around his right hand. Clearly he'd rejected any offer of help from Louis.

"What happened?" Claire moved to inspect the damage.

"A burn," said Louis. "It wasn't me!" He held up his hands, palms out. "One of the new apprentices, he—"

"It's not so bad," Hervé interrupted. "There's no need to fuss. Go up to bed. You must be exhausted."

"Don't be silly." Now she looked at him properly, Claire realized his face had a sickly pallor underneath the stubble. "Just how bad is this burn?"

Ignoring Hervé's protests, Claire sent Louis for the first aid kit. "Quickly, now."

When Louis returned, she took out gauze and antiseptic and a salve and laid them out on the table. Gingerly she unwrapped the makeshift bandage with light, quick hands, pretending not to hear the sharp groan from Hervé as she attempted to lay the wound bare. The bandage had stuck to the wound.

Sucking a breath between her teeth at the ghastly sight of raw flesh, she said, "Oh, Hervé. I think we need to get you to a doctor."

"No. It will be fine. Just . . . antiseptic." He winced at the mention of it, preparing for the pain. "I doused it with vodka but I guess it will be best if you use this stuff."

Stoic as he was, Hervé couldn't help flinching and crying out with pain as she swiftly disinfected his wound and applied a new dressing. She'd heard of people using fish skins to keep burns moist but she wasn't sure if it worked. And anyway, she couldn't go out to buy fresh fish until early the next morning. "You'd best come upstairs to sleep tonight," she said to him when she'd dismissed Louis and cleaned up the remnants of her handiwork.

Just barely, he managed to raise one side of his mouth in an attempt at a wicked grin, puffing out, "Thought you'd never . . . ask."

"I'll take the couch," she said, smiling and shaking her head at his joke. "Come on."

She grabbed a bottle of cognac on the way out—for medicinal purposes—and having locked up, took Hervé upstairs.

There was only a lamp burning in the entryway when Claire let them into the apartment. "The others must have gone to bed."

She switched on the lights, guided Hervé to her room, and told him to sit on the bed. She poured him a large glass of brandy, which he drained immediately. Kneeling at his feet, she took off his shoes and set them aside, ignoring his protests. "You can't do it. You won't be able to use that hand."

She sat back on her heels, deciding how best to proceed. "Stand up, I think," she said, rising to her feet.

Before he could protest, she was undoing the snaps of his suspenders and removing his trousers. "This isn't how I wanted this to happen," Hervé protested. He seemed to be laughing now, despite the pain. Maybe the brandy was working. Claire didn't know whether to be amused or exasperated.

"Quiet, you." Avoiding looking at him directly, she hung his trousers over a chair, then returned to unbutton his collared shirt. He wore a vest underneath, but she saw enough of his big chest to make her pause for an instant before resuming her nursing duties.

She made him drink another glass of brandy before saying, "Do you think you can sleep now?"

Muzzily protesting, he swung his legs onto the bed and let her pull the covers over him. She had to bank the pillows at his side so he could rest his injured hand on them.

What else? She was worried about the possibility of infection. She'd seen worse burns, but they could still be very dangerous, and a chef without the full use of his hands was no longer a chef.

Instead of sleeping on the couch as she'd intended, Claire decided to sit in the armchair by the window so she could be there if he needed her in the night.

Wryly, she smiled. Who could have guessed that the first night they'd spend together would be like this? She settled down to rest, and must have been asleep in seconds, because the first thing she knew, light glimmered at the edges of the curtains and she could hear sounds of Margot going about her usual morning routine in the kitchen.

"The brasserie!" Out of habit, Claire sat up, before realizing that it was Sunday and she didn't need to be anywhere, much less the brasserie, where she no longer worked. A second after that, she realized she was not in bed, as usual, but in an armchair.

Recollection flooded her mind. She looked over to the bed but it was empty. Someone—Hervé, obviously—had put an extra blanket over Claire as she slept. That was the wrong way around. She was supposed to be looking after him.

Had he left? She supposed he must have.

Rubbing her stiff neck, Claire went out to get coffee, and stopped short. The three of them—Hervé, Margot, and Gina—were sitting at the table helping themselves to Hervé's eggs Florentine.

"Tell me you didn't make that," said Claire.

"You don't think either of us did, do you?" asked Gina. "Anyway, that's beside the point. We both woke up to find a strange man in our midst. I think we are owed an explanation, missy."

"But it's not like that," protested Claire. "Hervé injured his hand last night. He was in a lot of pain, so I brought him upstairs."

Gina lifted an eyebrow.

"I slept in an armchair!" said Claire, half laughing, but also strangely close to tears.

"Well *that* was just silly," said Margot.

Hervé got up. "I'd better get moving."

"But it's Sunday," said Claire. And thank goodness for that. How would he manage at the brasserie?

Hervé shrugged. "I've got things to do." Then his eyes softened as he looked at Claire. "But if you'd like to come with me, I'd welcome the company."

Margot

On the evening of the masquerade, Claire took the night off from the restaurant and Gina put the cover on her typewriter. Margot did her own hair and makeup, but the other women fussed over her as if they were actually helping, and that was just as good. To feel pampered and cherished in this way was such a novel sensation, Margot savored every minute.

But she was regretting bitterly that kiss on the doorstep that she'd shared with Andrew Mountbatten. She'd politely refused his offer to be her escort this evening, fibbing that she had to be there early to oversee the final touches to the party arrangements. Charlie had understood and offered to send a car to pick her up, which she'd accepted gratefully and with relief. She didn't trust herself around Andrew Mountbatten.

When all was ready, Gina donned Margot's cotton gloves and helped her into the gown. As Claire did up her fastenings at the back, Margot felt like a princess in a fairy tale—one that could not help but end happily. That this was an illusion destined to last no longer than Cinderella's pumpkin coach was a thought she could put out of her mind for now.

"Magnifique!" breathed Claire. "But what are we missing?"

Gina stepped back, arms folded. Then she clicked her fingers. "Gloves."

She brought Margot the elbow-length gloves she'd worn to the embassy ball. "Pity we aren't the same shoe size. Those are divine." Margot's heels were Roger Vivier, bought with her staff discount from Dior. She lifted the skirt of her gown and pointed a toe, admiring the soft sparkle of diamantés on the slender strap.

Gina gave Margot's skirts a final tweak. "There. You are ready." The doorbell sounded.

Claire jumped up. "And just in the nick of time."

"Charlie said she'd send a car." Margot's stomach flipped over. In all of the excitement of getting ready, she'd forgotten to be nervous. "Will you ask the driver to wait a minute? I need to get my purse."

She snatched up the little clutch Gina had lent her and filled it with her things: handkerchief, comb, lipstick. What else? Money, just in case. Her hands were shaking as she closed the clasp.

"Get a grip, Margot MacFarlane." She whispered the words to herself but they only made her feel more wretched. She might pretend to be the same fun-loving girl she'd been the last time she was in Paris, but a lot had changed since then. What if tonight turned out to be a disaster? Charlie had been counting on Margot to help create something spectacular.

Her other fear, that mixing with the social circle to which Mountbatten belonged would be sure to end in her husband finding out where she was, had not gone away. However, the more time passed, the more often she saw people she knew at Dior. She had never heard one word from her husband following those encounters, and that had made her fear lessen as time went by. Besides, Gina was right. Even if he did find her, what could he do, after all?

Lifting her chin and straightening her shoulders, Margot looked at herself in the mirror. The young woman staring back was no Cinderella. Her belief in fairy-tale princes had shattered long ago. But that didn't mean she needed to deny herself happiness where she found it. No matter what, she meant to enjoy herself tonight.

Her white, lacy mask, which Béatrice had made for her out of remnants from the Dior ateliers, was positioned on a long stick. Originally, Margot had decided to attend only if her mask could be kept firmly in place, but she no longer wished to hide.

With a deep, bracing breath, she glided out to meet her driver.

On the drawing room threshold, she hesitated. Gina seemed to be making Charlie's chauffeur unusually welcome. She was in the process of handing him a martini. How odd.

Then the driver turned his head and with a shock, she realized why. Andrew Mountbatten stood there, dressed to the nines in a black tuxedo. His dark hair was brushed back from his face, but as if an impatient hand had already run through it, his fringe flopped over his right eyebrow.

Margot's heart gave a sharp, heavy pound. "What are you doing here?" She thought she'd made it clear to Charlie that she didn't want to accept Andrew's invitation to escort her tonight.

"Getting the third degree from us," quipped Gina with a smile.

"Speak for yourself," said Claire. "Me, I've been very pleasant."

"Wait till she's on her third martini," Gina said.

Andrew did not react to their banter. Margot could tell he hadn't been listening. He was too busy staring at her. "Margot. You look . . ."

"He's speechless," said Claire with delight. *"Margot est très jolie, monsieur, n'est-ce pas?"*

"'Pretty' isn't the word." He set down his glass and offered her his arm. "Shall we?" He nodded to Gina and Claire. "Delightful to meet you."

"Delightful," drawled Gina.

It would have been bad manners to dig in her heels and refuse to go anywhere with him, much as instinct told her to do so. Andrew Mountbatten didn't deserve to be rejected in front of her friends, even if he had overstepped the line Margot had so carefully drawn between them.

She slipped the thin chain of Gina's purse over her wrist, transferred her mask to the same hand, then tucked her other hand into Andrew's crooked elbow. This wasn't at all how she'd expected the evening to begin. In spite of her nerves and all the reasons she shouldn't encourage him, she couldn't suppress a giddy leap of the spirit as she went with him to the door.

"Have a wonderful time!" called Claire.

From Gina: "Don't do anything we wouldn't do!"

Margot was surprised to find that Mountbatten's vehicle of choice was an old Daimler, and that there was no chauffeur in sight. After helping her into the passenger seat, he slid behind the wheel. "Right," he said, putting the car in gear. "Off we go."

Margot grinned. "I'd expected something a little sportier." Her father owned a car like this back in Sydney and at this reminder of him, her heart ached. She would write to him and to her mother, too. It had been too long.

"Oh, this isn't mine," said Andrew, "but ball gowns don't tend to do too well in sports cars."

"Ah," she murmured. "My gown thanks you."

At a crossing, he stopped and turned to regard her. "It's not just the gown, and it's not just your beauty, either. You are sparkling, tonight, Margot. Every time I look at you, you take my breath away."

She was finding it hard to breathe herself. "Thank you," she managed to say. "You scrub up rather well yourself."

Her flippancy broke the tension between them. He laughed as they moved off again. "Thank you. I am not terribly keen on formal parties but my sister tells me this one will be memorable." He glanced at her, then shifted gear and smoothly took a corner. "You've been kind. She is quite lonely, here in Paris."

"But she has tons of friends," protested Margot. "She certainly brings flocks of them to the store."

"Hmm. But you know what those kinds of friendships are like. Flimsy, easily discarded. Volatile, even. I'm glad you've befriended Charlie—dare I say—in spite of your reluctance to encourage me?"

The last part of that sentence had been intended to fluster her. Coolly, she ignored it. "There is no need to thank me. I don't make friends out of kindness or charity."

"Will you allow me to thank you for your help with the party, then?"

She smiled. "That, I will allow."

"Here we are." The crunch of gravel under the car's tires heralded a long, tree-lined avenue that ended in a magnificent château. But rather than join the queue of vehicles processing like a train of caterpillars down the long driveway, Andrew rolled down the window and spoke to the attendant who stood at the barrier to a side road. A rapid exchange of French and then the attendant shifted the barrier and waved Andrew through. Margot swiveled to looked back and saw the barrier being replaced again after them.

"Where are we going?" she asked.

"Shortcut," said Andrew. "Well, usually I'd say it's the scenic route but tonight it will get us there faster."

As promised, despite skirting a small ornamental lake, they arrived at the back of the château in no time. Margot got out without waiting for Andrew to help her, entranced by the reality of the concept she had only visualized in her mind.

Instead of deciding on a Marie Antoinette concept, which had seemed to Margot quite an obvious choice, she had suggested Charlie choose a carnival theme, with an adult-sized carousel and traditional fun fair entertainment, from a coconut shy to pétanque, with the prizes all sourced from Dior's Grande Boutique. Fire-eaters on stilts and harlequins juggling clubs strolled through the crowd. A small fountain ran with pink champagne.

The atmosphere was lively and unexpected—even a little brash—but why go through life always being dignified? Everything had come together brilliantly. "Can I get you a drink?" asked Andrew, indicating the fountain.

"Yes, please."

As he moved away, Charlotte, resplendent in an azure silk gown complemented by the aurora borealis necklace from Dior, hurried up. She gripped Margot's hands tightly and bounced on her toes, her eyes sparkling through her butterfly mask. "Come and meet some people."

"But I'm waiting for your brother," said Margot.

Charlie followed the direction of Margot's gaze. "Oh, dear! He's been buttonholed by the British ambassador. You'll be waiting a long time."

By now, a group of men had gathered around Andrew. Having filled two glasses with pink champagne, he was laughing and angling his body away as if trying to extricate himself.

Really, Margot thought with an inward sigh, no man had a right to be that dashing unless he was arrogant or stupid as well, and Mountbatten was neither. To top it off, he loved books and he respected her opinions. Best of all—

"Enjoying the view?" Charlie's voice in her ear made her start. "Not that I can see it myself, but most women find him devastatingly attractive."

Margot swallowed, shook her head. "I was merely waiting for my champagne."

"He likes you very much, you know," Charlie said, and for once, there was a serious note in her voice.

Margot didn't know what to say. The truth would lead to expectations she couldn't fulfill.

"It's the first time I've seen him like that since Fleur," said Charlie. "The girl he wanted to marry."

That caught Margot's attention. The stab of jealousy she felt did not bode well. She must not forget she was a married woman, hardly free to indulge in romance or love. Or jealousy, for that matter.

"Oh, you needn't worry too much about her," said Charlie. "It was nearly a decade ago. Ancient history. The family forbade the match. Fleur was a divorcée and the Mountbattens, you know . . . We're direct descendants of Queen Victoria, so we're not allowed to marry anyone who has been divorced."

A stone dropped into the pit of Margot's stomach, cold and hard and heavy.

It shouldn't matter. It *didn't*. Then why was Margot finding it hard to catch her breath? Still she stood silently, hoping Charlie would continue, praying she wouldn't.

"Fleur died, you see," Charlie said softly. "Andrew was bitter and angry for a long, long time. He hasn't been serious about any other woman since. Until you."

As if he heard Charlie's words, Andrew glanced over and his gaze locked on Margot's.

"I'll leave you to it," said Charlie with a soft laugh, gliding away.

As if compelled, Andrew shouldered past his companions and moved toward Margot.

It was too much. The enchanted romance of the evening, wearing this wonderful gown, and a man like Andrew seeking her out with that look on his face.

With a great lump in her throat, Margot turned and started walking toward the coconut shy, where the crowd was thick. She threaded herself through the gaps, doing her best to elude Andrew's pursuit. She didn't look back to see if he followed her.

She reached the edge of the crowd and realized she'd been heading toward the place where Andrew had parked his car.

"Margot, wait!"

She turned to see him loping down the slope toward her, his hands now empty of drinks. "Is something wrong?" he demanded.

A lick of fringe was falling into his eyes. Impatiently, he thrust a hand through it to push it back. "What did Charlie say to you?"

"It's not anything that Charlie said." Margot met his gaze. "I don't belong here, that's all."

His dark eyes regarded her seriously. "You mean you don't belong with me."

"I'm not *with* you. Not in that way."

"Margot . . . I am utterly captivated by you. And call me arrogant but I can't be the only one who feels it."

"I'm married, Andrew." Her voice shook. "My real name is Margot, not Marie. Margot MacFarlane." She would never use her husband's name again.

He stared at her, stunned. Hoarsely, he said, *"What?"* If she'd ever doubted the sincerity of his regard, the horrified expression on his face convinced her. He stepped back, his hands dropping to his sides.

She longed to explain, to tell him all of it, that she'd left her husband behind in Australia and was never going back. That Andrew hadn't been mistaken in her feelings for him.

Suddenly she was furious, resenting the years that had been stolen from her. Had she really thought that a Dior gown—no matter how glorious—would turn back the clock, allow her to reclaim those lost years, her innocence, her ability to trust?

Somehow the fact that Andrew Mountbatten couldn't marry her even if she secured a divorce made it worse. Now it wasn't just a matter of overcoming the fears her husband had instilled in her; the very fact of having married him would taint her forever. Just when she'd begun to feel more like her old self.

Suddenly she realized she was weeping. She turned away, wishing she could run back to the apartment, but they were miles from Saint-Germain-des-Prés.

A hand settled on her shoulder. "Margot, my sweet girl. Don't cry." Andrew's voice was warm and steady. "Let me take you home." Wryly he added, "I promise I'll behave like a gentleman."

She'd expected that they would spend the drive home without speaking and dreaded it the way she used to dread the cold silences she endured throughout her marriage whenever she'd displeased her husband.

But as she stared, unseeing, at the moonlight glinting on the ornamental lake as they whizzed past, Andrew spoke. "Had any more thoughts about going into business as a literary agent?"

Glad of the change of subject, she answered, though with some constraint, "I thought I'd start small, with Gina's book, and go from there."

"If you'd care for some guidance, I'd be happy to assist," said Andrew. "No strings attached."

"I'd be grateful." But she had no intention of taking him up on the offer. That didn't seem like the right thing to do.

"I hope you won't feel awkward about it," said Andrew. Gently, he added, "I don't think my feelings will change, but I am well able to control them, you know." She sensed, rather than saw, him smile into the darkness. "That's one thing we British are rather good at, you know—repressing our emotions."

When at last they arrived at Le Chat, the brasserie was still buzzing with patrons. Margot got out her key and Mountbatten took it from her, sending a thrill of fear and anticipation through her. She couldn't help thinking of the last time they'd stood in this doorway.

He unlocked the door to the foyer of the apartment building. Handing the key back to her, he said, "Will you promise not to be a stranger? I do want to help you set up your agency. We can meet in my office if you like."

"Thank you," she said. She swallowed hard. "Thank you for not trying to push me or . . . or persuade me." It was a novel experience to have a man respect her decision when it went against his own interests.

His smile held a trace of self-mockery. "Oh, I haven't quite given up yet. You don't love your husband or you would be with him now, not with me." His voice roughened. "Damn it, Margot, I don't know how this happened. I want you more than I've ever wanted a woman before."

His words rocked her so hard off-balance, she had to put her back to the wall to steady herself. Before she could think of a response, he turned on his heel and walked away.

Chapter Nineteen

Gina

When Gina arrived at the Luxembourg Garden at the appointed time, she found Tommy Ledbetter already waiting for her by the Medici Fountain, as arranged. He was sitting on a park bench looking markedly out of place in his three-piece suit and fedora amid a forest of easels and art students bent on capturing the scene. Oblivious to the bohemian atmosphere surrounding him, Tommy was reading through a thick printed document, his black leather briefcase on the ground next to his feet.

Ahead loomed the subject of the artists' attention, a sculpture of Acis and Galatea, two lovers trysting, their pale marble limbs entwined. The pair were blissfully oblivious of the ominous and powerful figure of Polyphemus in weathered bronze, who glowered down at them from above.

"Working, Tommy?" said Gina as she approached. Why had he called her here without Hal? Maybe Tommy had been talking to Hal's father. Was he going to warn her off on Joe's behalf? That wouldn't work this time.

He looked up. "No rest for the wicked." He gestured to the space beside him. "Take a seat."

He set his briefcase on his lap, popped the clasps, and slid the document he'd been reading into it. Snapping the case shut, he returned it to the ground next to his feet. "I hear congratulations are in order."

Conscious of the fabulous diamond ring that was now back on her finger, Gina said, "I believe it's customary to congratulate the groom and to wish the bride happy."

Tommy smiled. He had a charming smile, and she wondered if there was a Mrs. Tommy back in Washington. "I'll take your word for it. And I do wish you happy. When my man Hal said it was you or no one, that was good enough for me."

"Oh, he's your man now, is he?" Gina tilted her head. Was Tommy no longer working for Joe?

"That's right." He nodded. "You know the thing I like about you, Miss Winter? You are quick on the uptake. We are about to launch Hal's campaign for governor."

"A little premature, isn't it?" Gina murmured. Why was Tommy telling her all this when Hal hadn't mentioned a word? "What with Joe's health in decline, I thought Hal was going back to run the company for a while."

"Joe wants to see him on the campaign trail before he dies." Tommy spread his hands. They were large. Quarterback's hands. He'd played college football with Hal, she seemed to remember. She'd bet he'd played dirty.

"And Hal agreed to this?"

Tommy missed a beat before replying. "Of course."

Gina noted the small hesitation and thought, *Got you*. "What's the problem, Tommy?"

"Frankly, Gina, the problem is you." He felt in his pocket and took out a cigarette case and lighter. "Want one?"

She shook her head, so he shrugged and helped himself to a cigarette and lit up. His eyes narrowed as he inhaled the smoke and blew it upward in a long stream. "What we need to do is rehabilitate you in the eyes of your peers."

"Really?" Gina ought to have seen this coming, she supposed. "How do you propose to do that?"

"Hal's already working on getting your father back on his feet. Looks like he'll succeed, too. We'll have Jay coming up roses in no time. Now you, Gina . . ." Cigarette between his fingers, he pointed at her. "You will need a small PR campaign of your own."

She wasn't angry . . . yet. Coolly, she said, "I suppose it will be the usual? Puff pieces in women's magazines, attending charity balls and lunches?" For Hal, she could do that much. Only she hadn't expected all of that to start so soon. She wasn't ready to leave Paris. And what about her book?

"Hal has already stayed in Paris too long," said Tommy, as if reading her thoughts. "But now he's got what he came for, I'll have him on the next plane out of here. Oh, don't worry," he said, as if anticipating her objections. "We'll give you a week or two to get everything squared away here, say goodbye to your friends." He eyed her casual trousers and striped shirt and added, "You might want to shop for a new wardrobe while you're here. I can set you up with someone from the embassy to advise you on appropriate styles. Pearls and twinsets, that kind of thing."

Fiercely Gina wrestled with herself. She wanted more than anything to tell Tommy to go to hell, but for Hal's sake, she kept a lid on her temper. "Pearls and twinsets. Roger that." She stared down at her hands, at the diamond on her finger winking in the sunshine. "Tell me, Tommy. Does Hal know you're talking to me about this?"

Laughing, Tommy held up a hand. "You got me. No, he doesn't. But he agrees with the general strategy. Come on, Gina. You've worked in D.C. You know the score."

Suddenly, she thought she knew all too well. The American. The shadowy figure who'd stepped out of the apartment building doorway when Gina and her friends had returned from the night-club that evening after they'd helped Margot move. He hadn't been looking for Margot.

"Are you having me watched, Tommy?"

After only a moment's hesitation, he nodded. "Hal doesn't know, or he'd tear me to pieces."

Wild with fury, Gina said, "I might just do the job myself!" Her voice rose enough to make a few people nearby turn their heads. "How *dare* you?" She felt violated, dirty, and only wished she'd re-alized sooner. She would have made sure to give Tommy and his watcher something to worry about.

Tommy looked her in the eye and spoke softly. "There's no point in getting mad at me, Gina. It was only for a few days. You know I had to be sure there wasn't any other man in your life, or any new habits you might have acquired in gay Paree that would make things awkward for Hal."

Gina refused to acknowledge anything of the kind. She was about to make a blistering retort, but Tommy held up a hand. "It's my job to get Hal Sanders elected, and the methods I use to do that . . . Well, he won't always like them, and neither will you. But you'll be thanking me when he's giving his victory speech come election night."

Will I? thought Gina. She had no ambition at all that centered on Hal's wealth or status. All she wanted was to be with him.

As it turned out, that was going to be more of a challenge than she'd dreamed. Even as her anger continued to simmer, she realized there was no point in arguing with Tommy—she might as well try to persuade a scorpion to shed its stinger. She'd worked in Washington and dealt with men like him before. She'd be more vigilant from now on. A good lesson to learn now, rather than later.

Her life with Hal was going to entail sacrifices, that was for sure. But it would all be worth it. She truly believed that. As long as she had Hal's support, she'd be fine.

Margot

Are you still talking to me? If so, I have a suggestion for you about starting your agency. Shall we say, my office at ten tomorrow? And bring a sample of your friend's manuscript if it's ready. Ten pages will do for starters.

Andrew
P.S. No funny business, I promise.

She couldn't help smiling at the last line. She knew without a doubt that if she didn't want a romantic relationship with Andrew Mountbatten, she should not see him anymore. But she'd just read the polished first half of Gina's manuscript and she was dying to show him. She knew he'd love it, and surely she could manage to keep things professional between them.

But when she arrived at the address he'd given her, a hôtel particulier near the Bois de Boulogne, she was doubtful and more than a little wary. It was clearly Andrew Mountbatten's private residence.

Andrew met her at the door, saying, "Don't be alarmed. I do live here but I haven't lured you under false pretenses. I have an office upstairs. Come up and you'll see."

Margot followed him up the cool marble staircase to the second floor, where double doors opened onto a space that was more like a library in a grand English country home than an office.

However there were two modern-looking telephones on the mahogany desk and a bank of filing cabinets behind it. Even more reassuring was the middle-aged woman who was thumbing through files in one of the deep drawers when they entered. She turned, letting fall her half-moon glasses, suspended by a chain around her neck.

"Miss MacFarlane, this is Mrs. Patterson, my private secretary."

If the older woman noticed that he'd stumbled a little over the "Miss" part of Margot's name, she gave no sign of it, but smiled and nodded. "How do you do? I'll send for tea." With that prosaic utterance, Mrs. Patterson excused herself and left. Andrew closed the doors behind her, then turned back, dark eyes gleaming with understanding. He knew precisely what wild thoughts had been rioting through Margot's mind before confronted with the sturdy Mrs. Patterson.

Mountbatten gestured to the comfortable-looking chairs grouped around a fireplace. "Do sit down."

He inquired politely about Claire and Gina. She asked him whether Charlotte had enjoyed the rest of the party. The whole time, his eyes seemed to burn through her. The expression in them

rendered their small talk ridiculous, but before things could become unbearably awkward, Mrs. Patterson came in with the tea
tray. "Cook made the macarons fresh this morning," she said with
a smile at Margot.

"Ooh, lovely," said Margot, thanking her.

"Shall I be mother?" asked the secretary.

"No, I'll pour," said Andrew. "Thank you, Mrs. Patterson." Dismissed, the secretary left the room.

Mountbatten poured their tea and offered Margot the plate of
macarons. She wasn't hungry. Being in the same room with Andrew
made her feel on edge, but she chose one of the delicate sweets
and set it on her plate.

"I brought Gina's pages." She fished out the envelope contain-
ing the sample pages of Gina's manuscript from the satchel she'd
brought. "I wasn't sure if you wanted them loose or . . ." She hadn't
exactly mentioned to Gina that she'd filched these from her desk so
she couldn't ask her how the pages should be presented.

He held out his hand for the envelope. "Give it here."

She passed over Gina's manuscript, saying, "You will think I'm
biased, but . . ." She trailed off as he frowned over the first page, a
coconut macaron suspended halfway to his mouth. He'd told her
he usually knew after the first page whether he would buy a manuscript or not. When he put down the macaron without tasting it
and turned to the second page, she felt a sense of hope tinged with
triumph. Pride glowed deep in her chest at his absorption in her
friend's work.

Margot sipped her tea and waited . . . and waited, while page after page joined the others in the "read" pile. Mountbatten was a fast
reader and finished in a few minutes, but Margot suffered through
agonies of impatience until he put down the final page.

Laughing, he looked up, shaking his head, staring at Margot in wonder. "I don't know why I'm surprised." He sat back. "When you told me about your friend, I expected I'd have to be . . . tactful."

"You mean you didn't trust my judgment," said Margot, narrowing her eyes at him.

"I mean your natural bias might have led you to see your friend's work as something it's not." He tapped through the manuscript pages with his finger. "But she's every bit as good as you said. If the rest of the book lives up to this sample, I think you have yourself a winner."

"Really?" Margot wanted to kiss him. "You're not just saying that?"

"I want to see the full manuscript the second it's finished," said Andrew.

"Oh, that's marvelous! Wait till I tell Gina. Thank you so much!"

"Maybe I ought to be thanking you." He hesitated. "Are you serious about becoming a literary agent? Really serious? You'd have to move to New York or London, you know."

She hadn't considered that, but what was stopping her? Of course, she'd miss Gina and Claire but the idea of setting up her own business, being her own boss, and talking about books all day long would be a dream come true.

"I'm meeting with one of my authors here in Paris next week. A debut novelist. Would you like to sit in?"

"Won't he mind?"

"I don't see why he should. He's on tour at the moment. Perhaps you've heard of him? Theodore Jones."

Margot gasped. "Really?"

"You know him?"

"*Know* him? I've read *The Rock Garden* three times." She went on to rhapsodize about his subtle use of metaphor, the book's difficult themes, the spare, evocative prose.

"I hear he's looking for a new agent," said Mountbatten. "Talk to him about his book the way you just spoke of it to me, and you might be in with a shot."

Someone of Jones's caliber would not look twice at a complete newcomer like Margot. *Would* he? And if he found out she had no experience . . .

"No, that's too much," said Margot.

"You don't want to represent him?" said Mountbatten. He raised his eyebrows. "Are you afraid?"

How was she supposed to take that? Pride made her say, "I'm not afraid, but if I am to go into business as a literary agent, I would like to stand on my own two feet."

Andrew laughed and shook his head. "Do you think anyone gets along in this business without help from one quarter or another? I certainly didn't. My mentor taught me everything I know, and I inherited his list when he retired." He shrugged. "Of course, one way to learn how to be an agent is to work as a junior for another agency. You would have to make the coffee, run errands, and if you're *very* lucky, you might be allowed to sell foreign translation rights . . ."

Margot tilted her head. "That wouldn't suit me at all." Part of the challenge and allure of being a literary agent was working for herself, representing only work that she loved, without answering to anyone. But Andrew was right. It was all about who you knew in this world. It was just that she was wary of accepting mentorship from a man who had made no secret of his romantic interest in her.

"I can only make the introduction to Jones," he warned her. "You would have to do the work of convincing him. And you'd have to come clean about your lack of experience and contacts."

While she turned that over in her mind, he went on. "The beauty of working with Theodore Jones would be that I've already signed him up for another two-book deal. So you won't have to do any of the negotiation for that first contract. It will give you a couple of years to gain experience before you have to negotiate his next deal. In the meantime, having him on your list will lend you real cachet."

She narrowed her eyes at Andrew. "I wouldn't go easy on you as a publisher just because we're . . . friends, you know."

His eyebrows lifted, but his eyes gleamed with laughter. "I wouldn't expect you to."

Margot was elated by the prospect. She might not be able to secure Theodore Jones as a client, but she'd be sure to give it her best shot. What did she have to lose? "When I sell my first novel, I will be sure to take you out to dinner to celebrate."

Andrew grinned back at her. "I'll hold you to that."

When he smiled at her like that, her heart turned somersaults. Her own smile faded. She wished he didn't have this effect on her! She wanted to remain professional but it wasn't easy when he looked at her like that.

As if sensing the return of constraint, he said, "Why don't we take a walk, you and I?"

"All right." She couldn't let this awkwardness continue. She needed to explain to him why she was holding back when it was so obvious to them both that she was falling for him.

In the street outside, Margot put on her hat and fumbled with her coat. Andrew took the garment from her and helped her into it, and she felt the fleeting touch of his hands at her shoulders all the way down to her toes.

"This way." They walked until they came to the gates of the Bois de Boulogne. Eventually Andrew stopped and turned to face her. "What is it? Tell me. Have I done something wrong?"

She didn't answer him immediately, rendered mute by the inability to put her feelings into words. As a younger woman, she'd worn her heart on her sleeve. But after living through that marriage, attempting to express any kind of emotion left her tongue-tied.

After a long pause, Andrew said, "Shall I give you my story, then?"

That made her look up. "Your story?"

"You needn't pretend my sister hasn't told you all about it," said Andrew dryly.

"She did mention something," acknowledged Margot. "But I hope you will believe that I didn't pry, and I didn't encourage her to divulge your private affairs."

"No. Well." He seemed to brace himself, and she knew it must be a difficult subject for him to talk about. "I loved a woman who died, you see."

"I'm so sorry," said Margot. This part she knew. "Was it in the war?"

He shook his head. "No, not in the war. She was thrown from a horse. The stupidest, most pointless accident. I was angry about it for a long time. Fleur had been married before. A mistake from the beginning, as it turned out. Her husband ran off with an actress within months of the wedding. I wanted to marry her but my family forbade it." He pressed his lips together. "You'd think I would have told them all to go to hell, but I'd been brought up steeped in tradition. Defying my family, the King . . . at the time, it was unthinkable. I did everything in my power to persuade them to let me flout that rule against our marrying divorcées, but it made no difference. To my shame, I gave her up." He smiled mirthlessly. "When she died, I raged at the world, but I blamed myself most of all for my cowardice." He huffed out a breath. "Believe me, Margot. I would not make the same mistake with you."

She was silent for a time while she digested this. "Do I remind you of her?" she asked, not really wanting to know the answer.

His somber expression vanished. "God, no!" He laughed. "Not in the least. I suppose I am simply explaining to you why I've been so . . . lacking in the usual British reticence, I suppose. Why I can't let you walk out of my life forever without a very compelling reason." He halted, and the wind rustled the new leaves above them as he searched her face. "Does that sound conceited? But I *know* you feel it, too."

I'm married. It would be simple to insist that was the reason for denying him, to lie and say she loved her husband and was never going to leave him. But it would be dishonest in a way that lying about her marital status never had been. She owed Andrew better than that.

Margot stared into his eyes. Could she possibly trust herself to love this man? She wanted to, quite desperately, but it was too soon. Only months after leaving her marriage, it wasn't safe for her to love anyone. Not yet, not with *his* voice still in her head, and the constant vigilance that was still as much a part of her as her blood and bone and breath.

On the bridle path that ran parallel to the footpath where they stood, the clop of horse hooves grew louder, then finally receded again, before she spoke. "I am smitten with you," she said. "I admit it. But really, that is part of the problem."

His face had lightened when she'd made the admission but now his expression grew intense. "I don't understand."

"I can't trust my feelings," said Margot. "Not anymore." Sadness welled up inside her, along with resentment that her marriage had made it impossible to trust any man—even one who seemed to be so considerate and kind.

She simply wouldn't survive if Andrew turned out to be just like her husband. If only she could give the man beside her some kind of test. But as she'd learned to her cost, a man could embody her wildest dreams at the beginning. Only time would tell if he would turn into a nightmare. "I thought I loved my husband and that he loved me," she said softly. "But he nearly destroyed me. I can't risk that again."

His expression darkened. She'd never seen the urbane Mountbatten look so forbidding. "What did he do to you?"

She pressed her lips together and shook her head. She was perilously close to tears and she didn't want his pity. With a deep breath, she forced the emotion down.

"Won't you give me a chance?" Taking her hand in a gentle hold, he looked down at it for a moment, then, as if it was difficult to admit, he added, "I know it sounds ridiculous and it's too soon and all the rest of it, but, Margot, I've fallen in love with you."

That made her feel even worse. He sounded so certain while her own emotions were all muddled and askew. If this was real . . . But how could she know?

She knew as well as anyone that there were never any guarantees when it came to love. How would she ever know if she'd be safe with any man if she didn't take a leap of faith and find out? But giving herself wholeheartedly to a man who took her love and twisted it to his own ends had ruined her. Better to remain alone for the rest of her life than to go through *that* again.

Gently, she withdrew her hand. "I can't," she whispered, mostly to herself. "I'm not strong enough. Not yet."

"Then I'll wait," he said. "However long it takes."

Claire

Hervé continued to make light of his injury, but Claire wasn't fooled. He couldn't even hold a knife and fork properly, much less run a restaurant. After a lot of soul-searching, she made her decision. Hervé wouldn't like it, but that was just too bad.

When she peered into the brasserie kitchen that evening, she knew she'd done the right thing. She found the staff in chaos, with Hervé trying to do everything one-handed and his staff dancing around him like ballerinas avoiding a baited bear.

One careless apprentice knocked Hervé's injured hand and he swore with such volume and eloquence that the brasserie patrons must have heard him.

Claire forced herself to stay out of the way, but when Hervé recovered somewhat and stomped out to the cold room, she gave him a few moments, then followed him in.

He had plunged his injured hand, bandage and all, into a bucket of half water, half ice chips. His big body gave a shudder—whether from the pain or the cold, she couldn't tell—and he bent a glare on her as she stepped inside.

"Don't say it," he said through gritted teeth. "I don't want to hear."

"I'm here to help," said Claire. "Just till you get back to normal."

He shook his head. "I don't want you here."

"You don't have much choice," said Claire. "If you continue this way, you'll get an infection, and then you'll be out of commission for even longer. There might even be permanent damage." She paused. "It's not just you now, Hervé. You have an entire staff relying on you for their livelihood."

"Don't you think I know that?" Hervé scowled. "But it doesn't mean you need to come back."

"I think it does," Claire said gently. "You know it, too."

"No. I don't," growled Hervé. "Do you think opportunities like the one with Thibault grow on trees?"

"I know that they don't," said Claire. "But family is more important. And now, you're my family."

He seemed as astonished at her words as she was. "Claire . . ." He shook his head, tried again. "Sweetheart, caring for your family doesn't mean you have to give up everything for them. Sure, it will be tough around here for a while, but I'll figure it out."

She shoved her hands in her pockets. "If I'm here, you won't have to."

"And what if something else happens in a few months, or maybe next year?" asked Hervé. "Are you going to run back to Le Chat to rescue me every time?"

His argument was a good one. She just wasn't going to admit it. "Well, that's not going to happen, is it? You hardly ever get injured or sick."

"But—" He broke off, looking thunderstruck, as if he'd realized something momentous. "You're scared. You really are."

"What? No! What do you mean, I'm scared?" Claire's heart was beating hard and fast.

"I mean, now you've got your dream, you're not sure you want it," said Hervé. "You're terrified of failing. And maybe, you're even more scared you might succeed with Thibault. You're frightened of what that will mean."

"I am not!" said Claire. But in the same breath, she whispered, "What if I'm not good enough, after all?"

Hervé threw back his head and laughed. "I've never heard such garbage in my life. Not good enough? Do you think Thibault was wrong about you? He wasn't. All of those other chefs were—*they* didn't even have the sense to try your cooking. They questioned your commitment, but they didn't see you getting up before dawn every day to practice your skills. They didn't see how much you want this. But I saw it, and Thibault could tell just from tasting that meal the kind of dedication you've poured into your work. Don't blow it now, Claire. You've got to go for it, and not let anything hold you back." His jaw tightened. "I'd rather put Louis in charge than see you back in my kitchen again."

He was biased. She shouldn't let his praise mean so much to her. And the fact that he was urging her to put her career first made her even more determined to help him keep the brasserie going. "Well, if I'm so brilliant, then Chef Thibault will wait," she said, not sure that she believed her own words. "He's already agreed to let me have time off for your sake, so don't let's argue any more about it. I'll give you two weeks and then I *promise* I will go back to Thibault."

Gina

Gina was typing as if possessed, although her fingers on the heavy keys couldn't quite keep up with her racing thoughts. She'd finished rewriting the final pages of *Liberty* in the early hours of the morning, but she'd been riding on such a tidal wave of creative energy, she couldn't stop. As she'd stared at the tall stack of pages that made up her story, an idea had burst into her brain that was so blindingly brilliant, she needed to get it down on paper as fast as possible.

Claire had risen early to check on Hervé at the brasserie before going to work. Gina hardly noticed when Margot left for Dior.

What seemed like minutes later, Gina heard the apartment door open and close. Claire must have come back for something, but both Claire and Margot knew not to disturb Gina when she was writing. Then the desk lamp switched on, making her jump. Incredulous, Gina realized it was evening already, but she couldn't stop. She needed to get as much done now as she could, before—

A hand on her shoulder made her jump again and utter a filthy curse. "Don't *do* that!"

"Such language," said Margot, laughing. "But I forgive you because this . . ." She held up the final pages of *Liberty* in one hand. "*This* is perfection." Gina blinked. When had Margot stolen them from under her nose?

After going through the various stages of denial, anger, and acceptance all writers face when their precious creations are thoroughly critiqued, Gina had ingested Margot's editorial comments and come up with ways to address her concerns. Once Gina was done, she had seen how much better and more nuanced these changes made the book.

"Perfection?" she repeated. A smile broke over her face. "Really?"

Margot nodded. "Really. I wouldn't change a single word. I'm going to ask for a week off to start calling publishers and sending out sample pages. I can't wait to start pitching!" She hesitated. "I wasn't going to tell you this because I didn't want to get your hopes up, but I gave Mountbatten a sneak peek at the first ten pages and he is clamoring for more."

"Really? That's terrific news," said Gina, sitting up straight. That an experienced editor with a New York publishing house liked her work was the kind of encouragement she needed right now.

Margot tilted her head to read the page in her typewriter. "But you're hard at work still? Don't tell me you've started another book already."

Nodding, Gina said, "As soon as the idea hit me, I had to run with it. Sorry, but I can't stop." She started typing again, afraid that if she didn't get the words down now, they'd leave her forever.

"You're still in your pajamas," said Margot. "Have you even eaten today?" When Gina didn't answer, she added, "Weren't you supposed to work at the bookstore?"

Gina hit the carriage lever and started a new paragraph. "I quit." Thank goodness she had, or she couldn't have taken advantage of this creative frenzy.

"What? Why?" Margot sat on the edge of the desk and peered into Gina's face. "Gina, will you stop typing and *look* at me? What's all this about?"

Sitting back, Gina blew out a breath and shoved her hands through her hair, then kneaded her aching neck. She ran her tongue along the backs of her teeth. Had she even brushed them that morning? "I quit the bookstore because I wanted to get *Liberty* finished. And once that was done, I had this terrific idea for a new book, and I had to start on that straightaway."

"What's the rush?" Margot asked. "You've always said writing novels is a marathon, not a sprint."

"You don't understand," said Gina. "I have to do this now, before I leave Paris."

Margot looked as if she'd been kicked in the stomach. After a long pause, she said, "I suppose we knew that was coming. How soon do you have to go?"

"Hal's leaving the day after tomorrow. He wants me to join him as soon as possible. I've got two weeks at the outside," said Gina, avoiding Margot's perceptive gaze. "So last night, I guess I sort of . . . panicked." She rubbed at her bleary eyes. On the one hand, she wanted to pour all her fears out to Margot. On the other, she was scared of what her friend might say in response.

"Well, even you cannot finish an entire novel in one day," said Margot. "Why don't you freshen up and I'll find us something to eat?"

When Gina came out of the bathroom, dressed and somewhat refreshed, she found Margot in the galley kitchen frowning mightily over a pan of what looked like it might once have been eggs.

"Are they fried or scrambled?" Gina asked doubtfully.

"Frambled?" Margot said. "It was supposed to be an omelet." She tipped the eggs into the trash. "Such a waste, but even my frugal great-aunt Mildred would not have eaten those."

"Bread and cheese will do for me," said Gina. "And wine. I bought a couple of bottles of bordeaux the other day."

They took their supper out to the drawing room. Gina sat on the sofa, tucking her legs up underneath her. Margot poured the wine and handed a glass to Gina before sitting down beside her. "You seem . . . a little desperate, dearest G. Are you sure marriage to Hal is what you really want?"

"Of course it is," Gina replied, helping herself to cheese so she didn't have to see Margot's doubtful expression. "Hal loves me and I love him. The rest . . . We'll work it out." She needed to believe that.

"All this time you've been focused on the change in your circumstances, and not being good enough for the position of Hal's wife anymore," said Margot. When Gina would have argued, she held up a hand. "Not that I agree with that, but . . . Have you ever stopped to ask yourself if being the wife of an up-and-coming politician is what *you* want?"

"I have. And it is." Gina bit off the words as if they were a day-old baguette. The fact that Margot was echoing the fear that had chimed in Gina's mind during that meeting with Tommy in the Luxembourg Garden only irritated her the more. "It's just that the timetable has been moved up and I wasn't quite ready, that's all. Hal's father is dying. He wants to see Hal's feet set on the right path before he goes."

"And are you fully aware of what's involved for you in campaigning for office?" asked Margot. "I can't imagine there'll be an awful lot of time to write." Margot seemed to be exercising a lot of restraint. Her tone was so calm and measured, she sounded quite unlike herself. "Hence today's output, I suppose?"

"I've managed to write a novel in Paris while holding down a job and freelancing on the side, haven't I?" Gina retorted. "I can certainly do it in between charity galas and political rallies." Restless, Gina got to her feet and paced, hugging herself.

"Will they even let you publish novels at all?" asked Margot. "I've never heard of a senator's wife having a career."

Stubbornly Gina refused to see what Margot was getting at. "You make it sound like I'll have no say in the matter. Hal won't let that happen. *I* won't let that happen." When Margot said nothing, she felt even more under attack, but she understood where Margot's concerns were coming from. "Look, I know you didn't have a good experience with marriage, but I'm . . ." She broke off, flushing.

There was an ominous silence. Then, "You're *what*, Gina? Different?" The words, soft and low, sounded dangerous. Margot held herself very still.

I'm not like you, Gina wanted to say. *I'm tough.* "The *situation* is completely different, is what I mean."

"You think you're stronger than I am," said Margot, rising to face her. "You think that if you'd been in my shoes, married to my husband, you would have put that man in his place, done exactly what you wanted, or left him flat when things got unbearable. *Don't* you? You can't even see that you're already compromising bits of yourself and you haven't even married Hal yet!" She crossed to the desk, snatched up the pages Gina had completed that day, and shook them at her. "You know it, too, or you wouldn't have been so desperate to get this story down before it's too late."

"Funny. I thought my literary agent would want me to be productive," snapped Gina.

"Gina, I want to be your literary agent for the long haul, not for one book," Margot flashed back. "But that's all you're ever going to write if you become Hal's wife."

Dimly aware that she was deliberately feeding her own fury, Gina whirled on Margot. "What about you? Andrew Mountbatten's head over heels for you and I'm pretty sure you love him, too, but you've led him on for weeks! And now you've broken his heart. Because you're a coward, Margot. Not during your marriage. I *never* thought that. But you're being one now."

There was a silence. Gina dropped her gaze to her hands, wishing with all her might that she could take back the words she'd just spoken. She didn't want to see the hurt she knew was written all over Margot's face.

"What on earth is going on here?" They hadn't heard Claire come in.

Gina simply stared at her hands, unable to put into words the pain that was in this room, the pain she'd created, the pain she felt. Worse than any accusation that had been hurled at her was the knowledge that she'd said such unforgivable things to Margot. She made herself raise her gaze to look at what she'd done.

Her face white, stripped of its sparkle, Margot sat down and drained the dregs of the glass of wine she'd left on the coffee table. Her hand shook as she poured herself another glass. A hard lump formed in Gina's throat. Why had she said those things? She hadn't even realized she'd been thinking them, and then, there they were, spilling like poison from her mouth.

She started to speak, but Margot forestalled her, suddenly demanding of Claire. "Why are you home so early?"

Gina glanced at the clock. It was eight thirty. Not even halfway through the dinner rush. Claire hadn't been fired, had she? That would set the seal on a truly awful day.

"Oh, I'm not. Home, I mean," said Claire. "I just popped upstairs to get something." She bit her lip, then lifted her chin, as if in defiance. "I'm working at the brasserie."

"What?" said Gina. "Because Hervé's injured? Can't someone else step up and support him? He has plenty of staff."

Claire shrugged. "Someone else didn't. Things weren't going so well, so I'm helping out."

"Isn't it a bit soon to be taking time off from the restaurant?" Gina pressed. "Was Thibault okay with that?" She was glad to get her mind off her own troubles and on to Claire's.

"You sound like Hervé." Claire rolled her eyes. "It's only for a couple of weeks. It will be fine."

Gina wasn't convinced. "During which time one of your underlings steps into your shoes at Thibault's and you come back to find yourself demoted or without a job."

"It's a chance I'll take." Claire's eyes sparked with anger. "Sometimes, we make sacrifices for the people we love."

Margot spoke. "You'd know all about that, wouldn't you, Gina?" She jerked her head toward Claire. "Tell her what you told me." But without giving Gina a chance to speak, Margot added, "Gina's giving up her future as a novelist to become a politician's handbag."

"No!" Claire stared at Gina. "But I thought you had all of that sorted out. I thought Hal understood."

"Just a few wrinkles to iron out," said Gina coolly. "Nothing I can't handle." She'd been on the verge of apologizing to Margot, but that snide remark had reignited her rage.

"*And* Gina's going to leave Paris as soon as Governor Charming crooks his little finger." Margot rose to her feet, setting her empty glass down with a sharp click. "Why don't you try to talk her out of it, Claire? Although if you've been kidding yourself you're actually doing the right thing by helping out at the brasserie when all you're really doing is running away from Thibault's, you're just as bad." Dark eyes blazing and filled with angry tears, Margot turned on her heel and headed for the bedroom.

"Well, at least you won't have to put up with me for much longer!" Gina called after her. She turned back to Claire, expecting an ally after Margot's attack on them both, but she found no sympathy there.

Claire was shaking her head at her, as if bewildered. "Gina, what have you *done*?" And it wasn't clear whether she meant to Margot, to their friendship, or to Gina herself.

Chapter Twenty

Margot

The second Andrew Mountbatten's housekeeper opened his front door, it occurred to Margot that she should have made an appointment. But if she'd telephoned ahead of time, her courage surely would have failed her. Gina's manuscript, her excuse for visiting Andrew that morning, was clutched tightly to her chest.

Last night's argument had left Margot hurt and furious. She'd spent a long time blaming herself for losing years of her life to a cold and manipulative man. In the months after she left Sydney, only her native practicality had saved her from living mired in anger and despair. Instinctively, she'd known regret and recriminations would only keep her stuck in place when she needed to move forward. She must put the past behind her if she wasn't going to waste even more precious time.

Gina had accused her of cowardice. If Margot hadn't leveled that accusation at herself a thousand times before, it wouldn't hurt so much. She wasn't quite ready to forgive Gina, but she knew that she would, eventually, just as Gina would eventually forgive her.

Was she a coward for refusing to give Andrew Mountbatten a chance? Margot had lain awake all night, trying to decide whether

Gina was right. Since that day he'd told her he loved her in the Bois de Boulogne, she'd ached for him with an intensity close to physical pain. In the contest between the yearning of her heart and the fear of becoming once again that beaten-down, powerless shadow of herself, which should be the winner?

She still hadn't decided when morning came. She only knew she needed to see him, and she couldn't wait.

"Ah, *bonjour*, mademoiselle," said the housekeeper, perhaps recognizing her from her earlier visit. "Won't you come in? Monsieur will be down in a moment. Shall I set another place for breakfast?"

Startled, for the first time that morning Margot checked her watch. It wasn't yet nine o'clock. She'd sped over here without even realizing how early it was—not so early for an Australian, perhaps, but in Paris, everything began and ended later. "Oh! Forgive me. I ought to come back some other time." She handed the housekeeper Gina's manuscript. "Would you give this to Mr. Mountbatten please? I . . . I should go."

"No, don't run away." Mountbatten's voice floated down from above them. "Join me, won't you?"

She turned to see Andrew jogging downstairs, fastening his cuff links as he went. He was coatless, but that was his only concession to informality. His gold tiepin gleamed against the crimson silk of his tie. His dark grey waistcoat emphasized his trim physique. He made Margot, who was usually a perfectionist herself when it came to the neatness of her attire, wonder if she'd even remembered to brush her hair before she'd charged out of the apartment, desperate to see him.

"I—I've already eaten, thank you," she blurted out. Which wasn't true, but she knew she couldn't touch a bite.

He smiled at her, and his smile held tender amusement at her disarray. "Shall we go onto the terrace? The weather is particularly fine today."

Andrew led her through the breakfast room, where the table was set and the sideboard filled with silver chafing dishes. Opening a French door for her to step through, he followed her out onto the terrace.

Wisteria wound through the trellis that ran along the eaves, framing a delightful prospect: a formal rose garden bordered with fragrant lavender and rosemary.

"Now. What brings you here this morning?"

With a start, Margot thought of Gina's manuscript, which she had left with the housekeeper. But now that it came down to it, she didn't want to make excuses. If only she could think of the right thing to say! *Come on, Margot,* she told herself. *Aren't words supposed to be your forte?*

When she didn't immediately answer, Andrew's lips twisted in a rueful smile. "I'm glad you've come. After our last conversation, I thought I might not see you again before I left Paris."

Her head jerked up. "You're leaving?"

In his eyes, she saw pain and longing and her heart twisted. He transferred his gaze to the garden. "First, I will introduce you to those authors I mentioned. If you still want me to, that is." He rubbed his chin with his thumb and his voice sounded strained. "I thought I'd take that trip to Bermuda, after all."

Following that, he would return to New York and she'd never see him again. Inside Margot, a voice screamed in protest. "But you said you'd wait," she blurted out, feeling wronged somehow, as if she hadn't tried to push him away at every opportunity.

He turned his head to look at her, and his dark eyes lit with hope. She had the feeling he was seeing her—really seeing her—as no man ever had before. "I thought it might be best to give you some space as well as time." A muscle in his jaw ticked. "Ah, Margot, you don't know how hard it's been to love you, be in the same city as you, and fight these feelings every day, forcing myself to respect your wishes and stay away."

Her heart melted at his words. She wanted more than anything for him to hold her, reassure her, give her some ironclad promise that everything would be all right. But there were no guarantees in love. Gina was right. Margot would have to be brave, take a huge chance, if she wanted Andrew Mountbatten in her life.

Watching her, he sucked in a breath. "The way you're looking at me . . . I'm having a hard time not kissing you right now."

Drawing on every ounce of courage she possessed, Margot gathered herself for the leap. "Then don't fight it," she whispered. Standing on tiptoe, she put her arms around his neck and pulled him down to her, pressing her lips to his.

He was gentle at first, but her response seemed to ignite something inside him and his kiss turned hot and hard—not what she'd expected from an English gentleman at all—and she felt the rush of breath leaving her lungs as he crushed her to him, lifted her off her feet. Still kissing her, he carried her to a love seat by the wall and sat down with Margot seated sideways across his lap.

When finally they broke apart, she cupped his jaw in her hand and whispered against his smoothly shaven cheek, "Don't go."

"Go?" he repeated, sounding dazed. "Who's going anywhere?"

She laughed and tilted her head back, reaching up to smooth his unruly fringe. "I *think* I've fallen in love with you, Andrew Mountbatten, but . . ." She hesitated, warmed by the fierce joy in his eyes. "After that kiss, would it sound very foolish if I said I'd like to take things slowly?"

"If that means I can't kiss you, we have a problem," he murmured. He dipped his head and pressed his lips to the sensitive skin beneath her ear.

She shivered and gasped, laughter bubbling up from her chest. "No, it doesn't mean that. But I want to make this clear. I am not going to marry again, ever."

"You mean you won't make an honest man out of me?" He kissed the side of her throat.

"Andrew! I'm serious." She smacked his shoulder with the heel of her hand and he stopped what he was doing to look down at her with a serious expression. "It's all right," he said softly. "Truly. I understand."

Margot rushed on, "I know you haven't asked me, and maybe you aren't likely to, but I just wanted you to know where you stand. I can't even make any real commitment to you—not yet."

She searched his face. "I'm not sure of myself yet, or of how the future will unfold. But when you said you were leaving, I . . . I realized I can't be happy without you. And I don't even want to try."

"How about we take it one day at a time?" said Andrew, tracing her lower lip with his thumb. "I've waited all my life for you, Margot. I can wait a little longer to make you mine."

Gina

After her fight with Margot and Claire, Gina couldn't sleep. She sensed Margot lying awake in the bed beside hers but they were both too raw with the wounds they'd inflicted on each other to break the silence. Eventually Gina couldn't stand it anymore.

She took a pillow and blanket and went to lie on the drawing room couch.

She woke the next morning to find both of her friends gone. Was this the end for them? She couldn't bear it if she lost Margot and Claire.

Margot's pointed remarks about Hal had hurt. Now a carousel of worries whirled in Gina's mind. Like carousel ponies, one concern rose, then another and another, and they spun faster and faster around her mind until she wanted to scream. If only she could go back in time and avoid that conversation altogether.

Hungry for reassurance, she dressed carefully and took a taxi to the Ritz hotel. Hal was due to leave for New York the next morning, and she'd spent the past forty-eight hours writing and arguing with her friends. What was wrong with her? She had to see him as soon as possible. Five minutes with him, and all her doubts would disappear.

Ordinarily Gina loved to visit the Ritz, reveling in the glamor and sparkle of its lush furnishings and winking chandeliers. Now she rushed through the foyer to reception and asked for Hal Sanders.

"One moment." The receptionist called and handed her the telephone receiver.

"Gina." Hal sounded relieved. "I've been trying to reach you. Come up." He gave her his room number.

Dimly she remembered the telephone ringing in the apartment late the afternoon before but she'd been too absorbed in her work even to consider answering. Guilt tightened her chest.

She checked her reflection in the mirror near the elevator. Despite her disturbed sleep last night, she didn't have bags under her eyes, thank goodness. She smoothed back a stray hair and checked her teeth for lipstick.

For the first time, it occurred to her that she was visiting Hal's hotel suite. She smiled to herself. Maybe she'd give Hal something to remember on those lonely nights in New York before he saw her again.

But it wasn't Hal who opened the door to the suite. Tommy stood in the doorway, a cold shower in human form, his index finger to his lips like a kindergarten teacher calling for quiet. "He's on the phone to the French Finance Minister." He led her into the sitting room of the suite.

The room was furnished in cream and fawn and pale blue, a restful palette. There was a painting of a young man on a horse over the mantelpiece and white roses in silver urns scattered about the room.

Receiver to his ear, Hal turned his head when she walked in. His eyes warmed when he saw her and crinkled at the corners. He made a gesture that was a cross between a wave and a stop signal, then turned his back and shoved a hand in his trousers pocket to continue the conversation. "Yes, Minister, I appreciate that, but we need your support on this issue . . . No, I do understand. What you have to remember in situations like this . . ." He launched into a confident explanation of United States economic policy. It sounded like he wouldn't be free any time soon.

From the three-piece suit Hal wore and Tommy's hovering presence, Gina deduced Hal wouldn't have much time for her today. Ordinarily she would have left him to it, but her failure to pick up when he called the day before and the fact that he was leaving Paris the next morning made her stay. She chose a magazine from the pile on the coffee table and flipped through it. Since she'd become serious about writing fiction, time had become a commodity she couldn't afford to waste. She began to wish she had a pen and paper handy. She could jot down some notes for her new book while Hal wrapped up his conversation.

Finally Hal ended the call. Gina looked up to see that he was beaming, not at her but at Tommy. "We've done it!" said Hal. "The Minister has agreed to meet this afternoon."

Tommy gave a hoot of victory and slapped him on the back. "See? What did I tell you? You're a natural." He turned his head to look at Gina. "Your future husband. Our future president!"

Hal gave a derisive snort. "Hardly. But that did feel good, I admit."

He seemed to remember Gina. "Give us a minute?" he said to Tommy.

"Sure." With a nod to her, Tommy let himself out of the room.

When the door closed behind him, Hal pulled Gina to her feet and into his arms. "Hello, you. Where've you been hiding?"

She smiled up at him, and with his arms around her, the tension began to drain from her body. "Not hiding. Writing. I lost track of time." She tilted her head. "Weren't you busy meeting with the Economic Reform Committee yesterday?"

"Yes, but I thought . . ." He blew out a breath. "I mean, I really wanted to see you last night, to talk over the day."

"Well, I'm here now," said Gina, linking her hands behind the small of his back. "Tell me."

The telephone started to ring. Tensing, Hal glanced at it but didn't move to answer. "I'm sorry, Gigi. I don't have the time today. My plane leaves tomorrow morning and I still have a mountain of calls to make."

She was disappointed but she only had herself to blame. "That's all right. We can talk as long as we want when I get to New York."

She smoothed his lapel. "Can I share my news? I'll be quick. Margot has found a publisher who likes what he read of my novel. She said he's champing at the bit to read the rest."

"Hey, that's great!" Hal hugged her to him, seeming genuinely delighted, but then he frowned as if distracted, his arms slackening.

She stepped back from his embrace. "It's a bad time. I'll go."

"No, no. Really, I'm happy to see you." One hand on his hip, he ran the other hand through his hair. "But I wish you'd checked with Tommy before you agreed to show your novel to a publisher."

"What?" She stared at him. "What do you mean?"

"I thought Tommy talked to you about this." Hal raised his gaze to the ceiling and she watched his Adam's apple move as he swallowed. "You're not going to like what I'm going to say, but I'll say it because I don't want to hide anything from you, Gina. What happened with your father . . . it's not a problem. At least, we're fixing it. But we need to shape the narrative from here on out. Do you see what I mean?"

Shape the narrative? Already he was talking like a politician. Slowly, Gina answered, "Tommy told me I have to start dressing the part and attending the right events." Her brows drew together. "What? Are you saying I have to run my writing by your people now? That's not going to happen. I can't believe you'd even suggest it."

Hal shook his head. "It's just a formality, a rubber stamp. Your book is a harmless novel about a couple of women, isn't it? I can't imagine there'll be anything divisive in a story like that."

"You mean because it's about women it must be trivial?" Gina felt her voice rising.

Hal frowned. "No! That's not what I meant. You're twisting my words. I mean, it's a novel, not a piece of hard-hitting journalism that might make things tricky for me politically."

"There is no way I'm letting anyone vet my writing before it goes to print."

Margot's words came back to her. *You're already compromising bits of yourself.* Margot had seen it. Hal had promised that Gina could be her own person despite the experience of a raft of politicians' wives who had gone before her. Margot had known exactly how marriage to Hal would be.

The trickle of doubt she'd felt in her meeting with Tommy swelled into a flood. "I can't do this," she whispered, her eyes wide. With trembling fingers, she tugged at her engagement ring. "I can't marry you, Hal."

"What? No!" Hal gripped her hands, trapping the ring in place. "After all we've been through, you're going to end it over this?" *Over a silly little novel?* were the unspoken words Gina heard.

"I can't do it, Hal." She said it more in sadness than in anger, her throat swelling with incipient tears. "I can't be what you need. I will always be one more problem to deal with if you want to make it to the White House one day."

She would never ask him to give up politics. Of that, he was well aware. She was disappointed to find that he didn't seem to understand what he was asking her to give up by becoming a politician's wife.

"But we've been through all this about you hurting my chances and I told you it's not true." Hal tightened his grip on her hands, and the engagement ring she'd loosened twisted, its large diamond digging painfully into the side of her finger. "Why bring it up again now?"

"Because I trusted you to stand with me against the Tommys of the world!" said Gina. "I didn't think it would be you and them against me." She blew out a long breath and tried to speak in a measured way so he knew she meant it. "If we cannot agree on something this fundamental from the beginning, there is no hope for our future. And if I'm honest," she said, tears welling in her eyes, "I would really, really hate being a governor's wife."

"But don't you see?" Hal said as a tear rolled down her cheek. "If I don't have you, then none of it matters. You are the most important thing in the world to me, you know that." Gently he took her face between his hands and wiped at her tears with his thumbs. How could she bear to lose him? He was staring down at her so tenderly. "I *love* you, Gina. And you love me."

Her heart felt shredded and bloody and she wanted more than anything to comfort him for the pain she was causing him. It would be so easy to give in, but today had been a sobering glimpse of their future together. For her, their marriage would have been full of battles like this, full of unwilling compromise and resentment on one side or the other—mostly on hers. She didn't want a life like that.

"I hate it as much as you do, but I have to accept it. For us, love is just not enough." Her voice trembling, she said, "You need to let me go now, Hal. Please."

His expression changed from tenderness to disbelief and then anguish as he seemed to comprehend the strength of her resolve, the finality of her decision. He swung away from her and paced to the window. Looking back, he said, "We could have worked it out. You could have written your novel, even kept your career as a journalist, within reason. I would have let you do anything you wanted."

And there it was. That one little word.

Let.

He would have given her permission, because once she married him, he would have ruled over her. And men like Tommy ruled him.

Hal paused, as if waiting for her to deny his claim. But there was nothing more to say. He wouldn't even understand that what he'd just said obliterated any lingering doubts she might have had.

It wasn't his fault that he was like this. It was centuries, millennia of attitudes passed down from father to son. It was the way of the world, the way his parents had been together, and hers, and on and on, back through the branches of their illustrious family trees, down to the very roots.

Gina didn't even know what a marriage of equals looked like. She could marry Hal and try to educate herself and him, and fight all those battles until she was scarred but victorious, but why should she have to? As a writer, she'd always be rowing against the tide while all the men around her cruised along with the current, their sails billowing with support from their wives. If she pursued a career as a novelist while married to a senator, she would have to do it in the teeth of opposition, from his family and hers, from his spin doctors and political masters, and from society at large. The prospect was exhausting. And that was before she even thought about bringing children into the equation.

She wasn't angry at Hal. The situation wasn't of his making. Deep in love with him, even she had disregarded these considerations when she'd agreed to be his wife.

"Hal, I'm sorry." The words couldn't begin to describe what she felt. She still loved him, and probably always would. He wasn't a bad person. He was merely a product of his upbringing, like everyone else. One day, he would realize she'd done him a favor, when he married a nice young woman who was content to be Mrs. Hal Sanders. There were plenty of those kinds of girls around.

She knew better than to say so. "I'm sorry," she said again. "I wish, so very much, that things were different." What she wished, deep down, was that he'd never even thought of going into politics. But she could no more demand he give that up for her than she could give up her dreams for him.

Hal stared at her as if her words were so inadequate, he couldn't believe they had come out of her mouth. A muscle in his jaw began to tick. He was holding his anger in check and she couldn't blame him for his fury, because for a long time before her father lost his money, she'd been content to cruise along in luxury at his side. It must seem the height of folly for her to insist on jumping overboard without a life preserver to swim against the tide.

The telephone's ring ripped through the silence.

"I'll go," Gina whispered. She placed the diamond solitaire he'd given her carefully on the mantelpiece. "You'd better get that."

Chapter Twenty-One

Gina

Meet us at Dior at five thirty sharp. Don't even think about not coming."

Gina read the note and shut her eyes. This was the second morning she'd woken with a sick feeling akin to dread. First that awful fight, then her painful parting from Hal.

The message, written in Claire's messy handwriting and left on Gina's bedside table, was Claire's way of forcing a resolution. Gina ought to be relieved. She longed for her friends more than ever, now that she had broken it off with Hal. But she'd been the one in the wrong when the three friends had argued that night and admitting it would not be easy.

She had hours to fill before their meeting and her mind raced with phrases of apology—all of which seemed grossly inadequate. When she wasn't trying to think of what to say, she was tormented with imagined scenarios where Margot refused ever to forgive her. She would have to leave the apartment, begin again, alone and friendless in Paris.

The writing went badly all day with the forthcoming confrontation hanging over her head. She was tempted to beg Monsieur

Florie for her old job back, if only to help pass the time, but she didn't think she had it in her to grovel twice in one day.

Doggedly, she plugged away at the typewriter, but for hour after hour, it was like wading through cement. Still she kept at it until finally, against all odds, inspiration struck and the story took flight. The next time she looked up, hours had passed. She'd have to hurry or she'd be late.

Gina made it to Dior in record time, breathless and windblown, a dire contrast to Margot, who didn't have a hair out of place. Margot wasn't wearing black this time. Either Dior had decreed a new dress code or she hadn't been at work that day.

Glad it was just the two of them—at least for now—Gina sped the last few steps and pulled Margot into a tight hug, overcome with a rush of gratitude and remorse. "I'm sorry! I'm so, so sorry. I didn't mean those horrible things I said."

Margot gave a small shudder that might have been relief, then let out a long, shaky sigh. "I know that. I know, my dear, darling friend. Although in some ways you were right." She squeaked as Gina hugged her harder. "Stop! You're crushing me!"

Gina let go, her laughter edged with tears. "Oh, Margot. It's been such an awful couple of days. You can't imagine."

Margot held up one finger in warning. "And we will talk about that, but not here. You know that Dior is only for the good news." Her eyes sparkled. "And I have some excellent news for you."

Gina's mind went blank. Then a glimmer of hope shone in the darkness. "Not the book?"

"Yes!" Margot gripped her hands. "I should wait for Claire but if I don't tell you this now, I might explode. Andrew Mountbatten read your manuscript—he canceled all of his appointments and tore through it in less than a day. He's excited, Gina. He agreed with me that *Liberty* is brilliant. He wants to offer you a book deal."

"*What?*" Gina couldn't believe it. Despite every miserable thing that had happened, she couldn't help the excitement that raced through her. All of that work, the writing and rewriting, and now . . . "Really? Are you sure?"

"I'm sure!" Margot rolled her eyes. "Oh, I know what you're thinking: Maybe he was humoring me, right? But he got straight on the phone to his colleagues in the United States. He's going to come back to us with a preemptive offer, because he knows that when they read it, the other editors will agree." She grinned and that old light of mischief was back in her eyes. "But do you know what? *I* think we should show it to other publishers, too. The Frankfurt Book Fair is coming up. We might even go to auction with it if there's enough interest."

"That sounds very grand," said Gina, marveling at how quickly Margot had become familiar with the publishing world and its jargon. "Won't Mountbatten be mad?"

Margot shook her head. "He knows my first duty is to my client." She winked. "That's you, by the way. And I'd be neglecting my duty if I didn't advise you that after the response he had to your book today, we ought to push this to the absolute limit."

Suddenly the news hit Gina with full force. Her story was going to become a real, solid book, with cardboard covers and marbled endpapers and printed pages in between! To see a novel, written by her, on the bookstore shelves . . . A surge of remorse made Gina blink hard to fight back tears. "I can't believe you did all of this for me when I was such a . . . so awful to you."

Margot frowned. "But, Gina, don't you know? You're my family. We might have our differences but we'll always, *always* have each other. Besides, now that I have a commission to earn, you're not going to get rid of me that—" She broke off. "Ah, there's Claire."

Gina's elation vanished like air from a popped balloon as she turned to see their friend striding toward them. She exchanged a look with Margot.

"We're sorry, Claire," Margot said, taking the lead this time. "You needed to be there for Hervé. We understand."

Claire's mouth twisted. "Well, I don't say you were wrong. And anyway, Hervé kicked me out of his kitchen after a couple of days, so . . ." She shoved her hands in her pockets and rocked on her toes. "I'm back at Thibault's, feet to the fire. Hervé's managing just fine."

Gina was glad. "I don't know what got into me that night. I wish we hadn't fought like that."

"We all said some things we regret," said Margot. "But I think perhaps we needed to hear some home truths, didn't we?"

Claire looked at Gina. "What about Hal?"

Sadness welled up inside her. "That's not something I can talk about here." She drew a deep breath. "But I have received a positive response to my book, thanks to Margot."

"*Vraiment?*" Claire's face lit up. "That's marvelous!" She threw her arms around Gina and rocked her from side to side. Margot put a hand on each of their backs, smiling upon them as benevolently as if she were the minister at a wedding.

"Now that," she said with satisfaction, "is what I like to see."

"But what about you, Margot?" said Claire, finally letting Gina go. "Are you with Andrew Mountbatten now?"

With the glint of mischief back in her eye, Margot nodded. "He has asked me to go back to New York with him when his sabbatical's finished."

"You're leaving Paris?" Gina exclaimed.

"I don't know," Margot answered. "I said I wanted to take it slowly this time."

Claire's eyes were wide. "But . . . you would not live with him in sin?" Clearly her Roman Catholic upbringing had not prepared her for such a shocking turn of events.

Margot winced and Gina sent Claire a warning glance. "If that's the way it has to be, we support you," said Gina. "He struck me as the real deal, and you can't wait five whole years to be free."

"Besides, there's the small matter of his not being allowed to marry a divorcée." Margot's mouth twisted. "He doesn't care about that, but I certainly do. And besides, I've been put off marriage as an institution, quite frankly." She laughed. "But we're all getting ahead of ourselves. I'm not committing to anything just yet."

"I liked him," said Claire. "Oh, but very much. And *I* have excellent taste in men."

"Oh, you do, do you?" Margot dug her in the ribs with her finger, making Claire giggle. "Are you and Hervé getting married, then?"

Claire nodded, grinning from ear to ear. She held out her left hand, letting the small diamond on her third finger sparkle and glint in the light of the setting sun. "But the wedding won't be for a couple of years yet. Not until I've gained more experience with Thibault."

"Oh, how wonderful!" cried Margot, catching Claire's hand to admire the diamond solitaire close up. "You must let me plan the reception for you, my dear, darling Claire."

Gina kissed Claire on both cheeks. "Congratulations, *ma chère*. I'm so glad we are to have a wedding, after all." She winked. "And I know exactly what you should wear."

EPILOGUE

Claire

Claire and Hervé's wedding reception was held in the private rooms at Le Chat-qui-Pêche. Instead of opening a separate restaurant serving haute cuisine, Claire and Hervé had sectioned off part of the brasserie for private parties, where the world's greatest gourmands came to appreciate the finest haute cuisine in Paris (according to the chef's papa).

True to his word, Hervé had bided his time, allowing Claire to develop her talents as a chef independently of him. She'd gained a wide range of experience at the highest level, catering for everything from state banquets to intimate dinner parties for movie stars. Hervé had waited some more while Claire struck out on her own as chef de cuisine for the Paris branch of an international boutique hotel chain, and watched as she discovered that what Hervé had said about working for hotels was true for her, too. She didn't like having to satisfy shareholders and boards and three levels of management. All she wanted was to create for her patrons unforgettable experiences that delighted every sense.

Finally Hervé's patience was rewarded and Claire returned to Le Chat. They spent the bulk of their time in the brasserie, but they took bookings for an extravagant private party one night every month. In very little time, they had established such a grand reputation that their private dining room was booked two years in advance.

Six months ago, they had finally achieved their dream of attaining a three-star rating from the Michelin Guide. The day the guide was published, they set a wedding date.

"At last!" said Margot, who was now living in New York with Andrew Mountbatten. "I get to plan this wedding!"

On the morning of the wedding, as Margot put the final touches to Claire's makeup, Gina brought in a box—dove grey with a white ribbon. Claire recognized it at once. "Dior?"

Smiling, Gina lifted the lid and set it aside. Then she put on cotton gloves and took out the embroidered and beaded stole that Margot had brought up to Gina's fitting all those years ago.

"You didn't!" Claire rose from the vanity and stared at the exquisite piece that Margot was carefully unfolding.

"We couldn't resist," said Gina.

"But how . . . ?" Claire stared from one to the other of them. The stole that matched this gown must have been sold long since.

Margot tapped the side of her nose. "I still have contacts. We asked a special favor and had this copied from the archives." She sobered. "I only wish Monsieur Dior was still here."

Tragically, Christian Dior had died in 1957 while on vacation in Italy. Madame Delahaye had foreseen a calamity should he travel to Montecatini, but this time she had warned him to no avail. Margot, Gina, and Claire had joined the sea of mourners at his funeral, their sadness at his passing only lessened by the knowledge that his legacy would live on.

It was the 1960s now and things were changing. Fashion lines were slimming down, hems were going up. But the beauty of their special gown was timeless, and the love and memories of joys and hardships that it held in every stitch and sequin would be with them forever.

Claire's happiness overflowed. She had everything she'd ever wanted, right here, under this roof.

"You are beautiful," said Gina, as she put the stole with tender care around Claire's shoulders. "Isn't she, Margot?" Blinking back tears, Margot nodded.

Claire had never in her life thought of herself as beautiful. But as she stared and stared at her reflection in the full-length mirror, she saw herself transformed. The warm, creamy tone of the silk complemented her skin. The happy light in her eyes gleamed as brightly as the rhinestone beads on her gown. Her red hair was shining and luxuriant, piled high in a becoming style only Margot could achieve.

Despite the long years she had waited to be his bride, Claire had never doubted that Hervé was the man she wanted to spend the rest of her life with. Only he understood and respected her passion and drive. With a secret smile, she reflected that the coming months would bring new challenges of a completely different nature from the restaurant and brasserie, but having established a firm foundation as to how their partnership worked, Claire was confident she wouldn't regret her decision.

"I'm ready," Claire said at last.

Gina

After the wedding ceremony, Gina and Aunt Vo-Vo squeezed into the back seat of Andrew Mountbatten's Aston Martin and they drove with the top down back to Le Chat.

"Perfect!" murmured Gina, lifting her face to the breeze. Paris had turned on the kind of spring day people wrote songs about. Gina was soon to go on tour to promote the second novel she'd published since her debut had won both critical acclaim and massive sales, thanks to Margot's astute negotiation skills and her passionate advocacy for Gina's writing every step of the way. Gina hated to say goodbye to Paris, but it would only be for as long as she could stand to stay away.

From the back seat she had a good view of the way Margot's head leaned toward Andrew Mountbatten's, the way he smiled at her as they sped along the cobbled streets. Margot's divorce had finally come through after five long years of separation, but there was no sign of a wedding on her horizon.

Margot always insisted she didn't want to marry again, and besides, she refused to be the cause of a rift between Andrew and his family if he flouted tradition by marrying a divorcée. She'd been heartbroken to discover that she couldn't have children, so the one reason she might have wished to marry no longer existed.

These days, Andrew and Margot were living in sin, as Claire termed it, in a lavishly appointed Manhattan apartment, and loving every minute of their work and life.

Still, attending a wedding always brought questions of marriage and commitment into sharp focus—at least, that tended to be the case for women, Gina supposed. The love of her life was now running for the Senate after a successful term as governor of New Hampshire. He was also married with three children. The thought of him made her only a little wistful, these days.

Vo-Vo, who spent the entire wedding ceremony looking like the cat who got the cream—or, more appropriately, the cat who had caught the fish—claimed she had planned Claire's triumph all along. "Who do you think asked Hervé if he wanted to buy the brasserie?" she'd exclaimed. "If only the silly girl had done this sooner, she could have had babies by now, but that's our Claire." She sighed. "I suppose we ought to be grateful that she gets around to things eventually."

Turning her head, Vo-Vo pinned Gina with her sharp gaze. "And what about you, miss? Are there any men in your life?"

Gina grinned. "There have been several," she said. "Does that shock you?" She had yet to meet the man for whom she would be tempted to surrender her independence, but she wouldn't rule it out. Life was good, and she earned enough money from her novels that she didn't need to moonlight as anything else. She'd bought her own apartment in Paris and spent part of the year in New York when she wasn't on tour.

"Hmph!" For the wedding, Vo-Vo had dyed her hair a spectacular shade of peach, which reminded Gina of sunset over the Seine. "Aren't any of you girls going to give me great-nieces and -nephews?" She poked at Gina's shoulder with a lacquered fingernail. "You'll end up like me at this rate."

Gina caught Vo-Vo's hand and gave it a quick squeeze. "Would that be so bad?" She grinned to think of herself aging into a Vo-Vo–like state, old and cantankerous, writing novels in a villa in the south of France. The only part she balked at was the thought of having a head like an Easter egg.

Margot

Margot sipped champagne and looked around her with satisfaction. Months of planning had come together in the most delightful way. The wedding reception was intimate and elegant and filled with love.

"I can't believe you're finally married!" Margot kissed Claire's cheek.

"And just in time." Claire patted her abdomen and winked, causing Margot and Gina to stare at each other, then burst out laughing.

"Talk about burying the lede," said Gina, pulling Claire gingerly into an embrace.

Margot rested a hand on Claire's arm. "How do you feel? You must be tired."

"I'm fine," Claire said, but put her finger to her lips as Vo-Vo called her over.

"And she teases *me* about living in sin," murmured Margot, making Gina chuckle.

"Speaking of babies, did you see who slipped in during the ceremony and sat all the way at the back of the church?" Gina asked. "Madame Vaughn! And she had the sweetest little girl with her, too. Dressed head to toe in Dior, if I'm any judge."

"Oh, I'm so sorry I missed her!" exclaimed Margot. "Claire told me she'd invited her but I know she likes to keep a low profile when she's in Paris, these days. I wasn't sure she'd come."

"She really was our fairy godmother, wasn't she?" said Gina. They had reignited their friendship and learned much about themselves because of that Dior gown. Living together in the apartment, which Claire and Hervé now owned, had been a precious gift.

Someone asked Gina to dance, and then Margot was alone. She watched the dancing, unsure of her feelings about the future. How had she missed Claire's news? Usually she intuited things like that. She'd been so busy with the wedding preparations, not to mention arranging the last-minute details of Gina's book tour and dealing with a million issues for her other clients, that any signs of Claire's pregnancy must have passed her by. Though delighted for her friend, sadness welled up inside her. She'd always wanted children of her own.

The insistent *chink* of a fork tapping on a glass broke in on her reverie. The music stopped. "It's time for the bride and groom to depart," announced Papa Bedeau. "But before they do, the bride will throw the bouquet."

Laughing, Claire turned her back as the unmarried women crowded around her, giggling and jostling, all eager to catch the bouquet. Margot wanted to tell them not to be in such a rush.

But when Claire threw her bouquet, the old gold roses and trailing tendrils of ivy bound with satin ribbon did not sail through the air in a graceful arc. It came like a bullet, aimed straight at Margot, and hit her squarely in the chest.

"Oof!" Automatically her hands came up and she crushed the blooms to her, holding the bouquet upside down.

A wail of disappointment from the unlucky single ladies mingled with laughter and clapping. Over the sea of guests, Margot's gaze found Andrew and their eyes locked.

As if that look had been an explicit invitation, he crossed the room to her in three strides and pulled her into his arms. In front of everyone, he kissed her as if he needed air from her lungs to breathe, as if he'd never let her go. "I will love you forever, Margot," he said in her ear. "That's my vow to you."

Blushing madly as she emerged from that embrace to catcalls and whistles from the rest of the guests, Margot laughed up at him, tears in her eyes. Almost imperceptibly over time, the wounds inside her had healed. She was ready to move into the future with him at her side.

"Forever." She put a hand up to his lean cheek.

He took the bouquet of flowers from her loosened grip and tossed it back into the startled crowd. Then he bent his head to kiss her again. "You know I'd marry you in a heartbeat," he murmured into her ear. "I don't care what my family says."

"I know that." And as long as she knew it, she didn't need him to prove it to her. They chose to be with each other every single day.

UPSTAIRS IN THE apartment, Margot and Gina helped Claire out of the Dior gown so she could change into her going-away outfit. "You can't imagine what it's meant to me, having you both here. I'll miss you so much," said Claire. "I can't believe we're spending two whole weeks away from Le Chat on our honeymoon!"

"I think Papa Bedeau is quite pleased to be back in charge," said Margot with a chuckle. Putting on her white cotton gloves, she laid out the Dior gown on the bed and went over it, inch by inch, taking note of loose threads and dangling beads for Béatrice to repair. A couple of small stains she spot-cleaned then and there with a secret preparation Béatrice had given her.

Then she carefully hung the Dior gown in Claire's closet. Later, she would take it to a specialist cleaner Dior used, before packing the gown away in tissue paper, adding sprigs of lavender and lily of the valley to the box. She couldn't help but feel it would be like laying out a body for burial. There was a tacit agreement among the three friends that no one would wear this gown again.

Well, perhaps not until Claire's daughter grew into womanhood. But that was a question for the future.

Gina sighed as the gown sparkled and gleamed in the light of the dying day. "Doesn't it seem like a lifetime ago that this beauty came into our lives?"

"And Dior brought us together again," said Claire. "Would we ever have found Margot without this gown?"

"I would have come crawling back here some time, I expect," said Margot. With a twinkle in her eye, she added, "But I'm glad you came across me sooner rather than later. The Pigalle was an awful place to live."

Gina laughed as she zipped up Claire's cream going-away dress. She set her hands on Claire's shoulders and looked past her at Margot. "Are you going to marry Mountbatten, after all? You nearly upstaged the bride and groom with that kiss."

"I can't believe he did that," said Margot, blushing all over again. "And *you,* Claire! You hurled that bouquet right at me."

"Well, I had to do something," Claire retorted. "You two would have gone on the same way forever if I hadn't, and I couldn't stand it one more minute."

"So . . ." Gina prompted. "What was the outcome of that passionate smooch, hmm?"

Margot shrugged. "We love each other. What more is there to say?"

"You're not getting married?" asked Claire, disappointed.

"No, but if . . . Oh!" Claire's going-away dress was formfitting, and when she'd turned side-on, Margot could see a small, sweet swelling where Claire's flat stomach used to be.

She jumped up and crossed to Claire. Bending over to address the bump, she said, "Hello, little bubba. You be good for your mamma now, won't you? Let her enjoy her honeymoon."

Gina watched this nonsense with a lifted eyebrow. "Here," she said, holding out the stylish swing coat that went with the dress to Claire. "This will cover everything nicely until you're ready to tell everyone."

Claire let Gina help her on with the coat, then she hugged her two friends hard. "Promise me we won't ever let another thing come between us. We won't need a gown to bring us together again."

"I'd say we're pretty much stuck with each other by now, wouldn't you?" said Gina as they left the apartment together. Her words might have been flippant, but her tone was soft and warm.

"Do you know what I think?" said Margot.

"No, what?" said Gina, but the quirk of her lips said she knew what was coming.

Margot grinned. "I think this *definitely* calls for champagne."

Then the three of them linked arms and went down to meet their future.

Author's Note

When I first began to write *The Paris Gown,* I viewed it as a delightful chance to return to the exquisite world of Christian Dior and his fashion house, a milieu I had grown to love while writing *Sisters of the Resistance.* However, as novels tend to do, this story became so much more: a celebration and acknowledgment of the vital importance of female friendship in every woman's life—particularly through times of hardship—and a loving tribute to my own dear friends.

As I wrote the story of Claire, Gina, and Margot, I also reflected on how often my close friendships have come in threes. In *The Paris Gown,* I have explored the dynamics of those tripartite relationships.

The gown around which the story revolves is fictional but based on the creation Dior designed for Princess Margaret for her twenty-first birthday party in 1951. The official portrait by Cecil Beaton shows the bespoke detailing chosen by Margaret herself; Her Royal Highness later described it as "my favorite dress of all."

Claire, Gina, and Margot are fictional characters, but the background for Claire's experience in the kitchen brigade comes from the impressive career and innovations of Escoffier, chef de cuisine at the Ritz Hotel, and also the story of Madame Brazier, who in 1933 became the first person awarded six Michelin stars—three at each of her two restaurants. Le Chat-qui-Pêche (the cat who fishes) is the name of a street in Paris. I liked it, so I stole it for Claire's brasserie.

Margot is inspired by Australia's answer to Nancy Mitford, Robin Dalton, whose excellent memoirs *Aunts Up the Cross* and *One Leg Over* are a joy to read. Dalton grew up in a mansion on the edge of Sydney's red-light district, Kings Cross. Margot's story about her father shooting himself in the leg with the pistol he kept in his surgery for protection against the unsavory characters who were sometimes his patients was gleaned from Dalton's memoirs.

Dalton divorced her first violently abusive husband, ran off to London in 1946, and fell in love with David Mountbatten, Prince Philip's cousin and best man at his wedding to Princess Elizabeth. David couldn't marry Robin because of the rule against direct descendants of Queen Victoria marrying divorcées but the two of them enjoyed a committed relationship in spite of this. After many adventures, including spying for the king of Thailand, eventually Robin became a literary agent and producer with an impressive list of clients: Margaret Drabble, Arthur Miller, Iris Murdoch, Joan Collins, Laurence Olivier, and Peter Weir, to name a few. The movies Robin produced include *Madame Sousatzka* and *Oscar and Lucinda*. Andrew and Charlotte Mountbatten are my fictional additions to the Mountbatten family tree.

To write about Margot's marriage, I undertook extensive research into the trauma caused by what is now called narcissistic abuse—sometimes known as coercive control. In my opinion, the best book on this subject written for laypeople is *It's Not You: Identifying and Healing from Narcissistic People* by Dr. Ramani Durvasula. For those who haven't experienced a form of abuse that can be so subtle and incremental and yet so devastating, it can be difficult to understand. Often victims feel very isolated, misunderstood by friends, family, and even professional therapists who are not trained in this area, so it is important to find the right help. Thankfully, this is more readily available today than it was in the 1950s.

Acknowledgments

The Paris Gown has been an emotional book for me to write, and I owe a debt of gratitude to Rachel Kahan, my editor at William Morrow, for her patience, guidance, and skill in helping me shape this story into what I hope is an emotional journey for the reader. My thanks also to my former editor, Lucia Macro, for everything she has done for me over the years—not least of which was brainstorming the idea for this novel—and for leaving me in such excellent hands.

I could not be more thrilled that a real Dior fashion photograph was used for the cover of *The Paris Gown*. Many thanks to the cover designer and the William Morrow art department, production, marketing, publicity, sales, distribution, booksellers, librarians, and all of the many wonderful people who are responsible for *The Paris Gown* hitting the shelves and getting into the hands of readers. To my lovely readers, thank you for devouring my books and telling me you enjoy them. I hope you share this novel with your own dearest friends.

To my unflaggingly stellar literary agent, Kevan Lyon, thank you for everything you do to support my books and career. You're the best!

And now to my own wonderful friends—Lucy, Vikki, and Yas, Jason and Ben—I couldn't imagine my life without you. Thank you from the bottom of my heart for our decades of friendship.

Last, but definitely not least, my love and gratitude always to my darling sons, Allister and Adrian—I'm so proud of the kind and caring young men you've become—and to my unfailingly supportive and loving family, Cheryl, Ian, and Michael.